A Season in the Highlands

JUDE DEVERAUX

A Season in the Highlands

JILL BARNETT

GERALYN DAWSON PAM BINDER
PATRICIA CABOT

POCKET BOOKS
New York Toronto London Sydney Singapore

This book consists of works of fiction. Names, characters, places and incidents are products of the authors' imaginations or are used fictitiously. Any resemblance to actual events or locales or persons, living or dead, is entirely coincidental.

An *Original* Publication of POCKET BOOKS

 POCKET BOOKS, a division of Simon & Schuster, Inc.
1230 Avenue of the Americas, New York, NY 10020

"Unfinished Business" © 2000 by Jude Deveraux
"Fall from Grace" (revised edition) © 2000 by Jill Barnett,
    originally published as "Saving Grace" © 1993
"Cold Feet" © 2000 by Geralyn Dawson
"The Matchmaker" © 2000 by Pam Binder
"The Christmas Captive" © 2000 by Patricia Cabot

ISBN: 0-7434-0341-X

First Pocket Books printing December 2000

10 9 8 7 6 5 4 3 2 1

POCKET and colophon are registered trademarks of Simon & Schuster, Inc.

Cover art by Dan Craig

Printed in the U.S.A.

Contents

Unfinished Business

JUDE DEVERAUX

One

Tyler Stevens set her coffee cup down on the glass-topped table, then dropped her head back against the wrought-iron chair, closed her eyes, and let the sun warm her skin.

"Playing Aunt Tyler again today?" came a voice she knew well.

"Yes!" Tyler said, smiling, but not opening her eyes.

"And wouldn't you rather saunter downtown to Union Square to pick up some fresh fruit and homemade muffins? Or wander about Central Park on this glorious day?"

"No," she said, then looked across her terrace at Barry. When she'd bought her apartment three years ago, she'd been concerned because her terrace was separated from her neighbor's by only a foot. Like the New Yorker she'd become, she was worried about privacy. But for a year she'd never even once seen the little old man who owned the apartment, and then he moved to Scarsdale to live with his daughter. When the apartment had been purchased by an unmarried man, Tyler had been concerned. Was she going to be fending off the attentions of some guy who wore gold chains? Or would he be a computer nerd and Tyler was his fantasy?

But when she'd seen Barry and saw that he wasn't going to be interested in *her*, she'd been enthusiastic in her

3

welcome. Barry owned a tiny, exclusive florist shop downtown, and within three months after he'd moved in, his terrace was lush with roses and greenery.

Then, about seven months after he'd moved in, he was sued by a young man who'd worked for him, and, even though it wasn't her field of expertise, Tyler had handled the case. The suit hadn't taken much of her time, and she wanted to be friendly with her neighbor, so when Barry had asked for her bill, Tyler had waved her hand. "Don't worry about it," she'd said.

Two weeks later, she'd returned from a business trip, and when she looked across her living room onto her terrace, she saw that it had been transformed into a beautiful garden of flowers, greenery, and even little trees in pots. Openmouthed, she was standing in the middle of the garden, staring, when Barry had leaned over the railing and said, "Like it?"

That had been the beginning of their friendship. Even though she'd been his lawyer on the case (and had won it), she'd kept her professionalism and they had shared little talk of their personal lives. But after Barry had transformed Tyler's boring terrace into a wonderland, they'd become friends. And after Barry had seen that Tyler didn't know how to take care of a garden, Barry had had a tiny bridge, complete with railings, made. He could slip the bridge into place so he could walk across to Tyler's terrace and weed and water. It wasn't long before the bridge never came down and they were taking care of each other's mail and even phone calls while the other was occupied.

Since, like so many New Yorkers, they were from other parts of the country, in a short time, they each became the only family in the city that the other had.

4

But that was until six months ago when Tyler's cousin, Kristin Beaumont, had moved to New York. Krissy's father was Tyler's mother's older brother, but, more than that, he was their "savior." Or at least that's what Tyler's mother always called him. When Tyler's father had been killed in an accident when Tyler was six, it was Uncle Thaddeus who'd stepped in and taken over. Tyler's father had been too young to think about such things as life insurance, so he'd left behind a penniless wife and child.

But Uncle Thad had opened his heart and his bank account. He'd paid for everything while his little sister went back to school and got her degree in elementary education. And years later, when young Tyler had shown interest in Uncle Thad's law profession, he'd encouraged her, and when she said she wanted to go to law school, he'd paid for every penny of her education.

So now, Uncle Thad had asked Tyler to "keep an eye on" his daughter when she moved to big, bad New York. Once a week Tyler went to Krissy's apartment for Sunday dinner. Tyler very much enjoyed the time spent with her young cousin. However, there was one teeny, tiny drawback: Krissy was the worst cook on the face of the earth.

"So what's on the menu today?" Barry asked, a watering can in his hand.

"Rocks, for all I know," Tyler said, shaking her head in disbelief. "The girl can take the finest cut of meat in the world and turn it into granite."

"No luck in introducing her to carry-out?"

"None. She says that if she wants to be a wife and mother, then she must learn to cook."

"Still on that, is she?" Barry asked as he stepped up

onto the bridge, then walked over and began to inspect Tyler's plants. "No hope in . . . ?"

"If you mean, is there any hope of turning her away from her obsession with her boss? As far as I can tell, there's no hope at all!" Tyler picked up her coffee cup again, saw that it was empty, then put it down. Uncle Thad had used his influence to obtain a high-level position for his beloved daughter as the personal assistant of Joel Kingsley, the founder and owner of the chain of DIY stores called Home Stores. Almost immediately after starting work, Krissy had decided that she was madly, passionately, and insanely in love with her charismatic boss. Never mind that Joel Kingsley was in his forties and Krissy was just twenty-three. And never mind that as far as Tyler could find out, Joel Kingsley didn't seem to think of Krissy as anything except an employee; Krissy still believed she was in love with him.

And as a result, Joel Kingsley was all that Krissy talked about. All. That's it. There had been three dinners in which not a word was uttered about anything other than Joel Kingsley.

Tyler had now spent twenty-four Sunday dinners with her cousin, and while trying to eat Krissy's inedible food, she'd had to hear everything there was to hear about Joel Kingsley.

For the first three visits, Tyler had tried to reason with her young cousin. She'd smiled indulgently. Krissy's gushing about her new job and, especially, about her new boss had made Tyler feel much, much older than her thirty-five years. "I'm sure that Mr. Kingsley"—she used the *Mr.* to emphasize the age difference—"is dashing compared to someone from back home, but—"

"Oh, Tyler," Krissy had gushed, "you've never seen him. He's so . . . so wonderful. He walks like . . . I mean, he . . . And he . . . Oh, you just have to see him to understand."

Tyler gave a weak smile. In her field of domestic relations—a "divorce lawyer," as she was more commonly called—she'd seen lots of men who walked like . . . And were so . . . But she'd also seen the way these dynamic men tried to leave the women with nothing after the divorce.

"And how many times has he been married?" Tyler asked quietly as she used the serrated knife to saw at the meat that Krissy had served her.

"Once, but that's all," Krissy said quickly. "Except for one other time."

"Does that mean that he's been married twice?" She was still trying to cut the meat but was having no luck.

"If you want to get technical, it does," Krissy said defensively, "but I'm not sure that first marriages count."

"They all count in a courtroom." Tyler's index finger was bending back painfully so she gripped the knife handle in her fist.

"You're too much like Daddy. You're too cynical. Would you like a spoon for that?"

"Spoon?" Tyler said, looking up, not understanding.

"For your macaroni and cheese," Krissy said as though Tyler were stupid.

Tyler looked down at the slab of black on her plate. "This is—?" she started, then stopped herself. She put down her knife and fork. "Krissy, honey, I know that New York must be exhilarating to you, and I'm sure that a self-made man like Joel Kingsley must be wildly exciting, but—"

"He's *not* exciting," Krissy said. "He works too hard to have time for anything except business. He never takes time off, and he does everything, oversees everything. If you saw him in the office . . . There isn't anything anywhere that is too small for him to notice."

Control freak, Tyler thought but didn't say. She couldn't help but look down at her plate. Macaroni and cheese? she thought, trying her best to see if she could make out the curve of the pasta. How did one get cheese to harden like that? She'd heard of blackened fish, but blackened *cheese?*

She looked back at Krissy. "There are a couple of young men in our office who I'd like you to meet."

At that Krissy angrily stood up, removed their plates, and disappeared into the kitchen. Her father had purchased his "baby" daughter an apartment. That the apartment cost more than Tyler's and that it had been professionally decorated, while Tyler's furniture had mostly come from auctions and estate sales, did rankle a bit. "Makes you, as Scarlett said, 'Pea green with envy,'" Barry had said when Tyler first described the place. "Of course if you didn't do so much *pro bono* work, you could afford an apartment like that," Barry had added fondly.

After that first Sunday luncheon, Tyler had done some research on Joel Kingsley. Unexpectedly, she'd found out that he seemed a nice enough guy. The truth was, that Tyler had expected to be told that he preyed on young and innocent girls. But, as Krissy had said, Joel Kingsley had been married when he was in college, but the marriage had broken apart just a year later. He'd remarried two years after he'd graduated and that liaison had lasted for fifteen years.

Tyler had called someone who had given her the number of someone else, so she'd gradually found a person who knew a little bit more about Joel Kingsley than was written in *Forbes* magazine. According to her informant, after fifteen years of being a "business widow," Joel Kingsley's second wife had divorced him and run off with her personal trainer. "Kingsley was generous in the settlement," Tyler had been told. "But Celeste Delashaw has her hands on him now."

"And who is Celeste Delashaw?" Tyler had asked.

"You aren't in the museum set, are you?"

"If you're asking me if I spend my free time going to thousand-dollar-a-plate benefits, no, I don't," Tyler had said more snappishly than she'd meant to.

"Neither do I, but I *read* about them," her informant had snapped back.

Tyler didn't reply to that. She hadn't much time to spare for reading about "society." And, besides, too many of her cases dealt with women who'd put men through school, while raising their children almost single-handedly. Finally, when the kids were out of the house and the man was a success, the wife was ready to enjoy what she'd worked for, but too often, the man then dumped her for a younger woman. Tyler had seen too many of these fifty-something women who were facing bleak futures alone.

"Celeste Delashaw is the former wife of Maximilian Aldrich. You have heard of him, haven't you?"

Tyler had looked at her watch. She was due in court in fifteen minutes. Thank heaven she was on her cell phone; she picked up her pace. "Sure. Steel."

"As in cars, boats, and planes."

"All I want to know is the character of this man, Joel

Kingsley. My young cousin works for him and she has a serious crush on him. Is he likely to take advantage of her?"

There was a pause on the other end of the phone. "I haven't heard those terms since I left Iowa. 'Crush.' 'Take advantage of her.' Are you asking that if she looks at him in invitation, is he likely to tell her that he loves her just so he can screw her on top of the copy machine?"

"More or less," Tyler said, her lips tight at such a thought about her beloved cousin.

"Not as long as Celeste Delashaw is after him, he won't."

"What about *him?!*" Tyler said in exasperation. "Not her. Him!"

"Keep your shirt on. I haven't heard anything like that about him. His wife left him because she never saw him, not because he was making the secretaries. However, he is a man. What's your cousin look like?"

Tyler didn't want to answer that. "Thanks," she said. "I owe you one"; then she pushed the "end" button on the phone and cut off the connection.

But, honestly, after that conversation Tyler wasn't much better off than she had been before. Joel Kingsley might be a good guy, but he was rich and powerful and he was probably surrounded with girls like Krissy who adored him. He wasn't married, but he was dating a rich woman who seemed to be protective of her "property."

"So why don't you take some food with you when you go?" Barry was saying now.

"I tried that. She puts it in the refrigerator and serves what she's cooked. Barry, *what* am I going to do about this? Uncle Thad expects me to oversee my cousin, but she's developed this infatuation with a man nearly twice her age. Krissy has always been so sheltered. She has no idea what can happen to her in this world."

"And you do?" Barry asked cynically. "It seems to me that you two are at opposite ends of the world. Your little cousin thinks that men can do no wrong, while you spend your days dealing with men whose only concern is how much wrong they can do."

"You aren't going to start on my love life again, are you?" she said, picking up her coffee cup, then standing. She was still wearing her heavy terry-cloth bathrobe.

"Can't start on something that doesn't exist, can I?" Barry called after her as she went inside the apartment.

Once inside her apartment, Tyler looked at the clock. There wasn't time to have another cup of coffee and to continue exchanging gibes with Barry. She had to get dressed to go to her cousin's for Sunday dinner.

Forty-five minutes later, Tyler was standing outside Krissy's apartment door and ringing the bell. The doorman had let her up, but now Krissy wasn't answering. Like the overprotective aunt Barry accused her of being, Tyler was instantly worried. Digging into her handbag, she removed the key to Krissy's apartment that she kept there for "emergencies."

Once inside, Tyler saw that there were no lights on in the apartment and there was no smell of burned food coming from the kitchen. In fact, when Tyler went into the kitchen, it was clean and neat, with no signs of food preparation. But the perfectly clean kitchen only added to Tyler's fears, for Krissy was a very conscientious young woman. If she invited someone to dinner, she'd not forget.

When Tyler heard a sound like a kitten mewling com-

11

ing from the bedroom, she began to run down the hall, her heels clicking on Krissy's inlaid hardwood floors.

When Tyler pushed open Krissy's bedroom door, she gasped, for there was Krissy lying in bed, her face pink with what looked like fever. Around her were three boxes of tissues, with a pile of used tissues on the floor. On the bedside table were four brown plastic bottles of pills, a thermometer, and two bottles of water.

When Krissy looked up at Tyler, she said, "I'm sick," in a congested voice.

"Why didn't you tell me?" Tyler said, annoyed but relieved to have found her cousin at last, as she felt Krissy's forehead. It was warm but not burning. "Why didn't you call me earlier? I would have come over and taken care of you."

"I know how busy you are, so I called Daddy and he sent a doctor to me."

Tyler looked at Krissy in disbelief. "You called Uncle Thad and he flew a doctor to New York?"

"No," Krissy said, weakly lifting her hand. "He got a doctor in New York to come to my apartment. The man was ever so nice, but he said that I have the flu and that I must stay in bed, so I can't go."

Tyler was still recovering from the shock of hearing that her Uncle Thad could get a New York doctor to make a house call. "Of course you can't go anywhere. You're to stay in bed and I'll take care of you. My law firm owes me about fifty weeks or so of vacation time, so I'll take some time off and I'll . . . I know, I'll introduce you to New York food delivery."

"But you can't!" Krissy said, then she put her hand to her head and flopped back on the bed. "You have to go to Scotland this afternoon."

12

Sitting down on the edge of the bed, Tyler picked up the medicines and read the labels. She wondered which drug was making her cousin delirious?

Putting the bottles down, she smiled sweetly at Krissy. "No, dear, I'm not going to Scotland this afternoon. Nor to Valhalla or even to Brigadoon. I'm going to stay right here with you, and—"

"No!" Krissy said, again rising out of the bed. "You have to go. It's the only way. Joel needs you. Me. He needs me, but I can't—"

Tyler pushed Krissy back against the bed. "Now calm down. Why don't I order in something for us to eat and after you've eaten, you'll feel much better. How about some fresh-squeezed orange juice and some bagels? Or maybe some chicken soup. Kosher. I know a superb deli that—"

"We don't have time to eat," Krissy said, and there were tears in her eyes. "You have to get on a plane and *go.*"

Tyler's voice was exaggeratedly calm. "Why don't you give me the name and number of that doctor Uncle Thad found for you so I can call him?"

"I'm not crazy," Krissy said, then she began to cry for real. Grabbing a handful of tissues from the box nearest her, she wiped her eyes, then threw the lot onto the floor.

Tyler looked at the other tissues on the floor. When you had the flu, you didn't usually have sinus drainage that called for this many tissues to be used. "Have you been crying?" Tyler asked. "Is this what all these tissues have been used for?"

Krissy opened her mouth to answer, but instead, she grabbed another handful and covered her eyes.

All her life, Tyler had been a sap about her pretty, young

cousin. There was twelve years difference in their ages, and Tyler had first seen Krissy when she was just three days old. Tyler had changed Krissy's diapers and helped her learn to walk. Many times, Tyler's mother had chided her daughter for saving her allowance and spending it on her young cousin, buying her things that Krissy's parents could easily afford to give her. But Tyler had so very much loved to see her cousin's dimpled smile when she opened her gifts.

When Tyler was fourteen, she'd started baby-sitting the two-year-old Krissy and the bond between them had strengthened. Tyler had been a serious child and she'd hated high school, with the girls backbiting each other as they competed for boys Tyler didn't want in the first place, so spending time with Krissy had been an outlet for her.

Tyler's mother had worried about her daughter, wanting her to socialize with her peers more, but Uncle Thad had watched his niece playing with his daughter and said, "Tyler listens to her own drummer. Quit worrying about her because she doesn't spend her life obsessed with boys and clothes."

So, in the end, Tyler's mother had given up trying to persuade her daughter to be a "normal" teenager and had instead used the time that Tyler was with her cousin to take up square dancing. And it was in the square dancing classes that she'd met the man who became her second husband.

When Tyler had gone away to a university to study law, the bond between her and Krissy had been stretched, for Krissy was as social as Tyler wasn't. The first year at college, Tyler had been worried about Krissy, thinking that she would miss her a lot, but at Christmas Tyler had seen that Krissy had already made many new friends.

As Tyler had stood by, watching Krissy playing happily with six other little girls, Uncle Thad had put his arm around her. "Aren't you a little young to be having empty-nest syndrome?"

"I'm glad she has friends," Tyler had said, but there was a catch in her throat.

Eventually, Tyler had become involved in her law studies and there were a couple of young men in college who interested her, but they'd received job offers in different states and neither relationship had held up over time and distance.

In the years since she'd passed her bar exam, Tyler had lived in New York and practiced domestic law. During that time, she had two serious relationships and had lived with one man for two years, but they'd split up because Tyler was doing better than he was. It hadn't been money that had angered him, but the fact that Tyler was always winning her cases. The final straw came when they had been on opposite sides in a courtroom and Tyler had trounced him.

So when Uncle Thad had called and said that Krissy was moving to New York and would Tyler look out for her, Tyler had been quite happy to do so. Aside from the food, Tyler enjoyed being with her young cousin. "Frustrated motherhood," Barry had said the first time Tyler had told him about her long relationship with her cousin.

Now, Tyler looked back at Krissy. "I so much wanted to go with him," Krissy said as she blew her nose, again throwing the tissues onto the floor. Of course "him" meant Joel Kingsley.

To hide her frown, Tyler bent over and picked up the tissues and put them into the wastebasket, but they wouldn't all fit, so she went into the kitchen to get a grocery bag. On the counter by the sink was an open notebook. "Tell him the *truth* about Delashaw," was written at the top of the page. "Take the black teddy and the red heels," was on the next line. "Pretend you like lawnmowers," was on the third line.

Tyler's frown was deeper when she returned to the bedroom, and when she saw Krissy struggling to get out of bed, her lips tightened into a thin, hard line. "Just what do you think you're doing?"

"I have to go," Krissy said. "He needs me. My date book has all the telephone numbers he needs and he depends on me."

"Down!" Tyler ordered as she pushed her cousin back toward the bed. Krissy's chest was hot, and she was sure that Krissy's eyes were more red than they had been a few minutes ago. "You aren't going anywhere. And I'm sure that Kingsley can find someone else to go with him."

"Not now," Krissy wailed. "Not at this late date. At least not . . . But even if he could, it doesn't matter. *You* have to go. You're the only one."

Tyler was tucking her cousin into bed, twisting the coverlet about her so tightly that she wasn't able to move. "Don't be ridiculous. What do I know about home . . . things?" she finished. Truthfully, even though Joel Kingsley's stores were all over the U.S., she'd never been in one of them, so she had no idea what they sold.

Krissy grabbed Tyler's arm. "Oh, Tyler, you have to do this for me. If I can't go, then Mr. Kingsley will call Marilyn, and she has the hots for Mr. Kingsley so bad that it's embarrassing. And she's really pretty. She changed her name to Marilyn because she looks like that other one, the old one."

It took Tyler a moment to think who Krissy meant. "You mean *Marilyn* Monroe?"

"Yes, that one. She wants Mr. Kingsley for her own, and she'll do something awful if she goes with him on this trip."

Stepping back from the bed, Tyler looked down at her young cousin. "How many of you in your office are after Kingsley?"

"Why, all of us, of course," Krissy said as though Tyler had asked a rhetorical question.

"And what about Ms. Delashaw?" Tyler asked. "Isn't Kingsley engaged to marry her?"

Krissy waved her hand in dismissal. "Oh. Her. She's old. In another six or seven years she's going to be *forty*."

Tyler had to turn away before she said something that would make her sound hurt. In a mere *five* years she was going to be hitting the big four-oh. She turned back to Krissy. "So you want me to go to Scotland to keep this Marilyn from getting her claws into your boss? You want me to save him for *you?*"

Krissy didn't seem to be aware that Tyler was being sarcastic. "Yes!" she said happily, glad Tyler at last seemed to understand the situation. "That's it exactly. I want you to go to Scotland in my place and make sure that that Delashaw woman doesn't do anything drastic and—"

"Such as?" Tyler asked in her lawyer-voice. *Drastic* was a word that frightened her. In her profession *drastic* could mean taking a chain saw to the living room furniture rather than letting the spouse have it, or it could mean kidnaping the children. *Drastic* was not a word that she liked.

"Marry him!" Krissy said in a near-shout.

"But maybe if he got married, then you girls—" Tyler began, but Krissy's screech cut her off.

"Could what?!" Krissy said in a voice that sounded full of pain. "Live without him? How could we do that? If you'd only meet him, you'd see what I mean. At least I think you'd be able to imagine. It's not as though he's *your* type, but he's the type of every other red-blooded female on this earth."

"Would you mind telling me exactly what that means?" Tyler asked, tight-lipped. "Exactly what *is* my 'type'?"

Krissy was not one to grasp subtlety. She took people at their word, not at their tone. "Oh, you know," she said, waving her hand in the air. "Like all those boyfriends you used to bring home. You know, uptight and rigid. Afraid to have any fun."

Tyler's back straightened. "I have no idea to whom you're referring," she said stiffly.

"Chester, Marshall, Phillip, and . . . What was that other one's name?"

"Brighton," Tyler said, narrowing her eyes at her cousin. How could such a nice little girl have grown up into such a— She stopped her thought as the door-bell rang, and, gratefully, she nearly ran from the room to answer it. "No fun!" she muttered. "How absurd!" Of course she'd had *fun*. Maybe not as much fun as someone like Krissy, who had studied what her father called "the home arts" in college, had had, but then Tyler had been working toward a profession and—

Opening Krissy's apartment door, she was greeted by a

very handsome man: tall, broad-shouldered, beautiful eyes. For a quick moment she thought that he was Joel Kingsley come to visit his ailing assistant. But this man was too young to be Kingsley. A quick glance downward and she saw that he was carrying a black leather bag.

"You're the doctor?" Tyler asked, incredulous.

"Yes," the young man answered; then Tyler saw his face turn red. "I, uh, I came by to, uh . . ."

"Check on your patient," Tyler said brightly, smiling as she stepped aside to open the door wide. And as she looked at this young man, she understood everything. Obviously, Uncle Thad was also worried about Krissy's growing attachment to her much-older boss. But instead of lectures and admonitions, he had used the opportunity of Krissy's illness to put her in contact with another man, a younger, more suitable man. "Right this way," Tyler said, still grinning.

In the bedroom, Krissy was out of the bed and standing in front of her closet. Even from the back she looked so weak that she might faint at any second.

"What are you doing out of bed!?" the doctor thundered, then went across the room in two strides, where he swept Krissy into his arms and carried her back to the bed.

Tyler stood to one side, watching with her eyes so wide open they hurt. In her entire life, no man had ever swept *her* into his arms and—

"I have to get up," Krissy said weakly as she looked up into the doctor's big brown eyes. "I have to get on a plane and go to Scotland because Tyler won't go for me."

At that the young doctor turned eyes that said, "How could you be so selfish?" toward Tyler. Instantly, her lawyer's instinct made her want to defend herself against this injustice. But as Tyler was thinking that she could not do this absurd thing of going to Scotland, she remembered how stubborn Krissy could be. Tyler wouldn't have put it past her cousin to, the minute after Tyler left, indeed get on a plane to Scotland. And if Tyler made her miss this flight, Krissy would just take another one.

On the other hand, if Krissy was left alone with this beautiful young man, maybe he could persuade her to forget about Old Man Kingsley.

"I, uh . . ." Tyler began. Both pairs of eyes were on her. "I'd have to pack and, uh . . . The tickets are in your name," she said.

"Actually, I called Daddy this morning and we talked about it, so . . ."

When Krissy didn't finish her sentence, Tyler, following her glance, looked toward the top of the dresser and picked up the two packets of plane tickets lying there. One was in Krissy's name, the other in Tyler's. Once again, Uncle Thad had accomplished the impossible.

"I know that you always carry your passport with you, so I took a chance," Krissy said. "And you don't have to pack. You can take my suitcase. We're close enough in size that you can wear my clothes. Everyone's always said that we look alike. Don't we, Jeff?"

The doctor looked Tyler up and down, and it was obvious that he did not think that she looked much like Krissy. In fact, if Tyler went by what she saw in this young man's eyes, she was ready for the glue factory.

"Sure," he said slowly. "With a little . . ." He shrugged as he turned back to Krissy. "I can't see you wearing clothes like that."

Frowning, Tyler looked down at her Sunday clothes: baggy khakis, a big loose-knit shirt, white tennis shoes. She spent all week wearing prim little suits, so on weekends she wanted to be comfortable. And, yes, she'd been told more than once that she dressed to be off-putting to men. And maybe they were right, but she wasn't interested in getting a man, so—

As she looked at the doctor bending over Krissy, Tyler had the idea that if she weren't in the room, that in another minute they'd be kissing.

"She isn't going to do this for me, so I have to get up and go," Krissy said, sounding as though she were a dying swan. "I can't let him down. I have to—"

"All right!" Tyler said. How could it be that she could go up against some of the biggest attorneys in New York and stand her ground, but her little cousin could wrap her around her finger? "But I really *must* go home and get my own clothes and—"

"There isn't *time!*" Krissy said with passion. "The plane leaves in two hours. You're barely going to make it to the airport and be able to check in. It is an international flight, you know."

Since Tyler had never been out of the U.S., no, she didn't know what Krissy meant. "I can't—" Tyler began again, thinking about the cases she had and what she needed to do on Monday and whom she had to see and whom she had to call. But then she looked at the two young people staring up at her. Krissy's eyes were pleading, while the doctor's were skeptical, saying that Tyler couldn't and wouldn't do it.

There was a suitcase on the floor, and she assumed it was Krissy's, packed with expensive clothes that Uncle

Thad had paid for. To Tyler's knowledge, Krissy had never bought anything on sale in her life. "You just don't have the choice that you do when the clothes are first put out on the racks," Krissy had said often. "But you don't have the bills that you do when you buy on sale," Tyler had replied.

"Stop thinking about all the bad things that could happen and just *go!*" Krissy said.

"I can't possibly . . ." Tyler said under her breath, still thinking about all the reasons why she couldn't do this thing. But one of her hands was on the suitcase and the other held the tickets and Krissy's itinerary.

She hadn't had a vacation in four years, not since she and Phillip had gone to Arizona together. But then, as Krissy said, Phillip hadn't been much fun. In fact, he'd eaten something bad the first night and spent most of the week throwing up.

"Mr. Kingsley booked three suites," Krissy said softly. "One for her, one for him, and one for me." She lowered her voice. "In a castle. The rooms are in a castle."

At dinner one evening, when Krissy was just four years old, she'd asked her father to buy Tyler a castle because all the books Tyler read to her were about castles. "She really, really, really wants one," Krissy had said to her father. As for Tyler, she'd been so embarrassed that she'd wanted to slide under the table. After that it had become a family joke. "Read any good castles lately?" her relatives would ask. Then her grandmother would turn it around and ask, "So when are you going to get a knight to live in the castle with you?"

Now, Tyler stood blinking at Krissy. She knew she was too old to be enticed by the thought of what was really just a building made of stone. But when she thought of her current cases and how her assistant could take care of everything . . . And when she thought of spending a few days in a real castle . . .

"Built in 1306," Krissy said, her voice barely a whisper.

Tyler started to say something sensible, but the next moment she closed her mouth, grabbed the suitcase, and ran from the apartment with only her hand raised to say good-bye. In the taxi on the way to the airport, she used her cell phone to call people and tell them that she had to go away for a few days on family business. "Emergency," she said and left it to their imaginations to conjecture what tragedy had called her away.

At the airport she bought a biography of William Wallace; then, when she boarded British Airways, she found to her delight that dear Uncle Thad had booked her a first-class seat. Smiling, Tyler settled back into her seat, took out her book, and read while sipping champagne.

Two

*S*cotland was much more beautiful than Tyler had imagined it to be. And when she took Krissy's suitcase out of the baggage claim area in Edinburgh and heard firsthand for the first time a Scottish burr from a gate attendant, she almost swooned with the sound of it.

There was a driver waiting for her—actually, for Krissy—with "Beaumont" written on the card he was holding up. Tyler nodded at him, and he hadn't asked questions about her identity. Truthfully, when she'd seen him, she'd been a bit afraid that he might say, "I expected you to be a bit younger," but instead, he'd smiled at Tyler in a way that made her feel, well, pretty.

The car was a luxury sedan, not a stretch, but plush inside. It was early morning and she was tired from the long overnight flight, but the minute they left the parking lot, Tyler came awake. Edinburgh was beautiful—old, its buildings blackened with age—and she could feel the weight of the years of the place. On a hill she saw a building that could only be Holyrood Castle.

Once they were outside the city, they traveled on a modern highway for a few minutes, but the driver kept looking at her in the mirror. "Like to see my country, would you?" he asked, smiling at her in the mirror.

His soft accent did something to the insides of Tyler, something that she wasn't sure she'd ever felt before. "Oh, yes," she said, and she knew that if anyone in her office had heard her gush like that, they would have been astonished.

The Scottish countryside was just as she'd always imagined it. There were rolling hills covered with heather, and she could see the foundations of many stone cottages that had been abandoned to the elements long ago. Twice they had to stop and let sheep pass across the road. And one time the sheep were driven by a man on a tractor who she swore was a dead ringer for a young Sean Connery.

As though he could read her mind, the driver smiled at her in a knowing way in the rearview mirror.

When they pulled into a driveway, Tyler leaned forward and strained to see what was ahead. When they turned a curve and she saw it, she let out a loud gasp.

"Your first castle?" the driver asked, amusement in his voice.

Tyler just nodded as she looked at the turrets, the great open gateway, at the stones that had been in place for hundreds of years. She knew the driver was laughing at her and probably thinking that all Americans were suckers for castles, but he didn't say anything.

And Tyler just absorbed the vision of the castle.

The interior turned out to be lush and gorgeous, with thick curtains hanging from each of the many stone-surrounded windows. A man carried her suitcase up carpeted stairs, then opened a huge oak door. When Tyler saw her room, saw the four-poster bed, she had to lean against the doorjamb to brace herself. She tipped the man a couple of heavy English coins; then he left her alone in the beautiful room. There was a giant wardrobe against one wall, a tall chest of drawers against another. Tyler knew that both pieces were antiques, and had they been for sale in a New York shop, they would have carried heavy price tags.

The bathroom was as big as the living room of her apartment in New York. There were two sinks in a marble topped cabinet, a modern shower in one corner, and along the far wall was a bathtub the size of a small swimming pool. As Tyler looked at the tub, she knew she'd never felt so grimy in her life, and so, smiling, she turned on the taps to fill the tub with hot water.

As the tub was filling, she went back into the bedroom and opened the suitcase that the porter had placed on the old blanket chest at the foot of the bed. "What in the world?" she said aloud as she looked at the clothes that she'd brought with her. Krissy's clothes.

One by one, Tyler started pulling things from the suitcase. As a New Yorker, Tyler knew that each garment she saw before her was expensive—as in thousands of dollars expensive—but the truth was, the clothes looked as though they were Frederick's of Hollywood crossed with Armani. On top was a little black dress—and the key word was *little*. The dress would have fit into a cigarette carton. There were tiny cashmere sweaters, little wool skirts, and a dozen packets of sheer black hosiery. The trousers she withdrew were made of beautiful Italian wool, but, holding them up, Tyler could tell that they were going to be snug. Except for one pair of exquisite, tall boots (the type made for looking at, not for walking), all the shoes in the suitcase were high heels. In the bottom was a red silk nightgown and a matching red silk robe. Or in this instance, Tyler thought, looking at the exquisite pieces, they should probably be called a peignoir.

Straightening, she looked down at the clothes spread out on the bed. Totaled, they probably cost more than she'd earned last year, but she wondered if the lot of them had as much fabric in them as three of her suits that she usually wore to work.

She grimaced. First she'd take a bath; then she'd go downstairs—wearing her baggy old weekend clothes that she had traveled in—then she'd find the nearest shop and buy something sensible to wear.

On the other hand . . . She reached out and touched the silk in the gown and the robe. Krissy really did have taste. Maybe it was the taste of a call girl, but certainly a top-class call girl.

Going into the bathroom, Tyler turned off the water, splashed bubble bath into the tub, then began to undress. When she was down to her underwear (plain, white, and all-cotton), she took out the pins in her hair and let it down. The mirror over the sinks was a bit steamy, so she wiped it clean and looked at her reflection. She wasn't beautiful, but she knew that she was quite nice looking, in a respectable sort of way. She had good skin that she slathered night and day with moisturizers, and her makeup was subtle. She darkened her lashes with mascara and added some liner, but she'd found that using anything other than the palest of colors on her lips, which were the best feature of her face, only made men look at her as though they were interested in something besides the case she was working on.

But as she looked at herself, Tyler pulled the band off her hair and let it fall about her shoulders. Her hair was her only real claim to beauty. "I wish I had hair like yours," were words she'd heard all her life.

Her hair was a dark chestnut with touches of red in it. Her hairdresser said that if he could clone her hair color, he'd be the most sought after man in New York. When he said things like that, Tyler just smiled. Her hair was very thick, but still fine and soft, and it reached all the way to her elbows, where it ended in great fat curls.

Long ago, Tyler had learned that if she wanted anyone to take her seriously, she had to keep her hair hidden. She had to pull it back from her face and do her best to hide it under a hat. Many years ago, when she'd first entered college, there had been so many remarks about her hair and so many young men had made "suggestions" about how they'd like to use her hair, that she'd had it cut short. But that had been worse, because, cut short, it framed her face in a way that created even more attention—unfortunately, the kind of attention that she didn't want.

After her hair had grown out again, she'd learned to

keep it hidden. Only in privacy, with a man she was intimate with, did she let her hair flow about her.

Suddenly, there was a knock on the bedroom door, and Tyler jumped, feeling as though she'd been caught doing something she shouldn't have been. The knock sounded again, this time louder, harder, more insistent. The clothes that she'd worn on the plane were on the floor, damp from bathwater splashed on them, and she saw no robe hanging in the bathroom. When the knock came a third time, Tyler ran into the bedroom and grabbed Krissy's red silk robe off the bed, then hurried to open the door.

There was a man standing there, his head down as he looked at a stack of papers in his hands. He was handsome in a seen-the-world sort of way. Like Harrison Ford is handsome, she thought. She was very aware that she was standing there with her hair down and wearing a bathrobe that was clinging to her as though it were made of plastic wrap. Red silk plastic wrap.

But the man didn't look up from the papers as he strode into the room. "What took you so long?" he asked, frowning, obviously annoyed. "I want you to call Larry and tell him that if Wallingford can't get the shovels to us by the tenth, then we'll go somewhere else. Fax the Westchester store and tell them to get the chain saws from the Portsmouth store. Overnight them."

He still hadn't looked up from his papers, and Tyler wondered what he was going to do when he realized that she wasn't Krissy. It was this moment that she'd not wanted to think about, this time when she had to try to explain what, even to her ears, was a ridiculous story. Would he fire Krissy?

"Tell Larry that, no, I don't want to buy more stock in

his cousin's company." He put the top paper on the bottom of the stack. "No," he said, shuffling another paper. "I do not like this design for the web site. Call that girl, that blonde, what's her name?"

He hadn't yet looked at Tyler. She took a guess. "Marilyn?"

"Yeah, that one. Call her and tell her to redo the new ads. They make us seem too old. I want to get the woman's market. Try it from that angle." He changed papers. "Tell Jonathan yes on all these figures. Tell him I want more on the Japanese store. I want more numbers. Did you get all that?"

Finally, he looked up at her. And Tyler waited for the explosion. Would she be put on the next plane out? But, worse, what would be his reaction to the fact that she was wearing a red silk robe that was more fit for a bordello than a family hotel—and her hair was down?

But Joel Kingsley—assuming that's who this man was—didn't so much as register surprise that he had just given orders to a woman he had never seen before.

If nothing else, Tyler thought, he should be asking if he was in the correct hotel room.

But when he said nothing, just stood there staring at her, she realized that he was waiting for her to answer his question, and it took her a moment to remember what he'd just asked her.

Well, she thought, if he could pretend that nothing was out of the ordinary, so could she. She gave him a little smile. "Every word."

He narrowed eyes that were a very dark blue. "Humor me," he said.

Tyler kept her little smile then repeated everything

he'd said to her almost word for word. She'd always been good at listening and remembering.

The man didn't make a comment about her good memory, but, instead, tossed the papers on top of a pink sweater on the bed, then turned and went to the door. At the door, with his back to her, he paused. "I have to go see the man about the lawnmower. Do what I told you to and be ready in an hour. And don't wear the heels." At that, he left, closing the door behind him.

For a moment, Tyler stood where she was, her mouth opening and closing; then she sat down on a chair beside the bed. Had he not noticed? she wondered. What sort of man could see that his assistant had been replaced by a stranger and not say a word about the exchange of people? Shouldn't he have at least asked about Krissy? For all he knew, she could have been run over by a truck.

Unless Krissy had called and told him everything, Tyler thought, then stood up. Yes, of course, that had to be it. She went back into the bathroom, meaning to climb into the tub full of hot water, but then she remembered all that she had to do in just one hour before she was to meet him.

With a sigh of self-pity, she let the water out of the tub. As she watched the water drain, she mimicked him, 'Do what I told you to,'" she said in a falsetto voice. One thing was for sure, she'd done the right thing in keeping her innocent young cousin away from that man. He'd eat sweet little Krissy alive.

Sighing, Tyler went back into the bedroom, picked up the telephone, and, using the papers he'd left behind, found the numbers and names she needed.

An hour after Joel Kingsley had walked into her room, Tyler was waiting in the hotel lobby to meet him.

It was all she could do to keep from tugging at her trousers because they were too snug. And the tiny cashmere sweater . . . Well, it rode up in front to expose her belly button. She kept hunching over to cover herself, but that made her feel like a hunchback, so she'd stand up straight again. But then her belly button was exposed.

"Where is the nearest clothing store?" she asked the man behind the desk.

Smiling, he glanced at her attire. "I'm afraid ye're a long way from a fashionable boutique."

"I don't want fashion; I just want something to cover myself up," Tyler said in exasperation.

"Now, that would be a shame," he said slowly, looking into her eyes.

It was a moment before Tyler grasped what he meant; then she felt herself blush. "I, uh . . ." she began, not knowing what to say. But she was saved from replying when just then Joel Kingsley came down the stairs, but he walked past her without a word and walked to the front door of the hotel.

He only saw me once, Tyler thought, so he probably doesn't recognize me.

But in the next second, he put his head around the doorframe and said impatiently, "Are you coming or not?"

Grabbing her handbag and the thin Mark Cross briefcase that she'd found in Krissy's suitcase, Tyler ran after him. There was a car waiting for them outside, and Kingsley was already inside it. Tyler got into the backseat beside him, but he didn't look at her. He was reading a stack of papers on his lap.

Part of her said that she shouldn't call attention to herself, but another part said that she wasn't sure he'd notice if she introduced herself as a maid from the hotel. "So what is it you're buying?" she asked.

"Beauty," he said without looking up.

"I beg your pardon?"

"Beauty," he said louder, as though she hadn't heard him the first time.

"I see." Several times on the plane she'd thought about her first meeting with this man and what his reaction would be when he discovered that she wasn't his assistant. She'd imagined everything from anger to amusement. But she'd *never* imagined that he'd *ignore* her.

And she had to admit that being ignored was more than a bit annoying. "So are we talking plastic surgery or a new kind of WeedWhacker?"

He still didn't look up. "Hardware," he said. "Drawer pulls. Toilet paper holders."

"So what do toilet paper holders have to do with beauty?" She was genuinely puzzled.

At that he put down his papers and turned to look at her. "Do you think that a Rockefeller has the same paper holder in his bathroom as Mr. and Mrs. America do?"

She looked back at him. He really did have the most beautiful eyes, and she could understand why all the girls at his office were half in love with him. But they'd die of starvation, she thought. This man was the coldest creature she'd ever met. "I can honestly say that I never thought about it," she said.

"Neither have most people. The drawer pulls and the paper holders and the doorknobs in the world of rich people are beautiful. Unusual. Different. Have you ever been in a New York designer's hardware store?"

"No," she said.

"What you would see inside one of them is a vast selection of hardware from all over the world, and they are truly beautiful. But they are expensive, very expensive. Do you know why?"

Tyler just shook her head.

"Design. That's it. Design. Those drawer pulls don't have better quality brass in them than the mass-produced items found in most hardware stores, but they have the advantage of great designers. Unfortunately, they're priced accordingly, and the average Mr. and Mrs. can't afford them. So I'm going to several countries and buying different items to sell in my stores. Beautiful things."

When he'd finished his little speech, he looked back down at his papers as though Tyler were dismissed, but she thought about what he'd just said.

"So who's the competition whose can you're trying to kick?" she asked.

There was a teeny, tiny smile at one corner of his mouth, and for a moment he hesitated as he turned a page. "Gilmore's Home Supply. They went after the women's market and started carrying appliances."

"I see," Tyler said as she leaned back against the seat. "And you think that cute little doorknobs will bring in the women?"

"You got a better idea, let me know," he said, and his voice was hard.

"I'll be sure to," she said in a voice that was just as hard as his.

Tyler closed the door to her bedroom behind her, then stood for a moment, leaning against the door and shaking her head. She had spent the last several hours with Joel Kingsley, and—

She didn't want to think about what today had been like. She wanted a strong drink, or maybe two of them; then she wanted that bath she'd missed earlier and—

She stopped thinking when the telephone rang, and she picked it up.

"Oh, Tyler," Krissy gushed. "You're finally there. I've called at least a hundred times. How is he? Was he angry that I didn't show up? Did he find the things he wanted to buy?"

"And I'm just fine," Tyler said sarcastically.

Krissy laughed. "I was going to ask about you, but you're always fine. You can take care of yourself."

"And that man can't? That man could take care of himself on a trip to the North Pole. Better yet, send him down the Amazon. He'd be better than an air conditioner."

For a long moment, Krissy didn't say anything. "You don't like him," she said flatly.

"Like him?" Tyler said. "Like him? Did you know that he detests any woman who he thinks is coming on to him?"

"Oh, yes," Krissy said happily. "He has to do that, as we're all in love with him."

"Kristin Beaumont," Tyler said slowly, "you cannot possibly entertain any romantic feelings for that . . . that . . ." She couldn't think of words strong enough to describe him.

"Tell me everything that happened," Krissy said eagerly. "Is that Delashaw woman there? Did you meet her?"

"Did you call him and tell him that you were ill and that I was going to be your replacement?"

"Of course I didn't," Krissy said, sounding as though that were an absurd idea.

"But the man made no comment at all when he saw me. He just—"

"—started telling you what needed to be done," Krissy said. "Yes, I would have guessed that's what he'd do. He has so much work to do that he doesn't have time for details."

"Details?" Tyler said, her voice rising. "Human beings are details to him?"

"Only pretty women," Krissy said. "Did he ask you your name?"

"No. In fact, he never addressed me once. He just handed me papers, handed me his cell phone, told me to call people. If I were a robot, he couldn't have treated me with less human interaction."

Again, Krissy was silent for a while; then she said softly, "He thinks you're pretty. Have you been wearing *my* clothes?"

Tyler knew the warning signs of approaching jealousy. She might think that Joel Kingsley was a jerk, but she knew that Krissy didn't feel that way. "So how are *you* feeling? Has the doctor been to see you again?"

"Yes," Krissy said hesitantly. "He came over last night and brought me something to eat. Tyler, you aren't falling for him, are you?"

For a moment, Tyler honestly didn't know whom Krissy meant. "Kingsley? Am I falling for a man who—" Once again she reminded herself that, whatever she thought of him, Krissy liked the man. Liked him too much, which was why she, Tyler, was here in Scotland. "No, Krissy," Tyler said patiently. "I'm not falling for Joel Kingsley. As you said, he's not my type at all."

At that Krissy laughed, her good humor restored.

"You're just like him, you know that? Both of you choose lovers who don't interfere in your lives. If you don't love, you don't get hurt."

At that Tyler pulled the receiver away from her ear, frowned at it, then put it back to her ear. "I really hope that you don't really believe that *I* am anything like Kingsley. He's a man without emotion. If you could have seen him tonight! We were in a pub and he was laughing it up with a bunch of men, but when a pretty waitress approached the table, he froze."

"She probably let him know that she was attracted to him. He hates that. And might I remind you of that man my mother introduced you to two Christmases ago? You weren't exactly warm to him."

Tyler was glad that she was on the telephone so her blush couldn't be seen. To this day, she couldn't understand what it was about that man that had turned her off. He was handsome, intelligent, a widower, and he had very kind eyes. He was a pediatrician, and it was obvious that children would like a man as gentle as he was.

But Tyler had stayed away from him as though he had a disease. Three times that evening he'd approached her, and the last time, she'd almost sneered at him.

"All right," Tyler said. This conversation had not gone the way she wanted it to. "Let's not get into that. Look, I need to take a bath and go to bed. I haven't had much sleep in the last twenty-four hours."

"Don't touch him, Tyler," Krissy said in a low voice. "I want him."

"You and half the female population of the world," Tyler answered quickly, then said good-bye and hung up.

But as soon as she put the phone down, she knew that

she didn't want to go to bed. She was too keyed up to want to sleep. And, besides, she was in romantic Scotland, in a castle, and ... With a smile, she reminded herself that she was off work and she was in Scotland. She went to a table set along the wall and picked up the hotel brochure. Was there any place that she could explore? Could she go wandering about the castle and see something besides a cell phone?

Reading the brochure, she saw that the hotel was in the "new" part of the castle, the part that was built after there was any real need for a fortress. But the older part of the castle had been restored, and during the day, there were tours conducted through it. There was a photo of a young woman in quasi-medieval dress pointing to a wall hung with an arrangement of swords and shields.

Going to the closet, Tyler looked at the assortment of clothes that she had with her. If she'd had her clothes, she would now put on a long wool skirt, a man-tailored white cotton shirt, and a thick cardigan. But there was no such thing in Krissy's wardrobe.

But then Tyler thought of the way Kingsley had turned away from that pretty barmaid this afternoon, and the way he'd acted as though Tyler didn't exist, and she also remembered the way Krissy had said that Kingsley didn't like "pretty" women. "What the hell?" Tyler said aloud, then pulled out a pair of black leather trousers. From a drawer, she picked up a pink angora sweater. It had a high neck and long sleeves, but the bodice was about half the length of what Tyler usually wore. Sure enough, when she put the sweater on, her belly button was again showing.

But as Tyler looked at herself in the tall, free-standing mirror, she could see that she didn't look so bad for an "old woman" of thirty-five. Her stomach was flat thanks to hundreds of hours in the gym, and her derriere was . . . Well, it would still pass. At least it hadn't fallen to the back of her knees yet, as her mother said it would do on her thirtieth birthday.

She put on her white sneakers, but they clashed with the black leather trousers, so she chose the lowest high heels from Krissy's wardrobe and put them on. And once she had the heels on, she didn't dare glance at herself in the mirror again or she knew that she'd never have enough courage to leave the room.

Downstairs Tyler asked the man behind the desk which was the way to the old part of the castle and could she visit it without a tour guide? At first he told her that the area was closed to the public in the evenings, but when Tyler looked disappointed, he smiled and said softly, "I'll see what I can do for you"; then he withdrew a key from a box behind the desk. "Follow me," he said quietly, and she did.

He unlocked a heavy oak door and opened it. "Turn on all the lights you want. They'll think it's the cleaners, but be sure to turn them off after you leave."

It was absurd, of course, but Tyler's heart was racing at the thought of being allowed to wander through a castle alone, with no guide telling her not to touch things. "I can't thank you enough," she said.

"Yes you could," the young man said very softly.

It took Tyler a moment to understand what he meant, but when he glanced down at her bare navel, she had to fight an urge to grab the too-short sweater and pull it down. But, instead, she . . . Well, she stood up straighter. "Perhaps," she heard herself say in a coquettish way, then thought, I make myself sick.

She fully expected the young man to laugh at her tone,

but he didn't. Instead, he gave her a warm smile, then opened the door wider for her. "Let me know," he said as she passed him.

When the door closed behind her, Tyler felt good. She'd never been the femme fatale type, but now she felt a bit . . . Well, she didn't exactly feel ugly.

Around her were walls covered in dark oak paneling. A suit of armor stood to her left. There was a long Knole sofa against a wall, the big tassels hanging halfway down its sides.

A castle, she thought, and it was all hers. On impulse, she reached up and pulled the tie from her hair and let it cascade down her back. There was no one here to see her, so if she was going to feel sexy, she might as well go all the way.

But ten minutes later, her good mood was broken. She was walking down an oak-floored corridor, reading a brochure she'd picked up off a table and looking at every object, when the door at the opposite end of the short corridor opened. For a moment Tyler thought about leaping behind the curtains to her left and hiding. After all, she wasn't supposed to be in here.

Through the door walked Joel Kingsley, and he looked as astonished to see her as she was to see him. "What are you doing in here?" he demanded.

In her opinion she was off duty and therefore she didn't have to kowtow to him. "I could ask you the same thing. This place is closed during the evening."

"I gave the owner three lawn tractors to test for me. What did you give to be allowed in here after hours?" As he said this, he looked her up and down—from her loosened hair to her bare midriff, to the black leather trousers, down to her high heels, then back up again. It was obvious what he was thinking.

"Sexual favors," Tyler said. "I have now been to bed with every man who works in this hotel. And was that one of *your* lawn mowers this afternoon? I think your gearshift bruised my back," she said as she put her hand to the small of her back as though to relieve the pain.

Once again she thought she saw the teeniest bit of a smile on his lips. "I'll speak to the manufacturer," he said solemnly. "I guess I should be glad I didn't send him WeedWhackers. You'd probably be suing me now."

Tyler didn't think that in her entire life she'd ever before indulged in this, well, sort of . . . sexual teasing. "Probably," she said. "But then—"

She broke off when she heard a sound from behind the curtain. Startled, she turned toward it.

Joel also heard the sound, and he threw back the curtain in one quick motion to reveal a deep window seat.

When Tyler saw the young man sitting there, she gasped, putting her hand to her throat. So much for being alone in the castle!

It was obvious that the young man belonged there, as he was wearing a huge white shirt made of a type of coarse cottony-linen fabric and a kilt that looked as though it had been through a lot of mud and washed repeatedly. Tall socks that Tyler could have sworn were hand knit covered his heavy calves, and his shoes looked to be real gillies. She had to give it to the staff; she'd never seen a more authentic costume.

"Ian McLyon," he said, nodding his head toward Tyler.

His accent was so thick that she barely understood him. He was certainly good-looking, with thick, black, curly hair and brilliant blue eyes. And now he was looking Tyler up and down in a way that was threatening to make her blush.

"I thought this place was closed in the evening," Joel growled at the young man.

Tyler turned to him, frowning. "From the look of him, he has more right to be in here than *you* do," she snapped.

"*I* made arrangements," Joel said, again looking at her in a way that made her feel sluttish. "I didn't do whatever you did to get in here after—" He broke off at the sound of laughter coming from the young man.

"Ah, true love," Ian said.

"We're *not*—!" That was all Tyler could get out, as the idea was so repulsive to her.

"Definitely not!" Joel Kingsley reiterated.

"Too bad," Ian said, smiling. " 'Tis a wonderful thing to be in love on a night like this. Look at that moon."

Tyler glanced up at the tall window, where she saw a full moon outside, lighting the beautiful, rolling land around the castle. Below them was what looked like an old-fashioned herb garden, set out in a pattern like a wheel. In the middle, the hub, was a birdbath. At the far end of the garden was a bench, and a girl was sitting on it, staring up at the window.

"Yours?" Joel asked, nodding down toward the girl.

"Ah, yes," Ian said, smiling sweetly.

Instantly, Tyler felt a bit of jealousy. What would it be like to have a man's face change like that when he thought of you? The instant that thought crossed her mind, she shook her head to clear it. People didn't "own" each other, as these two men seemed to think that they did. In her worst divorce cases she encountered men who thought that their wives "belonged" to them.

She opened her mouth to tell both men what she

thought of their chauvinistic attitude, but closed it again when Ian spoke.

"But alas, she's a bit upset with me now."

"How could she be?" Tyler said without thought; then when she saw Kingsley's frown, she took a step backward. "I mean . . ." she began, planning to backtrack, but, instead, she put her chin up. "I mean," she said softly, "how could any woman be angry at *you?*" She didn't turn to look, but she could feel Kingsley glowering at her. No doubt that later he'd have something to say about her flirting with a man she'd just met.

Ian laughed softly. "You do a man good, lass," he said, smiling at her, but then he turned his head toward the window, and his eyes were sad. "There are things between her and me that I can share with no other." He looked back at Tyler. "You wouldn't be willin' to take a message to her for me, would you? I have somethin' I need to tell her, and I . . ." Breaking off, he lifted his hands in a gesture of helplessness.

Tyler smiled. "I understand," she said, and reached out to touch his arm, but Ian turned to look at Kingsley before she could touch him.

"Would ye mind if your lady did this for another man? I would owe you forever."

Before Kingsley could speak, Tyler snapped, "He's my employer, not my lover!"

At that Ian turned wide eyes to look at Tyler, then back at Joel. "She's your maid?" he asked, his voice full of shock, but there was also an underlying tone of congratulations.

"Not quite!" Tyler said.

"Yes. Cleans the latrines for me every morning," Joel said, laughter in his voice.

Ian nodded solemnly, as though he didn't realize that Joel was joking. Tyler gave both men looks of disgust. No matter that they'd just met, there was that male bond between them.

Ian pulled his leg up onto the cushioned window seat, and when he did, his kilt rode up, exposing his leg up to his thigh. Tyler couldn't help but enjoy the view; he was a very good looking man. Pulling out a folded piece of paper from inside his tall sock, Ian looked at Tyler as though he could read her thoughts, and his look made her blush hotly.

She was sure that it was thanks to Krissy's too-tight, too-revealing clothes, but she was acting like a thirteen-year-old at a rock concert. After taking a tiny step backward, Tyler put out her hand to take the note from Ian. The paper was quite warm in her hand.

"Ye'll give it to her?" Ian asked softly.

"Oh, aye," Tyler said, unconsciously imitating his burr. Then, realizing what she'd done, she cleared her throat. Kingsley was looking down at her with one corner of his mouth lifted in an expression of disgust.

"I'd kiss you in gratitude, but my circumstances don't allow it," Ian said, amusement in his voice as he looked from one to the other. "Now ye must go, for her father will come for her soon, as he does every night."

There was such sadness in his voice at this last sentence that Tyler opened her mouth to ask him what the problem between him and his girlfriend was. And why was her father interfering? When she'd been in law school, she'd had some training in mediation. Maybe she could—

Putting his hand under her elbow, Joel half pushed her toward the door that was just to the left of the window

43

seat. "We need to do what the boy says and get the note to the girl before her father takes her home. It's probably past the bedtime of both of them."

"I don't recall that there was any 'we' involved in this," Tyler snapped as she jerked her arm out of his grasp. She looked around Joel Kingsley's big body to see Ian again, but he'd already drawn the curtain across the window seat, so she couldn't see him.

The old oak door opened to ancient stone steps that spiraled downward. After Joel flipped on the light switch, she went down first, her shoes fitting into deep grooves worn down by thousands of feet over hundreds of years.

Once they were outside, the cool air of a Scottish night hit them and Tyler shivered.

"If you wore something that didn't leave your belly hanging out, you wouldn't be cold," Joel snapped, then took off his jacket and handed it to her.

For a moment she looked at the jacket in question. But in that instant, she learned something. Girls who wore boxy wool suits didn't get offered men's jackets on chilly nights. But girls who wore black leather pants, high heels, and itty-bitty, teeny-weeny, fluffy pink sweaters were handed Italian leather jackets to slip around their shoulders. "Thanks," Tyler said, taking the jacket and slipping her arms into the sleeves. It was as warm from his body as the note she carried was from Ian's body. All in all, she thought, she didn't feel half bad.

But she wasn't going to let Kingsley know she was enjoying herself. When she smiled, she turned her head away so he couldn't see her.

They walked in silence across the lawn toward the herb garden and the girl. When they were about twenty feet from her, she jumped up and Tyler thought maybe she was going to run away, but instead, she held on to the arm of the bench and threw up.

"So now we know what the problem between them is," Joel said under his breath.

Tyler didn't take time to reply but hurried forward to the girl, meaning to help her, but the girl put up her hand to signal Tyler to stay away, so she did. The girl took a few moments to recover herself; then she sat back down on the bench. Her head and shoulders drooped in that way that Tyler knew was another sign of pregnancy—fatigue.

"Can we get you anything?" Tyler asked quietly. She had a soft, sweet look about her that made Tyler want to put her arms around her and take her home. Kingsley was right when he'd called her a "girl."

"No," she said, her voice hoarse. For a moment she lifted her head and looked up at the castle.

Following her eyes, Tyler looked back at the castle. There was a light here and there in the windows, but nothing but blackness from where she knew Ian was watching them. Tyler started to raise her hand to wave to him, but she didn't.

"Look," Tyler said as she turned back to the girl, "I know something about this sort of thing, and I believe I can help."

The girl acted as though she hadn't heard. "You have a message for me?" she asked tiredly, then held out her hand toward Tyler.

With a sigh, Tyler handed the girl the note. This wasn't her country, and it wasn't any of her business.

Tyler watched as the girl opened the folded piece of paper with trembling hands. When she read what was written there, tears filled her eyes; Tyler could see them glistening in the moonlight. Her heart went out to the girl: so young and pregnant. And by a man her father didn't seem to approve of.

Tyler wanted to try again to offer help, but the girl turned her head sharply, as though she'd heard something.

"You must go now," she said in a whisper. "My father comes."

"Maybe I should stay and talk to him," Tyler said. "I've had some experience in matters like this, and—Ow!" she said when Joel's fingers clamped onto her elbow.

"She doesn't want your interference," Joel said pointedly. "So leave the girl alone."

"It's none of your business what I do or do not do," Tyler snapped at him, trying to twist her arm out of his grasp.

"Oh, please go," the girl pleaded. "It will be harder for me if you are here when he comes. Please go."

Tyler couldn't disobey that plea. With a final twist of her arm, she removed it from Kingsley's grasp, gave one last look at the girl, then started walking back toward the castle, this time on a path through the herb garden. But her heel caught in a crack in the brick walkway and she couldn't move. It was with annoyance from her and smirks of "I told you so," from him that he bent down, grabbed her ankle, and pulled her heel out of the crack. "Thanks," she mumbled; then, with as much dignity as she could muster, she continued walking.

When she was almost to the castle door, she looked back at the bench, but the girl was gone. Tyler put her hand on the door latch to open it, then let it go. It was too late now to continue touring the castle and, besides, *he* might want to go with her. She'd had all she could take of Joel Kingsley for one day.

"I'm going to bed," she said, tight-lipped.

"Alone?" he asked instantly.

She started to defend herself—an occupational hazard—but then she waved her hand airily. "No. The cooking staff will be joining me. Cream cheese on the sheets, that sort of thing."

"Whipped cream," he said, looking down at her solemnly. "Whipped cream and sex go together. Cream cheese goes with bagels."

"Oh," was all that Tyler could think to say. It had to be the moonlight, but suddenly Joel Kingsley was looking very good. Without another word to him, she turned on her heel—which almost caused her to fall—and headed in the opposite direction, where she hoped the new part of the building and her nice, safe bedroom lay.

"Nine A.M.," he called after her. "I'll see you at nine in the lobby. And bring a pen this time."

Tyler kept walking.

Three

The next morning, Tyler searched out the most conservative clothes that she could find in Krissy's wardrobe, but there was nothing that covered too much of her. Or if she was covered, the way everything clung to her like the peel on a potato, she might as well have revealed skin.

With her head held high, she went to the lobby.

Kingsley wasn't there. "He said that he would be late," the young man behind the desk, a different one from last night, said.

"Hours late or minutes?" she asked.

"He didn't say," the man said, then turned away to answer the telephone.

Tyler looked at her watch. It was nine A.M.. Maybe there was a village nearby and maybe she could quickly get Kingsley's driver to take her into town so she could buy some decent clothes. Yes, that was a good idea, she thought. She could buy something that covered her body and—

"What time does the first tour of the castle start?" she heard herself asking.

"About five minutes ago," he answered. "It's right through that—"

"I know which door," she said as she hurried toward the oak door she'd gone through last night.

There were only three other tourists in the group that early in the morning, and Tyler wasn't surprised when she saw that Joel Kingsley was one of them. But when he glanced back and saw her, he looked like a schoolboy caught playing hooky.

For her part, Tyler acted as though she hadn't seen him and moved to the opposite side of the little group.

"Don't you have some work to do?" he said under his breath to her when they moved to another room.

"My boss is missing," she said sweetly without looking up at him. "Be quiet so I can hear."

Tyler found the tour fascinating and listened intently to every word about the building and the lives of the people who'd lived in the castle.

48

She followed the group, ignoring the fact that Joel Kingsley was behind her, into a small sitting room.

"Now here we have our love story," the guide said. He was an older man, wearing a kilt with an ease that made him seem like one of the Highlanders in the many portraits on the walls.

Joel touched Tyler's arm, and when she looked at him in question, he nodded toward a portrait on the wall, and when she saw it, Tyler's eyes widened. The man in the portrait was a dead ringer for Ian McLyon, the man they'd met last night.

The guide saw Tyler's look and smiled. "Ah, yes, all the ladies love young Rob. He was a handsome devil, wasn't he?"

"I thought his name was Ian," Tyler said, staring at the portrait. The young man they met last night must be a descendant of this man or one of the man's ancestors.

"I can see that you've been reading your guide book," the man said, obviously pleased. "And you have a good memory for gossip." His eyes were twinkling.

This made the other tourists laugh, but Tyler had no idea what he was talking about.

"Would you like to tell the story?" the guide asked Tyler.

Puzzled, she looked up at Joel, but he shrugged. "Ah, uh, no, thank you," Tyler said.

"Too bad. I would have liked a bit of a break," the guide said, again making the others laugh. "But you listen and you catch me if I make any errors."

Tyler nodded, but she really didn't know what he was talking about. A glance up at Joel showed that he was looking at her expectantly, as though he were wondering what she knew about Ian but hadn't told him.

"It was a very simple story," the guide began, "as so

many tragedies are. Young Caitlin MacAfee was pledged to marry Gilbert the Fair, a fellow clansman her father had chosen for her. But, as so often happens, she fell in love with a beautiful young man, a traveling musician, named Ian McLyon, and she secretly married him."

He paused to look at Tyler as though to ask how he was doing, but she just smiled so he continued. "But just after the marriage, the rejected suitor, Gilbert, went missing. The castle was searched, but only his bloody helmet and two of his rings were found in Ian's bed. So Gilbert's brother, Robert, accused Ian of murder."

The guide paused to look at the portrait on the wall. "Ah, poor Caitlin. Her father was not a wise man when it came to money, and he'd borrowed a lot from the family of the young man his daughter was to wed. We can only guess at how upset the man must have been when his daughter told him she'd wed a penniless musician."

The guide turned back to his audience and smiled in a sympathetic way. "I wonder if anyone believed that poor Ian actually did murder Gilbert? After all, Gilbert was a man who had survived many battles, and I doubt if he would have been easy to kill, especially not by a man whose hands were made to play a mandolin. But, alas, poor, unfortunate Ian was hanged anyway, and—"

He broke off because Tyler had let out an inadvertent gasp at this information, then she gave the man a weak smile. "Sorry," she mumbled. "Your storytelling is so real that I . . ." She trailed off, and the guide smiled at the compliment, then continued.

"After poor Ian was gone, Caitlin was married off to Gilbert's brother, Robert, and seven months later young Rob there was produced."

At that one of the tourists laughed. "Seven months?" she asked in a British accent.

"Oh, aye," the guide said, smiling. "But it was his child. Never mind that it was said that Robert was as ugly as a toad, Robert swore that his wife was a virgin when he took her to bed. Three weeks after he and Caitlin married, her father met with an accident. I believe he was thrown, er, ah, that he fell off the roof. And when Robert was master of the castle, he hanged anyone who was unwise enough to point out that his beautiful son looked nothing like him. So, now, shall we go into the next room?"

The others moved through the corridor, Tyler and Joel bringing up the rear. "Nasty piece of work that Robert," Joel said quietly so only Tyler could hear.

"Yes," she answered. "When do you think they have the reenactment? When does the young man playing Ian appear again?"

"I think he already has a girl," Joel said stiffly, then looked at his watch impatiently.

The next room was the last one of the tour, and there were several glass cases filled with objects that were of historical and personal interest to the family that had owned the castle for hundreds of years.

In spite of the fact that Joel looked as though he were now impatient to go back to work, Tyler took the opportunity to get the guide alone. "When is the reenactment?" she asked.

"I beg your pardon?" the guide said.

Tyler lowered her voice so the others wouldn't hear. "When does the young man playing Ian appear again?"

To her annoyance, Joel was standing behind her. "Forgive her American romanticism. She met a man playing a part and she now believes herself to be in love with him."

"I do not believe—" Tyler began but stopped as the other tourists said good-bye to the guide.

"Perhaps you could tell me what you mean by 'reenactment,'" the guide said softly.

"Last night we—" Joel began.

"We were *not* together!" Tyler said instantly.

Joel looked at her in a way that made her be quiet. "I realize that both of us were where we probably shouldn't have been last night, but we saw a young man who looks just like the man in the portrait. I'm sure he's a descendant, and Miss—" He stopped as he looked at Tyler in wonder.

"He doesn't know my name," she said with a smile to the guide. "Maybe I was wrong, but your story made me think that what we saw was a reenactment of the story of Ian and Caitlin, and the young man did say his name was Ian McLyon."

"McLyon," the guide said, looking from one to the other. "Perhaps you could tell me what you saw and where you saw it. I'd be most interested."

"Of course," Tyler said. "It was in the corridor back there. He was sitting behind curtains on a big window seat."

"Oh yes, I believe I know where you mean," he said as he started walking.

Turning, she followed the guide.

"What's your name?" Joel asked as he walked beside her, bending down so his lips were nearly on her ear.

"Krissy," she said, feeling impish.

"Not by twenty years," Joel said with a snort; then his next sound was a muffled, "Ow!"

When the guide turned back to look, Tyler smiled. "Sorry.

I stepped on his toe with my heel. It must have hurt a lot."

"There it is," Joel said, pointing to the curtain across the window seat; then he limped past Tyler, giving her a look that said she might have broken his foot. But she ignored him.

The guide moved the curtains back so they could see the empty window seat. "Could you tell me all that happened?" he said.

Joel and Tyler's words tumbled over each other as they told everything they had seen.

"And the girl was being sick when you saw her?" the guide asked.

"Yes. Poor thing," Tyler said. "If she's pregnant at her age, well, she needs some help. I think she was afraid of her father. Do you know where she lives? Maybe I could visit her."

Once again, the guide's eyes were twinkling. "I should think that she's past help now. Do you not realize that you've seen ghosts?"

At that Tyler looked at Joel, Joel looked at Tyler, then they both looked at the guide.

"Not quite," Joel said, smiling. "These were real people. Look, if we got in here so easily last night, I'm sure that some of the locals could too. I think maybe they were playing a prank on the American tourists."

"Ah. I see," the guide said. "Now, tell me again what you saw when you looked out this window last night."

"The girl—the young woman—was sitting on a chair at the edge of a large herb garden," Tyler said. Right now all she could see out the window was sky, but last night she had leaned forward. So now, she bent toward the window and—

Abruptly, she drew back.

Seeing the look on her face, Joel also leaned across the deep window seat to look below.

Where last night had been an herb garden, now there was a one-story building, an annex to the hotel. Behind it was gravel and parked cars.

Tyler didn't dare look at Joel.

"And how did you get down to the herb garden?" the guide asked.

"That door," Joel said, his voice low.

The guide opened his sporran, took out a set of keys, and unlocked the dark oak door they had used last night, then motioned for them to come and look.

Joel went first, then, turning, he looked back at Tyler. When she didn't move, he reached out, took her wrist, and pulled her forward. Behind the door were stone steps, just as they'd seen last night, but these steps had crumbled into rubble long ago. There was no way anyone could walk down those stairs now.

"Oh, my," Tyler said; then the next moment, she felt Joel's hand under her arm and he was hauling her upright. Her legs seemed to be turning to jelly under her.

"So?" she managed to say at last, doing her best to be an adult and not run screaming down the corridor. "What do we do now? Appear on the six o'clock news?"

"For seeing a ghost in Scotland?" the guide asked, amusement in his voice. "If we put all the ghost sighters on the telly, we'd have no time for the football scores, now would we?" Obviously, he was immensely enjoying the looks on their faces. He was going to dine out on this story for a long time. "Let me tell you about the two Americans I led round the castle one day," he'd say.

"Why don't I let you two have a nice quiet visit with . . ." he said, barely able to keep from laughing out loud, "with each other. Or Ian," he couldn't resist saying. "I have another group at ten. Maybe you can get Ian to appear then and give them their pound's worth." With that he turned and walked down the corridor. Obviously, he couldn't wait to tell his story.

"Wait!" Tyler called out after him. "What was in the note?"

"It's in the case," the guide said over his shoulder, then disappeared through a doorway.

It seemed awfully quiet in the room after he was gone. Slowly, she turned back toward Joel. "So. Maybe we should go back to work."

"I saw it," Joel said softly.

"Saw what?" she asked.

"In the case in that room, the last room we visited. There was a piece of paper in the case, preserved for hundreds of years."

She was looking at his face and saw that he was turning pale. "What did the note say?"

"'They hang me tonight,'" Joel quoted softly.

Four

"Joel, darling," came a voice from behind Tyler, and she turned to see a woman of approximately her own age staring at them. But age was the only thing that they had in common, for the woman was dressed in fashionable tweeds that, unless Tyler missed her guess, had been designed and made exclusively for her. The skirt was long, but it had a slit in it that reached halfway up the woman's thigh: conservative but sexy.

She had that groomed appearance of a woman who spent a lot of time in hairdressers' salons and in those spas that Tyler never had time to attend. The woman's hair was half a dozen shades of blonde, all carefully blended together and perfectly arranged, flowing softly onto her shoulders, which were encased in a silk blouse that probably cost what Tyler earned in a month.

The woman was staring at Tyler as hard as she was being looked at, and Tyler was very conscious of her sluttishly short skirt and her snug little cashmere sweater. Why hadn't she done what she'd planned to and spent this morning buying some proper clothes? she thought in regret.

"Joel, darling," the woman repeated, and Tyler was sure she'd had diction lessons, "is this your assistant? I must say that she doesn't look like your usual choices. I thought you were bringing that one . . . What was her name? Christine?"

"Kristin," Tyler said with a weak smile. "She's my cousin."

"Joel, you didn't tell me there would be a substitution."

"I didn't know," he said absently, as though he hadn't thought about the matter and didn't plan to.

Celeste Delashaw—for that's who Tyler knew the woman had to be—was looking from one to the other and frowning.

Tyler was trying to control the expression on her face, but she feared that she looked as she felt—as if she'd been caught doing something that they shouldn't have been doing.

Confirming what Tyler feared, Celeste said in annoyance, "What is wrong with you two? You look as though you've just seen a ghost."

At that, Tyler made a big mistake: she looked at Joel. Then Joel looked back at Tyler. First, Tyler smiled, then Joel smiled, then he let out a little sound that was like a laugh, then Tyler's usually stern face broke into a grin. Joel was the first to actually laugh out loud, then Tyler, too, began to laugh.

"We have," she said, holding her stomach against the laughter that filled her.

"We did," Joel said as he collapsed against the window seat. But the minute he touched it, he jumped away from it; then laughing more, he looked at Tyler, pointed at the cushion and laughed harder.

Tyler pointed out the window, her laughter so debilitating that she could hardly speak. "Two of them," she gasped.

"We even delivered a note to one of them."

"And it's now in a case, and it's hundreds of years old." Tyler leaned back against the window seat, Joel sat on it, and they fell against each other in helpless laughter.

After too many minutes of watching them, Celeste walked closer, looking as though she meant to put herself between the two of them. But she could no more wedge herself between them than she could stop their hilarity.

"Perhaps you could tell me who you are," Celeste said quite loudly.

"Tyler Stevens, attorney at law," Tyler said, trying to

contain her laughter as she held out her hand to shake Celeste's.

"Lawyer?" Joel said, holding in his laughter for a moment as he stared at her. "You mean I could have had legal counsel at assistant prices and didn't know it? Can I sue you for withholding evidence?"

This statement sent Tyler into new paroxysms of laughter. "Maybe I could have tried poor Ian's case and saved him," Tyler said, as she again fell against Joel.

"Really, Joel!" Celeste said in a voice that could have been heard over a tugboat horn. "You don't even know this woman. I think, Miss Stevens, that you should return to America."

It was that statement that sobered Tyler and made her remember where she was, who she was, and why she'd come there in the first place. "I . . ." she began, but when she stood up straight, she saw the way Miss Delashaw was looking at her, and suddenly, Tyler felt silly. What was a woman her age doing in the clothes of a girl? And maybe it was because of the clothes, but she felt as though she deserved a dressing down by this woman.

"You're right, of course," Tyler said, all laughter gone now. "It was presumptuous of me to have done this."

"Not to mention in poor taste," Celeste said, tapping the toe of her beautifully made shoe on the old oak floor.

"Will my cousin be dismissed?" Tyler asked softly. She looked at Kingsley, but he was staring off into the distance, no longer laughing, and back to being the man-who-wasn't-involved.

"No," Celeste said impatiently. "From what I've seen, the girl does her work well."

Feeling like a child who'd been caught with her hand

in the cookie jar, Tyler turned toward the door, but after a few steps, she looked back. Kingsley still had his back to her. "What about the work that I was—"

Celeste frowned. "I'm sure the hotel can find someone to take dictation and do . . . whatever it is that secretaries do. There will be an airline ticket waiting for you at the desk." After that, Celeste Delashaw turned her back on Tyler and walked toward Joel, who never so much as turned around.

Tyler wanted to say something to him, but could think of nothing to say. Should she start an argument with him, saying that he should have noticed that she wasn't his assistant? Should she—? No, she should go back to her room and pack, then return to the U.S. on the next available plane. The truth was, she didn't even have a right to blame Krissy for this humiliating experience. After all, it was Tyler who was the older, and supposedly, wiser person.

No, the only person Tyler had to blame for this fiasco was herself. She certainly didn't blame Miss Delashaw for being angry when she saw her fiancé laughing uproariously with another woman. If Tyler were in her place . . . Well, the truth was, Tyler had never been in Miss Delashaw's place. Actually, Tyler had never been enough enamored of a man to feel even the slightest twinge of jealousy.

Once in her room, the packing took but moments; after all, the clothes weren't very large, so it didn't take long to fold them. Tyler ran her hand across Krissy's pink angora sweater, thinking about last night and how a man had draped his jacket about her shoulders. With a sigh, she closed the suitcase, set it on the floor, then looked about the beautiful room, at the four-poster bed, at the big walnut wardrobe against the wall, at the deep-set window in the stone wall.

Would she ever again get back to Scotland? Would she ever again stay in a castle?

As she picked up the suitcase, she glanced at the telephone. She'd better call Krissy, she thought, and tell her what had happened. Dutifully, Tyler picked up the phone, then started to punch in the long set of numbers to make an international call.

So what was she going to tell her cousin? That Tyler, the woman Krissy thought could do *anything*, had screwed up? "Well, you see," she could imagine herself saying, "Joel and I saw a couple of ghosts, and—What do you mean, why am I now calling him 'Joel' and not 'Mr. Kingsley'? Look, Krissy, when you see ghosts with a man, when you see a young woman throwing up from early pregnancy and later you find out that the father of that girl's baby was hanged, and that both of them died hundreds of years ago, then—No, actually, he didn't fire me, his fiancée did. No, no, Krissy, I can stand up for myself, but in this case she was right. Kingsley and I were falling all over each other laughing and—No, no, Krissy, calm down, there is nothing going on between him and me. No, I'm not trying to take him away from either you or Miss Delashaw or even from Marilyn, but—"

Tyler put down the telephone receiver. There was no way in the world that she could explain any of this to herself, much less to her cousin.

And what about the people at her office? she thought. How was she to explain to them that she'd lied? Could she come up with something that anyone would believe?

She'd had a family emergency that lasted only two days? Stupidly, she'd told her assistant that she was going to Scotland. So how would she explain—

Tyler's head came up. Yes, it made sense that she'd have to quit Joel Kingsley's employment, but why did she have to leave Scotland? She had freed her work calendar and made arrangements for a two-week absence.

What was that thing that other people talked about? Ah, yes, she thought, it was called a "vacation."

Why couldn't Tyler stay in Scotland and take a much-needed break from her life of work and . . . Well, take a break from her life of mostly work and more work?

She again picked up the telephone, called the desk, and found out that her room was booked for ten more days. She thanked the man; then, smiling, she put the phone down. A vacation, she thought. Ten more days of nothing to do but sightsee and wander about the mountains and look at the heather. Ten days of sleeping late and eating too much and finding out about Ian.

At this last thought, she sat up straighter. Where had that idea come from? What did it matter to her what happened to a handsome young man who had died a couple of hundred years ago? And, the truth was, she wasn't totally convinced that the young man she'd seen had been a ghost. He'd been too real to be a ghost. Hadn't he? Weren't ghosts see-through white things that howled a lot?

One minute Tyler was sitting on the bed feeling sorry for herself, and the next she'd opened the suitcase and dug inside it until she'd found Krissy's cute little fanny pack. Ten minutes later, Tyler was wearing her own clothes, the contents of her handbag was in the fanny pack, and she'd taken a bottle of water from the tiny refrigerator in her room—and she was on her way up the hill to the old keep.

By the time she got there, she was out of breath and muttering about the young man at the desk who'd told her it was "just a wee walk" to the old keep. "Wee walk," she said under her breath. "Up a wee mountain, across two wee rivers, and across one wee canyon."

When she reached the keep, she leaned back against the stones and wiped the sweat off her brow.

It was then that the heavens opened up and sent a wee flood crashing down on her head. Frantically, Tyler ran through the nearest doorway, and with her hands shielding her eyes, she looked about for shelter. In the far wall was an overhang, a place that had at one time probably been a fireplace, and she ran toward it, her head down. But, fast as she had been, by the time she reached the relative dryness of the recess, she was soaked.

"Is it too much to hope that that thing includes an umbrella?" came a male voice from behind her.

Tyler nearly jumped out of her skin when she whipped around to see Joel Kingsley standing against the far wall and nodding toward her little fanny pack. "Are you following me?" she demanded.

"Yes," he said simply. "I followed you so well that I got here first."

Tyler knew that what she'd said was dumb, but she couldn't think of anything else to say. What she wanted to do was walk away from him, but Scotland was cold enough without wandering about wet. And right now it was so overcast that she wasn't sure she could find her way back to the hotel.

"So are you here because you saw me walking this way

or because you wanted to see where the victim died?"

She gave him a look of disgust. "You, of course. I have developed a mad passion for a man who didn't even notice that I was a different person than his usual assistant."

At that Joel snorted. "Right. With that hair. There's a B and B just down that hill. I saw it when I was looking around. Maybe if we go down there, we can get something to eat—unless you brought lunch in that thing." He again nodded toward the little fanny pack buckled about her waist.

Tyler was standing there blinking at him stupidly, still in shock over his statement of, "with that hair."

"Well, Krissy's Cousin, what's it to be?"

Tyler recovered herself. "Why don't you use your cell phone to call a car to come and get you, take you away from me forever; then *I* will make my way to the B and B and have a nice, leisurely dinner? By myself."

Joel smiled a bit, then pulled his pockets inside out and shrugged, showing that he had nothing with him. "Sorry. I came away empty. No phone, not even any money. If we get anything to eat, you'll have to pay. I'll reimburse you on your paycheck."

She opened her mouth to say that she didn't want a paycheck, but then she smiled at him. "I get three hundred and fifty an hour."

For a moment, he looked at her in speculation. "You have a good memory, and the shovels and the chain saws got where they were supposed to on time. And I liked the idea for the web site you gave Marilyn, even if you did lie and tell her that I came up with the idea. Yeah, all right, I'll pay you three fifty an hour. But no overtime."

Turning away from her, he looked out at the rain that was coming down hard and said, "Maybe someone at the B and B knows something about Ian. Are you ready?" But before Tyler could reply, he took off running through the rain.

For a moment, she stood where she was, not moving. Oddly enough, his praise, so honestly presented, had made her feel a bit warmer. However, she knew that if she had any sense at all, she'd return to the hotel alone.

But it was a long, long way back to the hotel. And she thought of the arrogance of Celeste Delashaw. It might do that woman a world of good to see the fiancé she kept under such strict rule walking back to the hotel with another woman.

With a smile of pure devilment, she put her hands up to shield her eyes and started running after Joel Kingsley.

"Oh, you poor dears," said the woman who answered the door of the pretty little cottage. "You're soaked through. Come in and get warm by the fire."

Joel stepped back, his head ducked down against the driving rain, as he let Tyler enter ahead of him.

When Tyler saw the kitchen, she stood there, freezing and wet, and gave out a little gasp, for the kitchen looked like a dream of a cozy, Scottish cottage. There was a huge fireplace with a brick hearth, a little fire burning merrily inside it. A big Welsh dresser stood against one wall, its shelves brimming over with mismatched, chipped dishes. The countertops were wooden and worn down from many years of use. In the center of the room was an old oak table surrounded by chairs with rush seats. Dented copper pans gleamed from their hanging places on the walls.

"You must be Americans," the woman said. She had gray hair and blue eyes and skin so white it looked as though she'd never been in the same country as sunshine. "All the Americans go a bit daft about the kitchen, says it reminds them of their ancestors. I don't know why all Americans seem to have descended from Scotsmen, but then we're a randy lot, we Scots. As for me, I'd like a new fitted kitchen with stainless steel appliances."

"No!" Tyler and Joel said loudly in unison, and that made the woman laugh.

"Here I am going on at you while you're standing there dripping. There," she said to Joel as she pointed to clothes on a hook by the door. "You put those on, and the missus will come with me and I'll sort her out."

Tyler started to say that she wasn't his "missus," but the woman didn't give her a chance. Her name was Mrs. McDonald, and she talked nonstop while she helped Tyler peel the wet clothes off her body, then discreetly turned her back while Tyler removed her underwear and pulled on cotton panties and, braless, slipped a cotton shirt on, then a thick sweater that had to have been hand knit. "We have little else to do here," Mrs. McDonald said cheerfully when Tyler asked about the sweater.

After Tyler put on cotton tights and a thick wool skirt, Mrs. McDonald ushered her back into the kitchen and held out a chair for her. Joel was already seated at the table, and Tyler had to admit that the rough Scottish workmen's clothes suited him. He wore a thick gray sweater and heavy corduroy trousers. His hair was already drying and looking as though he'd just stepped out of a salon.

As for Tyler, she felt grimy and wet and scraggly. Her

hair was still caught in an elastic band, but parts of it had escaped about her neck. She was sure that she had mascara running down her face even though she was constantly using the back of her knuckles to wipe under her eyes. In the bathroom, Mrs. McDonald hadn't given her time to look in the mirror to see how horrible she looked.

"So there, now," Mrs. McDonald said as she turned toward the stove, an ancient contraption that looked as though it belonged in a romantic photo in *House and Garden* magazine. Turning her back to the two of them, she ladled soup into thick pottery bowls.

Since Tyler had walked in the door, she'd been dying to ask the woman what she knew about the castle that was on the other side of the mountain or, as the Scots probably said, "the wee hill," but Joel spoke first.

"Have you lived here long?" Joel asked, and Tyler glanced at him, knowing what he was leading up to.

"All my life and all the lives of my ancestors," Mrs. McDonald said, smiling as she set two bowls in front of them. The soup was rich with beef and barley. There was a big, round loaf of bread on a wooden board in the middle of the table, with a crock of butter and a slicing knife beside it.

"Then you know people and . . . places around here?" Tyler asked, looking at Joel for encouragement. She wanted to lead up to asking this woman about what they'd seen, but she didn't want her to think they were crackpots.

Standing on the opposite side of the table, Mrs. McDonald looked down at them with twinkling eyes. "So which ghost did you see?" she asked.

Both Joel and Tyler looked up at her in astonishment.

"Oh, it's all right," Mrs. McDonald said, laughing as she

turned back to the stove. "Nothing you say will shock me. I opened my old house up because of so many tourists seeing ghosts, then walking to the old keep, getting hungry, and wanting dinner." Turning back to them, she put a platter of roast beef on the table. "Now, tell me. Which one did you see?"

"Ian," Tyler said.

"Ah. Ian," Mrs. McDonald said, and her face softened, her eyes looking dreamy. "That's all right, then. Only true loves see Ian. Ask you to carry a note for him, did he?"

"We're not—" Tyler began, but Joel cut her off.

"Is there anyway to make him stop?" Joel asked. "I mean, playing the same tragic happening over and over again for hundreds of years is a hideous punishment."

"Now, to that I don't know," Mrs. McDonald said. "You'd have to ask my brother Fergus about that. He was caretaker to the castle for thirty-two years, and he knows all the stories."

Tyler used the big knife to cut two thick slices of bread off the loaf, one for Joel and one for herself. "Where does your brother live?" she asked as she slathered butter on the bread.

"Here. When he's under a roof, that is. He could come in any time between now and six A.M., and you could have a bit of a natter with him."

At that statement, both Joel and Tyler looked puzzled.

"A chat. A talk," she said in explanation.

For a moment they looked down at their food, saying nothing. After the soup, there was roast beef and four vegetables, including mashed parsnips, a vegetable so delicious that Tyler wondered why Americans didn't eat them more often.

She looked up at Mrs. McDonald. "If you have so many people seeing ghosts at the castle, why isn't it called 'Scotland's most haunted' or something like that?"

"Too much competition for that title," Mrs. McDonald said. "And it would bring in the wrong kind of people, if you know what I mean. I must go out this evening, so there's summer pudding in the fridge and I'll make up the guest room for the two of you before I go, so you just make yourself at home."

"No!" Tyler half shouted, then calmed herself when Mrs. McDonald looked at her in question. "I mean, not for *us*. For me, yes. I'd like to stay here tonight so I can talk to your brother when he gets in. I have a few questions for him. But, anyway, about us, there isn't an 'us.' I mean, we're not married." Tyler knew that her face was red when she finished.

Mrs. McDonald smiled broader. "Oh, well, even in Scotland we've heard of the sexual revolution. Sleeping arrangements are your business, not mine," she said; then, laughing, she left the room.

In the stillness the woman left behind, all Tyler could hear was the crackle of the fire, but she could feel Joel's eyes on her. Defiantly, she turned to look at him.

"I'll flip you for the room," he said.

"And what about Ms. Delashaw—you know, the woman who fires employees for you—what is she going to say? Shall we look for a telephone so you can call and ask her permission to be out on your own all night?"

Joel put his finger in his ear and wiggled it. "Maybe my hearing is off, but you sound jealous."

"You *wish*," Tyler said.

At that moment they heard a car pull up outside.

Getting up, Tyler went to the tiny curtained window over the sink and watched their landlady get into the passenger side of the car, and it drove away.

Now she was alone in the house with Joel.

For a moment she stood at the window. It was still raining quite hard, and she didn't want to walk back to the hotel. Actually, she didn't dare to so much as leave the cottage or Kingsley would take her room. On the other hand, she could always give up finding out about Ian and what Mrs. McDonald meant by "true love."

But she wanted to know. She was on a holiday that included a castle in Scotland and seeing a romantic ghost. So was she going to return home and tell people that she didn't find out about the ghost because her young cousin's boss had eaten dinner in the same B and B where a man who knew about the ghost lived, so she hadn't—

She drew a breath. Barry would never forgive her if she didn't find out everything she could about the ghost.

Turning, she looked at Joel and saw that he had been watching her. "I'll tell you what. You go back to the hotel and I'll call you when Angus—"

"Fergus."

"Right. I'll call you when Fergus returns."

"How about if you go back, and *I* will call *you* when he gets here?"

"Think Ms. Delashaw will allow that?"

"Jealous. Yes, definitely jealous."

She wanted to make a smart, sarcastic retort to him, but she was too aware of being alone with him in the quaint little cottage to be able to think of a putdown. What was it about being in a foreign place that seemed to make a person forget the real world? She knew that the best thing she could do right now was get away from Joel Kingsley.

"Good night," she said over her shoulder as she quickly turned and went down the hall. Mrs. McDonald had pointed out the guest room to her earlier, so she knew where it was. She wasn't going to spend another minute in the kitchen wasting her time discussing whether or not she was jealous of a socialite like Celeste Delashaw.

The guest bedroom was as perfect as the rest of the house, with homemade curtains and a matching bedspread. Both were a soft mossy green, a color that fit so well with the surrounding misty countryside.

When Tyler closed the door, she saw that there was no lock. When she realized that this annoyed her, she chided herself. What did she think he was going to do? Try to kick her bedroom door in? The days of Rhett Butler were long over. In this day and time, men like Joel Kingsley—rich, handsome, heterosexual—had women running to them. Men like Joel Kingsley didn't have to do anything on earth to win a woman.

The bathroom was down the hall, and without a glance toward the kitchen, Tyler took the thick terry-cloth robe that hung from the back of the bedroom door and went to the bathroom. She had no more than closed the door when she heard a car pull up outside. Pushing aside the curtain, she looked out the tiny bathroom window and saw a long black car in the drive; then she saw Joel get into the back of it.

Tyler dropped the curtain back into place. It didn't take much to discourage him, she thought, then ran the tub full of hot water. She planned to soak until her skin shriveled.

An hour later she was regretting her impulsiveness in

deciding to spend the night at the little cottage rather than returning to the hotel. There was a tube of shampoo by the tub, and even though she was sure it wasn't included in the price of the B and B, she used it anyway. But there was no conditioner, so her hair was tangled and rough. Worse, she had no moisturizer for her face. As she got out of the tub and dried off, she could feel the tightness of her skin. Moving her mouth around, she tried to alleviate the feeling that her skin was cracking.

As she left the bathroom, she was frowning. Tomorrow she was going to regret this impulsive decision because tomorrow her hair was going to be flyaway, filled with static electricity, and her skin was going to be—

When she passed the sitting room, she jumped, startled, for Joel was sitting there, a book in his hand, a fire in the fireplace beside him. She opened her mouth to speak, but since he didn't acknowledge her presence, she didn't say a word but kept walking toward her bedroom.

But she hadn't passed the doorway when his words stopped her.

"Do you know what 'leave-in conditioner' is?"

As though someone had yelled, "Fire!" Tyler stopped in her tracks, unable to move. Her hand was still in her hair trying to pull the tangles out.

"And is Lancôme a good brand for face cream?"

As though she were a puppet and he her master, she slowly turned to look at him. He still had his head down, looking at the book, but in his left hand he held up a little shopping bag that said "Boots" on it. Even Tyler knew that Boots was the name of a fabulous drugstore chain in the United Kingdom.

For a moment she rolled her eyes skyward. If he'd

offered her three million cash, tax free, she could have laughed at him. She could have put on her best manner of insouciance and told him she didn't need him and never would. But conditioner? Moisturizer?

Tyler took a step backward, then two steps into the room. He had put the book down and was now rummaging inside the bag. From it he withdrew a comb and a brush. But it wasn't just any ol' comb and brush. No, these were by Pearson, the best of the best. She'd always wanted a set of those, but it had been one of those luxuries that she'd never gotten around to giving herself.

As she watched, he pulled a large bottle of leave-in conditioner from inside the bag, then three kinds of moisturizer: nighttime, day, and a tiny jar of eye cream. After that, he pulled out a small navy blue bag that zipped across the top, and slowly, as though he were an archaeologist examining puzzling but precious artifacts, he withdrew a complete set of cosmetics: mascara, eyeliner, blush, base, lipstick and, liner. Oh heavens! There was even an eyelash curler in there!

"All right," Tyler said, her mouth in a hard line. "What do you want in exchange? My soul? Firstborn?"

For the first time since she'd left the bathroom, he looked up at her, then smiled. "The couch in your bedroom. I'd like to be here when Fergus returns. I have a few questions I'd like to ask him."

With her eyes on the cosmetics, so very aware of her tight, dry skin and her tangled hair, she hesitated. Spending the night in the same room with him?

Joel held up the book he was reading. "I found this in the bookcase. It's about the ghosts of this area of Scotland." When she still didn't move, he said softly in a voice of enticement, "Ian is in here."

With a sigh of capitulation, Tyler stepped the rest of the way into the room and snatched the bag off the table, as though she feared that he might take it back; then she sat down on the chair opposite him. The room was so small that her knees were only a few feet from his. The only light in the room was the floor lamp by his chair and the fire. Tyler wasted no time in slathering her skin with night cream, rubbing it in well, and closed her eyes in almost ecstacy when the tightness of her skin stopped.

When she looked up, Joel was watching her as though he'd never seen a woman before. Truthfully, it was embarrassing to do something so intimate in front of a man she barely knew. "Don't tell me you've never seen a woman in her natural state," she said, trying to sound lighthearted. "Didn't I hear that you've been married, what? six or seven times?" She was lying, of course, but being the aggressor might keep her from being so aware of how alone they were and how attractive he was and how all she had on under the robe was a pair of borrowed panties.

"Eight," Joel said seriously. "And I don't divorce them; I mummify them and put them in a closet."

Tyler couldn't stop her smile as she squirted conditioner into her palm then began to stroke it through her hair. Try as she might, she didn't seem to be able to make him angry.

"And you?" he asked softly.

For a moment, she didn't know what he meant. But she picked up the hairbrush, and with her head turned toward the fire, she said, "No, I've never been married."

"Why not?"

She started to tell him that it was none of his business, but she didn't. "I seem to beat men at their own game, and they can't stand that. I make more money or I win more cases or I out-argue them. It's always something that I do to threaten them." She wasn't aware of it, but her voice was growing angrier with every word she spoke. "I guess I'm too much of a man for them."

When he didn't say anything, she turned to look at him. He was staring at her hair, watching her as she held it to one side and ran the brush through the long length of it. And there was a smile on his face that made her feel quite good. It wasn't a smile of lust—oh, that was in the smile, all right—but, better than that, he seemed to be laughing at the men in her life. And, most of all, he seemed to be laughing at her statement that she was like a man.

She had to turn away and stop looking into his eyes. Never before had she met a man who would do something so unselfish as to make a trip just to buy a woman cosmetics. Bottles of wine, or gin if he was in a hurry, yes, but not something as personal as hair conditioner and an eyelash curler.

When she spoke, her voice was husky. "So are you going to read to me or are you going to just sit there making puppy dog eyes at me all night?"

He gave a little snort of laughter; then he picked up the book and began to read.

Beautiful voice, was Tyler's first thought; then she forced herself to listen to the words of the story. There wasn't much that she hadn't already heard. Poor Ian had been hanged for a crime that no one, even back then, seemed to believe that he'd committed. But Robert was a powerful man and Caitlin's father was a very weak man, and Ian, just an itinerant musician, had been caught in the middle.

When he finished the article, Tyler turned to look at him. "What you said about Ian being punished was right," she said thoughtfully. "Wasn't being hanged for a crime he didn't commit enough?"

"Unless he wants something."

"Sympathy?" she asked. Her hair was still damp and, absently, she kept combing it.

Joel put the book down on the side table, then leaned forward, opened his legs wide, then silently motioned for her to sit on the floor between his feet.

Without thought, Tyler obeyed him. There was something intimate about the room, with its little fire and the rain outside, that made them seem as though they were the only people on earth.

Taking the brush from her, he ran it through her hair, and she closed her eyes to the sensation. Her mother used to brush her hair when she was a child.

"What do most ghosts want?" Joel asked, his big hands in her hair.

"I have no idea. But . . ."

"Yes?"

"I don't know anything about it, of course, but, like every one else, I've seen *The Sixth Sense.* Maybe Ian is asking for help. Maybe he wants us to . . ."

"What?"

"I don't know. If this were a novel, we'd walk through a door and find ourselves in the eighteenth century."

"Where they never had face cream and conditioner?" he asked, chuckling.

"Where *you* would have to wear armor and fight with a sword. And not a computer or cell phone anywhere."

"So I guess we'd better stay here," he said.

"Yes, let's." She was smiling, her head bent forward as he brushed her hair.

"What do you think Mrs. McDonald meant when she said that Ian only appeared to 'true loves'?" he asked softly.

"That her cousin is a justice of the peace and she's trying to drum up business for him?" Tyler said, not wanting to think about what the woman had actually meant. But when Joel didn't say anything in reply, she softened. "Why did you divorce your wives?" she asked.

"They deserved better than me," he said after a moment.

At that Tyler made a noise of derision. "I've heard that before. I'm a domestic relations attorney. I deal with divorces all day, year in, year out. When a man says that his wife 'deserves better,' it's because he feels guilty because he doesn't love her anymore and doesn't want her."

"Wrong," Joel said. "In my case it was because I never loved them and I knew that they knew it."

"If you didn't love them, then why did you marry them?"

He paused in brushing. "Truth?" he asked.

"Truth," she said softly.

"I hate dating," he said. "I know that all men everywhere are supposed to love going to movie premieres with a starlet on their arm, but I never liked that. I wanted . . ."

"What did you want?" she asked in little more than a whisper.

But before he could answer, a log in the fireplace fell, and Joel got up to put another one on and poke about in the fire for a few moments. When he turned back around, he sat on the floor across from her. There was a little brass bowl sitting on the hearth, and he picked it up, turning it around in his hands.

"Not many people have ever asked me what *I* want," he said softly, then when he looked up at her, his eyes were intense. "You see, I have the ability to make money and that's all that most people can see about me."

"Like Delashaw?" Tyler said, then could have bitten her tongue, for the words came out sounding bitter.

But Joel looked back down at the bowl in his hands and gave a one-sided smile. "Yeah, very much like Celeste." When he looked back up at Tyler, his eyes were twinkling. "So. Would you like to hear my life story? Like to hear about my failed marriages and all the trials and tribulations of a man who is on his way to becoming a billionaire?"

Inside her mind, part of Tyler yelled, "No!" but another part, the one that seemed to control her vocal cords, said, "Sure, why not? There's not much else to do, and the evening is still young."

Again, Joel smiled. "Did you know that all the women in my office think they're in love with me? Even your cousin Krissy gives great heaving sighs every time I walk into her office. If she weren't so fantastically good at cajoling people to do anything she wants them to, I'd fire her for being a nuisance."

Tyler blinked at his words. She felt great loyalty to her beloved cousin, but at the same time it was interesting to hear an outside opinion of someone she'd diapered.

"I doubt if she had much trouble getting you, an attorney, to fly to Scotland and take on her job," Joel said, smiling at Tyler.

She had to smile back. "I'm afraid you're right. She used every major emotion to get me on that plane—and they all worked."

"She does the same at work. Everyone thinks she's a sweet, innocent child, but I've seen her get the heads of companies on the line and talk them into meeting her for tea at the Plaza."

"That sounds like Krissy," Tyler said, drawing her knees up to her chest and hugging them. "You can't believe what she does to my uncle Thad, her father. My mother and I laugh about it until we cry. Uncle Thad prides himself on being the head of his household, but he has no idea that his pretty little daughter holds him in the palm of her hand. One time when Krissy was just six, she—Oh, well, you wouldn't want to hear silly family stories."

"You tell me your story, and I'll tell you what Kris did to get the strimmers into the Wichita store."

"I—" she began, then stopped and looked down at her bare feet peeking out from under her robe.

"You're thinking that we're enemies, so you shouldn't tell me anything about yourself, or listen to anything about me."

He had so perfectly read her thoughts that she had to laugh as she looked back up to him. "Exactly."

"I can tell you that it's been a novelty having a woman around who doesn't *like* me," he said, smiling, eyes twinkling. "You can't imagine what it's like being a single man surrounded by women who swoon over you."

"So why don't you fire them and hire all men?" she said, narrowing her eyes.

Joel laughed. "I must say that being around you has certainly been entertaining."

"If you're trying to seduce me, it won't work. I thought you were going to tell me about your marriages. How many were there? Ten? Twelve?"

"Is this professional curiosity?"

She hesitated. "Actually, no. I already know that you were generous in your settlements. That says a lot to me."

"So why did you check me out? No, wait," he said, holding up his hand. "Your cousin. You wanted to find out if Krissy was drooling over a bad guy or a good one."

Tyler turned away to hide her blush. "More or less."

"If you're so careful about your cousin, why aren't you more careful about the men *you* live with?"

"*Lived* with. Past. And there's only been one," she said, stalling for time. "I don't know. My mother once said that she thought that I was afraid to love a man because I was afraid that I'd end up like her." She looked up at Joel, the firelight behind him. "My father died when I was six, and it took my mother a long time to get over him. She loved him a great deal."

Joel seemed about to reply to that, but then he cocked his head and listened. "It's stopped raining. In the kitchen are wellies and flashlights. You wouldn't be up for a moonlight slog up the hill to the keep, would you?"

Lots of reasons of why she shouldn't do this went through Tyler's mind, but in the end, she wanted to go, just plain *wanted* to go. "Why not?" she said. "Krissy will, no doubt, be furious with me, and your Celeste will—"

As he got up, Joel cut her off with a laugh; then he reached down for her hands to help her stand. "So, tell me," he said as she stood up, "have you always had this obsession with Ms. Delashaw? Or is it new and just for my benefit?"

"If you're implying that *I* am one of the women who believes she's in love with you, you should be so lucky. Besides, my heart is already taken."

She'd meant it as a joke, but the minute she said it, Joel's face changed. "I thought there was no man in your life," he said sternly.

Tyler started to reassure him that she was uncommitted, but then she smiled. "What do you hope to find out at the keep?" she asked, as though he'd not asked her a personal question.

Joel shook his head at her, aware of what she was doing. "Go get dressed. Unless you want to wear just that. On second thought—"

Laughing like a schoolgirl, Tyler ran out of the room to the bedroom where, she put on her still-wet pants and the sweater that Mrs. McDonald had lent her; then she ran down the hall to the kitchen, where Joel was waiting for her.

Five

"You don't think we'll see any more ghosts, do you?" Tyler asked as soon as they were outside the cottage. She was draped in a waxed coat that was three sizes too big for her, and the green rubber boots she'd borrowed were loose on her feet even though she wore her tennis shoes inside.

"What I wonder is if what we saw actually was a ghost," Joel said over his shoulder to her.

"Maybe not, but the stairs were genuinely derelict and

the new part of the hotel was where we saw the girl."

"I was hoping you'd help me out," he said. "But I guess you have too much of a lawyer's mind to think of anything but the facts."

"What do you think he was—Ooof! Sorry," she said because she'd run into the back of him.

In one quick motion, Joel turned on his heel, threw his arm around her, and pulled them both down to the ground together. His arm was over her head, holding her down, his head beside hers; then, cautiously, he lifted his head to look up.

"What is it?" she whispered.

"There's someone there."

"Maybe it's Fergus," she said. "Maybe he's going home. Let's go talk to him."

Joel didn't let her get up but kept her pinned down beside him. "Something's not right. This person is slipping in and out of the stone walls."

"Maybe it's a cow and it's—" She stopped at his look. "Oh. You mean moving *through* the walls?"

Joel gave a curt nod, then ducked his head down, his arm still over Tyler's.

"Let's go back to the cottage," she said. "Nice ghosts sitting on window seats are one thing, but they found a man in that place who'd been shut inside a wall. If it's his ghost, I don't think he's going to be a happy spirit."

"I don't think it is a ghost," Joel whispered, his face close to hers. "And he's moving through the windows in the walls, not the stones themselves. I think it's a man, and I think he's doing something that he shouldn't; that's why he's sneaking about. Stay here and let me go see what's going on."

Before Tyler could reply, Joel was up and running across the moonlit field toward the towering stone tower. Tyler kept her head down and her face covered. Already, she could feel the cold seeping through her clothes, and she thought with longing of the cheerful little fire in the cottage. What could she think of to keep her mind off her present circumstances? Wonder what was going on back at her office? Would Barry remember to water her plants? How was Krissy doing? Did she still have the flu?

When Tyler heard nothing from Joel, she lifted her head and looked up. Nothing. She didn't hear anything or see anything. Silence.

"Kingsley?" she whispered. No answer. "Joel?" she said louder. Still no answer.

She lifted her head higher and listened. Still no sound. Cautiously, she got up and stood in a crouching position to make herself smaller. When she still heard or saw nothing, she ran across the open space toward the rock wall, then flattened herself against it and waited. Nothing. No sound of any kind.

Cautiously, she stepped through the doorway into the keep and instantly, a hand grabbed her ankle and pulled her down. She would have screamed, but another hand was put across her mouth, and in the next second she was drawn down under Joel Kingsley's big body and held there.

"Quiet!" he said into her ear, then removed his hand enough so she could turn her head. To her left she could hear soft sounds coming from the opposite side of the old keep. Sheep? she wondered. Or was it a smaller animal?

"Oh, Davey," came a female voice across the wind.

With eyes wide in question, Tyler looked up at Joel as he still lay nearly on top of her. He nodded down at her in answer. They had stumbled upon a couple of lovers having a tryst in the old keep, and from the sound of their voices, they were quite young.

Joel put his finger to his lips to motion for her to be quiet; then he rolled off of her silently and took her hand in his. Tyler stood, and as quiet as she could be, she followed Joel back through the doorway, on their way out and back toward Mrs. McDonald's cottage.

But one of them stepped on a rock, and it went tumbling down the hillside.

"What was that?" came the girl's voice.

"Nothing," came the voice of a boy who was obviously in the throes of passion.

"No, Davey, I heard something. If it's my father, he'll murder both of us."

"Your father is as like to leave his bed as I am to leave you."

When Tyler looked up at Joel, she could see that he was smiling; then he led her another step, but a second rock went rolling. Grabbing Tyler, Joel pulled her back against him and they froze in place.

"I heard something. I did, I tell you!" came the girl's voice.

"It's just the ghost, so get back down here."

"I don't like ghosts," she said, "and I'll not be performin' for them."

"Nessa, it was just a joke. There are no ghosts here. They're just for the tourists," the boy said, pleading. "You know that."

"I know no such thing. Wasn't it my own mother that saw the lady walk through that picture on the second floor?"

"Aye, and didn't Fergus show you that that picture has a hinge on the back? Your mother had probably been drinkin' again and—"

After that statement there was the unmistakable sound of flesh hitting flesh as the girl slapped the boy across the face.

"What'd you do that for?" the boy asked.

"For sayin' my mother was a drunk." There was a sound of clothing being moved about, as though the girl were dressing.

"I said no such thing. I like your mother. She's the best cook in the village. Her barley soup is the best in the world."

"And you know *why* her soup is so good, Davey McAllister? It's because she puts a pint of whiskey in it," the girl said, defiance in her voice.

"Ah, well, that explains it," he said.

"And what does that mean?" the girl asked.

"I mean that whiskey would make anything taste good. Come on, Nessa, we haven't got all night."

"You can be sure of that! And you don't have to tell me that *your* mother is at the kirk more than the vicar is. But then *my* mother would be too drunk to attend services, wouldn't she?"

"Lord help me, but how did we get onto mothers?" the boy said, exasperated. "Come on, Nessa, let's enjoy ourselves tonight and—"

"You mean, let you have your way with me, don't you? And what do you plan to do with me afterward? Leave me fat and pregnant while you marry someone else, someone closer to your station in life? Someone who doesn't have a drunk for a mother?"

Joel and Tyler heard what sounded like the girl turning and walking off, with the boy close behind her. For a while they stood still as they listened to the boy pleading with the girl not to go, but the girl seemed to make no answer as, eventually, their voices faded from hearing.

"Well, at least it wasn't a ghost," Tyler said at last.

"Or a cow," Joel said seriously.

Stepping away from him, she turned toward the doorway. "It's late and I think that after that any ghosts that were here would have gone home by now," she said seriously.

All Joel said was a noncommital, "*Mmmm*"; then he followed her when she started down the hill toward the cottage, in the opposite direction from the young couple.

Neither said anything for a few minutes as they made their way down the wet path; then Joel said, "Come on, Nessa, give us a kiss."

"After what you said about my mother!" Tyler said. "I'll have you know, Davey McAllister, that my mother never so much as touched a drop of liquor in her life."

"Oh? So she had all those men while she was sober, did she?" Joel said.

"At least she's wanted by men. Your mother's face is so sour it'd scare angels away."

"Ah, but it's your mother who sees angels," Joel said.

Tyler stopped walking, put her hands on her hips, and glared at him. "Only one angel. And only on alternate Saturdays. And he only comes to visit her to give her feathers to use in her dust mop."

Joel opened his mouth to reply to that, but then he laughed. "Her dust mop," he said, laughing. "I concede. I can't top that. What kind of dust mop would need feathers from an angel?"

"To dust the altar at church, of course," Tyler said, sounding as though he were an idiot.

That remark made Joel laugh harder, and Tyler turned around to start walking again. "So much for our finding out anything about Ian," she said. "But, all in all, I'm glad we didn't encounter the ghost of that man who was walled up."

"Or the lady who walked through the hinged picture."

It was Tyler's turn to laugh. "What do you think Nessa's mother was doing? Nipping at the Lagavulin when someone used the door hidden behind a picture frame and she thought it was a ghost?"

"Think she threw her apron over her head and went running?" Joel asked.

"Or was she like us and ran errands for the ghost?"

"And walked down stairs that were crumbling. To think, if we'd waited a few minutes, we could have seen Caitlin's father, the one who sold his daughter to Robert the Vile."

"Robert the Ugly," Joel said in mock seriousness.

They were almost to the cottage and Tyler glanced over her shoulder at him, then started laughing. She didn't want to admit how frightened she'd been when Joel hadn't returned from inside the keep.

"What did you think had happened to me?" he asked, lips twitching in merriment.

Again, it was as though he'd read her thoughts. "That you'd fallen in a hole and were being held hostage by a flock of sheep. Or, more likely, you were being attacked by young secretaries who had fallen in love with you. Hey! Maybe we should have let Nessa see *you;* then she would have forgotten all about young Davey."

"Why, you——" Joel said, then made a lunge for Tyler. She sidestepped him, but he gave chase.

She ran down the rest of the path as quickly as she could, laughing all the way, Joel on her heels. When she reached the cottage door, she flung it open and ran inside, for a moment blinded by the light in the kitchen. Joel skidded to a halt just behind her.

"There you two are," Mrs. McDonald said. "I was wondering where you'd got to. Go up to the keep to have a midnight cuddle, did you?"

Tyler looked at Joel, and he looked back at her; then they both burst into laughter.

Mrs. McDonald was smiling also. "Come on, sit down and tell me what you're laughin' about. I could use a good laugh."

"We saw—" Joel began, but Tyler reached up and put her hand over his mouth to silence him.

"We didn't see anything," she said.

Mrs. McDonald looked from one to the other of them. "You saw some of the village boys and girls up there, and you don't want me to know who they were. Let's see? Was it Aggie and that young Colin?"

Tyler removed her hand from Joel's mouth. "No," she said.

"Mmmm," Mrs. McDonald said. "Innes and Katie? Now, she's a mad flirt and . . . No? Nessa and Tommie McAllister?"

"Close," Joel said, smiling.

"Tommie and . . . No? Ah, then, Nessa and someone else?"

"You had half the name right," Joel said as he cut two slices of bread from the loaf still on the table, then buttered them.

"No!" Mrs. McDonald said in shock. "Not Nessa and *Davey* McAllister!"

"Yes!" Joel and Tyler said together, smiling.

"Ah, well, that girl has set her sights high. I hope she didn't ... Well, I hope she didn't finish what she started."

"No, she didn't," Tyler said.

"She picked a fight with him, then used it as an excuse to run away from him. Poor boy was running down the hill behind her begging her to come back," Joel said cheerfully, his mouth full.

Mrs. McDonald let out a cackle of laughter. "The girl has more sense than I gave her credit for. She'll get him if she keeps on like that, and she probably does want him."

"Not Tommie?" Tyler asked, eating the bread Joel had cut and buttered for her.

"Not enough ambition for her. Nessa is pretty. She has a drunk for a mother and a lazy, no-good for a father, but she has plans for herself. Davey is smart. He's not good-looking, not like Tommie is, and Davey is a fool when it comes to women, but he's smart. He's home from university just now, and my guess is that Nessa plans to go back with him."

Mrs. McDonald looked at Joel and Tyler with a smile. "You two are learning more about Scotland than you wanted to. First a ghost, and now you find out secrets about the village. So you must tell me *your* secrets."

"Not in this lifetime," Joel said cheerfully. "Heard anything from your brother? He wouldn't have left any books around here, would he?"

"Boxes of them," Mrs. McDonald said, looking from Joel to Tyler, then back again. "So which of you is staying in my guest room tonight?"

"I am," both Tyler and Joel said in unison; then Tyler blushed and looked away.

"We worked out—"

"Don't tell me," Mrs. McDonald said, holding up her hand. "Now what do you two want to do? Play cards? Watch the telly?"

"I'd like to see those boxes of books," Joel said, looking in question to Tyler.

But she stepped away from him. "I think I'll go to bed," she said softly. "It's been a long day, and I—"

She didn't say any more, but after a brief "good night," turned and nearly ran down the hall to the bedroom. There had been something too intimate about the way that Joel had said that they had "worked out" the sleeping arrangements, something that had made Tyler know she had to get away from him.

But once inside the bedroom, she leaned against the door and closed her eyes for a moment. She'd had a very good time tonight. She'd sat between Joel's legs and he'd brushed her hair. They'd walked together up the hill, and they'd laughed together all the way back.

There was something about him that brought out the silliness in her, she thought. And silliness was not something that she came by easily. All her life she'd been told how much her mother had loved her father and had been devastated by his death. "You're the strong one now," she'd been told when she was just six years old. "You have to help your mother. You have to be a good little girl." Tyler had never had the freedom to be like Krissy and demand this and that from the adults in her life. No, as a child Tyler had always been aware that if she weren't absolutely perfect, she was going to hurt her mother more than she'd already been hurt. "And more pain might kill her," Tyler had heard a thousand times.

Being perfect and thinking that not being perfect might kill your mother, had made Tyler not feel free to be silly, free to laugh, free to make up stories about angels and dust mops.

So what was it about Joel that made her feel this freedom? She'd certainly never felt like this with the other men in her life. But then she'd been in competition with them, hadn't she? She wasn't in competition with Joel Kingsley.

Annoyed with herself, Tyler grabbed the bathrobe from where she'd tossed it on the back of a chair and left the bedroom to go down the hall to the bath. Ten minutes later, she left, wearing a nightgown that Mrs. McDonald had left draped over the tub and that Tyler hoped had been intended for her; then, without looking into the little sitting room, she went back to the bedroom and climbed into the bed.

For all that her mind was full, she was asleep as soon as she lay down.

She awoke to the sound of a loud bang, then felt the bed jar as something hit it. Or maybe it was someone.

"Ow!" came a male voice very near her.

"Are you hurt?" Tyler asked sleepily, lifting her head.

The next moment there was another slam into the bed, another exclamation of pain; then all of Joel Kingsley's big body fell on top of her, slamming her into the bed and nearly knocking the breath out of her.

"Sorry," he said into her ear as she struggled to get him off of her so she could breathe.

Joel seemed to be trying to get off of her, but he was so clumsy that she was sure he was drunk. He lifted himself up on one hand, but that hand caught her at the side of her chest in a way that made him cup her breast.

"Excuse me," he said, his voice full of apology as he removed his hand. But when he moved again, his knee went between her legs and his face fell forward into her neck.

"Are you *drunk?*" she asked in disgust, pushing at him.

"No, but I had umpteen cups of black tea with our landlady. The woman is an animal when it comes to cards. It's just that this bed is—Oh, pardon," he said as he again touched her breast. "I didn't mean to be so—Oops again."

Tyler finally understood that his clumsiness was an act. He had not stumbled onto the bed by "accident," and he certainly hadn't touched her body parts by "accident." Part of her knew that she should tell him to get away from her, but she couldn't resist the game. There wasn't a lot of laughter in her job. In truth, there wasn't a lot of laughter in her life.

"I'm sorry," she said as she brought her knee gently up between his legs. "Did I hurt you?"

"Uh, no," he said. "Not actually."

"Are you sure? Maybe I should check and see." At that she put her hand between his legs and massaged gently. "Are you *sure* I didn't hurt you?"

"I think I'll be all right in a minute," he said huskily. "But—"

"Maybe I should kiss it to make it well," she said under her breath.

"In that case, I have cuts and bruises all over my body," he said.

"You too?" she said as though surprised. "I nearly fell down that hill on the way here, and I think I'm going to need lots of kissing in lots of places."

"I will try to oblige," he said softly; then he tangled his hand in her hair and brought her lips to his. "I've wanted to do that since the first moment I saw you in that red thing with all that hair floating about you."

She arched her neck so his kisses could reach all of her skin. "You didn't even notice that I wasn't your regular assistant," she murmured.

"You do have a keen sense of humor," he said, then began to unbutton her nightgown. "Have you ever been made love to for six hours straight?"

"Let me think . . ." she said.

"No, I don't think I will let you think. Not for six hours, anyway," he said; then his lips took hers again.

Six

When Tyler first awoke, she didn't remember where she was; then she felt the warm body next to hers and she wanted to snuggle back under the covers and stay there forever.

But in the next second, she was rolling to the far side of the bed and putting her feet on the floor. She didn't dare look at Joel. She didn't dare allow herself to remember what had happened last night. She certainly didn't want to remember that last night had been the best sex of her life.

There had been caressing and touching, as well as passion. But most of all, there had been laughter. Three times, she'd told Joel to be quiet, that Mrs. McDonald would

hear them. "Old bat probably has one of those baby listening devices under the bed," he'd said, making Tyler giggle like a girl.

But now, last night was over and, as they said, it was
now time to pay the piper. What she'd done last night was
going to have repercussions unless she could, somehow,
stop it from continuing. To keep on with Joel would
alienate Krissy, which would alienate Uncle Thad, a man
who had given everything to Tyler and her mother. And
to Tyler, family was a great deal more important than a
one-night stand.

As quietly as she could, she pulled on the khakis that
she'd first put on to go to Sunday dinner at Krissy's apartment in New York. How very long ago that seemed!

Then, on tiptoes, she left the bedroom and went
toward the kitchen. She jumped when she saw a man sitting at the table eating a breakfast that would feed half a
dozen people. The smell of bacon, eggs, tomatoes, mush-
rooms, toast, and butter made Tyler want to sit down and
join him.

But at any minute Joel might come out of the bedroom; then they would talk; then . . .

"Mornin' to you," the man said.

Again Tyler had to stamp down the impulse to sit and
ask the man questions, for surely this was Mrs.
McDonald's brother, Fergus.

"Good morning," she said as she headed for the door
to the outside. "I, uh, I hate to leave so quickly, but I—"

"You the one saw Ian?" he asked.

Tyler paused with her hand on the door handle. "Yes,"
she said, then took a deep breath. Maybe she had time for
one question. "Why do you think he has to do that?

Wasn't being hanged for a crime he didn't commit enough?" There was anger in her voice, but she knew the anger wasn't about Ian but about her stupidity of last night.

Fergus gave a snort of laughter. "Maybe he needs someone to tell him that while he was passing notes to his girl, the man he's supposed to have murdered was screaming inside a stone wall up on the hill."

His image was so graphic that Tyler could feel her stomach turn over. She opened her mouth to reply, but she knew that if she asked even one more question, she'd ask a hundred, and while she was talking, Joel would wake up, and then—

"The problem is," Fergus continued, "people don't find out that Ian's innocent until *after* they see him. And far as I know, no one has seen him a second time, so they don't get to tell him about the man inside the wall."

Tyler started to say something, but then she thought she heard a noise from down the hall. Maybe Joel had awakened. So she raised her hand in farewell to Fergus, then hurried out the door.

It didn't take her long to pack her single suitcase, and the man at the desk was very obliging in booking her a seat on British Air and ordering her a car to take her to the airport. Within minutes of returning, she was standing at the desk, ready to leave to return to the U.S. as soon as the car arrived.

While she was standing there, she saw the tour guide enter the old part of the castle. When he saw Tyler, he smiled and said, "Saying good-bye?" in a way that let her know that he was laughing at her.

She gave a little smile in return, then the guide went through the door, chuckling.

But as she stood there, Fergus's words came back to her. No one had ever seen Ian a second time to tell him that the man he was supposed to have killed was probably still alive.

The man at the desk was on the telephone and she knew that the car would wait for her, so Tyler hurried through the doorway into the castle, then ran down the hallway toward the window seat. She was thankful that she had on her sneakers and so didn't make a sound.

Sunlight was streaming through the window across the cushioned window seat. Of course there was no ghost there, and part of Tyler breathed a sigh of relief. But then, after a quick look about to make sure that she was alone, she climbed onto the cushion and pulled the curtain closed.

"Ian," she said in a whisper, "I don't know if you can hear me or not, but the man you're supposed to have killed has been sealed inside a wall in the old keep. If you get him out before he dies, I think you can clear your name."

When she stopped speaking, there was silence, and that stillness made her feel silly. She was talking to the air, and, worse, she was trying to communicate with a ghost.

After again making sure that no one was near, she drew back the curtain and climbed down to the floor and started back toward the hotel wing. But she hadn't taken more than a couple of steps when she thought she heard something behind her. Turning quickly, she looked back at the curtain. Was it her imagination or did the curtain move? Did it seem to be falling back into place as though a hand had just pulled it aside?

Tyler waited for several more minutes, but she saw nothing, heard nothing; then, with a sigh, she went back down the corridor to the hotel. The man at the desk told her her car was waiting. Following the porter with her suitcase, she went outside and got into the car. And as it was leaving, she saw Joel walking up the hill to the hotel, and she leaned forward in the seat so he couldn't see her. That part of her life was finished now, she told herself. She was going to leave the romance of the Highlands and return to the real world.

Seven

Six Weeks Later

Still missing your little cousin?" Barry asked as he moved around Tyler's terrace watering her plants.

"Yes," Tyler said. She hadn't seen Krissy in the six weeks since she'd been back from Scotland, for Joel had called Krissy and demanded that she get there as soon as possible. About the time Tyler's plane was landing, Krissy was boarding the next flight to Scotland.

"No calls? No letters?" Barry asked, obviously fishing for information.

"A couple of postcards," Tyler said, volunteering no more information.

But Barry wasn't going to give up that easily. "Why do you think that Joel Kingsley transferred his base of operations to Scotland? I thought he was only going there for a vacation?"

"Maybe he liked it there," Tyler said, sipping from her coffee mug and not meeting Barry's eyes. Maybe he's marrying Ms. Delashaw, she thought. Or maybe he's marrying my cousin.

"Oh, by the way, did you see the FedEx package that came for you yesterday?" Barry asked.

"Depositions," she murmured, uninterested.

"Actually, it was from Scotland, and Kingsley's company's name was on the return address."

Slowly, Tyler put down her mug and looked up at Barry. Without any doubt in the world, she knew that he had purposefully kept this package from her, hoping that she'd open it in front of him. Since she'd returned, he had plagued her night and day about why she had gone tearing off to Scotland and why she'd returned in such a hurry and why she'd been in such a blue funk ever since.

"Get it," she ordered Barry in her lawyer's voice, the voice that made her opponents know that she meant business.

With his hands raised, palm upward, Barry went into Tyler's apartment and, moments later, returned with a thin letter-size FedEx package.

Tyler wanted to tell Barry to go home and to let her open the package in private, but that would mean that she thought it was something personal from Joel. But in six weeks there had been nothing from him, not a postcard, not a call, nothing. Of course she had acted like a child and run away, hiding from him, not even paying him the courtesy of telling him why she was running.

But on the other hand, wasn't the world full of women waiting for the man to call her back after their one night together?

In spite of her trying to be logical about the matter, her hand shook as she pulled the string to open the package. Inside was a magazine. No letter, nothing handwritten. Even when she shook the magazine, nothing fell out.

Trying to hide her disappointment, Tyler put the magazine on the table and picked up her mug.

" 'The Royal Historical Society of Scotland,' " Barry read as he picked up the magazine, then opened it. " 'Mystery Revealed,' by Joel Kingsley," he read from the table of contents.

Tyler nearly missed the table when she slammed her mug down on the table's edge and grabbed the magazine from Barry at the same time. Nearly tearing the pages from the magazine, she hurried to find the article.

At the top of the page was a photo of the portrait of Ian. Quickly, she started to scan the article.

"Well!" Barry said, trying to see over her shoulder. "What does it say?"

"It says that Joel Kingsley has spent the last six weeks in Scotland, aided by an army of research assistants, and has found out that Ian McLyon was probably not hanged after all. It says that Joel Kingsley believes, via new documentation that has just come to light, that Ian was accused, but that a passing farmer heard the shouts of the man Ian was supposed to have killed. The farmer thought he was hearing a ghost, but when the source of the sound was investigated, Gilbert the Fair was released from the wall where his brother had put him."

Tyler read further before she spoke again. "It is now believed that Gilbert's brother, Robert, was the man who was actually put into the wall and it is Robert's skeleton on display in the castle, not Gilbert's, as has been thought all these years. And . . ." Tyler read the next paragraph with a smile. "The librarian at the castle, a man who has written three books on the history of the family, says that he believes the documents found by Joel Kingsley and his staff are forgeries. 'All I know is that they weren't there last week,' the librarian said."

"Do you think that Kingsley forged them?" Barry asked, eyes wide.

"No," Tyler said softly. "I think that those papers didn't exist before six weeks ago. I think that . . ."

"That what?" Barry asked eagerly.

"I think that maybe Ian was warned and that he somehow got a message to someone to check the keep and that Gilbert was found before it was too late."

"But—" Barry began, but Tyler didn't hear what he had to say because she had just seen that there was a page on her fax machine. How long had it been there?

Tyler had to read the fax three times before she could comprehend it.

I'm engaged! I'm going to have a wedding so big it'll take Daddy two years to pay off the debt. Start thinking about the dress you want to wear when you're my maid of honor. I want to see you so very, very much. We'll be arriving tonight. Could you please, please, please take a taxi to the airport and meet us? I've ordered a stretch to meet us so we can all ride back to the city in style.

Krissy

Krissy's plane information was at the bottom of the fax.

"Are you all right?" Barry asked from behind her. "You look like you're going to faint."

"What time is it?" Tyler asked.

"Nearly five, why?"

"I have to go meet a plane."

"No one in New York meets planes," he said, as though he were teaching her the proper etiquette needed to live in the city.

"I am," Tyler said, and she knew it was something that she had to do. She had to face up to this once and for all. For the past six weeks she'd watched *Entertainment Tonight* religiously, hoping but dreading to see something about Joel Kingsley marrying Celeste Delashaw. She told herself that if he did marry, she would be overjoyed. If Joel were married, then Tyler could forget him and go back to work and her friends—and her life.

Such as it was.

After she'd returned from Scotland, Tyler had gone back to work, but her heart wasn't in it. Truthfully, she didn't seem able to recover from her encounter with Joel Kingsley. It was absurd, of course, because who in the twenty-first century paid any attention to a one-night stand? And that's all it had been, she told herself again and again.

Of course there was the fact that she'd never shared a ghost sighting with anyone else. Nor had she shared laughter such as she'd shared with Joel Kingsley.

And there was something to be said for plain, old-fashioned human contact. That night they'd sat together before the fire, when he'd read to her . . . She'd lived with a man before but never had she once felt so . . . so content as she'd felt sitting there that night with Joel. The other

men she'd allowed into her life had been there just to alleviate the loneliness. But after she'd broken up with them,
all she'd felt was relief.

She'd spent much less time with Kingsley than she
had with her live-in boyfriend, so why did she . . . did
she . . . well, miss him? Weeks later, she was still thinking of
things that might make Joel laugh. When she watched TV,
she found herself wondering which shows Joel watched.
Or did he work too hard to get to do something as ordinary as watch TV? And if that was the case, how could she
help him relax?

But he wasn't "hers" to do anything with.

So now, somehow, her beloved cousin Krissy had
"caught" him, and Tyler was going to be gracious about it.
If it killed her, she was going to be happy for her cousin.

As Tyler grabbed her handbag off the little table in the
foyer, Barry said, "You can't go to the airport looking like
that."

"Yes, I can," Tyler called over her shoulder, then ran
out the door.

Tyler was sure that the few minutes she spent standing
in the airport waiting for the passengers to arrive was the
longest of her life. What was wrong with her? Had she run
out of her apartment like that because she was so eager to
see Joel again that it didn't matter that he was going to be
with another woman?

Before Tyler could clarify her thoughts, there was
Krissy, grabbing her and hugging her, and complaining
that she hadn't answered any of her calls or called her back,
and Tyler hadn't called "Daddy," or anything. Was she okay?

As always, Krissy gave Tyler little time to answer any

question, but it didn't matter because Tyler had no answers to give.

Krissy stepped back. "Here he is," she said proudly.

Expecting to see Joel, and preparing herself to put on a display of surprise, Tyler looked up to see a young man standing there. Tyler looked behind him to see Joel, but he wasn't there. "Where's—?" she began.

"Here!" Krissy said, laughing. "You don't remember him, do you?"

It was then that Tyler looked up at the young man standing in front of her. No, she had no idea who the man was.

"Dr. Shipley," Krissy said; then when Tyler still looked blank, Krissy said, "Do you really not remember him? He's the doctor my father sent to me when I had the flu. He was there the day I asked you to go to Scotland."

Tyler wasn't understanding. "You were still ill, but you went to Scotland anyway?"

At that Krissy laughed and looked at the doctor. "You'd never believe that Tyler is the brainy one in the family, would you? *Hello.* Tyler, this is my fiancé. We're to be married. Remember my fax? Marriage. Remember?"

It still took Tyler several moments to comprehend. "You're marrying *him?*" she asked softly.

"Yes. I told you that in my fax. You obviously got it or you wouldn't be here."

"You didn't say *who* you were marrying," Tyler said in a voice that was little more than a whisper.

"Oh. Didn't I? Well, my dear cousin, if you'd called me back any of the hundred times that I called and left a message, I would have told you all about him."

"Once," Tyler said. "You called and left one message, and I did call back. Didn't the hotel tell you?"

"Oh, well, maybe they did," Krissy said, waving her hand in dismissal. "To tell the truth, I was too busy with Jeff to have time for much else. So? Aren't you going to give him a hug and welcome him into the family?"

It was finally beginning to penetrate Tyler's brain that Krissy was not going to marry Joel Kingsley. Tyler wasn't going to have to spend every Christmas for the rest of her life looking at him across a dinner table and pretending that . . . She didn't want to think about what she was not going to have to pretend.

"I think we should get the bags and get out of here," the doctor said, his first words since they'd arrived.

For the next half hour, as Tyler went with them to baggage claim and waited while the doctor got the bags and put them on a cart, Krissy kept up a nonstop run of chatter about how Jeff had flown to Scotland the day after she'd arrived. Krissy recounted their courtship hour by hour, talking about starry nights and moonlit walks.

"That is when Kingsley let any of us have any time off," Krissy said, then threw a dreamy look at the back of her fiancé. "Jeff wants me to quit. He wants me to stay home and have a dozen babies."

Not even this remark could get a rise out of Tyler. It was as though there was no more emotion left in her. She'd tried to stamp it down, but now she knew how very hard it had hit her to think that Joel was going to marry someone else.

Tyler managed to contain herself until they got to the car. A long black stretch limousine was waiting at the curb for them, a uniformed driver sitting in the front. Dr. Shipley put Krissy's luggage in the back, and as soon as the three of them were in the back, the car pulled out of the airport.

"It was so wonderful," Krissy said. She and Jeff were sitting on the seat facing forward, while Tyler had taken a seat at the side. "Did I tell you about——?"

"I bet your boss wasn't too happy about your leaving, was he?" Tyler said, and immediately wished she hadn't said anything, but she wanted so much to know.

"Happy?" Krissy said. "He doesn't know the meaning of the word."

"True," Jeff said as he held Krissy's arm close to his. "I can't believe Kristin ever thought she could love a sour old man like him."

"And, Tyler dear, I apologize for ever subjecting you to——"

"What happened?" Tyler said sharply, cutting Krissy off.

"Well . . . After Ms. Delashaw left——"

"Left?!" Tyler exploded, then cleared her throat nervously, and she gave a little laugh. "I got the idea they were a pair," she said as though it didn't matter at all. "Or did she just leave temporarily?" Tyler had to keep from looking at Jeff, as he was watching her with an intensity that she found disturbing.

But Krissy was oblivious. "Oh, no, one of the hotel staff told me there was a huge fight." Krissy leaned forward as though she were sharing a secret. "Over another woman. It seems that Mr. Kingsley spent the night with another woman."

"How did she find out?" Tyler asked quickly, still ignoring the intense stare of the doctor.

"I was told that he *told* her. Mr. Kingsley *told* Ms. Delashaw that he'd been to bed with someone else; then he told her he wanted her to leave."

"Scotland or his life?" Tyler asked quickly.

"I don't know," Krissy said, "but I would guess that he meant his life. Why do you ask?"

"Because—" Tyler began; then she could think of no reason for having asked such a question. But both Krissy and the doctor were staring at her, waiting for her to give an answer. "Because—"

To Tyler's horror, she then burst into tears. "I'm sorry," she said, covering her face with her hands. "I didn't mean—"

Immediately, Krissy was by her side, putting her arms around her cousin. "Tyler, honey, what's wrong? Has something happened to you? Did someone do something bad to you?"

"I fell in love," Tyler sobbed. "It was awful. I didn't mean to. I thought you were going to marry Joel, and I thought he'd be at the airport, and—"

"You thought *I* was going to marry my boss?" Krissy said as though that were a ridiculous idea.

The doctor handed Tyler a tissue from the box in the tray, and she blew her nose. "Don't pretend you weren't in love with him just six weeks ago," Tyler said as sternly as she could manage. "You told me he was *yours.*"

"Well, maybe I did have a bit of a schoolgirl crush on an older man, but—"

"He's not an 'older' man!" Tyler said fiercely as she wiped her nose. "He's wonderful! He has the most wonderful sense of humor in the world, and—"

"Kingsley?" the doctor asked in disbelief. "Joel Kingsley has a sense of humor?"

"Yes," Tyler said. "He is a very funny man."

"I heard lots about him while we were in Scotland but never that," Jeff said.

"Jeffrey, please," Krissy said. "Tyler is upset, and sometimes when you think you're in love with someone, you can't see that person's flaws."

"*Think* I'm in love with someone?" Tyler said, glaring at Krissy. "Have you ever before heard me say that I was in love with anyone?"

"Not even a movie star," Krissy said. "Aunt Sarah said she didn't know how she'd given birth to such an unromantic person as you."

"My mother said that about me?" Tyler said, and the tears began to flow again. "What else does she think is wrong with me?"

Jeff gave Krissy a narrowed-eyed look for having put her foot in her mouth. "I don't think your mother meant it that way. I think she was hoping that someday you would fall in love with a man."

"Well, I wish I hadn't," Tyler said. "I hate it. I hate feeling like this. It's awful. And he doesn't even know that I'm alive. I was a . . . Well, I wasn't important to him at all. Why is the car stopping?" she asked, looking up. The limo had pulled off to one side of the highway, into the lane that was reserved for "emergencies only."

"I don't know," Krissy said. "Maybe we have a flat tire."

At that moment the door to the limo opened and the driver said, "Out! Both of you!"

In shock at a driver speaking to his passengers that way, Tyler looked up to see both Krissy and Jeff scrambling to get out of the car. Tyler moved to get out with them, but as she reached the door, the driver bent down and looked into the car.

It was Joel.

"I think we need to talk," he said; then he got into the car and shut the door behind him.

But they didn't talk. Instead, Joel pulled her into his arms and began kissing her, and it wasn't until the highway patrol stopped to ask if they needed help that they broke apart.

Jeff drove the limo back into New York, Krissy beside him, Tyler and Joel alone in the back.

But they still didn't talk. Talk would come later.

JUDE DEVERAUX is the author of twenty-five *New York Times* bestsellers, including *High Tide*, *The Blessing*, *An Angel for Emily*, *Legend*, and *A Knight in Shining Armor*. Her newest novel, *The Summerhouse*, is forthcoming in hardcover from Pocket Books. She began writing in 1976, and to date there are more than thirty million copies of her books in print. Ms. Deveraux lives in Connecticut and is currently at work on her next novel.

Fall from Grace

JILL BARNETT

Dear Reader,

Welcome to the Highlands! "Fall from Grace" was originally published as part of a Scottish collection titled *Highland Fling,* which has been out of print for years. Creating Colin, Grace, and her inept band of Highland outlaws was great fun. I can still remember laughing at them. In answer to your many requests, Pocket is republishing the original story, with a few additions—special moments I always wished were in the story the first time around.

Enjoy the fun,

Jill Barnett

The Devil is always good to beginners.
—*Auld Scottish proverb*

One

*T*he man was out cold.

Grace McNish sat on his chest, looking down at him. Well, she thought, her head was surprisingly clear considering she had just slipped and fallen from an old rowan tree, and had had the blessed good fortune to land upon a dastardly McNab.

She did remember him riding up the trail as if he owned it, the vile McNab plaid wrapped around his large frame and billowing about him like the devil himself. She remembered pulling her dirk. She even remembered taking a step onto a lower branch so she could leap on top of him at the exact, perfect moment. The trouble was, she never remembered that exact, perfect moment.

She leaned closer, her dirk clutched in one fist, and scowled at him, trying to look mean and arrogant and cunning. Like the McNabs.

She searched his face for signs of a trick. It was known throughout the Highlands that a McNab could not be trusted. They had an unending hunger for land, and anything else of value, particularly if it belonged to the Clan McNish, which they fed on the same way leeches fed on blood.

She placed the blade of her dirk close to his neck.

He did not move.

Was he dead?

She bounced on top of him a couple of times.

His breath came out in a soft whoosh.

She watched him closely. Very closely.

He slowly inhaled in that shallow way of those who were asleep or unconscious. On his forehead there was an egg-sized knot, just above his thick, dark brows.

She rubbed her own forehead and winced. His knot matched hers. She'd knocked heads with him. She supposed that fact might delight her grandfather, since he'd often commented on ways for her to put her hard head to good use.

She pressed the point of her dirk against the man's neck.

If he moved, she would stab him.

She looked around the glen, searching for signs of more McNabs. Sometimes they traveled alone. Sometimes in packs, like wolves scouting for wee lambs to gobble up.

But the glen was empty. In fact, the only change at all in the small clearing was a spot of trampled bracken where his spooked horse had fled.

Leave it to a McNab to be too cattle-handed to control one poor wee horse.

She gave snort of disgust. The horse was probably stolen anyway.

She leaned a wee bit closer, until her nose was almost touching his. His breath was soft and warm and sweet, as if he had just eaten an apple. She was so very hungry right now she would have eaten an apple core and been happy. With her free hand she searched his upper body in case he had something to eat tucked away.

No apples. No bread. No cheese. Not even an apple core.

At that moment, she decided that she truly despised this man who couldn't handle his horse, because the animal most likely carried some food in its saddlebags.

She leaned down and gave him a look that should have cooked him. She swiped the hair off his cheek so she could look at him and send curses on his heartless soul with her eyes.

Most of the McNabs were uglier than sin. This one wasn't.

His brow was broad and his blond hair was long, almost to his shoulders. His face was strong and craggy, like the mountains in the distance. He had a square jaw that was clean-shaven, an oddity for the McNabs, who usually wore beards to hide their weak chins.

He exhaled again. His breath swept across her lips and nose.

Apples. Apple cake. Apple pudding. Apple tartlets. Apple jam. Stewed apples. Scones with apple butter. Roasted plovers with apple stuffing. . . .

Her belly growled. She knew hunger well, knew that it made people do things that they might not do otherwise. She looked at him long and hard to see if he was really awake and only faking.

But his breathing was shallow, so she relaxed.

A twig cracked in the woods near her right.

She froze. Her grip tightened on her dirk. Without moving her head, she cast a sly look to the right, then to the left.

She recognized a familiar mutter and rolled her eyes. Not more than a second later it sounded as if someone were swimming through the nearby bushes.

Swimming or drowning in them.

"Fiona," Grace called out.

"Aye! 'Tis me. I'm stuck." It sounded as if a team of oxen were tramping through the woods.

Grace waited.

Fiona McNish stumbled out of the bushes, twisting this way and that, mumbling and spinning like a dervish while she tried to free herself and her plaid from a thick bramble bush.

Grace didn't know if she should laugh at her or yell at her.

Finally free, Fiona turned and tiptoed over to Grace's side. She knelt beside the man, leaned over, and peered down at him. After a moment she turned and looked up at Grace, running her hand nervously through her curly red hair. "Is he dead?" She looked back at him. "Oh, Lord in Heaven above, Grace McNish! Please, tell me that ye've not killed the mon."

Grace slid her small dirk back into her belt. "He's not dead. Only knocked senseless. 'Tis a fine state for a McNab."

Fiona wasn't laughing with her. She looked as if she were about ready to run back to the old laird with fresh tales of Grace's latest mistake.

Grace reached out and gently placed her palms on either side of Fiona's head. She turned it so she could speak into her left ear, since Fiona's right one was nearly deaf. "Lucky for us, Fiona McNish, that this man *is* out cold, since you just made enough noise to wake even Old MacAfee."

Fiona frowned. "Old MacAfee is dead."

"Aye, my point exactly."

Fiona stared at her, confused; then she said, "Oh. I was very loud? My plaid got caught."

"You were supposed to stay hiding in the broom bush across the road until I called for you."

"I was hiding in a bush."

"Not where I told you to hide."

"Aye, but I was worried about ye."

"Worried about me? Now, why would you be worrying about me?"

"He's a big mon, Grace."

She poked a finger into his chest. "This oaf? Och!" She turned away and crossed her arms in disgust. "Scotland would be a finer land with one less McNab."

" 'Twas not him that had me worrying, Grace, but ye."

"Me?"

"Aye. Ye screamed so loud I heard ye with my right ear."

"Scream like a frightened woman? Me? Hah! I would never!" Grace waved a hand in the air as if her throat weren't still raspy and sore, as if she hadn't screamed her bloody lungs out when she fell. "You needn't be worrying yourself about me. The blood of ancient warriors runs through my veins. True and brave. I *am* the laird's granddaughter."

"I thought ye broke something."

"I did. I broke him off his saddle." She laughed and laughed. She did think that was quite amusing.

Fiona was still not laughing.

"Don't be worrying about me. Look here. I've nabbed a McNab." Grace faced her. "I promise you. Nothing will go wrong this time."

Fiona looked at Grace as if she had just promised to fly to the moon.

"He *is* a McNab, Fiona. Look at the plaid."

"Aye. I can see he's a McNab. I'm not doubting that. I believe ye think all will be well, but there is a vast difference between what ye think, Grace, and what happens." Fiona's expression grew dour. "What I see is trouble coming."

"The only trouble coming is called *McNab*," Grace shot back, then tried to stand.

Something stopped her and she landed back on his chest with a *plop!* Her plaid was caught underneath the oaf. She reached around and grabbed it, then tugged so fiercely she could feel her face turn red.

A moment later there was a loud rip.

"Damn heavy McNab. . . ." she murmured through clenched teeth as she wadded up more of the fabric in her fists and pulled again.

"Do ye think he'll wake up soon?"

Grace finally got the plaid out from beneath him. "I don't care if he never wakes up." She stood and planted her feet on either side of his waist. A pose of the conqueror over the conquered. She had seen the same stance in clan paintings that had hung in the old castle before the McNabs raided the place and stole everything. Those paintings had showed past McNish lairds standing proudly over downed stags and boars, in the days before the clan war.

She stared down at him. Even unconscious the man looked healthy as a milkmaid. "Look at him. All hearty and muscled. The McNabs aren't starving for food."

"Aye, from those shoulders and thick legs, I'd say the mon has not missed many meals."

"He and his brothers have probably been stuffing themselves with McNish mutton. *Stolen* McNish mutton." Grace was suddenly quiet, for a wonderful idea had just popped into her head. A scant minute later she grinned and resisted the urge to rub her hands together in wicked glee.

"I know that look, Grace McNish!" Fiona made the sign of the cross and started to back away as if she were facing the monster from the loch. "Ye've got yerself another idea, haven't ye? 'Tis a frightening thing, that look."

"Wait!" Grace ran around and blocked Fiona. *"This* is a good idea."

"So ye always say." Fiona tried to sidestep around her.

Grace grabbed her arm. "Listen."

Fiona gave a resigned sigh and looked at Grace.

"There shall be no puny ransom for this McNab."

"What are ye thinking?"

"We will not demand a ransom sum the usual way. No, we'll not calculate the price on his head based on how many lambs they've stolen." Grace smiled in anticipation. "We shall collect the ransom by weight!"

Fiona stared at her. "Weight? What weight?"

"His weight. Look at him."

They faced the man together. Grace studied him for a long time. He had wide, plaid-covered shoulders and a narrow waist and hips. His thick muscular legs were covered in expensive trews that were worn only by those with a high rank in a clan. He also wore soft leather shoes—ones with woven silk laces. "Think of it, Fiona. A ransom by his immense weight should be enough to feed the clan for a long, long time."

"Yer grandfather is not going to like this. Do ye not remember what he said? The Campbell himself, Lord of the Isles, is coming in less than a fortnight. All of the clans are trying not to make trouble now. Not a single one of them wants to kindle the powerful Campbell's bad side."

"Och!" Grace spun around and then began to pace, her hands waving angrily in the air as she spoke. "As if I care one wee bit for the almighty Campbell's good or his bad side. We've not seen any help from *Himself*, the great and powerful Colin Campbell."

"But yer grandfather warned you just this morn. 'Grace,' he said. 'We'll have none of yer tricks for the next fortnight.' "

"Poor Grandpapa." She sighed. "His mind is addled from lack of meat."

"Grace . . ."

"You tell me what the almighty Campbell has done for us. Anything?"

"No, but—"

"Aye! Has he cared enough to intervene for us these past years when the McNabs were raiding?"

"No, but—"

"Aye! So . . . why should I care for his bad side? You know as well as I that if he cared a whit for us, then he would have stopped the McNabs from stealing everything we had. And *I?*" She jabbed a thumb into her chest. "*I* should be worrying about whether we might kindle the Campbell's bad side? *Och!* If I had my way, I would light a bloody bonfire under it."

She paced again, her jaw growing tighter and tighter with each step. She faced Fiona, her hands on her hips. "He hasn't done one single thing."

"They say he's a busy mon."

Grace snorted. "Aye, he's so busy belly-crawling to the

Sassenach king or chasing after those wild MacGregors that he cannot have a care for the wee troubled clans."

She stared quietly down at her plaid, where a new hole had just formed that morning. She rubbed her hand over it as if that one motion could hide all the shabbiness of her clothes. She stared down at her bare feet. Silk shoelaces? She didn't even *have* any shoes. "The clan won't make it through another winter with no food, no cattle, nothing but the thin, puny clothes on our backs."

She stood proudly—at least, she felt it was as proudly as one who was four foot eleven could. Grace knew that she lacked stature. She tried to make up for it with spirit.

Her grandfather called her spirit a vivid imagination with more pigheaded obstinance than a Sassenach has lies. But she believed that she held generations of Highland spirit deep inside her heart and that was why she felt things so strongly; it was in her very blood to have such strong emotions.

She would be as stubborn as an old ass if by doing so she could save her clan. It was the motive behind everything she did.

Someone had to do something. Her grandfather might believe that the almighty Campbell would help them, but she did not. She adjusted the folds of her tartan so they hid the thin tatters and holes, those places where during cold winter days the icy Highland wind would blow through and chill her to her bones and remind her of the shame of her father and her grandfather, of all the McNish.

She faced Fiona. "My grandfather's first duty is to the clan. I am certain he will not give up the fine prize of a McNab to ransom."

"I believe that ye're thinking a prize McNab might make yer grandfather forget about the fire."

Grace didn't respond, but what Fiona said was true. It had been her fault that all their winter wood and small pots of coal had burned up.

Fiona shook her head dismally. "If I take a deep breath, I can still smell the smoke. If I close my eyes, I can still see the old laird's red face. I am not certain which was redder, yer grandfather's face or the flames."

Her grandfather had been truly upset with her.

"Even I wouldna give Seamus flaming arrows for his old crossbow."

Grace raised her chin. "We have to protect the clan from the vile McNabs. My grandfather can do little with but one leg."

"He does not need two legs to shout," Fiona said. "And shout he did. Even I heard him."

"The McNabs didn't cut out his tongue," Grace said in a bitter and dry tone. "But they took his leg. They killed his sons and his pride. We are the only hope the clan has." Grace paused, then waved a hand casually in the air. "Besides, I told Seamus to aim toward the loch."

"He *was* aiming for the loch."

"See? That just shows you that he needed the practice. It seemed very logical to me that if the arrows were lit on fire, then Seamus could see how far from the target they landed. And the target was the water."

"But he did not hit the water."

That was very true. He had hit the outbuildings. Grace felt guilty, terribly guilty, especially afterward when she had watched her poor grandfather hobble into the woods, a crutch in one hand, an old saw in the other. His shoulders were bent in defeat as he began to slowly try to replace months' worth of chopped wood.

Grace had wanted to cry. Instead she ran after him and tried to help, but he did something he had never done before. He told her to go home and stay there. When she had argued, he had just ignored her and limped away.

She faced Fiona. "I cannot undo the damage, but we can feed the clan with the McNabs' Michaelmas provisions. This is the chance we've been waiting for. It's time we started stealing back some of what they have so easy stolen from us. I'll not let this opportunity pass."

"I dinna know if this is such a fine idea." Fiona looked as if the sky were about to fall down. On her.

"Fiona. Tell me why you do not see it."

"See what?"

"God's plan. Right here before our very eyes."

Fiona looked completely confused, which Grace figured was a good thing.

"Think about it. I fell at the exact moment this McNab was riding past. Surely you . . ." She paused, placing a hand over her heart innocently. ". . . you would not have me question the Lord's way? I fell right on top of him. What else could it be but God's plan?"

"Clumsiness?"

Grace waved a hand. "You might think that, but remember the tinker who came to the isle for the first time in years. He told me about the McNabs' Michaelmas plans. The way I see it, I was supposed to fall on him, Fiona. We are *supposed* to ransom him. You cannot say there will be trouble when it is God's plan instead of something I just dreamed up."

Fiona stared at Grace in complete silence, then turned

121

and looked at the fallen man. She turned back toward Grace and stared at her as if the truth would be written on her face.

A loud clap of thunder echoed from the clouds around Ben Lawers like God's own voice.

Grace resisted the urge to laugh at her fine timing and crossed her arms over her chest. "See, there? Heaven speaks. God agrees with me."

Fiona paled.

"Surely you will not question a Higher Power?"

Fiona shook her head vigorously.

"I thought not." Grace turned back to the oaf.

Fiona took a step closer to him. "He doesn't look much like a McNab." She pointed a finger at his face. "Look there! He has a chin!"

"Aye."

"I've never seen a McNab with a chin."

"Most likely it came from some poor ancestor with strong blood. One who was probably kidnapped, then forced to marry an evil McNab."

"Which one of them do ye think he is?"

"One too many."

Even Fiona laughed at that.

Grace glared down at him. "Old Donnell McNab has twelve sons. How should I know which one he is? They're all sniveling, murdering cowards who maim old men and steal from women and children."

"Aye, that they are."

Grace leaned closer and said, "Did you know that the loch monster was once nothing more than a cruel McNab?"

"He was?"

"Aye." Grace stepped closer. "The man's deeds had been so very evil, himself so mean, a fairy of the moor mist changed him into a beast and doomed him to forever live in the loch." She slowed her speech and lowered her voice. " 'Tis said . . ." She paused for effect. "No bogey. No ogre. No evil warlock is as horrible as a McNab!"

Grace moved a step closer to the man, leaned down close to him, then hunched over and looked up at Fiona with an expression she hoped was fierce and mean and ogrelike. "Hell has two McNabs who guard its gates so no one can escape. Those vile McNabs ride across the flames on the River Styx astride wild, mad, frothing kelpies. Ugly kelpies. Did you know that the devil himself looks exactly . . ." She lowered her voice to raspy whisper. "I mean *exactly* like the laird of the Clan McNab."

"The tales are true?"

Grace nodded. "McNabs cut out their captives' livers . . ."

Fiona gasped.

". . . and throw them to the wolves." She waved her arm and spun around, mimicking a McNab in the act. "The same wolves that follow them like pet dogs, slobbering, mad wolves. *Hungry* wolves."

Fiona looked at the oaf and slowly eased two steps backward.

In a truly sinister tone Grace said, "They *skin* their prisoners alive . . ."

Fiona stepped back again.

Grace began slowly moving in a circle, her elbows high and her hands clawlike and pinching the air. "They scalp their captives' heads bald." Grace picked her way over to Fiona with giant, monsterlike steps and wiggled her fingers near Fiona's curly red hair.

Fiona grabbed her hair with her hands. *"Nooooo."*

"Aye, they do. And worse . . ."

"Worse?"

"Aye. To the women." Grace waited, pausing for dramatic tension. "To the women. 'Tis said, they strip them *naked,* then have their way with them."

"No!" Fiona shivered, hugging herself.

"Aye," Grace said with a smug nod. "They do."

There was a long pause before Fiona dropped her hands to her sides and gave Grace a direct look. "What does that mean?"

Grace was trying to think up her next grim detail.

"Grace?"

"Hmmmmm?"

"I asked ye what it is."

Grace looked up. "What what is?"

"McNabs having 'their way with' women."

Grace had no idea, so she planted her hands on her hips. "Well, if you don't know what it means, I'm not going to tell you."

"Do ye know?"

"Aye." Grace gave a sharp nod. "Of course. I am the laird's granddaughter. I have to know these things."

"Then tell me."

"I cannot. You are not the laird's granddaughter."

"I'm yer friend *and* a distant cousin."

Grace shook her head. "And as your friend, a true friend, I'm going to spare you the gory and gruesome details. Now stop pestering me and help me tie this devil up."

Fiona frowned at her. "How do ye do that?"

"Do what?"

"Manage to twist yer argument until ye make sense?"

124

" 'Tis gift from God," Grace answered over one shoulder as she knelt beside the man and struggled to push him onto his side. "He has to weigh close to fifteen stone!" She sat back on her heels and muttered, "Must be that hard and heavy McNab head. Come, help me push him over."

After a few hard shoves and grunts, they managed to move him onto his side, and Grace wedged her knees beneath him to prop him off the ground. She extended one hand toward Fiona. "Hand me the rope."

When her hand remained empty, she glanced at Fiona, who just stood there, frowning; then she turned her left ear toward Grace.

"The rope! Give me the rope."

Fiona turned this way and that, searching the area. "Where is the rope?"

Grace scooted backwards and dropped the man's shoulder.

He thumped to the ground like a sack of rocks.

She turned, stunned. "What do you mean, 'where's the rope?' "

"Don't ye have it?"

"No. You were supposed to have it."

"I don't have it."

"But I told you to get it."

"When?"

"Before we left."

"Ye did?"

"Aye. I told you to get the rope from the stables."

While chewing her lip uneasily, Fiona put her hand into the sporran that hung from her belt, felt around for a moment, then pulled her hand out and opened it for Grace to see.

In her palm was a brown waxy ball the size of a walnut.

"What is that?"

"The soap from the table."

Grace groaned. Fiona had misheard her . . . again. "Well, what's done is done. I still need something to bind him with." She stood and began to search the area. "Stand over him, and if he so much as moves, clobber him on the head with that broken branch."

"What broken branch?"

"The one that's lying next to him."

"That branch? Me?" Fiona's voice was barely a squeak. She took two more steps back.

"Aye."

"What if I kill him?"

Grace just looked at her.

"I cannot kill him."

"He's a McNab. You couldn't hit him that hard."

Fiona just stood there.

"The Lord, in His infinite wisdom, would not have broken the branch if He didn't want us to use it."

"I thought you broke the branch."

"I did, but it was God's plan. I just happened to be part of it. Now . . ." she said, thoughtfully tapping a finger against her pursed lips, "what can we use for a rope?"

Fiona stood over the man, the branch held in her quivering hands.

Grace eyed the belt that held Fiona's plaid in place; then she looked down at her own. A belt would bind him well. But he, too, had a belt. Why should their plaids be left to billow in the icy Highland air? Let this McNab freeze.

She knelt beside him and began to unbuckle the belt; it was fine wide leather, ornately tooled, the buckle itself a solid piece of heavy, expensive silver. It almost broke her heart to look at it and think of how many meals that buckle had cost.

After the hard years they had suffered, all she saw was how many people the cost of such an ornament would feed. She could vaguely remember her mother wearing jewels and precious metals, but that was back in the days when Clan McNish had power and wealth. What little finery the clan owned had been stolen by the thieving McNabs or sold and bartered for food.

She looked at the man, this McNab, knowing he represented everything cruel in her world, everything stolen from them.

She began to unbuckle his belt.

A minute later, when her empty stomach growled loudly, she scowled down at her enemy for a flicker of a second, then braced her knees and grasped the belt tight with two hands.

She pulled the belt flap back just a wee bit too hard (with all her might).

The man grunted when the belt tightened a good three notches.

"Grace McNish!" Fiona screeched, jumped back and almost dropped the branch. "Are ye trying to wake him?"

"I couldn't help myself. Come closer, Fiona."

"Why?"

"Because I am going to use his belt as a rope to bind him. Come, now. Help me."

"How?"

"You guard him while I try to pull this belt out from under him." Grace started to roll him over again. "Remember. If he so much as opens an eye, clobber him."

Two

*H*e'd like to clobber her.

Colin Campbell, Earl of Argyll, Lord of the Isles and a descendant of the King of the Scots, lay surprisingly still as the little shrew tried to belt his hands together. He was the second most powerful man in all of Scotland, yet he lay there and willingly played the captive, eyes closed, his breathing deceptively even . . . except for the moment she had near halved him with his own belt. She must have pulled it a good five notches tighter.

She was strong. Probably had bulging arms and a chest like an ox, then skinny legs and no butt. A woman shaped like a tree, with the kind of face that went with that mouth of hers. Grace McNish would have ruddy skin, a crooked hook of a nose, a wart or two, straggly brown hair, and small, sneaky eyes, black to match her humor.

"There," she said brightly, as if she had just tied a ribbon in her hair instead of binding the hands of the man who held her very precarious future in them. He heard her brush her own hands together with a couple of cocky claps. She stood next to him and shouted, "Put the branch down, Fiona, and help me turn the oaf."

Colin's jaw tightened. Oh, did he want to teach her a fine lesson about whom she called an oaf.

Two pairs of small hands gripped him; one pair tentatively held him by his left shoulder. Fiona.

One pair pinched viciously into his left hip. Grace, the shrew, whose future was looking dim.

With a few grunts and gasps, they rolled him over and

onto his back, where he rocked slightly on top of his bound hands. He listened for their next move and thought about when he should make his.

"Grace!" a lad shouted from behind them; then there was the sound of running feet thrashing through the nearby bracken.

The thrashing ceased with a loud *thud!*

Twigs, mud, and damp leaves splattered the side of Colin's face. He didn't flinch, but he could feel a wet leaf slowly slide down his cheek and stop in his ear.

The lad scrambled to his feet, sending more mud this way and that. "They're coming. Grace! The McNab supply wagons! They're almost here! And there's no guard!"

"I've captured their guard, Duncan." The shrew placed a small bare foot atop his belly and pressed hard enough to make him grunt.

He could feel her look.

He kept his breath even and shallow—something that wasn't easy with that little foot jabbing into his gut.

He could feel them all staring at him. He wondered what they would do if he just leapt up. If his hands hadn't been bound, he would have done it, too.

Grace took her foot off his belly. "There is no time to stand here and gawk at him. Where are the others?"

So there were more of this little McNish band of thieves. Colin waited to see if they mentioned how many.

"They are still in their hiding places," Duncan answered.

"Quickly, then! Drag this stupid oaf into the bushes and hide him well."

"The bushes?"

"Aye. You'll have to use the really big bushes over there. Then get back into your positions."

"What about his feet? They're free." Duncan took a step closer to him.

There was a long moment of silence.

"Tie his shoes together with those silk laces," she said. "Tie them in knots."

Colin mentally swore. She was a wise little witch.

A moment later, with his cloak and beltless plaid dragging and bunching beneath him, they hauled him through the sharp bracken while he began to covertly work his wrists free. He needed them free so he could wring her scrawny neck.

They stopped after dragging him over a sharp rock, then dropped him into a thicket of bushes.

He lay there listening to their muted voices, to the shrew shushing the others, and the sounds of them shinnying up the nearby trees.

Then there was nothing but nature's silence, the same deceptive silence he'd blindly ridden into like a damned green fool. On a damned green and foolish horse.

His own stallion had turned lame in the same fall that had ruined his cloak and plaid and forced him to borrow these at the last inn.

If he had been astride Torquay, instead of some hired, skittish nag, he wouldn't be lying in a thicket trussed up like a Michaelmas goose with his own belt. His men would find this vastly amusing, fodder for jests that he would not easily live down. His men should have been scarcely an hour's ride behind him, and, luckily for him, the belt was loosening.

Soon this Grace McNish would care very much about his good and bad side.

The call of voices and the creak of wagons came from

the road. He turned over, using their noise to camouflage any sound his movement might have made. He opened his eyes for the first time.

Through the bushes he could see three heavily loaded provision wagons as they lumbered up the grade. Their drivers were only servants, old men who tossed a wineskin between them, drinking and laughing and jesting as they drove right into a trap.

The lead wagon edged past.

Colin looked up at the nearest tree. Sunlight caught the glint of metal—a dirk pulled.

The dirk moved. The branches shifted.

A moment later, a battle cry that sounded like the howl of a sick hellhound shrieked from that tree.

"A McNish!"

A flash of wild black hair and bare, wiggling legs flew through the air.

Past the driver . . .

Past the wagon . . .

Past anything remotely near her target.

She landed with all the grace of a tangled puppet. Right into a huge mudhole.

He bit back a bark of laughter.

She lay sprawled there for no more than a blink, then scampered up, covered in mud from head to toe.

She launched herself at the driver. Somehow she managed to get her dirk poised at the man's throat. "A McNish!" she shouted again.

"A McNish!" came the answering battle cries of her band, and they began to fall from the trees on top of the other wagons.

Fall, not jump.

There was a loud thud and a curse.

"Duncan?" the shrew called out.

"Aye?"

"Is all well?"

"Aye." He paused for a long telling moment, then said, "I missed."

So did she, Colin thought, amazed that they had managed to capture these wagons at all. But they had. The old men driving them looked stunned as they wobbled on their seats, so drunk they looked ready to keel over.

A truly awful screechlike, hellish bellow rent the air; it sounded like a wildcat dying.

Colin winced, shook his head slightly to get his ears to stop ringing, then turned toward the racket.

Standing in the road beside the first wagon was a red-haired lass, the reed of a bagpipe between her lips and her cheeks puffed and red as plump autumn apples.

Fiona.

She blew on the thing again.

The blare rang clear through his teeth right down to the very bones in his toes. His jaw fell open in surprise and pain.

The mud-covered shrew flinched, her shoulders hunching almost to her ears, while the old driver closest to him pounded the heel of his hand against one ear.

Fiona started to blow on that damned thing again. It was such an awful sound Colin almost leapt up and bolted from the bushes to stop her himself.

But Grace reached out with her free hand and grabbed a cord on the drone pipe, pulling it away from the girl's mouth before she shouted, "Fiona!"

The lass looked up.

"Enough pipes! Why are you blowing on them?"

" 'Tis our battle hymn. Could ye hear it?" Fiona asked with a frown. "I couldna."

Colin's teeth were still ringing. Hell, you could have heard those pipes in Edinburgh.

"Aye, Fiona. We can hear it. Next time sling the pipes from your left side, next to your good ear. Then you can hear it, too."

A deaf piper, Colin thought. Now, why didn't that surprise him?

"Duncan?" The mud witch spoke through clenched teeth, and she gave the lad in the next wagon a sharp look.

Duncan was a lad of about sixteen, whose hair was covered in leaves and his face freckled with specks of mud. He held an old claymore on another of the drivers, who was so drunk he fell forward and began to snore loudly.

"I had thought those pipes were . . . *lost*," the mud-faced Grace said pointedly.

Duncan fiddled nervously for a moment, then opened his mouth and took a step at the same time. He tripped on a goose cage before he could speak.

The geese in the back of the wagon began to honk so loudly Colin almost longed for the sound of Fiona's bagpipes.

Clumsy Duncan. Colin watched the lad try to shush all the geese, which made them honk all the more.

"I found my pipes this morning," Fiona said brightly. "When ye were still in bed. Ye'll never guess where they were, Grace."

"Probably not." The shrew had trouble keeping the sarcasm from her voice. "Where were they?"

"They were in an old arms chest with a *big* lock, and that was beneath a blanket, which was under a pile of wood and *that* was behind an old table, behind a huge haystack, way, way, *way* over in a corner of the stable loft." Fiona paused, then added in a puzzled tone, "I dinna know how on earth my pipes got there."

The shrew turned and mumbled something that sounded like, "I don't know how you found them."

Fiona tore her gaze away from the bagpipes and looked at Grace. "Did ye say something?"

"No," the shrew lied. "Put the pipes down now, and go guard the road." She looked around the glen, then called out, "Iain! Seamus! Is all well?"

"Aye!" two lads answered at once.

Colin glanced toward the third wagon, which was farther back than the first two. Two boys of about twelve stood guard at it. One of the boys held a pike, and the other one had a rusty crossbow. Both weapons were aimed at the driver.

The pike was about a century old and so bent with age it looked as if one good wallop would break the thing in two. Colin doubted the crossbow had been used in the last three hundred years.

But it didn't matter, since the lad had the arrow cocked wrong.

Colin wiggled his hands more and felt them finally slip from the belt. He shook his head. Never had he seen a more inept band of reivers. Had the drivers been anything else but drunken old men, this band of McNish outlaws would be the captives, that is, if they were very lucky and weren't dead instead.

Their clothing was as poor as their reiving skills. Every

plaid was ragged or torn. The lads' shirtsleeves were too short, the seams split and gaping, the saffron color faded to a pale yellow. And there wasn't a single pair of shoes worn among the pack of them.

He shifted his position and began to untie the wad of knots they had tied in his own shoes.

"Hold still, you devil's lackey of a driver, or I'll cut out your drunken McNab liver and feed it to the wolves!"

Ahhhh, the shrew speaks.

He glanced at her.

She had her dirk against the driver's neck. Her face was covered in brown mud that was beginning to crack. Leaves and twigs hung from her long hair. All he could truly see was that tangle of black hair and the whites of her eyes. "Get down from that wagon, you drunken fool!"

The first driver wobbled drunkenly, then hiccuped twice before he climbed down.

She followed him, her dirk waving madly this way and that.

The other driver joined him in the middle of the clearing, prodded along by the lad with the pike, which he kept near the man's throat while the other lad fiddled with the crossbow and arrow, stopping every so often to scratch his head and frown in frustration.

Grace turned to Duncan. "Wake up that driver over there!"

But Duncan couldn't move easily. Two of the caged geese in the second wagon had his shirtsleeve gripped in their bills, and every time he'd tried to pull it loose, a third and fourth goose would stretch out their long necks and nip him.

135

Grace walked over and pinched the snoring driver on his leg. The man sat up quickly, blinking and cursing as he looked around, his hand rubbing his leg.

"Get down!" She poked him with the point of her dirk, and he slid from the wagon, then, at knifepoint, staggered over to join the others.

"The McNab isna going to like this," one of the drivers told her.

She laughed. "And I care what Donnell McNab likes?"

One of those fools started to move toward her.

She spun around with dervish speed, and mud flew in clods from her face and hair. She looked like a leper, mud clinging to her skin in spots, as she stalked the drivers in a circle, her dirk slicing back and forth through the air.

The old man jumped back out of the way. "Watch out with that thing!"

"You watch it." She grinned, a surprisingly pleasant smile with its straight white teeth. "Tell the McNab that the Clan McNish greatly appreciates his gift of the food in these wagons. 'Twill be a bonny fine Michaelmas at the Isle of Nish this year."

She laughed, but there was little humor in that sound. Her shoulders went straight and her chin went up.

She strolled by each servant and waved the dirk beneath his nose. "And be sure to tell him we have taken one of his oafish sons."

"His son?"

"Aye," she said. "The big one that doesn't have the wee sense needed to control a horse."

Colin took a slow, long, deep breath.

"Tell him—" she continued, "tell him that he'll see the

cattle-handed lug in hell if a McNab sets one foot on what's left of McNish land!"

The servant shook his head as if he were trying to comprehend; then he looked to the other two, who shrugged. "I dinna ken which—"

"You do not need to understand. Go! Take my message to Old Donnell. Tell him to wait to hear our ransom demand!"

The old men looked at each other.

She fanned the dirk in their faces again. "If you favor your livers, get your scrawny legs moving!"

One of the men started to speak. "But—"

An arrow shot past the shrew's nose with a deadly whine. She gasped and froze.

The old men ducked, cursing.

Colin hit the ground, flat as an oatcake.

The deadly arrow struck the tree next to him.

He lay there for a moment, still feeling the wind from that arrow. Slowly, he turned and looked back through the bushes toward the glen.

The McNab drivers had straightened and were standing there slack-jawed. That arrow had passed just inches from them, too. Their faces were very pale. A second later they ran down the road as if chased by the devil himself.

"Seamus?" The shrew's voice sounded controlled. She turned slowly. Very slowly.

The deadly crossbow lay in an empty spot, the same place where the lad had been standing only a moment before.

She looked at the boy with the pike.

He turned quickly around and dropped the pike, ready to run, too.

"Do not move, Iain," she warned, walking toward him. The lad looked ill.

"Where's Seamus?"

"I dinna ken, Grace."

She took a threatening step toward him, one that placed her right in front of him.

"I saw nothing! I swear." He held his hands up.

She stepped past him, searching the woods as she called out, "Seamus?"

A bush near the road quaked like an aspen.

"Seamus?" She moved closer to the wiggling bush.

The bush stilled.

"Seamus. . ."

The bush sneezed.

She took two more steps closer and then stood over it. "Seamus. I know where you are."

" 'Twas only a wee slip of the trigger!" said a voice from the quivering bush.

"Come out of the bush, Seamus."

"I hit a tree." His voice was cheery, as if hitting anything were quite the accomplishment.

"Come out, Seamus."

"Be ye vexed, Grace?" the bush asked.

"Aye. Come out now, Seamus."

The bush was silent and still.

"Seamus!"

His head popped up from the bush, looking like that of a wide-eyed weasel.

"Grace! Grace!" Fiona came running up, something clutched in her hands. She skidded to a stop in front of the shrew and held out her hands. "Here. Look. I have it!"

Grace frowned and looked down. "What?"

"The toad," Fiona answered proudly.

"What toad?"

"Ye ordered me to hoard the toad. It wasn't easy to find, either." She lifted it up. "This is it. I kept it close to my chest. Although why ye want to hoard toads, I'll never know."

"I said . . . 'guard the road.' "

"Huh?"

Grace leaned toward the girl's other ear and yelled, "I said 'guard the road!' "

"Oh." Fiona stared at the toad for a long moment, then dropped it and wiped her hands on her old plaid. She gave a relieved sigh. "Thank heaven, I was afeared ye were turning to witchcraft."

Colin sat there, watching another one of their trout-brained conversations go on and on. When he glanced at the shrew, she had moved to a water barrel in the back of one of the wagons. Her back was to him as she toweled the mud from her face and hair.

He smiled without humor, prepared to face the ugly mud witch, the shrew from the Isle of Nish.

She tossed the cloth away and turned around.

Colin felt the smile fade from his face. He just sat there, frozen in that bush, not moving, not breathing. "Good Lord . . ." he muttered. For the mere glimpse of a face that lovely, a man would make a bargain with the devil himself.

Her skin wasn't pocked and ruddy, but the color of Highland snow, the kind of skin that looked soft enough to make a man crave its touch, crave its taste, crave the feel of it against his own.

Her features were proof of God's perfection—a heart-shaped face, fine high cheekbones with a barest hint of a blush, full pink lips that turned his thoughts carnal, and eyes that slanted slightly upward, misty, exotic eyes that fired lust in a man, because men knew that a woman's eyes turned slanted and misty when she had been loved long and well.

He rested his hands on his bent knees and took a deep breath, then just continued to stare at her, unable to will himself to look away. She was the most exquisitely perfect young woman he'd ever seen.

"Duncan!" she hollered. "Go over to those bushes and check on the oaf!"

Except . . . for her mouth.

Quickly Colin reached beneath his cloak and unfastened the Campbell broach hidden beneath his borrowed plaid, then retrieved the belt and twisted his hands into it so it looked as if they were tightly bound. He lay down, eyes closed, his breathing slow and shallow, the broach clutched in his fist.

The bushes about him rustled. There was a moment of telling silence when he could feel the lad looking at him.

"He's still unconscious!" Duncan shouted.

"Good." Her voice was coming closer.

Colin waited.

"We'll lug him to the wagon," she said finally. "Iain? Seamus? Come help us."

Soon he felt four pairs of hands try to lift him; one small set of fingers dug deeply into his shoulder muscles. He knew where Grace McNish was.

Colin let every muscle in his body relax. At six foot three and thirteen stone that was plenty of dead weight.

She grunted, and the lads groaned and staggered a little.

He heard her mutter a curse on the black soul of the McNab who "had sired the heavy lummox"; then they hauled him toward the wagon.

As they went past the bushes that lined the road, Colin dropped his broach, a sign for his men to find.

They fumbled and stumbled repeatedly with his limp body, stopping to catch their breath and grunt and groan.

At this rate, his men could be here before they had him loaded into the wagon.

He had nothing to fear, other than becoming deaf from a blast of those bagpipes. Then he remembered that arrow, the one that had just missed his head. He decided that these fools could surely kill or maim him, but if they did, it would be by accident.

Duncan and the shrew had climbed into the back of a wagon, and now they tugged on his shoulders, while the other lads tried to heave him up. Grace sat down as she pulled his head and shoulders into her lap.

She smelled of lusty wet Highland earth and female musk. One side of his face was cradled against a soft woman's breast. He thought of that face. Perhaps he didn't want his men to come soon, after all.

"He's a brawny one, he is," one of the lads said.

" 'Tis all that stolen mutton and beef they eat," Grace said, still cradling his head.

He moaned and turned so his mouth rested against the tip of that breast. Then he groaned loudly against it, trying not to laugh when she gasped and scooted away.

There was a another telling moment of silence. He could feel her face just inches from his, searching his for a sign he was awake. He could feel the warmth of her breath when she finally breathed. Then she moved away.

"He's waking up. Don't just stand around! Iain and Seamus! You take the last wagon. Fiona!" She raised her voice. "You'll ride up here and guard the oaf." She paused, then asked, "Did you hear me?"

"Aye. Guard the loaf. Where is the bread?"

"The *oaf!*"

"Oh . . . him."

"Aye, him. But first go fetch that branch again. Duncan, you take the second wagon." Grace paused, then whispered, "Is Fiona gone?"

"Aye," Duncan replied. "She went over by the tree to pick up the branch."

"Good."

"Why?"

"First chance you have, Duncan, hide the pipes again. Over in the wagon with the geese. She's afraid of geese."

Soon the wagons were lumbering down the road, wheels rattling, axles creaking, and in the back of one of the wagons, amid sacks of oat flour and barrels of ale, lay the Lord of the Isles, a wee ghost of a smile on his lips.

Colin Campbell hadn't laughed this much in years.

A little while later a group of armed men entered the clearing. The man in the lead dismounted and knelt on the ground, carefully examining the footprints and the wheel ruts.

He looked up at the others. "An ambush."

Another man was walking the circumference, eyeing the broken bracken, tree branches, and bushes. He pulled the broach from the bush and held it up. "Look at this broach!"

142

They did look.

One man knelt on the ground, his gaze following the wagon tracks. He stood and mounted his horse quickly. "Ride this way!"

A moment later they rode from the clearing in swift pursuit.

Three

*H*er stomach growled again.

Grace looked down into the wagon bed at her prisoner, who was still unconscious. Since he was a McNab, she lifted a water bucket and dumped the whole thing on him.

He didn't sit up coughing as she'd hoped. He didn't even flinch. He just slowly opened his eyes as if he had all day, as if he were dry as summer air instead of dripping icy water from a nearby brook.

He stared straight at her from eyes that were not a cold blue, as she had expected, but an odd shade of yellow gold—the eyes of a Highland wildcat, sharp and keen.

He gave her the most unsettling look she'd ever received.

For a brief instant she forgot he was a McNab.

She forgot to breathe.

She forgot to move.

But she would never forget that look.

Some weak part of her wanted to turn away, but she couldn't, wouldn't. Their gazes were suddenly weapons, each one of them trying to overpower the other with a look.

Her chin came up, yet she didn't blink. She would not let herself look away or even blink. Not first, anyway.

She couldn't guess his thoughts, but had the uncanny feeling that he knew hers better than she did. Why was it that he was her captive, yet she felt like the hunted?

"Grace!" Duncan shouted. "Come here!"

She blinked. "I'll be there in a moment."

He smiled mockingly, arrogantly.

She drew her dirk and smiled back slowly, arrogantly.

He didn't react.

She moved the dirk toward him, waiting for some reaction from him: fear, a tensing of his muscles, a tightening of his jaw. She got none, yet her own heart began to pound in her ears.

He never took his gaze from hers.

She felt her smile slowly fading. She moved the dirk down, pausing above his heart.

No response. His manner was completely unchanged.

She moved the dirk to his belly.

Still nothing, not a flinch, not a sign that he was aware of her weapon.

Her bluff wasn't working. She took a deep slow breath and moved the dirk lower.

She waited. No man wanted a knife of any kind near their groin. What would they think with if something happened to it?

Time felt as if it had stopped. The tension between them grew rapidly until the air was as taut and silent as a war ground before the battle charge.

"Grace!" came the impatient call again.

Damn his eyes for never flinching. She raised the dirk high. *What will he do now?*

He didn't even blink.

Damn her, she thought, for giving in. She sliced the small knife downward toward his feet and cut right through the knotted shoelaces.

"Get down." She waved the dirk in his face. "And if you try to run away, you'll find this dirk in your back." She gripped the splintery rim of the wagon bed with one hand and leapt to the ground.

She never saw the exposed nail.

Two steps and the sound of tearing fabric ripped through the air. She turned.

Her plaid had a hole in the back of it that was the size of the oaf's grinning blond head. She jerked the brown plaid fabric from the nail, spun on a heel, and marched toward the others, her head high as she ignored his snort of laughter.

"McNish!" His voice was so deep it sounded like the thunder in Cairngorms. In fact, it took her a moment to realize that God was not calling her.

She took a deep and settling breath, but did not turn around.

" 'Tis no more bonny and rosy a view in all of Scotland!"

She stopped. View? What view? She cast a glance over her shoulder to see what he was braying about.

He stared at her back, grinning.

She tried to follow his gaze, but couldn't see over her shoulder. With a sinking feeling of pure dread, she reached a hand around, over the plaid. Over her hip. Over the tail of her shirt . . . and lower.

She touched bare skin. The hole was right over her rump. She jerked the folds of her plaid, adjusting them in her belt. She stuck her chin high and marched off, calling vivid and vile curses down upon the obnoxious and hard-headed McNab.

His head wasn't the only thing that was hard.

Colin's grin faded as he watched her stomp off. He leaned against his bent knees that were still stiff from lying prone for so long in the hard wagon.

An interesting last few moments, he thought. He was used to battles of pride, as much as he was to the kinds of tactical wars carried out in the world of politics, the games he'd played with clan chieftains, ambassadors, and kings.

But he'd never had to do this kind of staring battle with a woman, at least not with a catapulting banshee who could easily have gelded him with that dirk of hers. He must be daft, to be toying with her.

He jumped down to the ground.

She stood by the other wagons talking to Duncan while Fiona burrowed through the supplies like a ferret on the scent of a hare.

"Have ye seen my pipes?" Fiona shouted.

Grace shook her head, gave the lad Duncan a conspiratorial smile, then, as if she'd felt Colin's stare, turned toward him.

Her smile faded.

For some reason he cared not to analyze, that annoyed him.

Her chin went up a notch; then her hand slid to the handle of her dirk. She gave him a look that said, "I won."

One for her.

He leaned casually against the side of the wagon, crossing his ankles in nonchalance before intentionally staring right at her butt. He slowly let his gaze roam up from her bare feet, stopping every so often to smile knowingly and linger on another intimate part of her anatomy before traveling on.

By the time his gaze reached that incredible face, it was bright red and glaring. And then she turned away.

One for him.

Colin laughed, using his loosely bound hands to shove away from the wagon. He twisted his wrist so the belt became tighter. It wouldn't do for it to fall off in front of them.

He took a step.

"Don't move!" warned a wee and shaky voice.

He looked over a shoulder and froze.

Seamus stood nearby, pointing the quivering crossbow at him.

It was, Colin noted, perfectly loaded this time.

One for Seamus.

"Don't move!" the lad repeated.

Colin didn't intend to move. He liked living. "I'm not moving, lad."

"Och!" cried Fiona from a wagon. "Look! Here they be!" A moment later screeching pipes bellowed through the small glen.

Colin hit the dirt.

Seamus's arrow whizzed overhead. It disappeared into the thick green forest.

When Colin looked back, a familiar pair of bare little feminine feet stopped in front of him. Grace McNish.

Across the way, Fiona hit the pipes again. He thought the top of his head might blow off.

"I thought she didn't like geese," he said.

"Sharp ears, McNab."

"Sharp tongue, McNish." He looked up at her then, slowly, past her bare legs, past the ragged plaid, past the cracked belt where she rested her small fists, to that defiant and amazingly beautiful face.

"You move quickly, McNab, for someone who cannot even control a poor wee horse."

"Not so quickly, McNish, that I cannot see a nail." He paused. "Or feel a draft."

Her eyes narrowed and her face flushed a familiar rosy color that made him grin. "I'll not banter with a sniveling devil who steals from poor women and wee bairns!"

Colin gave the wagons a pointed look. "The Clan McNab has no women and bairns?"

"Don't spend your breath or your sly mind trying to make me feel guilty, McNab. Your clan's not starving. You're not living on a rocky, barren isle in the middle of an icy loch, where there's little game and nothing grows but hunger and the tears of your clan. Did you have to watch a powerful, brave man you loved become old because his sons were murdered, his body maimed, and his clan driven away in shame? I do not think so."

She gave him a look so full of contempt that he almost forgot that he was not a "vile McNab." "Your clan is living off McNish mutton and beef, off vegetables grown on fertile land that once belonged to the McNish. Off plump geese, off those priceless oranges and honeyed figs in that wagon."

Whipping around, she grabbed a fat brown sack from the wagon, then bent over him, her face but a foot away, her jaw jutting out and her body shaking in anger. "Starving people would crawl on their swollen bellies up the craggy granite face of Ben Lawers for the wee crumbs of a month-old bannock."

She dropped the bag in front of his face with a heavy plop. "Starving people don't dine on these! You want me to feel sorry for a clan who has plump bags of honeyed figs? Fie on you and your clan, McNab!"

He watched her walk away, her head high, her shoulders and back as straight as a Scotch pine. She had sheer determination in every movement of her body, this shrew with a dagger-sharp tongue, Black Scots temper, and the face of an angel. He saw that Grace McNish had a clear and true love of her clan, a loyalty that was fast fading among many Scots, what with England's slow pervasion of Scotland.

The constant warring between the clans rendered Scotland an easier land to conquer subversively, with devious plots—hungry men's schemes to control the Scots throne.

Loyalty was something Colin understood, and respected.

He sat up, thinking to end his game and tell her who he was, but before he could stand and go after her, Iain approached him.

The lad waved a heavy claymore near Colin's nose. "Ye're to move over there. By that tree." He nodded toward a large fir at the edge of the small clearing. "Where I can keep a better eye on ye."

Colin stood, towering over the lad, whose wrists were too thin and frail to support even one strike of that heavy sword. "Where's your pike?"

The lad glanced at the claymore with silent doubt, then looked at Colin and nodded toward the last wagon, where Duncan stood with Seamus's crossbow slung safely over his shoulder while he instructed him on how to hold and maneuver the long pike.

"Seamus had a wee bit of trouble with the crossbow," Iain said.

An understatement.

"Duncan will use the crossbow instead."

Colin remembered being splattered with mud when Duncan tripped. He remembered the lad's losing battle with those geese, and his ambushing the wagon and "missing." Colin watched the bumbling older lad play weapons tutor to Seamus, and he thought of Duncan with the crossbow.

Colin decided he would keep on ducking. He turned back to Iain, who was struggling to hold the sword on him. The claymore was not easy for a brawny man to wield, much less a thin lad. Taking pity on him, Colin moved over toward the tree and could hear the lad trudging in his wake.

Colin pointed at the tree, and asked, "You want me here?"

Iain nodded, keeping his wary eyes on Colin, who sat down on a pile of crisp fallen needles at the base of the pine. Iain moved a distance away, slapped the claymore onto one narrow shoulder with a grunt, and began to march back and forth like a sentry on a castle wall.

Colin relaxed, leaning his head against the tree trunk, and he watched the lad march.

A shower of green pine needles softly drifted to the base of a nearby tree. Colin did not move. He listened. Someone was in that tree.

From the corner of his eye, he caught the barest hint of

movement high in the tree's thick branches. He faked a yawn and rolled his shoulders, then winced as if he were feeling stiff. The motion allowed him to change the direction of his gaze without arousing suspicion.

High in that tree was the familiar glint of polished steel—a broadsword.

Slowly, with little movement, he edged his hands out from the twisted belt. He leaned his head back against the rough trunk, feigning sleep, and he listened.

Behind the tree, and from nearby, came the soft sound of tentative steps. It was the sound of another warrior's tread—quiet, stealthy, and deadly.

Four

You must be getting old, Mungo. I could hear your tramping a good twenty feet away," Colin said quietly, keeping his eye on Iain, who was marching like a sentry about twenty feet away.

There was a familiar grunt from behind the tree. "I'd like to see how bloody quiet ye'd be after ye've had an arrow shot in yer foot," came a gruff reply.

Colin tried not to laugh. The captain of his men-at-arms, a seasoned warrior, while hiding in the surrounding woods, had been shot in the foot by Seamus. "You've been here that long?"

"Aye," Mungo whispered. "We've been following ye for a while. Until that damned arrow, I figured ye had nothing to fear. Except perhaps for yer hearing."

"Ah, Fiona's pipes," Colin said.

"I thought the gates of hell had opened and the devil himself was coming. Which one of them is the piper? I'll get him first."

"It's a lass."

"Which one?"

"The one with the red hair."

"That sweet-looking lassie?"

"Aye."

Mungo muttered something, then whispered, "Who are they?"

"McNishes."

"Which one is the archer?"

"A lad called Seamus."

Mungo grunted, then said, "Damned arrow came out of nowhere."

"You're not badly hurt?"

"No. Just a slice in me foot that makes me feel meaner than usual. Shall I cut ye loose so we can go after them together? I want this Seamus all to meself."

Colin didn't answer, just found himself looking at Grace McNish.

"We're ready whenever ye say."

The silence continued, and Mungo said, "Donnell McNab is expecting ye for Michaelmas. Ye know he's complaining that it's been too long since he petitioned you for the right to take the last of the McNish lands."

Looking at these McNishes in their bare feet and ragged plaids, their bodies a bit too thin, lent more credence to Grace McNish's claim that theirs was the clan that was suffering, not the McNabs, as their laird suggested. "Aye. McNab is right," Colin answered. "It has been long since he petitioned me to do something, but I'll not be rushed into choosing sides."

Mungo grunted in agreement.

Colin watched Grace rummage through the food in the McNab wagons with the others. She picked up the bag of honeyed figs and opened it, looking inside with a look so covetous that he forgot what he was thinking. She took a deep breath, squared her shoulders, and closed the bag, placing it back on the wagon with a quick look of longing.

He realized why she didn't eat one when she obviously wanted one so badly. She was saving them for the clan.

After another speculative look in her direction, Colin said, "I want you to ride ahead to the McNab. Tell him I've been delayed. And watch him, Mungo. See what you can find out about this feud, where it began and why. Find out what his charges are against the McNish."

"An' what about ye?"

"Leave me be," Colin said. "I want to see for myself if the McNish clan is as much of a problem as McNab claims."

"Ye want to stay with them?"

"Aye."

There was a long moment of silence. "Well, if that is what ye want."

"It is."

"I heard a rumor at the last inn that MacGregor's been seen about."

The MacGregors had been causing too much trouble of late. To Colin they were little more than outlaws out to divide the Highlands.

" 'Tis good to know. I'd love to get my hands on Peadar MacGregor."

Mungo placed a hand on his shoulder and gripped it, a signal he was leaving. A moment later, from behind him, Colin heard the high whistle of a lark, but he knew the sound well; it was not the call of a bird but the signal of his men. Slowly and silently, they disappeared from the trees and bushes and into the deeper forest.

He continued to watch Iain, who, under the weight of the sword, had slowed his pacing to the speed of a slug.

Colin rested his head against the tree trunk, closed his eyes, and let the steady methodical sound of the lad's marching lull him to sleep.

Grace stood in front of McNab, a bowl of food in her hands. Duncan, Seamus, and Fiona had gathered in a circle between the wagons and were busy eating. They were as famished as she was. They'd had only one meal in the last three days, and that had been just a few berries and an old bannock soaked in water.

"Go and get yourself something to eat, Iain. I'll guard the lummox."

At that the McNab slowly opened his eyes and looked at her.

"Here's some food." She shoved the bowl toward him.

"I didn't think filling my stomach was of your concern."

"Unlike you McNabs, the McNishes are humane. We don't starve our enemies . . . not that you look like you'd starve."

"Ah, like what you see, do you, McNish?"

She felt her cheeks turn red, and she swung the bowl up high enough to heave it at him.

"Throw it," he said.

She wanted to throw it, until he told her to. She lowered the bowl instead and held it out to him.

He said nothing.

"Do you want it or no?"

He gave her a lazy, winner's smile. "I can't take it. My hands are bound."

She looked at his mocking face, took a deep breath, and knelt in front of him, determined to remain calm, unannoyed. One didn't give in to the devil. Kneeling in front of him only brought home to her the fact that even when he was sitting, he was still a good head taller. It was as unsettling as his staring games, and made her feel as if she had to be even more defiant, to show him he couldn't intimidate her.

"Undo my hands," he suggested too lightly for her taste.

"So you can escape? I don't think so. I'll feed you."

He laughed again, as if this were only a game. "I would think you'd prefer to let a McNab starve."

"A part of me would, but I would not let you starve." She jabbed the spoon into the bowl.

"Why not? Isn't it what we McNabs deserve?"

"Aye. It is, but your ransom price will be figured on your weight. You lose weight. We lose gold." She sat back on her heels and studied him for a moment. "I'd say your head alone is worth a small fortune."

"Och, McNish. What does it take to close your shrewish mouth?"

She held up the spoon. "Och, McNab. What would it take to open your big one?"

"Are you referring to my mouth?"

It took her a moment to understand him. She felt the

155

heat of a blush that showed she'd understood his meaning too well.

Then the devil opened his big mouth and gave her a look of feigned innocence. She knew that look. She'd used it often enough herself.

From the sparkle in his eyes she could see he was enjoying this immensely. For just one moment she asked herself if she could dump the bowl on his head. But someone who knew true hunger could never waste food.

She lifted the spoon toward his mouth, anxious to get the deed done.

He watched her expectantly.

Her hand had slowed as if he could control her with his very eyes.

She fed him and it was unnerving. Not once did he look away. She resisted the urge to squirm and looked back down at the bowl instead of at him. It was a game, her feeding him and him giving her a look that felt as if it could melt her.

She took a deep breath and lifted the spoon toward his mouth, not knowing that she moved with it, closer, her mouth still parted. He moved toward her simultaneously, and his eyes shifted to her mouth.

She could smell the scent of leather and man.

He moved closer and closer with each bite.

His face was so very close, but she refused to back away from him. She would not.

"Thank you, Grace McNish, for the food. 'Twas sweet of you."

No one had ever called her sweet.

Before she could think or move, his mouth touched hers and moved softly, tenderly, in a touch she'd never known. A kiss. Her first kiss. She forgot who he was and just let herself feel this thing that she had wondered about.

He licked her lips. It made her shiver.

He shifted so his hard thighs were suddenly outside hers; then he edged her back until they were shielded from the others by the tree. Before she could react, his tongue filled her mouth, and he pinned her against the tree with his body.

He kissed her for a long time that way. She had no idea how long.

He surprised her and broke it off.

She wanted his mouth back.

His lips drifted like snowflakes over her face.

She opened her eyes and looked at him.

He looked somewhat dazed. There was no calculation in his expression, just surprise, and something more elemental—power, possession, and passion, an intensity that excited and frightened her at the same time. And there was a small bit of doubt, as if he didn't believe she was real.

She understood the feeling all too well.

He knew this feeling not at all, this violent consuming need to possess her. It was a deep and passionate urge that felt as if it bordered on obsession.

They panted little clouds of ragged mist. He watched her close her eyes in an effort to deny what had passed between them.

But it did no good. It was undeniable to him, too.

Her eyes were tinged with dampness, and her cheeks had begun to blotch. She was fighting to control her tears.

Pride he understood. "Go on, shed your tears," he said with grudging respect. "To cry is not shameful, McNish."

"I do not cry," she said fiercely.

But she wouldn't look at him. Instead, she scrambled away. "Do not touch me again, McNab." She stood quickly—a power play if he'd ever seen one—and then she did look down at him. "I think you are the very devil himself."

She spun on a heel and walked away, her pride high, but he knew she was not as strong as she tried to be. She had to work too hard at it. In fact he'd never before seen anyone who worked so hard to be what she wasn't.

He'd been on the verge of telling her who he was, but she'd walked away. He leaned back against the tree trunk then, adjusted his belted hands, and closed his eyes. He dreamt of muddy shrews and she-devils, of black-haired women who looked like heaven and could capture a heart with only a kiss.

Five

Colin awoke to the godawful wailing sound of Fiona's piping.

"Fiona!" Grace shouted.

Fiona was standing on top of one of the wagons. She heaved a mighty sigh and looked down, a prideful and dreamy expression on her face. "Doesna the sound stir yer braw heart wi' the pride of the Highlands?"

No, he thought. It was enough to send a loyal Scot fleeing to England.

"Put the pipes down and tell us what's in the wagon," Grace said. "I'm making a list."

The lass brightened. "I'll play for ye later, then." She gave her bagpipes a pat that made them groan sickly and looked down in the wagon.

Seamus, not Iain, was now on guard duty. Colin watched the lad walk twenty times the length Iain had, pike resting atop a narrow shoulder. He would reach the edge of the glen and turn sharply, marching back past Colin and past the wagons to the other side.

Seamus turned sharply, and the pike knocked the needles from a pine with a whack! Yet on he went, marching back and forth, pivoting when he reached some imaginary boundary only he must have known.

"Ten hams in this one!" Iain shouted down from one of the wagons.

"Aye," Grace acknowledged, then turned toward the next wagon, where Fiona stood. "What's in your wagon?"

Seamus marched past, stepping high, the pike on his shoulder. It was amusing.

"A barrel of pickled herring," Fiona called out. "Three barrels of ale, fifty partridges, and apples!"

Seamus pivoted and marched past.

"Fifteen mean-as-the-devil geese!" Duncan shouted from the goose-wagon. He was trying to jerk his sleeve from the bill of one of the birds.

"Three barrels of oat flour!" Duncan called out, then added "Duck!"

"How many ducks?" Grace casually asked.

"Duck!" Duncan hollered.

Colin looked at him in time to see him leap in the air just as Seamus turned and his pike whipped under Duncan's feet.

Duncan landed back down on a goose cage and shouted, "Seamus!"

Completely oblivious, the lad halted mid-pivot, the long pike still on his shoulder. It was barely a foot from Grace's head.

"What, Duncan? Where be ye?" Seamus called out, searching.

Unfortunately he spun back around toward Duncan, who didn't move quickly enough. The pike hit him in the back.

There was a loud thud.

"Oh!" said Seamus, looking down at his feet. "There ye be, Duncan. What're ye doin' lyin' on the ground resting while we're doin' all the work?"

Duncan's face turned from red to purple.

"Look there," Seamus added, pointing at the shattered goose cage next to Duncan. "Ye let that goose get away." He moved toward the wagon. "Gie me the crossbow and I'll shoot it!"

"No!" everyone shouted at once, including Colin.

The goose calmly waddled off into the forest.

For over two hours the cumbersome wagons rattled and bumped over a mountain road. The higher they traveled, the thicker the forest and the mist. Duncan drove the lead wagon, Iain the second. Seamus drove the last, alongside Fiona, while Grace sat in the wagon bed and kept a watchful eye on the McNab.

Reaching up to the heavens like the bruised arms of

some enormous god were the purple crags of Ben Lawers. Grace used the mountains as a reference. She knew they were only about six more hours from Loch Earn, and from the crumbling old castle atop a barren rocky isle that was the only land left to the Clan McNish.

In the four bleak and desolate years since the Battle of Boltachan, her clan had suffered under the conquering sword of the McNabs. She'd been barely fourteen at the time, and had never known what had sparked so blazing a feud.

There was more food than her clan had seen in years inside these three lumbering wagons. They desperately needed this food—the geese, hams, and oat flour. And she wanted to see the bairns' faces when they tasted the oranges and honeyed figs.

She smiled when she thought of their faces.

"What are you thinking, McNish?"

That deep voice went through her as if it flowed in her blood. Only the sound of his voice made her feel these things.

Annoyed, she looked at him.

He was reclining, kinglike, atop some bags of oat flour. When she'd last looked at him, he'd been asleep. She wished he still were. "You're awake."

"Aye."

"I wonder how a man who is responsible for almost destroying a whole clan can sleep so peacefully. Have you no conscience?"

"My conscience is clear, McNish."

She snorted.

"You didn't answer my question."

"I've forgotten it," she lied.

161

"I asked you what you were thinking."

"Why do you want to know, McNab?"

He shrugged. "Humor me."

"I was thinking about the clan." She paused. "The bairns."

"Do you have bairns?" he asked her.

She looked him straight in those gold eyes. "If I said aye, would you look to steal them on your next raid?"

"I don't steal children." His voice was disgusted.

"No, you just kill their fathers."

"So bitter. Did you lose a husband, McNish?"

"I am but eighteen."

"So? That is old enough to have been wed for two years, perhaps three."

The silence stretched between them.

"I'm not wed," she finally answered.

He watched her in a way she did not like. "Did you lose a father, then?"

"Aye. My parents are dead."

His expression relaxed a bit. "Tell me what it was about the bairns that made you smile so."

"It wasn't killing their fathers."

"Where, lass, did you get that mouth?"

"The same place you got your cowardice. I was born with it."

His expression changed so swiftly she almost flinched. Those yellow eyes of his glittered with a fierce hardness, and he seemed to be choosing his words carefully. "Men have died for calling another a coward," he said with a calm that she sensed was deadly. "I suggest you not use the word coward to me again."

"I'll say whatever I like, McNab. You're the captive, not I."

Neither of them spoke. He looked as if he was counting.

Good. Be angry. I could not care less.

She ignored him and fiddled with the ragged edge of her plaid for the tense minutes that followed.

Finally he broke the silence. "I wonder that you cannot find the courage to look me in the eye."

Her head shot up, and she met his challenging look with a stubborn one of her own.

"Nor can you answer a civil question."

"What is this, McNab? Now that you're a captive you seek to suddenly become humane? Civil? Plaguing me with questions. Why should you suddenly care about the widows and children of the men you killed?"

He just looked at her, waiting for an answer.

"Why should my thoughts concern you?"

Again he said nothing.

Cursed man, she thought, but finally answered him. "There are McNish bairns that have never tasted the kinds of food as these wagons carry for one holiday feast."

She stared at her hands for a moment, rubbing them together, seeing the ragged nails and calluses she had from hoeing granitelike ground that would grow nothing but scrawny turnips. "I want to see their eyes when they taste for the first time the sweetness of an orange, the juicy meat of plump roast goose, the pure pleasure of a honeyed fig. That was what made me smile." She faced him. "I want their mothers to sing to them, their fathers to toss them high in the air. But most of them no longer have fathers, and their mothers have nothing to sing about. I want to see my grandfather laugh. I cannot give him back his leg, I know that, but I'm the only family he has left. Perhaps I can give him back his pride. I want life to be as it was before."

"How was your life before?"

"Warm and safe and happy."

So his instincts about her had been correct, Colin thought. Her clan was her life, and her need to right the wrong done them, whatever that be, was what compelled her to do and say the things she did.

He knew of that kind of compulsion himself, fighting the wrongs done by others. He'd spent a decade doing the same. It had taken him ten years to rebuild the Campbell name and the title of the Earl of Argyll.

The title was his by inheritance. The respect was his by merit.

His uncle, the last earl, had spent much time and effort inciting the clans, thereby ensuring his services to a king who preferred his kinsmen to be busy feuding with each other, rather than causing trouble to him and his precious throne.

Colin had inherited the title at fifteen, and it had taken him years to gain respect and, more important, to regain trust—years to repair the damage done by a man who cared nothing for loyalty, heritage, respect, but only for the amount of gold paid him to divide his own homeland. It was not an easy thing, living down a traitor.

He felt her looking at him and glanced up.

She scowled and turned away, digging beneath her and coming up with a dark red apple. She took out two more and handed one each to Seamus and Fiona, then pulled out her dirk and began to peel the remaining fruit.

'Twas like watching a child with a toy, he thought. She slowly drew the blade round and round so the peeling curled downward. When the entire peel was only one long dark bouncing spiral, she grinned and cut it off, lifting the peel up to eat.

Then she noticed he was watching her and flushed as red as that apple. She stuck her chin up.

He found her game with the apple charming. He didn't care whether she looked at him or not. He enjoyed watching her.

Perhaps it was the expressiveness of her features, the way every thought in that obstinate little mind flickered across her face as clear as spring water. She was in a fine temper, and Grace McNish was lovely in a temper, in spite of her scowl, in spite of her zeal to chew the bloody apple from here to kingdom come.

He smiled.

She looked at him out of the corner of her eye, and he winked. She looked away quickly. He stared at the back of her head, and after some time she looked at the apple in her hand, then muttered something about McNab.

"I cannot hear you, McNish, when you speak to the forest," he said, watching her cut off a chunk of the fruit.

Still she didn't look at him, but shouted, "I said . . . would you like some apple?"

"Sounds familiar, a woman offering a man an apple ..." He let the sentence hang.

She spun around as he'd expected she would, her eyes narrowed in understanding. "I see no man, McNab. Only the serpent."

"If only you knew how badly I want to say something right now."

165

"What?" she asked, her expression suspicious and curious. 'Twas an interesting combination to watch—stubbornness and innocence. He shook his head and tried not to smile.

"Say it."

"No. I don't think so."

"No courage, McNab."

"Just being politic, McNish."

"Bah!" she said, and tossed the piece of apple at him.

With rapier speed, Colin sat up and caught the small chunk of apple in his open mouth. He heard her gasp of surprise and leaned back against the oat bags, grinning at her while he chewed.

For one brief second he thought she might smile, but she didn't.

He swallowed, then nodded, looking at the apple. "Is that one wee morsel all you're going to give me?"

She cut off another chunk and tossed it high in the air again.

He watched the piece of apple fall, then smoothly moved and caught it the same way he had before.

She flicked a third piece.

He caught it.

And another.

He caught it, too.

Faster and faster, chunks of apple flew through the air as quickly as her dirk could slice. Cheeks bulging, he caught the last one, and she burst out laughing. It was the sound he'd wanted to hear, innocent and clear as the lilting skirl of the bagpipes.

He chewed, grinning.

She sagged back against the wagon bed, smiling. It was

the first sincere smile he'd seen on her face. "Och, McNab, I was right; you do move quickly."

"It is not speed that counts, McNish, but agility and patience. There are some things, some situations, when slow and easy is better."

He saw that she did not understand what he meant, innocent that she was. But he had to give her credit for covering it well. She stuck up her chin, her expression suddenly filled with certainty. "Aye. Slow can be better." She paused thoughtfully. "Certainly better for torturing prisoners."

She always had to have that last word.

Fiona's bagpipes bellowed overhead, playing the tune of an old Scots victory song that in her hands sounded like a dying animal. After one particularly spine-raking note, the poor geese in the second wagon honked loudly and all the sounds echoed off the mountains around them.

Grace had decided that for the sake of annoying the McNab, she would let Fiona play. He had cringed every time Fiona hit a note.

The road had narrowed into a steep climb and become more pocked with holes. As the three wagons climbed the grade, they had to slow to a crawl because it was more difficult to keep the wagons to the center of the rough, steep road.

They neared the crest of a hill, and Grace slowly craned her neck over the side of the wagon to look down at the long drop below, where a river ran through a wooded area. It was a *long* drop.

Her belly fluttered uneasily. She didn't like great

heights, especially when seen from a lumbering wagon. Her hands gripped the wagon rim tighter, and she glanced back at McNab.

He appeared not the least bit concerned with the rough ride, which made her even more determined not to show that she was. In spite of her churning belly, she straightened her shoulders and let go of the wagon rim, then calmly folded her hands in her lap as if she were sitting in a chair.

The wagon wheel beneath her hit a deep groove in the road. Fiona missed a note, a painful experience for anyone nearby.

"Och! That wasna right, was it?" Fiona asked, pausing, so that the only noise was that of the honking geese. She played another wrong note, frowned, and shook her head, then tried four or five more.

"Well." Fiona gave a deep sigh. "I will have to start all over again from the beginning." She started again, playing so loudly that she couldn't possibly hear the groans of the others.

McNab winced, then turned to Grace, who was taking in deep breaths to calm her sick stomach.

He shouted, "Have you thought about hiding those pipes in a loch? A very deep loch?"

Quickly she pulled her hand back from the rim of the wagon, where it had been gripping the side despite all her intentions.

I will not show him I'm afraid.

The wagon hit a deep rut and bounced hard.

Grace slipped. "Oh, God . . ."

She slid right over the side of the wagon, but made a desperate grab for the wagon rim.

Splintery wood dug into her palms.

She hung on with everything she had. Her body dangled helplessly over the crag and banged against the side of the bouncing wagon. She screamed for help, but her voice was drowned out by the skirling squeal of Fiona's bagpipes.

Suddenly McNab was there. His hands held her wrists. His powerful grip pulled her upward and into his arms.

She knelt atop the barrel, holding on to him so tightly she could barely catch a breath. She was crying, so she buried her face in his neck.

"Your safe, *m'fheudail.*" His hands rubbed her back so soothingly. His powerful hands, the ones that had saved her, now were calmly, tenderly rubbing her fears away.

Those big strong hands.

His big, strong *free* hands.

She pushed herself away and looked at him, kneeling there with his hands free. "You devil's spawn! Your hands aren't bound at all!"

"A fact that just saved your neck, lass."

Angrily she jerked back, pulling him with her.

The barrel beneath them wobbled and teetered.

Seamus drove the wagon into a hard, deep rut.

"Damnit to hell!" McNab swore as he lost his balance and fell right into her with all of his weight.

They both went over the edge.

Six

With an uncanny sense of acceptance, Grace waited to die.

Suddenly McNab's big arms clamped tightly around her as they fell. He twisted in midair, his body protecting hers.

Just below the cliff, the hill sloped, and they slammed into it so hard that both of them grunted; then they rolled together, down and down over grass and dirt.

Sharp rocks scraped and gouged her and must have done the same to his arms, which were still wrapped protectively around her. Grace could feel him try to take the brunt of the battering, try to keep his body between her and the slick hillside. Shale splintered and scattered with them as they slid until they splashed to a stop in a shallow river.

The water was like ice.

Head dripping, McNab came up coughing. "Damnit, woman! Can you do nothing without throwing your whole body into it?"

She sat for only the time it took to blink, then pulled out her dirk and flew at him, water splattering with her. "No! I can't! Watch this!" And she hit him with her whole body.

He fell back with another splash, Grace astraddle his chest, her dirk on his neck. He opened his eyes and looked up at her, his gaze moving from her face to the dirk poised once again at his neck. She grinned down at him. She had him.

After a moment during which the idiot appeared to be fighting back a laugh, he said, "Och, McNish, we have to stop meeting like this."

She remembered the last time they'd been in the same position. Under the tree. "You were awake!"

He flipped her onto her back so swiftly she lost her breath.

Stunned, she stared up at him, her body pinned between his splayed thighs, his hand gripping her wrists so tightly above her head that the dirk plopped uselessly into the trickling water.

He grinned down at her. "Aye, McNish."

"Nay, McNab! You'll not take me without a fight!" Her knees battered his lower back, and she twisted upward, trying to unseat him.

He tightened his thighs, holding her more firmly, and he pinned her struggling wrists. She jerked her head from side to side, water spraying up with each motion. She fought wildly, until her breath came in exhausted pants and her chest heaved.

He could read the panic in her face and feel the rapid beat of her pulse in the wrists he held so tightly. Her desperate gaze left his face and turned toward the escarpment. She was searching for help.

In the distance, the weak wail of a bagpipe could be heard. Her band of reivers had no idea they were gone.

He watched the play of emotions upon her face.

"Go on." Her chin went up. "Do it," she said in an emotional rasp; then she closed her eyes, sighed, and her body went surprisingly limp.

He knelt there, watching her, confused.

She held her breath for a long time, her eyes still closed. She turned her head away, then exhaled dramatically. "I'm ready." She took another deep breath and lay there very still. After another minute of silence she cracked open one green eye, peering at him suspiciously. "What are you waiting for, McNab? Do it."

"Do what?"

"What you McNabs always do. Have your vile way with me!" She shut her eyes and flopped her head back in the most dramatic gesture of submission he'd ever witnessed.

He did a fine job of holding back his smile. "Ah, yes." He nodded. "I'd forgotten." He just let the silence drag on. "Now, how was I supposed to do that?" He frowned as if he couldn't for the life of him remember what to do.

"You have to strip me naked first, you oaf!"

There was that mouth again. He nodded, then cocked his head thoughtfully. "There are alternatives. I could cut out your liver."

She eyed him, her face no longer so fierce.

He paused, then pointedly looked around. "But there are no wolves to throw it to."

She exhaled.

"Perhaps you are right. I should just strip you naked and have my way with you, since I cannot seem to think of anything else. Although it seems to me there was something else we 'vile McNabs' do." He stopped, then muttered, "I cannot think of it."

Her eyes grew round, and he could see her trying not to let her fear show. He decided she'd had enough teasing and released one wrist, then quickly snatched up the fallen dirk before she could beat him to it.

Dirk in hand, he turned back toward her.

She screamed loud enough to crack heaven.

He sat on her to keep her from squirming away. "Hold still!"

172

"Oh, God . . . Please don't skin me alive, or scalp me! Please!" All her bravery gone, she fought and wiggled and battered his back again with her knees.

"Damnit, McNish! Hold still!" He gripped her flailing wrists just as a knee rapped his back hard. "I'm not going to hurt you!"

A second later she stilled, looking up at him with a surprised expression. "You're not?"

He stood up and looked down at her, holding out a hand. "No, I'm not."

Stubborn to the last, she ignored his outstretched hand and scrambled to her feet on her own.

She rammed her shoulders back and stuck her chin up high. "I was right. You are a coward," she said with complete stupidity.

He counted to ten, slowly, very slowly. Finally he looked up the hillside, searching for the best path back to the top. The sound of splashing water came from behind him. He turned.

She stood there wringing out her sodden plaid. Her black hair hung damply down her back, and her shirt and plaid clung to her wee body. The cloak and plaid he wore hung about him in a sodden mass, and his trews were wet from the thighs down.

He watched her twist the water from her clothing. She wrung out each section of fabric with the same zeal that he would have liked to use to wring her stubborn neck. She didn't look up, didn't acknowledge him, yet he knew she was aware that he watched her. Finally he turned back and eyed the hillside again.

"What are you going to do with me?"

She had purposely waited until he'd turned before

speaking. He sought more patience—something that was running thin. He turned. "What do you think I should do with you?"

"I'm not a McNab. I couldn't think that cruelly."

He leaned back against the rock face and eyed her, deciding whether or not to tell her that he wasn't a McNab. "What would you say if I chose to remain your captive?"

She gaped at him, then quickly covered her surprise. "I'd say you were a coward *and* an idiot."

Her mouth made the decision easy for him. She didn't deserve to know the truth until she learned a few lessons, lessons he'd take great pleasure in teaching her.

With a narrow-eyed look of suspicion, she asked, "Why would you do that?"

"To prove to you that all McNabs aren't what you think." He turned his back on her.

She snorted. "More than likely you are doing it to spy on us."

He counted to fifty this time and surveyed the hillside.

After a few more too quiet minutes, she said, "I don't believe you."

He ignored her and stepped back so he could better see the face of the cliff.

"What are you looking for?"

"A way back up to the road."

She followed his gaze to the steep hillside covered with slick rock. The mist was slowly dropping, and wisps of fog hovered near the top of the cliffs. "They'll come back," she said with a confidence he did not feel.

He headed for a small break in the rock. "Come this way."

"I think this way is better," she said, and moved in the other direction.

He turned and grabbed her by the shoulder. He nodded in his direction. "This way."

"But this way looks easier," she argued.

He ground his teeth together. It kept him from killing her.

She tightened her jaw and lifted her chin in defiance.

He'd had enough. In one swift movement he picked her up, ignoring her yelp of protest. He set her on the ground directly in front of him, turned her around so she was facing the right direction, and said, "Walk."

She scowled at him over a shoulder, then foolishly opened her mouth to argue.

"Now!" he barked, leaning over her and using his size to try to intimidate her.

She glared at him, muttering something about fools that made him itch to toss her back into the river, but she walked toward the path he'd found. They traveled about ten yards and hit a section of sheer rock.

She turned around and planted her fists on her hips. "So now what, McNab?" Her tone said, *I told you so.*

Colin counted to a hundred this time, then scanned the hillside for alternative routes. He didn't like her smug grin. He liked her casual humming even less. When she began to mutter about hardheaded McNabs, he wondered why God gave this woman the gift of speech.

If he hadn't wanted to observe the circumstances of the Clan McNish for himself without their knowledge of who he was, he would have told her that he wasn't a hardheaded McNab but a powerful Campbell and he'd teach her to care more than a whit for his good and bad side.

"Come here," he said.

"Why?"

"Because I told you to."

"I don't wish to." She crossed her arms and stood there.

"But I wish you to. Now."

"No."

He saw red and took a long step toward her.

She wisely balked no more than a second longer and then slowly took a few steps toward him muttering, "I'm coming. I'm coming."

A long hour and many arguments later, during which Grace McNish luckily escaped with her neck intact, they reached that narrow road and both sat back down, waiting for her cohorts to come back for them.

There was no sign of returning wagons—no dust cloud above the road, no jangle of harnesses, no thud of horses' hooves, no creak of wagon wheels, and most telling, no bellowing bagpipes. Nothing.

"They'll be coming soon," she said for the tenth time.

The minutes moved like glaciers. She took to drawing circles in the dirt with a finger. He took to pacing.

"You'd have thought they'd have noticed we were gone when the song ended."

She looked away.

He looked down at her. "How long is that song?"

After a pause she said, "If Fiona can get through the entire thing with no mistakes, perhaps ten minutes."

"And if not?"

"She always starts over from the beginning."

He groaned, then sat down next to her on the hard ground.

She scooted over, scowling at him.

He stretched his long legs out and rested his arms atop his knees. "It's going to be a long wait."

"You're wrong, McNab. They'll be back."

It was sunset when Colin finally stood again. He dusted himself off and, without a word, started to walk up the road in the direction the wagons had gone.

"Where are you going?" she called out.

He ignored her.

"McNab!"

He kept walking.

"You're my captive! Remember? You cannot just up and leave!"

It wasn't long before he heard the sound of her running feet. He grinned and lengthened his stride.

She scurried up to him, grumbling.

He looked down at her. "Learned your lesson, did you?"

Her mouth thinned and her eyes narrowed. She looked straight ahead and made a fierce attempt to match his pace. Her wee arms pumped and her feet scurried, but never once did she lower her determined chin. He caught her covert glance just before she said, "No McNab could ever teach a McNish anything."

"Och! I could teach you something, McNish."

"No doubt some inspiring tidbit, McNab." She paused, which put her a few steps behind him.

He could hear her running to catch up.

She rushed by him and stuck her chin up, still staring straight ahead. "Perhaps you can instruct me on how to command a horse."

"Perhaps I can teach you how to land where you aim."

She spun around, the ragged damp plaid whirling

about her. He caught her flying fist in one hand before it hit his chin.

He held it tightly and looked down at her, his patience gone.

She glared up at him, raised her chin a notch, and tried to punch him with the other fist.

He ducked under her fist and at the same time flung her over a shoulder, pinning her flailing legs with one arm.

"Perhaps, McNish," he shouted over her squeals of protest, "this will teach you when I've had enough."

He kept on walking, one arm clamped across the back of her thighs. He ignored her struggles, ignored her fists beating at his back, and did his best to ignore that mouth.

Seven

Grace was quiet for the first time since McNab had decided she was a sack of oat flour. Unfortunately her screaming hadn't sparked a single response from him, other than that obnoxious whistling. The man thought he was a lark.

He had finally put her down a little while ago. She turned back toward the small glen near the road, where a covey of grouse were feeding. Her stomach growled. She could just see them roasting on a fire. She was so very hungry, but she wouldn't admit it to him.

McNab looked at her for a moment, then at the birds. He quietly stepped toward the bushes. He turned to her and raised a finger to his lips, pointing at the birds.

She glared at him. Did he think she didn't know enough to keep quiet?

He picked up a rock and threw it.

They had one grouse.

He picked up another stone and threw it. They had dinner for two.

He started to walk toward the fallen birds. Grace grabbed his arm and shook her head. Then she raised a finger to her lips and frowned, as he had.

She picked up a rock that filled her palm. "My turn," she mouthed, and resisted the urge to throw it at him when he crossed his arms and appeared to be holding back a laugh.

Grace heaved a rock at another grouse.

"You hit it," McNab said in surprise.

She dusted her hands off and swaggered past a group of hazel bushes. "Of course. You needn't sound surprised."

"Nothing you do surprises me, McNish." He walked over to the birds and squatted down.

She stopped swaggering. He'd just called her predictable.

"I pretended it was your head."

He looked up at her and laughed as if he had expected her to say exactly that.

"Mine's the biggest one," she added smugly, and pointed at the two smaller birds that he'd killed.

He didn't answer, but gathered up the birds, then suddenly stilled.

"The puny ones are yours," she goaded.

Colin stood, then grabbed her arm and pulled her into the forest.

"Where are you going?" she shrieked, tired of his man-handling.

"This way. Hurry!"

"But that's the wrong way."

"Be quiet." He glanced back just as she gave him a dire look.

"That road leads to Loch Earn! If you think I'm going this way, then you must think me a bigger idiot than you."

"Shut up, McNish."

A horse whickered from the road, which was followed by the sound of laughter.

"They've come back for us!" She wrenched her hand from his and marched off for the road, her words echoing in her wake. "I told the stupid oaf they'd come. But does he believe me? No."

His big hand closed over her mouth and he jerked her back against him, holding her still. She screamed in protest, but the sound was muffled against his hand.

"Be quiet, damnit!" he hissed into her ear.

He was going to try to take them all prisoner, she thought. She kicked him. He grunted but held her more tightly. He turned around, dragging her with him into the thick brush. "Look, McNish!"

What she saw sent a chill down her spine. A small band of men moved on horseback onto the road from the dark forest opposite. They had the look of those who had sold their souls to the devil.

A big man with wild gray hair and a red beard stabbed his pike into the road and turned. "Naught but an empty road, Tom."

"Aye," said a man wearing a red scarf about his head. "So where's this fine quarry ye told us about, Tom?"

A small, beady-eyed man with a collection of knives strapped to his belt turned to the man with the red kerchief. "They were coming this way, Sim."

Then he turned to the big man and whined, "I seen 'em meself, MacGregor."

"Dinna mind him, MacGregor," said Sim. "Auld Tom's been seeing kelpies and fairies ever since he polished off that jug earlier. What's a few wagons when yer pot-eyed?"

All the men laughed except the beady-eyed Tom, who pulled a long dagger and leapt toward the other man, slashing out and calling him a vile name.

They fell into the road, and the others gathered around, cheering and shouting and calling for a kill. The huge man called MacGregor slowly walked into the fray, watched the men cut at each other, then planted his pike between them while he pinned Tom's wrist to the ground with his filthy boot. "We've wasted enough time."

The men grumbled slightly, but turned, and within a few moments they disappeared like wraiths into the forest.

Grace turned to McNab. "Were they looking for us?"

"Appears they were looking for the wagons. It's a good thing that band of yours didn't come back to find us."

Grace glanced back at the road and thought of her friends and what might have happened. She shivered slightly.

"Come along, McNish. We need to fetch the grouse, but this time, stay away from the road." He stood over her and held out a hand to help her up.

She placed her hand in his and let him pull her up. Just this once.

* * *

The night was black and moonless, but it wasn't silent. An owl hooted and insects chittered. However, Grace was quiet for the first time in hours. They'd traveled well into the depths of the forest and even farther away from her home. And she'd told McNab so, many times.

Once she was certain he wasn't heading for McNab land, she let him pull her along until he said he thought it was safe enough for them to make camp. He had his broad back to her as he reached for some more branches for the fire.

She watched him, conceding that he didn't seem to have the McNabs' hot-blooded temper.

Oh, she'd tried everything she could to spark rage in him. But he'd ignored her.

She huddled deeper into her plaid. So now she had decided not to say anything. Silence. That ought to get to him, she thought.

She glanced covertly at him. She should have hated him, for she hated everything that was McNab. That hatred was a part of her, the one thing she'd clung to when it seemed as if there was no hope for the Clan McNish.

But she was having trouble hating this man. She couldn't look at him and see the pain of her clan. She looked at him and she saw—oh, God . . . She closed her eyes at the thought. She saw him as a man.

She refused to think of him as "handsome," but there were the strong lines of his profile, his firm mouth, his strength, and the frustrating way he calmly reacted to almost everything she'd done to bait him.

She wanted to remember vengeance. What she remembered was his kiss, his taste. She remembered him acting so silly and catching those apple pieces. She remembered laughing for the first time in so very long.

And she remembered his grabbing her wrists and pulling her into the wagon. His hands on her back. How, when they fell, he had tried to protect her in some odd, gallant way.

A McNab? Imagine that.

He'd kept her from foolishly walking into a pack of thieves, which she would have done. She needed to hate him. But she didn't.

She sat there, hungry, trying not to think about him as he roasted the birds, trying not to look at him, and concentrating on every past cruel act of his vile clan in the hope that she could dredge up some spark of fight against what she was feeling.

In the distance a wolf howled, and Grace pulled her plaid tighter around her. A woods owl called out.

The fire crackled as he added wood. "You must be hungry."

"No. I'm not hungry." Then her cursed belly growled loudly.

He looked up at her while he turned the three grouse they had caught on a spit he'd made. "You're wrong, McNish. You are hungry. Your belly tells me so about every few minutes."

"I wasn't wrong," she said, forgetting to be silent. She crossed her arms over her plaid. "I'm never wrong."

"I suppose that wasn't your empty stomach calling out just now?"

"Aye, it was. But I wasn't wrong," she added stubbornly. He looked at her until she admitted, "You just happened to be right for a change." The Grace McNish rule: Never admit you were wrong. "Don't worry yourself about me, McNab. Hunger is a normal state for a McNish." She

183

looked away from the meat, unable to watch it cook. She was so hungry she'd almost have eaten it raw.

She sat there, miserable because she had lost control of everything, even her belly. The rich smell of the roasting birds finally got to her. "Aren't they cooked yet?"

He chuckled. "Almost."

"Remember the big one is mine."

There was long silence; then he asked, "I take it you're talking about the grouse?"

She should have seen that one coming. "You are a sick man, McNab."

He shrugged. "If you want the big one, you can have it. Just ask."

She straightened and put her hands on her hips. "My stone hit the biggest grouse, and we both saw it. I want it understood. The bird in the middle is mine."

"Are we having another challenge, McNish?"

"I don't know what you mean. I was just pointing out which bird belongs to whom. You McNabs have trouble keeping your hands off things that don't belong to you."

He waited a moment before calmly and arrogantly responding, "Who struck the first kill?"

"Why . . . you did," she said sweetly. "Don't the McNabs always kill first?"

He looked as if he had a murder on his mind. Hers.

She decided this time it would not be a good idea to grin smugly—she did have some sense of prudence, after all—and she changed the subject instead. "The birds are burning."

He looked down at the spit, where the two outer birds—his birds—were aflame. He swore and jerked the spit from the fire.

184

She held out her hand and asked sweetly, "May I have my bird, please?"

His narrowed gaze met hers.

She pointed at the spit. "That nice plump one in the middle. The one that's not burned. That one is mine."

He used her dirk to pry off a charred bird. It crackled and the burned legs and wings crumbled to the ground. She almost felt sorry for him when she saw how he stared at it. Almost, but not quite. A McNab should understand what hunger was.

"I'm waiting," she said brightly.

He stabbed the dirk into her bird, and the meaty juices ran out, sputtering as they dropped into the hot ashes. He slid the bird from the spit and held it up for her to take.

She plucked it off the dirk before he could do anything rash, like steal it for himself. She ripped off a leg and just stared at it for a moment because it looked as good as it smelled.

She tasted it and closed her eyes. It was heaven. She chewed slowly, savoring the flavor. She licked her lips and sighed as she swallowed. She opened her eyes to find him staring at her with the look of a man starved. She quickly hugged the bird to her chest. "This is my bird, McNab."

"What bird?" he asked distractedly, still looking at her mouth.

"This bird!" She held it up in front of her face.

Scowling, he viciously bit into one of the charred birds. His expression changed. He looked like someone who had just eaten a big lump of Lowland coal. He stopped chewing. It looked as if his eyes were tearing, and she could have sworn that his jaw twitched.

"Mmm." She took another plump mouthful and oohed and aahed over how perfect it was.

He crunched down on blackened meat, then paused, blanching slightly before he chewed again, very slowly.

"This is *soooo* good."

He swallowed, hard, then grunted something about his being only a little well done.

"Mine's perfect, McNab." She leaned over and looked at his bird. "Look. I believe there's a piece of meat right there." She paused and pointed toward the breast of his bird. "A wee one that's not too well done." She looked up. "See it?"

"It's fine," he growled, and bit off another bite before tossing the carcass over his shoulder.

"So's mine." She bit into the meat with great relish. *"Hmm, hmm, hmm."*

He frowned at the second bird, then tossed it and the spit over his shoulder, too.

The look he gave her said he knew exactly what she was doing and didn't like it one bit.

Just the kind of look that sparked her to say, "Delicious." She ducked her head to hide her grin. She munched some more and heard him stand. *Och,* she thought. *Can't take it, McNab.* She ignored the quiet sound of his footsteps and finished her delicious meal, then turned and tossed the bones into the fire.

She turned back around and looked up—her third mistake. Her second had been ignoring his footsteps. Her first had been pushing him too far.

He towered above her. "So torment is your game, now is it, McNish?"

"Aye, McNab," she said, returning his look evenly.

He pulled her up with such speed that her vision blurred. He held her fast against him. "You're about to learn a new game, *m'fheudail*."

She fell right into his trap and opened her mouth to speak.

He kissed her into silence. She struggled for barely a moment—less fight than he'd expected.

While he used his hand to firmly hold the back of her head, he filled her mouth with his tongue.

She stilled and almost instantly raised her fists, which barely reached above his shoulders.

Then slowly she opened her hands, lowered her warm palms, and slid them around his neck. She held him the way he held her.

After a long and passionate kiss, she pulled her mouth away from his and rested her head against his chin. "Och, McNab. What are you doing to me?"

He pulled at her plaid. "Stripping you naked and having my vile way with you."

She shook her head. "Nay." But then her lips moved over his softly. Her tongue darted past his, kissing him back passionately.

He moved his other hand down her back, over the soft roundness of her buttocks, and felt her arch her body against his; then her hand slid down around his waist.

No meek, submissive woman here, he thought. He moved his hips against her, catching a mating rhythm old as time. She moved with him, responded as she had to every challenge he gave her.

His lips never left her mouth, that mouth that pushed

his patience to the limits; now it pushed his passion beyond anything he'd known before.

Her hands gripped him tighter, and she matched him, hip to hip, tongue to tongue, movement to movement.

He could feel her need to hold her own sense of power in this, as she did in everything.

His hands moved lower, up under her plaid and shirt, then skimmed the back of her legs and moved to touch the warm soft skin of her inner thighs.

She gave a gasp at his touch, a sound he wanted to hear again. Her skin was silky, like touching a rose petal. He stroked downward until he held the back of her knees and pulled them up around his hips.

She moaned something against his mouth, half plea, half cry. Her hands tugged the back of his clothes up; then she slid her palms inside his trews.

Holding her tightly, he sank to the ground with her beneath him. He broke the kiss for the first time and straddled her, running his fingers over the soft skin of her eyelids, down her jaw. "Och, *m'fheudail.*"

She opened her misty eyes, and he ran his finger over her damp lips.

He was lost in the look she gave him, and he wasn't sure he wanted to find his way out.

Just as he had done to her, she reached out then and traced his jaw, then ran two fingers along his cheek to stroke his eyelids, his brows, then touch his lips.

He drew her hand away, holding it while his other opened her plaid and her shirt and stroked the white skin of her neck downward to her belly.

She caught her breath at his touch; then her eyes grew misty and she moistened her lips.

He parted her clothing more until her breasts were bared, and he teased them with a slow fingertip. She tried to sit up, her hands moving to mimic his touch, but he slid his arm under her back and pulled up so she arched toward him. He lowered his mouth to her bare waist, sucking until he had made his mark on her.

The whole time, her hands were busy pulling at his clothing, baring his chest.

His lips closed over her breast, taking as much of it into his mouth as he could.

He straightened and laid her back on the ground. Her nails scored his flexed thighs. He touched her again and felt her body rise with the tide of passion his touch brought.

"Such fire, McNish," he whispered into her ear. "Such hot fire. Burn for me." He cupped her low and touched her so she moaned.

He slowed his caress, and she cried out and ran her hands over him through the rough wool of his trews.

He shifted out of her reach and slid his arms under her knees, lifting her to his mouth. He blew on her, then kissed her there for the longest time.

She gave a thin moan of pure pleasure, then pulsed hard and fast. Before she had barely stopped throbbing, he did it again.

He lowered her legs to his hips and jerked down his trews, moving over her, placing his hands by her head. He shifted slowly up and down, rubbing against her.

He kissed a path up her belly, ribs, and breasts. His mouth moved up her neck, and he paused, the swollen tip of him settled barely inside her.

Her eyes grew wide, and he slowly entered her, watching her face for fear or pain. She jerked his head down and filled his mouth with her tongue. He inched inside more, her tightness closing around him until he met her maiden-head.

He stilled, then slid his hand between them. She found another quick release, tightening around him. He broke the kiss, closed his eyes, and threw his head back.

With a swift thrust, he broke the barrier, possessing her where no man ever had.

She screamed, and punched him in the jaw.

"Damn . . . McNish." His eyes shot open and he froze; then he shook his head and flinched slightly before look-ing down at her. "What the hell did you do that for?"

She glared up at him, accusation in her eyes. "You hurt me!"

"I had to."

"Why, because I am a McNish?" She sounded as if she were going to cry.

Christ! He gritted his teeth together and took a deep breath. "It only hurts the first time."

"Oh." She paused, then looked up at him, her eyes nar-rowed in suspicion. "Are you in pain?"

"No," he answered without thinking.

"Then you've done this before?"

Oh, hell . . . The answer to that question would proba-bly get him more than a swift punch in the jaw. He moved his hands to hold her head and kissed her slowly, then moved his mouth to her ear and whispered, "It doesn't hurt the man, McNish. Only the woman." He looked down at her, his lips almost touching hers. "Does it still hurt?"

She appeared to think about this for a moment, then wiggled her hips slightly.

He counted in Gaelic, searching for control, praying that he wouldn't have to stop.

"No."

He shifted, pulling back and watching her face for signs of pain.

"Don't leave me," she said in a panicked rasp, her small hands holding on to his buttocks.

"I'm not leaving you, McNish. I'm becoming part of you." He slid forward. "Slow and easy." He slid back, beginning a timeless rhythm.

Within moments her eyes drifted closed.

"Feel me . . . as I feel you."

Her hands slid up his forearms and gripped them tight.

He ceased all motion and asked, "Am I hurting you?"

She opened her eyes, misty, slanted, green as the dark depths of a Highland forest.

"No." She shook her head; then, as if to prove it, she tightened her knees on his hips.

He loved her in long slow strokes that drew out the sensation, that taught them the feel and texture and pleasure of each other. Primitive need made him want to come, but he didn't want to leave. He wanted to stay inside her forever, feel the tightness, hear her murmurs, revel in her until he died from the intensity of her.

"More," she softly chanted with each breath, impatiently prodding him with her body to move more swiftly.

He gritted his teeth and continued just as slowly. She opened those misty eyes and watched him, her expression half dare, half pleasure. She gripped his hips tightly and tried to quicken the pace.

She drew a long breath that he felt to the very depths of her. "Quicker, McNab."

191

"Slower, McNish." He edged in and out so slowly, savoring each inch, the slow and easy friction that he knew would prolong their pleasure.

She pushed up, hard and strong, and a slight smile touched her lips when suddenly he was inside her as deep as anyone could be. She closed her eyes and moved against him. He matched the motion, but grasped her hips and slowed the movement as he bent to run his tongue over her shoulder and to tease down to a breast.

She arched up, and he slid an arm under the small of her back, his hips beginning a slow, deep grind that made her moan and reach to grip his forearms again. He licked a path up her white belly and across each rib, then shifted his hold so his hands held her by the waist and he pulled her up against him as he knelt, until she could do little but cling to his shoulders.

Not once did either of them miss a motion, a beat. He could feel every inch of her with each withdrawal, could feel the swollen woman's point that ran like a small tongue over his shaft.

Her release came hard and fast and on a scream that sent him far over the edge.

When he came around, he was sure he was blind. He opened his eyes, expecting blackness, and he got it. Her black hair was wrapped around him, as were her warm legs and her warm, soft body. Had he been blinded, it would have been worth it.

He took a long, slow breath. The air was filled with the musky scent of their loving and the clean pine smell of the woods in which they'd lain.

He watched her eyes slowly change. She stared up at him and murmured, "My God . . ."

If she were the only woman he could ever make love to, he'd die a happy man. He realized then with sharp clarity that he'd just lost the one battle he had thought he could win.

She stared up at McNab's face. He looked as though he'd been hit with a caber. She turned away, feeling exactly the same way.

She had liked it. Liked it? She wanted to live forever in his arms. How could she?

Traitor. Weakling. Coward. She could have stopped this.

She should have. But she didn't. She closed her eyes against the sharp pang of guilt that struck her. He was her enemy. A McNab. But the true horror was something she could no longer deny—he was a man she could love.

"We need to talk," he said, his deep voice wrapping around her like chains. He reached out to brush the tangled hair from her face, and she flinched. He paused, something unreadable flickered through his eyes; then he looked down at her. "I hurt you again."

She looked away and shook her head, then pushed at his shoulders. He moved off her, and she jerked her clothing down, grasping the front of her plaid and shirt with one tight fist. She scrambled to her feet.

"McNish?"

That voice, oh, God, that voice. She couldn't face him. "You didn't hurt me. I hurt myself." And betrayed my clan, she thought, imagining her grandfather's face when he found out. A McNab.

"There's something I need to tell to you." He stepped toward her, his hands out to her.

"Not now." She turned her back to him.

His hand touched her shoulder, and she stiffened. God . . . she was going to cry. She never cried.

"McNish."

"Not now. Not ever, McNab!" And she did something else she'd never done.

She ran.

Eight

Where the hell is she?" Colin muttered, stumbling through the dark depths of the forest. No one could disappear that quickly. "Damnit, McNish!"

He walked farther, searching the bushes, the trees, every dark and dank nook and cranny.

A man's shout pierced the forest silence.

Colin froze and released a branch of a thick bush.

"You devil's spawn! Let go of me!"

He'd have known that mouth anywhere. He edged closer to a thick copse of trees.

"Ouch, damn ye! Catch her, Sim! The wee bitch bit me!"

"I'll do more than bite you, you vermin! *McNabbbb!*" She kicked one of the thieves.

Colin drew his dirk and stepped into the clearing. "Let her go."

The two thieves turned, still struggling to hang on to her. He cast a quick glance to make certain she was unharmed.

"It's about time, McNab!" She glared at him.

There were times when she didn't have the sense to be afraid. This was one of them.

She turned to the two thieves. "He's a McNab." Her face took on that stubborn look of challenge. "Surely you've heard about the McNabs. They'll cut out your liver and feed it to the wolves!"

Colin groaned. "McNish . . ."

"He'll skin you alive, you thieving cowards!" She jerked her arm away from one of the men and grabbed his hair in both fists, then yanked hard. "And scalp you bald!"

"Jesu! Get this viper off me! And get her hands out of me hair. Another minute and I'll be bald!"

"You'd best let go of her," Colin ordered, although he wasn't quite sure who needed saving most. McNish or the thieves.

"Aye, you sniveling, belly-crawling—"

"McNish! Be quiet."

Thankfully she clamped her mouth shut and released the man's hair. The men quickly let her go. With a sharp tug, she straightened her clothing, then stuck her chin up and strolled toward him. She stood next to him, then muttered, "It certainly took you long enough."

"Sometime later I'll teach you what long is," he said, ignoring her snort. He pinned the men with a hard look. "Where's the rest of your band?"

The smaller man glanced slyly at the other, then responded meekly, "There be no others. Only we two poor souls. She attacked us, she did."

McNish jammed her fists on her hips and shouted, "That's a lie! We saw the others! And the big one named MacGregor!"

195

"Goddamnit, McNish!" Colin grabbed her with his free hand and shoved her behind him. "Be quiet!"

Indignantly she turned to him. "Well, we did!"

"Thank you for telling them."

His sarcasm hit home. Her face flashed with guilt for an instant; then she shrugged. "Oh, well, too late now," she said. "And you know, McNab, you don't have to be so sarcastic."

Before he could say or do anything, something sharp poked him in the back.

A knife.

"Dinna move! Neither of ye!" came a gruff voice from behind them.

"Well, McNab," she muttered, "you wanted to know where the rest of them were. I'd say the knives that are poking in our backs right now are your answer."

The group of thieves took Grace and McNab to a clearing, where she saw they also held her McNish band captive along with those wagons and the provisions so important to her clan. Fiona, Iain, Seamus, and Duncan all sat nearby, tied, but looking unharmed. Grace counted eight thieves, excluding the big one called MacGregor, who couldn't be seen anywhere in the camp.

She and McNab had been tied, too, and forced to walk to the camp at sword point. Grace was gagged.

The rest of the thieves huddled near a large fire and watched her through sly eyes. She glared back at every one of them.

"What have ye there, Tom?" one of them asked. "A wee bit of skirt fer the men? I might want this one for meself."

Tom and Sim both looked at Grace and shuddered. "We don't want her, Lem! But neither do ye!"

"Ye're fools, then. She's a beauty!" Lem walked toward her, and she swung a foot back, planning to kick the fool when he got close enough.

Tom jerked the gag from her mouth.

"Stay away from me, you pocked rat!" She thought she heard Colin groan just before Duncan and Iain cheered.

"Ah," Lem said. "I like 'em with fight."

"Good!" She spat and kicked him hard.

"Get him, Grace!" Duncan shouted.

Scowling down at her, Lem raised a fist.

McNab stepped in front of her.

Lem paused, then looked up at McNab. He was almost twice as big as Lem and threatening, even with his hands bound.

"Don't," her McNab said with deadly calm.

Grace grinned at his broad back.

"If you touch my wife or the other lass, I will kill you, and if I don't, there are plenty of others who will."

Grace's mouth fell open. His wife? What possessed him to say that?

"His wife?" Duncan squeaked in disbelief.

Lem turned a suspicious gaze on Duncan, who flushed red, then Lem turned back to her and asked, "Yer friend there sounds surprised. Are ye his wife or no?"

'Twas worse than hitting her in the face. If she said yes, it would be a public declaration, stated by both McNab and her, and according to Scottish law they would then be legally man and wife.

She stepped beside Colin and looked up. He had to

know if she said anything, if she agreed, then they would be bound together.

There was something unreadable in his expression.

'Twould serve him right if I agreed, she thought stubbornly.

His face held a sudden challenge, as if he knew she'd say no.

Her eyes narrowed. She looked Lem straight in the eye and said, "Aye! I'm his wife!"

Nine

Colin smiled. She'd done exactly as he had thought, and he could see in her colorless face that she'd just realized it.

Tom the thief stepped up to him, careful to stay out of McNish's range. He removed his battered hat and placed it over his chest, then patted Colin's shoulder. "Me heart goes out to ye, lad." Shaking his head, he shuffled away with Sim, muttering about hell on earth.

Lem looked at McNish first, then at Colin.

"You will not touch these women." Colin did not flinch.

After a few moments, Lem made a sound of disgust. "Get over there with yer woman and the others! And keep her quiet or I'll gag her again."

Grace stepped toward him. "You wouldn't—"

"Be quiet, wife!" Colin nudged her forward with his knee hard enough to make the men laugh.

McNish didn't. She waited until Lem had walked away,

then whispered, "You tricked me, McNab. You'll be sorry."

"Most likely, I will, *m'fheudail*," he muttered as he watched her walk away.

Colin took in the lay of the camp as he crossed the clearing to join them. He stood over McNish. She scooted around until her back was to him. Her band stared up at him in awe; then Duncan foolishly said, "Grace. You just wed a McNab."

One blazing look from McNish, and he hunched over slightly and looked away.

Colin sat down next to her.

She scooted away.

He leaned to where Duncan huddled with Iain, Seamus, and Fiona. "Where are your weapons?"

"Over by the last wagon," Duncan answered, nodding toward the wagon that sat about twenty feet away. The pike, the claymore, and the crossbow were stacked by the wagon wheel. It was about equal distance between the wagon and the campfire.

Colin leaned closer to McNish. She started to scoot away again, but he said quietly, "You'll hold still, wife, if you want to escape."

She turned to him, her face as stubborn as that of an old ass.

He edged back until he was alongside her and partially blocked from his view of the campfire. "Your dirk is inside my plaid. Don't look at it! Just move your hands back. Aye, that's right. And feel around behind you for the handle."

She moved back a bit and reached inside.

"That's not it."

She froze.

"The dirk handle's smaller."

Her elbow jabbed into his stomach. He faked a cough to cover his grunt, and she slid the dirk out.

He shifted and raised his bound hands slightly. "Cut the rope."

She shoved the dirk handle into his hand. "Cut mine first."

"McNish," he warned through a clenched jaw, "now is not the time for this."

She didn't move.

"You will obey me . . . wife."

"It is not very smart of you to remind me of that mistake when I have a dirk in my hand, McNab. 'Twould be easy enough to make myself a widow. Besides, there was no ceremony where I promised to obey."

"Cut . . . the . . . damn . . . rope."

She waited just long enough to push his patience over the edge; then she did as he demanded, handed him the dirk, and raised her hands. "I'm ready."

Colin leaned toward Duncan and had the other lads scoot closer so he could cut their hands loose, with a whispered warning to keep them hidden behind them until the time was right. He tucked the dirk into his waist.

"Do me," she leaned over and whispered harshly.

"Not now."

"What do you mean, 'not now'?"

"Be patient, wife."

"Damn you, McNab!" she hissed.

He ignored her mumbled curses and scanned the camp. The men, who had already been drinking heavily from an open ale barrel, now began to sing.

"Sing along with them," Colin said, and joined in. He watched them, seeing that they were reasonably drunk and careless.

They all finished an old Scots ballad, and Colin shouted, "What you lads need is some piping. The red-haired lassie's a truly fine piper!" Colin ignored the gasps of the McNishes.

One of the thieves cheered and said, "Gie the lass the pipes!"

"Aye," said another.

Colin leaned toward a grinning Fiona and whispered into her left ear, "You can help us escape, lass, just play as loud as you can, then run and hide behind the wagon. Do you understand?" Her eyes widened, and she nodded seriously.

Tom had risen and went to get the bagpipes that were sitting on a wagon seat. Colin leaned to the others. "When she plays that first note, run for the weapons. Duncan, take the pike. Iain, take the claymore. Seamus, you take the crossbow."

"Seamus and the crossbow?" they all asked in unison.

"Aye," Colin said in a tone that brooked no argument. "Don't forget to keep your hands hidden when he brings the pipes here. Everyone understand?"

They nodded.

"What about me?" McNish asked.

"Quiet. He's coming," was all Colin said.

"Raise yer hands, lassie," Tom said to Fiona. He cut the rope, then handed her the pipes.

Colin had shifted earlier, so he was squatting, the dirk hidden in the folds of his cloak and plaid.

The thieves all looked at Fiona expectantly. She raised

the reed to her lips and hit the loudest note Colin had ever heard.

The thieves stood frozen in shock.

"Now!" Colin yelled. He grabbed Lem just as an armed Duncan turned from the wagon with the pike and ran toward them. He tripped, and Colin threw Lem to the ground. Duncan fell atop him, pinning him down with the pike.

One down.

Colin grabbed a thief in each hand and slammed their heads together. As they fell he glanced at Iain, who was struggling to raise the claymore. "Rest it on your shoulder, Iain!" Colin shouted. Iain let the claymore fall onto his shoulder, conking the thief that was just sneaking up behind him on the head.

Four down.

A screeching flash of long black hair sped past him as he grabbed another one. McNish made a flying leap at Tom's back. She missed his back but managed to sling her bound hands about his neck as she went flying past him.

Tom screamed like a man being chased by the devil, with Grace hanging from his back. She jerked her hands and choked him.

Colin watched him struggle with her and almost felt sorry for him. She was kicking and biting and jerking her bound hands about the man's throat while he staggered around coughing and choking.

Sim was trying to sneak up on Colin's right; Colin spun around and punched Sim as hard as he could.

Sim fell back and tripped Tom, knocking both men down with Grace flailing like a dervish on them.

Colin started to step in, but Grace was doing fine with–

out any help from him. A moment later she had managed to knock both men unconscious with her feet.

Six down.

Colin sidestepped a kick from the man and punched him just as Seamus loaded the crossbow.

The lad turned and took aim.

"Seamus is aiming the bow!" Colin shouted.

He and the McNishes hit the ground flat.

The lad pulled the trigger, and the arrow shot out and pinned the last thief to a thick pine tree.

Colin took a deep breath and glanced around the camp. All eight down.

"McNaaaab!" came a muffled shriek.

He turned and saw two bare feet kicking from beneath the unconscious bodies of Tom and Sim. He slowly walked over and watched her feet kick the air for a moment.

Her head finally popped out from under Tom's arm. She scowled up at him. "Well, don't just stand there, you grinning oaf! Get them off me and cut these ropes on my wrists!"

Colin stood there a second, then bent down. Such a sweet wife he had.

A dirk flew just over his bent head and stuck with deadly force into the side of one of the wagons.

Colin hit the ground next to McNish and quickly freed her hands.

"I've been waiting for this for a long, long time." MacGregor's deep voice sounded from the edge of the camp. He stood there casually tossing Colin's broach in his left hand.

"Aye, MacGregor. So have I," Colin said, then lunged for MacGregor's knees.

The huge man thudded to the ground. He grabbed Colin in a bear hold and squeezed.

Colin kneed him and ducked a hammy fist.

"Get him, McNab! Punch him in the gullet! Kick him in the privates! Choke him!"

Colin looked toward McNish. She had burrowed out from under the men and sat atop them, punching the air with wicked fervor. "Get him!"

He turned back just as MacGregor connected with a hard punch, knocking Colin to the ground. He rolled and shot back up, seeing nothing but stars.

"Break his nose! Blacken his eyes! Strike him in the belly!"

Colin threw his hardest right and felt the satisfying crack of MacGregor's jaw.

The man fell like a cut tree.

"Nice one, McNab!" McNish clapped her hands. "I knew you could do it."

Colin picked up a fallen dirk and held it over MacGregor, who shook his head and looked at Grace, then back at Colin. "Who the hell is that she-devil with the mouth?"

"My wife."

MacGregor scowled. "Who is 'McNab'?"

McNish swaggered over to him and stopped, planting her hands on her hips and sticking her chin proudly in the air. "He is McNab!"

MacGregor howled with laughter as Colin and the lads tied his hands and feet.

Grace looked at the laughing MacGregor and frowned. "What is so amusing, you cur?"

MacGregor looked at Colin and said, "It might be a good idea, Campbell, if ye told yer wife yer real name."

" 'Campbell'?" McNish repeated. She stared down at the broach that lay on the ground next to MacGregor. She bent and picked it up, then turned a stunned face toward Colin. The broach declared him Lord of the Isles, Earl of Argyll. She looked at him. The color drained from her face. She wobbled slightly.

"Aye, he's no McNab," MacGregor said. "He is Colin Campbell himself."

There was a loud thud.

The Countess of Argyll was out cold.

Ten

With the MacGregor and his band of outlaws taken care of, it took Colin a very short time to realize that his wife's clan needed his protection badly. He had ridden onto the Isle of Nish and almost instantaneously was ready to kill Donnell McNab and his greedy sons with his bare hands.

But it was when he saw Angus McNish hobble out from the old run-down castle, his white head as high as when he was a younger man with two good legs and a plaid without holes in it, that he understood well his wife's fierce nature.

Colin had closeted himself alone with Angus McNish, then rode directly to the McNab stronghold. Luckily for the McNabs it took a day to get there, so his temper had cooled. Before that, he had been ready to send the lot of the McNabs on a ship to a land so savage they would have been lucky to survive.

Instead, he made it clear that it did not matter that

Grace McNish was his wife, although it would serve the McNabs well to remember that fact, but that if he ever heard they stole even an apple from anyone, he would confiscate their remaining lands and exile the whole lot of them with nothing but the clothes on their backs.

While he could not take away the pain of the past, he did charge the wealthy McNabs exorbitant fines, payable for years to the descendants of the men and families whose lives they had destroyed, and confiscated more than half their cattle to give back to the Clan McNish, along with all McNish lands. He also took control of all the borders of McNab land, to ensure they kept to themselves in the future.

In the true way of cowards, the McNabs groveled quickly. By the time he and his men rode out, Old Donnell and his sons were ready to kiss the ground Angus McNish hobbled over.

But when he had arrived back at the crumbling old McNish castle, his biggest problem was not the McNabs or clan wars. Grace had locked herself in the tower and refused to have anything to do with him.

She now stood across the tower room from him; her expression mulish from the moment he had walked into the room.

"How long are you going to punish me?"

She did not answer him.

"I would think, wife, that finding out I'm not a McNab would be a good thing."

"Then that is your mistake, my lord."

"What?"

"Thinking, my lord."

"Will you stop 'my lording' me?"

" 'Tis what you are, is it not? Colin Campbell, Earl of

Argyll and Lord of the Lies." She turned about, standing there with her back to him.

He knew she was trying to make him angry. He closed the distance between them and stood over her.

She didn't turn around or even look up at him.

"I see, McNish. You have never told a lie."

She rounded on him, then, her face fierce. "You knew who I was when you married me, *my lord*. I didn't lie about something so important."

"So you admit this marriage is important to you, *m'fheudail?*"

"Do not call me your darling."

"You didn't answer me." He slid his arms about her and pulled her against him, resting his chin on her head.

She stood there stiffly.

"Is this marriage important to you?"

She burst into tears and shoved away from him, sobbing and sobbing.

It was so unlike her that he just stood there. It was a pitiful thing to see, her shoulders hunched and her hair hanging down to cover her face. Her sobbing grew louder, and he winced at the sound, wanting badly to hush her up. In the great hall below they must have thought he was beating her from all the howling she was doing.

"McNish?" He had no idea what he should say to her.

The longer he stood there, the more she cried.

"Do you want me to leave?"

"Aye . . ."

He turned to leave.

"Nooooo . . ." she said on a wail.

He stopped.

"I don't know. . . ."

He stood there. *What the hell was he supposed to do?* "Are you so very unhappy?" he asked finally.

"I don't know," she sobbed into her hands.

"Perhaps if you look at this logically, you might not be so upset."

"Logically?" She cried even harder.

"Do you regret our marriage?"

She didn't say anything.

He waited so long he thought his hair might have turned gray. "You're not going to answer me," he said sharply. When she said nothing again, he added, "I'm leaving then, until you can stop being so unreasonable."

"Unreasonable?" She spun around, her face tear-streaked and red and blotchy.

"I'm tired of this. You're making me angry."

"I am making you angry? And *I* am unreasonable," she said very slowly, enunciating every word.

A moment later he went running back down the stairs, ducking the three pewter goblets, two platters, a coal bin, and brass ewer that came sailing down the stairs after him.

He walked into the great hall to see Angus McNish wincing as the last goblet clattered down the stone stairs behind him and rolled into a corner with a loud clunk in the telling silence.

The men were all sitting around a huge oak table before a raging fire, every last one of them looking at him.

Mungo stood to his full six feet six inches and set down his wine, then tossed Colin his sword. "Here. We thought ye might need this to protect yerself from yer wife."

The men laughed as if it were the most amusing jest.

"Aye, we thought you were beating her, with all that howling. We dinna know she was beating you!"

"Aye, next time ye'll hae tae take a band of guards wi' ye."

"I'll be happy to be one of 'em if I can find me grandda's armor."

The jesting went on for a few minutes. Finally, Colin slumped into a huge chair and stared at the fire.

His men grew quiet, and slowly, one by one, they left until there were only Angus and Mungo left at the food-laden table.

Angus came over and handed him a goblet. "Have yerself some wine. It dulls the senses, particularly the ears. I could hear my granddaughter shrieking at you from down here."

"I suspect they could hear her in London."

" 'Tis one hell of a goose egg ye've got on your noggin," Mungo said, staring at Colin's brow, which was throbbing.

"I didn't duck quickly enough." Colin pressed his fingers against it and winced.

"She is a spirited lass, like her grandmother before her," Angus said. "Ye'll never be bored, laddie. I never was."

"Someone should have beaten her," Colin grumbled into his wine.

"Aye, but she always could outrun me, even before I lost this leg."

"I suppose I won't ever be bored, but I don't understand her."

"Gie it time, laddie. Ye'll see how to handle her spirit. Yer a smart lad."

"I dinna want a handful of a lassie," Mungo said in passing conversation. "I want to come home to a little peace and quiet. Gie me a lass with a sweet manner. And I'll be happy as a lark."

Colin stared at Mungo, a man he'd known for twenty

years and who was a grizzled warrior who had never married. As far back as Colin could remember, Mungo hadn't much time for ladies. And here he was talking about peace and quiet and a home?

Colin thought for just a moment that the world about him was mad and he was the only sane one in it.

Mungo chewed on a hunk of bread and some meat; then he looked up at Colin and said, "Come, eat something, and let yer lady's temper cool."

"Yer man is right, lad. She'll come around soon enough. Her grandmother always did."

Colin helped himself to some of the roast goose and more wine, while they all talked about women, wives, war, and other trying battles.

He had no idea how much time had passed, but the fire was dwindling and he and Angus had risen to put logs on it more than once.

So it surprised him when Fiona came downstairs. She looked at him, then cast a quick glance at Mungo and smiled shyly.

Ah, he thought. So that is the way of it. Mungo's strange talk of sweet lassies.

Then Colin frowned. Now there was a match, the redhaired lass with more sweetness than honey and a man who was a good twenty years older and almost twice as big, with battle scars on his cheeks and arms and a hand that could knock a man unconscious with one whack.

Colin thought about Fiona's bagpipes. He wondered what kind of peace and quiet Mungo would have with that instrument in his house.

But when he looked at Mungo, Colin saw he wore a silly grin that made him look as if he had been cold-cocked. He knew the feeling well. He also knew then that the bagpipes wouldn't matter to Mungo any more than Grace's shenanigans mattered to him.

Fiona curtsied. "Me lordship, I have a message for ye from yer wife."

Angus poured more wine into Colin's goblet. "Ye'll be needing this, lad. Take a good stiff swill of it, before the lassie speaks."

Fiona opened her mouth, but Colin raised a hand to stop her. He downed the whole goblet of wine, then faced her. He waved his hand, "Speak, lassie."

Fiona looked away from Mungo back to Colin and straightened her shoulders. Then a blank look came over her face, and she stood there, silent. Frowning, she said, "Gie me a moment." She looked down and mouthed a few words; then she nodded and looked up again.

"Are ye ready, lass?"

"Aye." She took a deep breath. "Her ladyship, Countess of Argyll, granddaughter to Angus, laird of the Clan McNish, wife to Himself, Lord of the Isles, wishes his lordship to know that she has no regrets."

Colin felt his heart soar. She didn't hate him. She didn't want to dissolve their marriage, which was what he had thought she wanted.

"She also said to tell ye that, 'Even if she did have regrets about marrying ye—which she does not even one, wee bit—ye must be bloody daft in the head to think that she would ever admit she was wrong'."

Grace's stubborn-to-the-last message hung in the air.

A moment later, the men were laughing.

Epilogue

*I*t had been twelve years since Colin Campbell had brought his bride home to Findon Castle. Over the years, he proved again and again that as Lord of the Isles, he was wise in the ways of men. Peace had come to the Highlands, but there was not always peace within the walls of Findon.

It was Michaelmas, a very special time at the home of the Earl and Countess of Argyll. The bells rang and called the brood of Campbell children to come to the great hall for the official cutting of the huge Dundee cake, a sweet treat filled with currants, dried fruits, and, best of all, honeyed figs.

Outside, one small, eight-year old girl hollered a battle cry, *"A Campbell,"* as she fell from a huge rowan tree onto the back of her eldest brother, a tall young man called Gavin who had the patience and intelligence and, luckily, the strength of his father.

"Are you going to just keep walking with me on your back, Gavin?"

"Aye, Annabella. That I am."

"Good," she said, grinning and sliding her arms around her big brother's braw neck and hanging on. Now she knew for certain that she would get to the hall before her other sisters so she would get the first piece of cake.

Another Campbell son, ten-year-old Lucas, joined them at the steps to the huge doors. He, too, held the promise of their father's stature and temperament. Both boys were patient lads, something they needed to be with four younger sisters who were exactly like their mother.

The three walked into the great hall and caught their parents kissing. Annabella jumped down from Gavin's back and walked over to the cake. She had just picked up the knife by the cake when her father took it from her and scooped her into his arms, then swung her around until she was giggling. He hugged her to him and said, "You know you must wait for the others, sweet."

Their mother smiled at them and moved over to put her arms about each of her sons. "We have news for you. Next spring you all will have a new brother or sister."

Secretly both Lucas and Gavin said a prayer that it would be a boy. There were too many girls in the house as it was.

The doors banged against the wall and six-year-old Bridget came barreling into the hall with her twin sister, Isabel, in her wake. Bridget skidded to a halt, elbowed in front of her brothers, and gave Isabel a smug grin. "I was first!"

"You cheated! You locked me in the cellar!"

"You're just angry because you didn't think of it."

Isabel stuck her chin out like a mule. "You're worse than a vile McNab!"

While they were arguing over who would get the first piece of cake, two-year-old Marta ignored them all, ran right through her father's legs, and made a dive for the huge cake.

She landed in its center face-first.

Cake went everywhere. A glob of icing on Gavin's forehead. Cake crumbs in Lucas's right eye. Icing speckled Bridget's face like freckles and dripped from Isabel's long black hair. Annabella was picking sticky nuts off her plaid, and her father's shirt was covered with currants.

Not a crumb had hit Grace, a fact that had her laughing at all of them.

Marta popped her head up and licked her lips, then looked at everyone with a wide, cake-crumbed grin and said, "Mine!"

No, there wasn't much peace within the castle walls, but there was love. There was always love, and never once were there any regrets.

JILL BARNETT is the author of fourteen acclaimed novels and short stories. Her newest novel, *Sentimental Journey*, is forthcoming in hardcover from Pocket Books. Her work has appeared on many national bestseller lists and has been published in fourteen languages. She is a recipient of the PERSIE Award for Literature and the National Waldenbooks Award.

Cold Feet

GERALYN DAWSON

One

Scottish Highlands, 1886

Rand Jenkins was lost.

A bitter wind whipped across the snow-covered moors, blowing drifts as high as his horse in places. The cold dry air caused his eyes to tear and his lips to chap, and he hadn't felt his toes all morning. All in all, he was miserable.

Then a woman rode up beside him, and his morning went from miserable to downright sorry.

"We're lost, aren't we?" asked Sarah Ross, the estranged wife of the Marquess of Weston.

Rand scowled in reply. If not for her he'd be sipping iced tea on his front porch in San Antonio today instead of freezing his posterior off in the Highlands of Scotland. Funny how weather changed a man's perspective. A trip somewhere cool had sounded good last August when he'd agreed to do a friend a favor by escorting this lady home to her husband. Five months and thousands of miles later, a good ol' Texas summer day sounded mighty fine.

Sarah Ross shook her head in disgust. "We should have reached Rowanclere Castle by now. I told you we should have stopped for directions at that last farm. We're lost."

He set his teeth. "No, we're not lost. I'll bet Rowanclere

is around the next bend." *Please, God, let it be around the next bend.*

"That's what you said three bends ago," Sarah complained, her breaths fogging on the air like miniature smoke signals. "We're lost and it's freezing and we'll be lucky if it doesn't start snowing on us any minute now. The Widow Norris didn't know how lucky she was to awaken ill and unable to continue the trip as my chaperone this morning. She's warm in her bed at that pretty little inn, and we're lost and freezing in a foreign country."

Rand's eyes crossed as frustration bubbled inside him. *Nag nag nag.*

The woman had harped at him all the way from Texas, and his temper was getting thin. He realized that her attitude was mostly bravado, so he tried to be understanding. Hell, he'd be cranky, too, if he faced a reunion with a spouse he hadn't seen in almost a decade. But the fact remained that her harping wore on his ears. He was more than ready to get to Rowanclere, turn her over to her marquess, and head home.

Of course, he had to find the blasted castle first.

He gazed up the road, searching, and shivering from the cold. A wisp of smoke rising into the air caught his attention. "Look, off to the north. There's something . . ."

Sarah stopped and stared. "That's a cottage, not a castle, but it looks like someone is home. This time we're stopping for directions, Rand, whether you like it or not."

With that, the Marchioness of Weston gave her horse a nudge and guided him toward the thatched-roof stone cottage nestled at the bottom of a snow-covered hill.

Rand sighed heavily, then followed. By the time he reached the cottage, she had dismounted and was approaching the door. "Hold up, there. Let me do it. It's not safe for a woman to go knocking at a stranger's door."

"I'm told they have a tradition of hospitality in the Highlands," she said, rapping her knuckles against the wood. "Besides, it's not safe for a woman to get lost in a snowstorm, either."

"You're not lost and it's not snowing." Even as he said it, a snowflake landed on his nose. When she arched a brow his way, he narrowed his eyes and declared, "These are just flurries."

"Flurries liable to become *just a blizzard* any moment now."

Rand just shook his head. *If her husband can live with this woman and not cut out her tongue, he's a better man than I.*

A gust of wind blew a dusting of snowdrift from the roof and it floated down upon them as the door creaked open. "Aye?" asked a melodious feminine voice. "Yes, may I help you?"

Rand couldn't reply. He was too busy being smitten with lust. After one look at her, he halfway expected the snowflake on his skin to turn to steam.

She had fairy princess features with a saloon girl figure. Her hair was the color of midnight, long and free flowing. The cold air kissing her cheeks brought a becoming stain of color to a fair and flawless complexion. And her eyes ... oh, her eyes ... Rand swallowed hard. Long, curling lashes framed eyes a pure, crystalline green. A bewitching, other-worldly, ageless green.

He thought he might lose himself in the spell of her eyes right here and now.

Rand's gaze drifted downward, drinking in the lovely view of a full bosom, narrow waist, and gently flaring hips packaged in a plain woolen dress. He couldn't remember the last time the mere sight of a woman had affected him this strongly. It was almost scary.

Sarah jabbed him in the side with her elbow and said, "I'm sorry to bother you, but I'm afraid we're lost. Is this the road to Rowanclere Castle?"

The beauty smiled pleasantly as she replied, "Nae, this road leads to Laichmoray. The turn to Rowanclere is aboot ten minutes south."

Sarah shot Rand a triumphant look, but before she could say *I told you so,* he patted her shoulder and said, "See, I told you we should stop for directions."

Sarah choked, then coughed. The beauty clicked her tongue. "Ach, you puir thing. It is a cold December day, and a puir one for travel." She opened her door wide. "Please come in and warm yourselves by my fire. I am Annie Munro and I wish you welcome in my humble home."

"Thank you, ma'am," Rand said, placing his hand on Sarah's back and propelling her inside. "We're much obliged. My name is Rand Jenkins, and this is Lady Weston. She's on her way to join her husband who is kin to the owners of Rowanclere Castle."

"Weston? Would you be his American wife, then?"

"Yes," Sarah said with a sigh. "Of course, he was plain old Nicholas Ross when we met, so that's how I think of him no matter what his title."

Annie Munro smiled widely, then took Sarah's hands and gave them a squeeze. "I've known Nick since we were both children. Your husband was the very devil at playing pranks, Lady Weston, but he has grown to be a fine mon. It's pleased I am to meet you."

"Please, call me Sarah. At this point in my life, I find a little friendly familiarity pleasing."

Rand noted that her complexion had taken on that familiar greenish tint it developed whenever Lord Weston's name was mentioned. Every mile closer to Rowanclere, the deeper the shade of green, too. Damned if he didn't feel sorry for her, viper tongue and all. He felt the urge to reach out and ruffle her hair like he did his little sister's.

The lovely lass beamed. "Very well, Sarah. Then I insist you return the favor."

As Sarah and their hostess exchanged pleasantries, Rand took a curious look around Annie Munro's small but welcoming cinnamon-scented cottage. A long table divided the single room in half. One side appeared to be a work area, with dozens of baskets and jars placed in neat order on shelves that lined the walls. Dried plants hung in bunches suspended from the ceiling, and on the table sat a mortar, a pestle, knives, and pots in a variety of sizes. Interesting, he thought.

Not as interesting as the other, more personal side of the house—mainly because he didn't see any signs of a Mr. Munro. A man's natural curiosity caused him to probe a bit. "This is a nice place you have, Mrs. Munro. I'm awfully grateful to you for giving us somewhere to warm ourselves for a bit. Being from South Texas, I'm not accustomed to all this snow and cold. I haven't felt my toes in three days."

She laughed. It was a lovely laugh, light and melodious like a chime.

Rand blinked twice. Where the hell had that come from? He never had those flowery sorts of thoughts about women. Must be the cold.

"It's Miss, sir, and by all means, please take a seat before the fire and warm your puir toes. In fact, if you are not offended by informality, I suggest you remove your shoes and we'll hang your stockings up to dry."

Rand pursed his lips. He could easily sink into a fantasy in which this goddess asked him to remove his clothing. Of course, he wouldn't stop with socks.

She offered refreshments and seats in front of the fire. Sarah requested tea while Rand accepted the suggestion of something stronger. While their hostess put a kettle on the stove to heat, he and Sarah stripped off their shoes and socks and stuck their feet toward the flames. Soon delicious warmth seeped into his skin and thawed his toes. Rand groaned in pleasure. "Miss Munro, you are surely a saint."

She looked up from pouring Sarah's tea and smiled. "Oh, I'm no saint, sir. Quite the opposite, in fact. I'm a witch."

Annie watched the braw, bonny man's eyes widen with shock, the woman's light with intrigue. *By my fegs.* What had she done? She stuck out her tongue, her eyes crossing as she looked down. Yes, that was her very own tongue in her very own mouth that had just uttered the dumbest words ever spoken.

"I'm kidding, of course," she said, pasting on a smile and avoiding their eyes. "It's something the villagers tease me with from time to time."

Sarah sighed. "That's too bad. If you were a witch I would ask you to cast some spells for me. I've a few people in my life who I'd like turned into toads." She gazed pointedly at Mr. Jenkins and added, "I believe their bodies should match their personalities."

He gave his companion a droll look, then drawled, "Aren't I lucky, then, there's no such thing as witches."

Her interest engaged by her visitors' exchange, Annie resumed pouring the tea. Casually, she asked, "You dinna believe in witches, sir?"

"I do not."

"What of fairy folk or ghosts?"

"Figments of the imagination, that is all."

Sarah wiggled her toes toward the fire and shook her head. "You're wrong, Rand. Otherwise, how do you explain the repeated presence of supernatural traditions in separate cultures all over the world?"

"Easy." He folded his arms and crossed his long legs at the ankles, a confident man completely at ease with himself and his opinions. "Mankind uses tales of witches and ghosts to explain away that which he doesn't yet understand. Think about it, ladies. The more scientifically advanced a society, the less willing it is to accept tales of the powers of shamans and sorceresses. I predict that in another generation in more advanced cultures, belief in such nonsense will have almost disappeared."

Sarah sniffed. Her eyes glimmered with disdain as she met Annie's gaze. "Just one little spell. That's all I need. Can't you just picture a toad in a cowboy hat?"

Annie couldn't help but smile, especially when Mr. Jenkins tipped an imaginary hat toward his companion. "I respect your viewpoint, Mr. Jenkins, but you winna find many like thinkers among the Highlanders. We have a long history of belief in supernatural beings. While I've never personally met a witch or an elf or a kelpie, I believe it is possible they exist. What is your viewpoint on fortune and fate? Do you take mind of superstition and tradition like we do here in the glen, especially during this time of year?"

He nodded. "I believe in luck. Have seen runs of it—good and bad—often enough to prove it. I don't hold with many superstitions, but I will admit to upholding tradition. I think traditions are good for family and country, alike."

"Like the traditions of Christmas," Sarah said with a sigh. "We spent it traveling, I'm afraid. We had hoped to make it to Rowanclere in time for the holiday, but that was not to be. However, I can vouch for Rand being a traditionalist." She lifted her hand to her hair and touched an attractive tortoiseshell comb. "This was my Christmas gift from him."

" 'Tis lovely," Annie said, both gaze and tone admiring as she handed Sarah her steaming cup of tea.

"They were all I could find in Inverness," he drawled. "The shops were all out of mouth gags."

Amusement twinkled in Sarah's eyes, even as she childishly stuck her tongue out in his direction. "I see a frog with a cowboy hat who croaks with a South Texas twang."

Smiling, Annie reached for a bottle of whisky to pour Rand Jenkins a drink, then paused as her gaze lighted on her special holiday bottle of Athole Brose. As was her family's custom, three days before Christmas she had mixed honey, oatmeal, and cream, then combined it with two pints of whisky plus her own addition of a pinch of heath pea. After stirring it with a silver spoon 'til it frothed, she'd bottled it. But this year, the first holiday season since her mother's death, she'd had no family with which to share it.

Realizing this company here today might well be her only visitors of the holiday season, Annie decided to mark the occasion, albeit privately. She uncorked the Athole Brose and poured a glass for Mr. Jenkins. Handing it to him, she said, "So you are from South Texas, then? Would you speak to me of your home? Jake Delaney's stories have given me a fascination for Texas. 'Tis a grand desire of mine to visit there someday."

She joined them before the hearth, and as the bitter wind swirled around her cozy cottage, she listened to tales of her visitors' homeland. Mr. Jenkins talked of cattle drives and rustlers, of rattlesnakes and tarantula spiders and stinging scorpions. Sarah spoke of the high society weddings she oversaw in her role as a professional wedding consultant.

While they conversed, Annie's sable-colored cat, Midnight, emerged from a cozy nap in the mending basket. While the kitty wound herself around Mr. Jenkins's ankles, her mistress listened and dreamed of living in a place where one's reputation had more to do with personal character than with whom one's ancestors had been.

"Will you be returning to San Antonio, Mr. Jenkins?" she asked as Midnight leapt into his lap.

Seconds later, the man sneezed. He immediately lifted the cat and returned her to the floor. "Oh, yes. I'm definitely going home. I'll visit with the Delaneys at Rowanclere for a week or so, then head that direction. Hopefully, the weather will cooperate with my plans. I don't relish traveling through blizzards."

They discussed Highland weather for a bit after that, then the conversation drifted to Rowanclere Castle and the people who lived there. Sarah nibbled at the biscuits

Annie offered, and after admitting that she and her husband had been estranged for some time, asked a few questions about Nicholas. Annie had just refilled Rand Jenkins's glass and scolded Midnight for continuing to bother him when a knock sounded on her door. She answered the summons and swallowed a groan. It was Maggie MacGregor, Annie's best customer. She couldn't turn her away.

"Annie, Jamie is giving me some troubles aboot the wedding. I need more of the love potion. Can ye brew—"

"I have visitors, Miss MacGregor," Annie interrupted, cutting a significant gaze toward the Texans.

"Oh." The young woman's fair skin colored as she donned a false smile and said, "Hello. Sorry to interrupt yer visit. Annie, if I could get a bottle of that . . . um . . . medicine for cough. Our chimney clogged yesterday and smoke backed up into the house. Mother's cough has worsened."

"Your puir mama. Smoke is coorse on delicate lungs like hers. Luckily, I blended more of the tonic she prefers just this morning. Let me get it for you."

Attempting to act as if nothing were out of the ordinary, she filled two bottles with two different liquids from her stores, then handed them to Maggie MacGregor and accepted payment in return. She saw her customer off, then turning to the Texans, attempted to escape back into the subject of weather. "The clouds are breaking up," she said with a smile. "With luck, you'll find the remainder of your journey to Rowanclere pleasant."

Mr. Jenkins stood and crossed the room to her worktable. *He has big hands,* she thought as he picked up a medicine bottle and read its label.

"You're a healer?" he asked, interest gleaming in the blueness of his eyes.

She nodded. "Knowledge of the usefulness of native plants has been passed from mother to daughter in my family for generations. Though we now have a doctor in the area, many villagers continue to come to me to receive treatments for their common ailments."

"Like cough medicines."

"And love potions," added Sarah. "How delightful. Could you give me something to give my husband? Not a love potion—heaven knows, that's the last thing I want. I'm thinking more of an anti-shouting elixir."

Mr. Jenkins snorted. "Don't be ridiculous."

Delicate eyebrows arched. "You don't think Nicholas will shout at me?"

"I don't think Miss Munro, here, makes love potions. That's nothing but silly superstition at work. She's an herbalist who treats coughs, not a witch who casts spells and such. Right, Miss Monro?"

Annie's chin came up. "I'm not a witch at all. That is a false, wicked rumor that persists as a result of events that happened two hundred years ago."

"But you gave that woman—"

"Get your shoes on, Sarah," Mr. Jenkins suddenly interrupted. "We'd best take advantage of the blue sky and get going." He reached for his socks and began to tug them on.

Scowling, Sarah said, "But Rand . . . oh, my . . . what's wrong with your eyes?"

Annie looked. The man's eyes were teary and as red as the Ross clan tartan. He sneezed twice in quick succession before saying, "The cat swished its tail in my face.

Close contact with cats often . . . *ahchoo* . . . gives me . . . *ahchoo* . . . fits."

Annie opened her mouth to offer a remedy for his malady when Midnight distracted her by climbing the furniture, then leaping onto Mr. Jenkins's broad shoulder to purr loudly in his ear. "Enough!" he snapped as he grabbed the cat around the middle and lifted her away. Keeping her at arm's length, he crossed the room to Annie and shoved Midnight at her. *Sniff, sniff, ahchoo.* "Miss Munro, thank you for your hospitality, but we must be on our way. The road to Rowanclere is back to the south a ways, you say?" *Ahchoo. Ahchoo.*

"Aye." Midnight twisted in her arms, meowing petulantly, but Annie held on tight. What was wrong with her pet? Ordinarily, the kitty was almost placid. "Look for the burn off to your left and the small bridge that spans it. That's the road to Rowanclere. It's not much bigger than a trail, but you canna miss the bridge if you watch for it."

After thanking Annie again, Mr. Jenkins signaled for Sarah to hurry and fled the cottage at which point Midnight's loud meows faded to purrs. Sarah donned her shoes and coat, then said, "I've enjoyed our visit. I hope we have the chance to do it again before I return to Texas."

"I am counting on it," Annie replied, meaning it. She'd enjoyed this departure from routine, and she hated to see it end.

Sarah gave Midnight a pet, then flashed a smile and sailed out of the cottage, calling over her shoulder as she went. "And if you find the time to mix up a potion for me to use on my husband, just let me know. Bye-bye."

"Safe journey," Annie called after her. She stood in her doorway, scratching Midnight behind the ears as she watched her visitors ride away. Puir Mr. Jenkins, plagued as he was by the sneezing and watery eyes. Had he not rushed off so fast, she could have offered him a tonic to provide relief.

Although, on second thought, she may have used the last of that particular blend. "I'll need to brew up more," she murmured.

The two horses turned onto the road. Then, just as Annie prepared to shut the door, twin streaks of color and movement against the snow caught her attention. Her eyebrows arched as a pair of cats—one gray and one white with tawny stripes—sprang onto the road and fell in line behind Mr. Jenkins's horse. Then, before she knew it, three more cats appeared from seemingly out of nowhere.

How strange. Annie had seen dogs follow a horse before, but never cats.

Midnight suddenly lifted her head. She let out a loud howl, then wriggled from Annie's arms. The moment her paws hit the floor she took off, a flash of black against pure white snow, until she'd joined her fellow felines so that now a regular clan of kitties trailed Mr. Jenkins's horse.

"How very strange." She'd never seen cats run in a pack like that. Neither had she seen Midnight have much to do with others of her kind. What was happening here? What was it about Mr. Jenkins that appeared to attract every cat in the area?

How completely, exceedingly strange.

Her lips pursed in thought, Annie shut the door, then crossed to her work shelves. She removed the cork from the bottle of Athole Brose and sniffed. "Hmm . . . it smells right."

Next she moved to the hearth and picked up Rand Jenkins's glass. She sniffed it, then brought it to her mouth and touched the rim with her tongue. Honeyed cream and whisky. Aye, it *was* Athole Brose. She hadn't confused her bottles.

Frowning with concern, she removed an old, well-worn book from a shelf and set it on her worktable. Opening the volume, she began to skim the handwritten pages inside, absently clicking her tongue as she read. "Adder's-grass, benweed, cat peas," she murmured, searching. "There, heath pea."

The tubercles of the root may be dried and chewed to sweeten the breath and prevent drunkenness. Good against disorders of the thorax. Repels hunger and thirst for extended periods of time. May be used as a substitute for bread when necessary. Makes an agreeable fermented liquor.

Annie grimaced as she flipped the book shut. "It disnae say one word about cats."

Replacing her herb book upon the shelf, she reached for a second, ancient-looking tome. Just for argument's sake, she'd see what it had to say about cats in the other book she'd inherited from her mother.

The one titled: *Spells and Incantations.*

Two

*R*and rode toward Rowanclere Castle accompanied by one nervous wife and seventeen mewling cats. It was the damnedest thing he had ever seen. He'd had half a dozen on his trail when he rode into Rowanclere village, and he'd collected eleven more by the time he rode out. Who ever heard of cats behaving this way, following a man around like he was the Pied Piper of Pussycats? Through the cold and snow, no less? Didn't most cats hate getting their feet wet? This made absolutely no sense.

And if the yowling of seventeen cats wasn't enough, he had the added pleasure of having to listen to Lady Weston's agitated babbling. Between the two rackets, his ears felt ready to fall off.

As he approached Rowanclere Castle's front door, he said a quick prayer of thanks for having finally reached the end of this journey. Now if he could only beat the damned cats inside.

He might have stood a chance had Sarah not dragged her feet about dismounting. He wanted to go on without her, but he couldn't make himself act in such an ungentlemanly manner. At least, he couldn't until one of the cats decided to use his leg as a climbing post. "You have to the count of five to get down from that horse," Rand said to Sarah, giving his cat-wrapped leg a vigorous shake. "Otherwise I'm dragging you down."

"Oh, all right."

He waited beside her horse to assist her, then had to nudge away the felines milling about his ankles to give her a clear place to step.

"What is it with you and these cats, Rand?" she asked. "It's not natural."

He took a step toward the castle, tripped on a tabby, and groused, "What it is, is dangerous. I think I'd better check and make sure I don't have a big fish in my pocket. Might be catnip, though. Miss Munro had all those herbs

233

hanging around. Could be something fell into them in her cottage."

Speculation sparkled in her eyes. "Maybe she put a spell on you."

"Very funny. Let's go inside, Sarah. Your husband is waiting."

Dread melted the delight from her expression, and Rand winced in pity. Poor Sarah. Here was one more good example of how marriage can mess up a person's life. He gave her hand a reassuring squeeze, then pulled her toward the front door, stepping carefully over the milling meowers in his path.

They were halfway to the door when it opened to reveal his friend and former law partner, Jake Delaney, who immediately ushered them inside the castle while managing to shut out the majority of the felines.

Rand had not seen Jake in three years, and their reunion was a collection of handshakes, claps on the back, insults, laughter, and bad jokes. Jake introduced his beautiful wife, Gillian, with obvious pride, and the welcoming smile she offered Rand warmed him like summer sunshine.

He couldn't help but note how Gillian's smile dimmed considerably when he introduced Sarah. Though he could tell she tried to be pleasant when exchanging courtesies with her brother's wife, Gillian had the look of someone sucking a lemon and trying to pretend it wasn't sour.

"Nicholas expected your arrival a good six weeks ago," she said stiffly. "He awaited you here at Rowanclere as long as possible before returning to England to spend the holidays with his English family."

"He's not here?" Sarah asked, her mouth dropping open in shock. "I came all this way, and he's not here?"

Rand knew the woman well enough by now to realize she was fixing to blow. Thinking to head off the explosion, he said, "Well, how about that, Sarah? A reprieve. How did your husband know just the perfect Christmas gift to give you?"

He knew his strategy worked when her eyes softened with relief.

A footman took their coats—after Rand checked his pockets for leaves, twigs, or other foreign objects—and while Gillian showed Sarah upstairs to her room, the men retired to the library for some catching up and a drink. "What's your pleasure?" Jake asked, waving toward a decanter-laden table. "We have a wide selection of local whisky, but I've also laid in a store of bourbon for when I'm feeling a touch homesick."

"When in Rome . . ." Rand said, gesturing at the whisky. He crossed the room to warm his hands before the fire. Then after his friend handed him his drink, he tried to take his seat.

He sat on a cat.

Eeee-yeow! The critter squalled like a child and they both leapt toward the ceiling. Sighing heavily, he shoved the feline out of his way. "Is this your animal?"

Jake shook his head. "No. We don't keep cats here at Rowanclere. We have a two-legged dachshund that demands all our attention."

Ahchoo. Ahchoo. "A two-legged dachshund?"

"She broke her back, and her hind end is paralyzed. But don't tell her. She doesn't seem to know it."

Rand started to ask more but was distracted by the sting of cat claws digging into his shoulder. The dratted animal had snuck up behind him and climbed up on his shoulders. Frustrated beyond words, he peeled the cat away and tossed it onto a nearby settee. "Do I smell?" he asked Jake, wiping his watering eyes.

"What?"

"I'm wondering if that first cat was in heat and left a scent on me. Something is attracting these animals."

"You're right about that," Jake agreed. "Another is sneaking up behind you this minute. I'd like to know how he got into the room since the doors are all closed. Two more are scratching at the window, and look at that." He gestured toward the fireplace where a black cat appeared as if emerging from behind a solid wall. "That one found Rowanclere's secret passages. Our dachshund, Scooter, will have a fit."

"This is ridiculous." *Ahchoo*. Rand stood and turned a deaf ear to the chorus of meows his movement engendered. "How about we continue our visit later, Jake? Right now I think I'd better get a bath and change my clothes."

Unfortunately, that didn't solve the problem. The animal assault continued the rest of the afternoon and even at dinner that night despite the fact the Delaneys saw the room cleared of cats twice. Rand didn't know how the pests kept getting inside. It was damned unsettling.

As he sat at the dining table attempting to enjoy his meal, one cat rubbed around his ankles, and a second kept jumping into his lap and bringing on the sneezes. A third stood beside him on his hind legs and played thief by swiping a fish fillet from his plate while Rand was busy wrestling with the first two cats. The bouts of sneezing and watery eyes were bad enough, but when he glanced down at his hands and saw hives rising on his skin, he reached his limit. "That's it," he said, scratching at his arms. "Now I'm angry. That woman did something to me."

"What woman?" Jake Delaney asked as he calmly salted his potatoes.

"Miss Munro. We missed the turn and stopped at her cottage for directions. This trouble started after we left her home."

Sarah Ross sipped her wine, then shook her head. "No, Rand. It started in her home with that cat of hers, remember? And if I'm not mistaken, her Midnight and the one who just stole your supper are one and the same."

"Really?" Rand studied the black cat who now sat at his feet daintily licking his paws. "How can you tell?"

"Look at her eyes, Rand. That one's eyes are spooky."

She was right. This black cat had bright green eyes that did look . . . well . . . haunting. And in a way, familiar. Unease crept up Rand's spine like a spider. "Maybe she put something in that drink."

"Excuse me." Gillian Delaney cleared her throat. "May I clarify something? Are you saying that you visited Annie Munro's cottage? You drank something there?"

"Yes."

Gillian and Jake shared a significant look. Jake winced and slowly shook his head. Gillian reached across the table and patted Rand's hand. "Dinna fash yersel'. It will be all right. I'm told few of them are permanent."

"Few of what?"

"Annie Munro's spells."

Rand's dinner turned to lead in his stomach. No, he wouldn't believe that superstitious nonsense. "Come on now, Gillian. Don't tell me you think that woman is a witch. Surely you don't set any store in that sort of thing."

She gave the black cat a sidelong stare, then shrugged. "I'm a Scot. We have a long tradition of 'that sort of thing.' Did she tell you she is a descendant of the last woman burned as a witch in Scotland?"

No, she hadn't mentioned that.

"It doesn't . . . *a-a-ahchoo* . . . matter." Rand would have argued with her more, but a particularly violent bout of sneezing hit him hard, and he couldn't get a sentence out. Plus, the itching had spread up his arm to his chest, and he thought if he didn't scratch soon he'd die. He choked out an "Excuse me," then hurriedly left the dining room. Without bothering to retrieve his coat, he headed straight outside into the fresh air of a bitterly cold night.

He shuddered and shivered and swore and scratched. Finally, he stripped off his jacket and shirt, and plunged his hands into a snowbank. With teeth chattering, he wiped the wet, chilling snow on his arms and chest. His breathing eased, as did the itching, except for his back. He leaned up against Rowanclere's stone wall and tried to scratch, but it didn't help the itching nearly as much as the snow had. Finally, he gave up. Marching over to the snowdrift, he stretched out his arms and tipped himself backward.

Lying bare-chested in the snow, a cold wind swirling off the castle's towers and turrets and sweeping over him, Rand had never been so cold. His teeth chattered nonstop, and he knew his skin must be turning blue. But at least he'd quit itching. And sneezing. His eyes continued to water, but he figured that was from the cold, rather than the cats. At least tears were too salty to freeze on his face. Weren't they?

Icy air stung his lungs as he inhaled a deep breath, then

blew it out in a rush. How the hell had he ended up in such an undignified position as this? He was a lawyer for heaven's sake.

True. And undoubtedly, lots of folks would think lying half-naked in a cold snowbank to be the perfect spot for lawyers. Was Annie Munro one of those people? Had he inadvertently put himself in the middle of a feud she had with a Scottish advocate? Is that why she'd sicced her cats on him?

And *how* had she sicced her cats on him? With a spell? He didn't believe that. He didn't believe in spells and incantations and witches. Still, she had to have done something, and now that the cold had cleared his head, Rand knew what that something was.

Pharmaceuticals.

Had to be. She had used her herbal expertise and slipped a drug into his drink to attract a plague of cats his way.

Rand crunched his stomach muscles and sat up. About that time, the snow between his legs started moving and two pink ears rimmed with grey fur popped into the air. He stared at the cat in silent wonder. Whatever the drug, it had to be damned strong.

The cat clawed its way forward through the snow, then softly, warmly, laid its head right atop Rand's privates.

"Get off!" Rand shoved to his feet, glaring down at the cat.

The last place he needed hives was his crotch. He grabbed for his shirt and shrugged into it, grumbling through chattering teeth. "Tomorrow. First thing tomorrow I'm gonna go back to that winsome witch's lair, and I'm gonna say her familiar got too damned familiar, and

I'll demand an antidote to whatever concoction she dosed me with. I won't leave until I get it, either."

But as he turned to reenter the castle, he glanced down at the cat who only seconds ago had lain sprawled between his legs and Rand couldn't help but wonder. Could the drug be adjusted in such a way that instead of attracting cats, it attracted women? Good God. Such a thing would kill a man for sure.

But what a way to go.

Annie Munro dreamed of cactus and armadillos and a broad-shouldered cowboy with sky blue eyes and a molasses drawl. She awoke with a smile on her face, an unusual yearning in her body, and a secret wish in her heart. If only she could somehow convince Mr. Jenkins to take her back to Texas with him.

Annie had trouble here at home. All her life she'd been an outcast due to her family history, but she'd had her mother, her aunt, and her grandmother, so it hadn't mattered too terribly much. Then three years ago, trouble came and left her aunt and grandmother dead. Last winter, influenza had claimed her mother, leaving Annie alone.

It was a sorry way to live, and Annie soon determined to change it. She put aside every penny possible to fund a new life somewhere away from the rants and rumors of folk who made use of her skills while disparaging her with their voices. Her stash of monies was still too small to see her safely settled in a new place, but recent rumblings in the nearby villages made her wonder if she dare wait much longer.

Maybe if she approached the problem with care, Mr.

Rand Jenkins could be convinced to provide a solution to her troubles.

The morning dawned cloudy with the scent of snow in the air. Annie nibbled on a slice of Yule-kebbock, savoring the taste of caraway seeds mixed into the special holiday cheese as she went about her morning chores. Periodically she went to the door and called for Midnight, though she knew it to be a futile effort. Midnight would come home when she wanted to come home, and nothing Annie did would change that. Still, she was lonely and a little worried about her pet's absence, and the effort made her feel better.

During the next hour two customers called, a concerned mother needing a bogbean tonic for her colicky infant, and a young man in search of a wayburn leaf poultice for a burn. Having been treated, the young man departed in the direction of Rowanclere village, and watching him go, Annie had an idea.

Perhaps she should pay a visit to Rowanclere Castle and see if Midnight had followed the Texans all the way there. What would be wrong with that?

The more she thought about it, the more she warmed to the idea. She could take Yule gifts with her. It would be a neighborly thing to do. She'd take a selection of aromatic sachets for Gillian and for Jake . . . well . . . Annie frowned and thought for a moment. What could she give Jake Delaney that he might like?

She glanced around the work area of her cottage and made a mental inventory. "A gift. What type of gift would a man like Jake . . ." her voice trailed off as her gaze lit on a bunch of allheal.

Annie smiled. Of course. Jake Delaney wouldn't care

that allheal, otherwise known as mistletoe, was a sacred plant to Druids and believed to have numerous miraculous qualities. Oh, he might find it interesting that in days of old, enemies who met beneath a mistletoe in the forest would lay down their arms, exchange friendly greetings, and keep a truce for a day. But the reason she considered giving Jake Delaney a gift of ribbon-bedecked mistletoe was the current tradition that had developed from the old—kissing beneath the mistletoe.

From what she'd observed, Jake took every opportunity to find an excuse to kiss his wife. Mistletoe would be the perfect gift.

Pleased with the idea, Annie went to work. She had filled a basket with sachet and attached ribbon to four sprigs of mistletoe when a knock—or to be more precise, a pounding—sounded at her door.

"Miss Munro!" *Pound. Pound. Pound.* "Miss Munro, are you home? You'd dang well better be home. We have a problem."

Recognizing the unmistakable accent, Annie's mouth went dry. She rinsed her hands, then grabbed a cloth and wiped them dry as she hurried to answer the door. She froze at first sight of him.

Hands braced on his hips, Rand Jenkins glared down at her, his eyes snapping blue fire. The clue to his temper clung to his back, her head peeking up over his left shoulder, her tail curled beneath his arm.

"Midnight, naughty girl," Annie scolded. "I've been fretful about you."

"You've a right to worry. This cat's life is in danger."

"Danger!"

"Yeah. If it doesn't leave me alone, she's not gonna

make it to her ninth life. Neither it nor all these others." With a theatric flourish he pointed behind him where nine cats sat in a line like well-trained dogs.

"Why, that's amazing. I've never seen cats act in such a manner. How do you get them to do it?"

"Me? What do you mean 'me'? This is all *your* doing."

"I beg your pardon?"

"I should darn well hope you would," he announced, shedding himself of the cats, then sweeping past her into her home. "In the past eighteen hours I've been sniffed, scratched, bitten, and spit on. My eyes have watered enough to fill one of your lochs, and I haven't gone five minutes without sneezing. When I woke up this morning I had a cat stretched across my neck, one on my stomach, and another in a place I won't mention in polite company. And that's not all. I asked for milk with my breakfast. Milk! It's damned humiliating. Next thing you know I'll be coughing up a furball. And it's all your fault!"

He searched her shelves, grabbed the Athole Brose, then stalked toward her. Holding the bottle right in her face, he spoke through clenched teeth. "I don't know what sort of drug you put in this, you little witch, but I want an antidote and I want it now!"

"I'm nae a witch," she defended automatically, even as her mind tackled the problem. Annie had done nothing out of the ordinary to the Athole Brose, except for adding the pinch of heath pea to the recipe as she preferred. She'd had two glasses of the drink herself with no ill effects. No, whatever had brought this cat condition upon Mr. Rand Jenkins, she had nothing to do with it.

"Your accusations are misplaced, sir. I shall prove it." Keeping her stare locked on his, she swiped the bottle from his hand, yanked the cork, and took a long sip straight from the bottle. She licked her lips with relish and said, "Delicious."

He stood mere inches away. Midnight once again clung to his back and shoulder, but the man didn't seem to care or even notice. His gaze had dropped to her mouth and stayed there.

Suddenly, Annie felt a rush of heat course through her veins that had nothing to do with the whisky in the drink. The air between them hummed with tension and anticipation. Again, this time because her mouth had gone bone dry, she wetted her lips with her tongue.

Rand Jenkins groaned. He leaned forward and she felt his breath against her lips. His spicy, masculine scent teased her and her senses swam. Then, with his mouth poised above hers, he murmured, "You really are a witch, aren't you?"

Three

Their lips were less than an inch apart when the cat swiped his paw between them. A claw hooked the tender flesh between Rand's nostrils and tugged. Pain burst through his head like fireworks.

"Yeow!" he yelled as Miss Munro jumped back. He grabbed the cat around the middle and tried to hold it still, but the damned animal twisted and squirmed, each movement an agonizing yank that brought tears to Rand's eyes.

"Help me," he demanded. Begged. Pleaded. The claw was stuck but good.

"Oh, Midnight, you naughty kitty." Annie Munro reached for the cat's paw and attempted to free Rand. The cat protested and held on, its *meows* a definite scold at its mistress.

Rand considered mewling right along with the cat, so sharp was the pain. Instead, he tried to reason with the thing. In a soft, gentle tone that belied his words, he said, "Good kitty. Let go now, kitty. Let go or I'll take you outside and smother you in a snowbank, kitty."

"Mr. Jenkins!" Miss Munro scolded. "Don't you threaten my Midnight."

"No threat, just a pro—Yeow!" The cat pulled Rand's head around and sharp teeth nipped the tip of his nose. Then, just as Rand contemplated wringing its neck, the claw retracted and the beast sprang to the floor. Rand grabbed his handkerchief from his pocket and brought it to his nose. Pressure both helped stop the bleeding and muffled the pain. "Stupid cat. This hurts."

"Oh, quit acting like a bairn. If you can be patient for a moment, I have something that will help."

He watched closely as she walked over to her stores and removed a jar from the shelf. "Do you think I'm crazy? I'm not letting you come near me with any more of your concoctions. Look what happened from a few simple sips of a beverage."

"It's a pain-killing ointment made primarily of willow bark," she said with a theatric roll of her eyes. "Apply a thin coating to the wound and it will help promote healing as well as providing you ease."

"Willow?" he asked, suspicion in his tone as she

spooned a dollop of ointment from the jar. "Aren't witches' broomsticks supposed to made from willow?"

"I wouldn't know, and besides, I didn't think you believed in witches. Shall I do this or would you prefer taking care of it yourself?"

"I don't believe in witches, and yes, thank you very much, I will take care of it myself." Rand couldn't believe he was putting himself at her mercy this way, but hell, his nose burned like fire. "If you're not being straight with me, Miss Munro, and this stuff has something in it that brings dogs sniffing after me or something, we'll both be in trouble."

"The medicine is perfectly safe, as was the drink I served you yesterday. You have my word."

"Your word. That's the crux of the problem, isn't it? Can I trust your word?" He gazed deeply into those enchanting, indignant green eyes and tried to judge her honesty.

Ooh, she looked madder than an old hen in a wool basket. Considered herself falsely accused, did she? Well then, he guessed he did believe her. At least, he believed that *she* believed it was safe. Still, the fact remained that the cats started coming around after his visit here. Something had to explain that.

Cautiously, Rand doctored his wounded nose and all but moaned in pleasure at the near immediate relief. In fact, the cream soothed his fresh cut so well he decided to use it on some of yesterday's scratches. To that end, he shrugged out of his coat, then began unbuttoning his shirt.

"What are you doing?"

"I like that stuff. Figure since I'm already taking the

risk, I might as well cover all my sore spots." He peeled off his shirt, then spread the ointment across the dozen or so scratches across his chest. Then he turned to Annie Munro and asked, "Get my back for me, would you?"

She hesitated, and Rand got the distinct impression she didn't relish touching him. Rather than being insulted, he was intrigued. Could it be she didn't want to touch him because she *wanted* to touch him? Possibly. Even likely. She'd been ready to kiss him, hadn't she? Why, if not for the damned cat, he'd know for a fact what those cherry lips tasted like.

It was a piece of information he realized he craved learning.

Her finger touched his back with a feather-light stroke and Rand couldn't hold back a groan. "That feels good."

"I told you the ointment was soothing."

He wasn't referring to the ointment.

Rand shut his eyes and enjoyed the sensation of feminine hands gliding across his skin. He'd missed a woman's touch. Due primarily to the extended travel, he hadn't had a woman in months. His mouth quirked in a half smile, he mentally added, *And I've never had a doctor like Annie Munro.*

He found himself wishing for a dozen more scratches that needed tending.

The pleasant interlude ended when the black beast tried to climb his leg yet again, which forcibly yanked Rand's thoughts back to the matter at hand. "Miss Munro . . . Annie . . . may I call you Annie?"

She nodded.

He grabbed up his shirt and slipped it back on. "Annie, I'm willing to accept the idea that you didn't intentionally

247

dose me with a pharmaceutical that caused the beasts to swarm. However, the fact remains that prior to my walking into this cottage yesterday, cats didn't particularly like me. Since I walked out, I've been a six-foot two-inch block of catnip. I've been flooded in felines. Something happened while I was here, so it's only right that you fix it."

"But I don't know what happened. I don't know how to fix it."

"Well then, sugar, I reckon you'd best get to work on figuring it out." With that, he sat down, propped his boots on the table, and sneezed three times in a row. "I'm not leaving here until you do."

The man took up way too much space.
The man had almost kissed her.
The man's bare chest was a feast for the eyes.

These thoughts and more ran like a litany through Annie's thoughts as she attempted to ignore Rand Jenkins and go about her normal business. Her efforts went for naught; the man simply refused to be ignored. When she tried to finish the gifts she'd begun for the Delaneys, he critiqued her bows. When she added vegetables to a broth she had simmering on the stove, he appropriated both a spoon and a taste and declared it short of salt. When she adjourned to her work station and set about preparing the betony for Mrs. MacAfee's nerve tonic, he pulled up a seat beside her and proceeded to question every move she made.

Annie's nerves had stretched to their breaking point. "Mr. Jenkins, you will have to allow me some room."

"Call me Rand, please. Short for Randall. Never have

liked the entire name. Possibly because my daddy's name was Randall Jenkins and he was a mean sonofagun." He reached across her worktable and picked up a small dried plant. "What's this? What's it used for?"

"Fumitory," she replied tightly. "Or in Gaelic, *lus-deathach-thalmhuinn*. Some believe that when burned, its smoke has the power to exorcize evil spirits. I am thinking of burning some for you."

"For the cats?"

"To make you go away."

"Aw, Annie." He grinned, set it down, then picked up a jar. "What's in here?"

When she tried to ignore him, he stuck the jar in front of her face. Identifying the herb inside, she rolled her tongue around her mouth and tried not to smile. "Now that might be just the thing to rid you of the cats. In fact, I do believe you should try some."

"Yeah?" He held the jar up to the lamplight and studied it. "You really think it will work? What does it do?"

"Its name is self-descriptive. Hot arsemart is always effective."

"Hot. . . ." He returned the jar to the table with a shudder and a bang. "Shame on you, sugar."

She did allow herself a soft giggle at that, but her amusement was interrupted when movement above her caught her eye. A cat she didn't recognize was crawling along the rafters of her roof. Then she spied a second kitty slinking along the base of the wall and a third crept up her work shelves. Annie's heart sank. "Ach, trouble is upon us. Midnight will tolerate other animals outdoors, but not in her private territory."

Her words proved prophetic. No sooner had she finished her sentence than the cottage erupted in a full-blown cat fight. Meows and yowls and spits and hisses—a whirlwind of fur flew through the room.

The crisis escalated when Rand decided he should break up the battle. When it was done, Midnight was the only one left standing—or in this case—sitting. Sitting atop Rand's stomach, calmly licking her paws while he lay flat on his back muttering beneath his breath, the three feline intruders successfully vanquished from the cottage.

"Guid fegs, do you know nothing about dealing with such battles?"

"I've had some experience with cat fights." He shoved Midnight off his stomach and sat up. "'Course, they always involved women and not animals."

"You're bleeding again."

He glanced down at the scratches visible through tears in his shirt and grimaced. "You might need to make a new batch of that ointment, Annie. Does it work on hives, too? I'm starting to itch again."

She sighed. "I'll need you to draw me more water before I do anything. You spilled my crock, Mr. Jenkins."

"Rand," he corrected. Standing, he scratched at his belly and added, "Shall I dunk myself in snow again or do you have something to stop this itching?"

Although Annie was tempted to tell him to visit a snowdrift, he looked so miserable she took pity on him. She plucked a jar from one of her shelves and handed it to him. "Wipe the welts with snow, then before the skin dries, use a thick layer of this."

"Great. Where's your well?"

She handed him a bucket. "I draw my water from the burn that runs behind the cottage off to the left."

Cold air swept into the room as Rand marched out. Annie viewed the mess sullying her home, shook her head, and sighed. She had a good hour of work ahead of her to clean up the damage, more the result of the Texan's "help" than anything else. Yet, as she turned herself to the task of righting furniture and mopping up the floor, she did so with a spring in her step. For all the trouble he brought, Rand Jenkins did add some excitement to her life.

He'd almost kissed her.

Annie shivered at the memory. It was a pleasurable itchy-coo that had nothing to do with the cold and everything to do with the man who heated her with a look.

A knock at the door interrupted her musing, and she bit back a smile as she crossed the room to see what the Texan needed now. "What trouble have you gotten yourself into—?"

It wasn't Rand. The scent of whisky hit her like a fist as a young man from the village strode into her home without a by-your-leave. The look he turned on her was glassy from drink, predatory. *Oh, no. Not again.*

"I granted no permission to enter my home, Johnny Hart. Leave now."

"Nae," he said grimly, swaying on his feet as he spoke. "Not without getting what I've come for."

He advanced on her, and Annie darted behind the questionable protection of her worktable. "The tale you heard is naught but a lie, Johnny Hart. You'll gain nothing from hurting me."

"It disnae have to hurt. I've had experience. I know what to do with a virgin."

Annie removed a knife from a drawer. "The only thing you'll be doing with this virgin is leaving her be."

"Nae, I've need of your powers, witch. I'll lie with you and for twenty-four hours have control of all you say and do. I've a mind to own my own castle and perhaps a house in Edinburgh, too. I've a fondness for that town. All I need is your virgin's blood and a lock of your long black hair to burn at the altar of St. Paul's Church."

"You'll not have it. I'll defeat you just as I did the two who came before you."

"Will Henderson and Thomas Keith are not as big and strong as I."

"True. But they were not as drunk. Or afraid. You're afraid, aren't you, John? You needed bottled courage to approach me. What's the matter? Are you a'feared I'll put a withering spell upon your manhood?" With that she narrowed her gaze and stared hard at his breeks.

Though this same strategy had worked in the past, this time the villain only laughed. "Your evil eye winna work on me, witch. I was warned and have taken steps to protect myself. I've sprigs of rowan and ivy in my pocket. My staff winna wilt before your threats, Annie Munro. Now put down the knife and let's see the deed done."

Nervousness skittered up her spine as he rounded the table. For the first time in her life, Annie cursed the fact that she wasn't truly a witch. "You're being a fool. Don't do this. You will not like the consequences."

"Actually I think I will like them very much. You are pleasing to a mon's eye, Annie Munro. I believe I shall enjoy this verra much."

"Only if you like pain," she told him as he grabbed for the knife. Reacting swiftly, she managed to hold onto her weapon and administer a cut across his palm while doing so.

He yelped with pain, and brought his hand to his mouth to suck at the wound while his eyes flared with fury. "Ye'll pay for that." He lunged for her, but Annie danced away, her mind working feverishly. She could throw the knife and hope to stab him, but that was risky business. She could scream in hopes that Rand would come running to save her, but that went against the grain. Independent by nature, she preferred to save herself.

So how to do it? He stood leering at her, swaying from exertion and the effects of drink, and Annie slowly shook her head in disgust. Three such visitors in the past ten days. *By my fegs.* If she knew who'd started this ridiculous rumor she'd dose them good with hot arsemart.

Then John Hart did something his predecessors had not. He pulled a knife of his own. Seeing it, Annie froze. He took advantage of her distraction and pounced.

She felt a tug at her scalp and heard a tearing sound. He came away with a long lock of her hair and Annie's anger blazed. Her hair was her one true vanity, and she didn't appreciate his brazen taking of it. "You should nae have done that, Johnny," she warned as she darted for her work shelves and grabbed a most effective weapon—a bottle containing the juice extracted from foalfoot roots. "I give ye one last warning before I hurt ye."

"I have the lock of hair," he said giddily. "Now for the fun part, the virgin's blood."

Annie sighed. Shaking her head, she yanked the cork and threw the contents in John Hart's face. Almost immediately he began to yell as the acidic liquid brought blisters to his skin. "Ye've blinded me!"

"Nae, I aimed not for your eyes. Now leave my home and never darken my door again."

"But it hurts! Help me."

"The best treatment is to cover the sores with snow and hold it there until it melts. Repeat the process until you reach the village. By that time, you should enjoy some relief."

Fleeing for the door, the man halted just long enough to glare at her and say, "Ye are a wicked witch, Annie Munro. I should have come to ye at night when ye were sleeping like I was advised to do. I'd have done the deed before ye awoke. But nae, this is the treatment I get for trying to be nice."

Right outside the door he paused to scoop up a handful of snow. Holding it against his face, he hurried away, bumping into Rand who was returning with a bucket of water. "Hey," the Texan called as water sloshed over the sides of the bucket. "Watch where you're going."

Annie turned away and after tucking the now straggling lock of hair back into her plait, began to carefully clean up the puddle of foalfoot juice from her floor.

"What was wrong with that fella's face?" Rand asked as he hauled the bucket inside. "It was red as a springtime sunburn."

Annie didn't respond. Now that the danger was over, reaction had set in, and it took all her concentration to keep her hand from trembling. Johnny said he should have come when she was sleeping. If he'd come when she was sleeping, he might well have succeeded with his vile plan. And someone had advised him to do it that way. Next time, someone might.

Next time.

She dropped her cleaning rag onto the floor and said, "It can't happen. I won't let it happen."

"Let what happen?" Rand asked as he emptied the water bucket into the crock. Then, after hanging the water bucket on its peg beside the door, he looked at her more closely. His brows dipped in a frown as he asked, "Annie, are you all right? You look a little . . . upset. Did that fellow do something to you?"

"No," she said vaguely. "No, I'm fine."

It was true. She was fine. Fine for now. But how long could that last?

Rand apparently took her word for it, because he turned his attention to her supply shelf and read aloud a selection of labels before asking, "Are you ready to get down to business? I'd just as soon avoid another cat fight, and judging by the mess, I imagine you'd prefer that yourself. So, where's my antidote? Do you have one already made or will you need to cook it up?"

As Annie met his questioning gaze, she suddenly felt the urge to do something she'd never done before. The idea came on like a tidal wave that swept her up and took control, flinging her forward without giving her time to think it through. Words formed on her tongue, and before she could bite them back, slipped out. "I didn't drug you with the Athole Brose, Rand Jenkins. I put a spell on you."

Four

Rand gave her an incredulous look. "Excuse me?"

"You're bewitched."

"No, I'm bewildered. Why are you throwing out this ridiculous story?"

She marched over to a chest beside her bed, opened a drawer, and removed an old and worn-looking book. Carrying it over to the table, she made a performance of setting it down reverently, then gestured for him to approach. "I should not show you this, but under the circumstances, I think it's the fastest way to convince you. Read the title, Mr. Jenkins."

"Rand," he automatically responded as he scowled down at the gold lettering that adorned the binding.

"Spells and Incantations," Annie read aloud, emphasizing her point. "Feel free to glance through it, but I do ask you to take care. This book has been passed down through my family for generations, and most of these pages are hundreds of years old and quite delicate. Also, I should warn you against attempting a spell yourself. Unless, you perchance have witches in your family tree, too?"

Ahchoo. Rand grabbed his handkerchief and wondered what the woman was up to. Why the sudden about-face? She'd been adamant before in her denial of the charge of witchcraft. Why change?

Something had to have happened with that last customer of hers. He'd bet his favorite hat on it. "Do I need to go after that fella who just left here and beat the tar out of him?"

"What? What does that have to do with witches in your family tree?"

"I don't have witches in my family tree." He had a few bitches, but that wasn't the type of thing a man said to a lady, not even a lady whose enchanting eyes flickered with deceit and whose hands nervously twisted the fabric of her skirt.

Her smile was forced as she said, "I do. You can ask anyone. You can ask your friend Jake Delaney. His wife knows all about me."

"She knows you lie through your teeth?"

Now those green eyes flashed with temper. "Look at the book and call me a liar."

Rand sneezed once more, then opened the book and slowly flipped through the pages. "A spell to cause sickness. An incantation to bring rain. A recipe for a love potion. Oh," he thumped a finger on the page. "This is the one Sarah wanted—a spell to turn a man into a toad."

"It is one of our most popular spells."

Rand's lips twisted in a grin at that. "Why didn't you mention it when she asked?"

Annie sniffed. "I prefer not to interfere in marriages."

"Smart way of thinking, that," Rand mused as he slowly turned the brittle pages. "I have to say, Annie, this book offers a strong argument toward your witchiness. It really is old, isn't it?"

"Aye."

"Where's the cat spell?"

"I don't keep all my secrets in one book," she said with a shrug, then jumped when he suddenly slammed the book shut, folded his arms, and glared down at her.

"All right, Weird Sister, what's your story? What trick are you trying to pull with this nonsense?"

"Weird Sister?"

"Shakespeare. The witches from Macbeth. Didn't the Thane of Cawdor live around here somewhere? Maybe your great-whatever-grandmother knew him."

Annie folded her arms. "Very funny, Mr. Jenkins. However, rest assured this is no nonsense or trick. I did put a spell on you, and I am willing to remove it—under certain conditions."

"Certain conditions," Rand repeated, arching a sardonic brow. Reaching into his pocket, he removed his wallet and thumbed through the bills. "I wouldn't have pegged you for an extortionist, Miss Munro. Guess I'm not the judge of people I thought I was. Is this your usual way of working? If so, I'm surprised you have any customers at all. So, how much do I have to pay for the cat antidote?"

"I don't want your money."

"I won't do anything illegal or immoral, I'll tell you that right now." He paused for a moment and his gaze made a lazy trip from her head to her toes, then back up again. "Well, we might find some room to negotiate on the morality issue."

Annie rolled her eyes. "I'm not asking you to do anything illegal."

"Good."

"Or immoral."

"Can't win 'em all."

"I want you to take me with you when you leave."

"Pardon me?"

"I want you to take me to Texas, the sooner, the better. If you will agree to that, I will rescind my spell."

Rand's mouth quirked up in a half-smile. "All right," he agreed. "I accept. Now, get rid of it."

Obviously his quick acceptance caught her off guard because she eyed him suspiciously. "Well, I can't do it right now."

"Why not? I'm ready." He squared his shoulders, puffed out his chest, and extended his arms at his sides, palms out. A look of pure frustration flashed across her face, and he'd have laughed had he not wanted the damned antidote so badly.

Annie shook her head. "If I remove the spell now, what guarantee do I have that you'll uphold your end of the bargain? You might leave and I'll never see you again."

"But you're a witch. Couldn't you track me down and turn me into a toad or something if I didn't hold up my end of the deal?"

"It doesn't work that way."

Of course it wouldn't. Because the woman wasn't a witch and she had no special powers beyond an apparently extensive knowledge of the way various plants act upon the human body.

Rand allowed his arms to drop back to his side. "Well, looks like we have a problem, then, because the cats are bound to swarm again and I'll be hanged if I'll take another snowbank bath. A man could catch pneumonia and die from doing that."

"I suggest we compromise. I could cook up a potion that would prevent the welts from rising on your skin, but—"

"What about the sneezing and watery eyes? It's damned embarrassing for a man to walk around all the time looking like a crybaby."

"The tonic will relieve the sneezing and watery eyes, too."

"And it'll get rid of the cats?"

"If you'd allow me to finish without further interruption, I will tell you." She waited, giving him a pointed look, until he nodded. Then she continued, "The potion I will give you will relieve your symptoms. However, it will not affect the cats. I will not remove the cat attraction spell itself until we board a ship bound for America."

Sneaky girl. Must be two separate types of antidotes. "So you're telling me I'm gonna have cats climbing on me until I leave Scotland?"

"Aye."

"That's not acceptable."

"It's my best offer."

Rand had to admire the woman's spunk, but he wouldn't, couldn't let her get away with it. Even if the cats didn't make him itch, he still didn't want them around. He didn't like cats. He liked dogs. Big dogs. Useful dogs like a bird dog or a bloodhound. A dog listened to a man, minded him. Talked back with a deep, resonant bark, not a wimpy meow. Dogs didn't pounce unexpectedly from the top of doors or furniture. They didn't draw figure eights about a man's ankles and trip him when he stood. They damn sure didn't sink their claws into a man's nose and nearly rip it off.

Rand's years as a lawyer had taught him well in the art of negotiation, and he recognized that sometimes arguments were won in stages. Considering that the woman was attempting extortion, he didn't mind lying to her one little bit. With that in mind, he nodded. "Very well, I accept your terms. Now give me the medicine."

"Oh, I cannot give it to you now. This is an infusion that works best when it is first made. I'll need time to prepare it." She glanced at the mantel clock. "Return this time tomorrow and I should have it ready by then."

Rand's stomach sank. "You don't have it ready? But I want it now. I can't stand another day of this."

"Certainly you can. Why, you're better now than you were when you arrived. Your eyes are not nearly as red and you've only sneezed twice in the past five minutes."

"That's because that cat of yours is busy protecting her territory by keeping the others chased away. Who knows how long that will last. Shoot, chances are the minute I sit down she'll leap into my lap and it will start all over again."

He scowled with disgust and raked his hand through his hair. "You know, I hate it when this happens. The ink is hardly dry on our agreement and it's already time to renegotiate."

"But—"

"No 'buts' about it, Annie. If I have to wait twenty-four hours for my antidote, then I demand you provide me a potion to keep the cats away until then. It's only right."

It might also solve his problem entirely. Were her skills with herbal remedies such that she could create a temporary fix, or would she cure him with the intention of poisoning him again the next day, which he would make certain didn't happen? Either way, Rand would be ahead.

Quickly, he smothered the smug smile that threatened.

Annie Munro proved she possessed the ability to match him scowl for scowl. "I am sorry, sir. What you ask for is impossible. However, in an effort to lessen your symptoms until treatment is ready, allow me to suggest that you avoid closed rooms and even sleep with a window cracked if you are able to tolerate the cold. From what you've described to me, your symptoms are worse when you come into physical contact with cats, so anything you can do to prevent their actually touching you will help prevent the worsening of the manifestations of your condition."

He scratched his head. "That's funny. Annie, you sound more like a healer than a witch."

Damn, the woman was pretty when a blush stained her cheeks.

Stiffly, she crossed the room and retrieved his coat from the hook beside the door. Holding it out to him, she said, "You'd best leave now. Our days are short this time of year in the Highlands. You'll not delay if you are to reach Rowanclere before dark."

Rand eyed the coat in her hand, but didn't move his feet. After a moment, Annie helpfully opened the door. Cold air rushed in; half a dozen cats made a move to follow. Annie's black devil-cat, Midnight, pounced from out of nowhere to plant herself solidly in the doorway. Her hisses and spits sounded enough like a South Texas rattlesnake to make Rand look twice. "Do witches' familiars change shape?"

"Midnight, move." Annie tried with only minimal success to scoot the cat out of the way. "You're blocking Mr. Jenkins's way and he needs to depart."

Rand eyed the cats outside, the peat fire within, and shook his head. "Nah, he doesn't. Shut the door Annie. While I agree with your suggestion about fresh air helping with my sneezing and itching, I think leaving the house wide open is overdoing it."

"But—"

He took his coat from her fingers and returned it to

the hook. Reaching around her, he pushed the door closed, then turned with a smile. "So, sugar. What's for supper?"

She shot him a look that could only be described as the Evil Eye.

"On second thought, don't worry about feeding me. I'm pretty sure my appetite just died."

One good thing about being a "witch," Annie didn't have a reputation to lose. Having a man spend the night in her cottage would cause no uproar, no scandal, no outrage. It was something Annie had long bemoaned and one of the things she hoped a relocation to America would solve. She yearned to be Respectable.

But in the meantime, she'd accept Rand Jenkins's presence in her home without protest. After the incident with Johnny Hart, she was glad to have the company.

She put the Texan to work assisting in the preparation of the sneeze-relief tonic. While she prepared an emulsion of swine thistle seeds, she instructed him how to crush twigs of poisonberry to extract the juice that would be added to her emulsion. Though he balked a bit upon hearing the name of the plant with which he worked, Rand did as he was asked. While they worked, they conversed, something Annie had not enjoyed since her mother's death. She'd forgotten how pleasurable shared tasks could be.

"Tell me more about your home, Rand," she encouraged. "Since I'm to be living there, I have much to learn. You said you were in business with Jake Delaney. So do you live in the town of San Antonio where he is from?"

"Used to. Not anymore. I've recently settled in Fort

Worth, which is how I ended up being the one to bring Sarah to Scotland. Fort Worth is her home. Or, *has been* her home, I reckon I should say. Who knows what this reunion with Lord Weston will bring. I like Fort Worth, though. It's a nice little town that has just enough of the frontier left in it to make it interesting."

"What about San Antonio? Did you dislike something about the place? Is that why you left?"

"No." He shook his head. "I got run out of town."

A swine thistle seed spurted from Annie's grasp. "Run out of town?"

He shrugged and offered a crooked, self-deprecating grin. "I'd been calling on a young woman, the mayor's daughter, in fact. Her family thought it was time to put a ring on her finger. I resisted. Past experience has made me wary of ever putting myself through that particular trial again."

Again? He was married? "Are you a widower?"

"Oh no. Not that lucky. The she-devil is still alive and kicking and living off the fruits of my labor up in Austin, I'm afraid. I'm divorced."

"Divorced?" Annie repeated, her eyes going wide. "That's almost as bad as being a witch!"

He chuckled and tossed a crushed poisonberry twig onto the small pile his work had slowly built. "Help me out here, Annie. Coming from you, was that an insult or a compliment?"

"Neither one. It was a comparison."

His brow furrowed and he thought about it for a moment. "I'm sorry. I can't figure out how divorce and witchcraft are linked. I might refer to my ex-wife as a witch upon occasion, but it's just a figure of speech."

Annie set down the wooden spoon she used to stir her mixture and looked at him in shock. "They say divorce is an abomination. It's considered a scandal, a disgrace, an outrage. A divorce is improper."

"So is living with a woman who dishonors her vows by cuckolding her husband."

"Oh."

"Yeah, oh." He held up the small glass jar containing the poisonberry sap and asked. "Is this enough?"

"We need twice that amount."

He nodded, then returned to work. Annie fumbled for something to say. Curiosity urged her to ask about his wife, but she didn't wish to be rude. Luckily, Rand solved her dilemma for her. "It was a hard lesson to learn. I loved my wife. Or at least, I loved the woman she pretended to be. Finding out she was nothing more than a liar, well ..." he shrugged. "Let's just say I won't be so gullible again. That's why I wouldn't take it all the way to the altar with the mayor's daughter. I wanted to trust her, but ... well ... I have cold feet."

Annie glanced down. "I'm surprised since Midnight is stretched across your boots."

He followed the path of her gaze, scowled, and gave his foot a shake. "Stupid cat." *Ahchoo.* "You misunderstand, Annie. I meant cold feet in the figurative sense, not the literal. I meant that I want no part of women who lie. I figure it'll take a near miracle for me to trust one enough to marry after my last experience."

"I see." For the next few minutes, Annie busied herself with gathering from her stores the rest of the materials to be added to the cooking pot where the thistle seeds simmered. While she worked she pondered the information her guest had revealed. It was a good thing she only needed escort service from Rand Jenkins and wasn't looking to marry him. She'd told more lies in the past hour than she had in the past year. Five years. Maybe even her life.

Rand lifted a blue and white checkered cloth from a basket of clean towels, leaned a hip against the counter and wiped his hands. "Your turn. I've told you my deep dark secrets, what about you?"

"I already told you I'm a witch."

"I'm not talking about that. I want you to tell me why you want to leave your home so badly that you'd spin a . . . that is . . . that you'd put a spell on a poor stranger to try and make it happen."

Annie took a long time to answer. Though she couldn't say exactly why, she realized she wanted Rand to understand. Perhaps it was because he'd opened himself to her and given her a glimpse of the man behind the handsome face and muscular body. Or maybe it was the intimacy created by deepening shadows on a snowy afternoon. Most likely it was her own guilt for lying to the man. For whatever reason, she waited until she'd added the final ingredients to the cooking pot, checked the heat on her stove, then poured herself and her guest a drink from a bottle of whisky given her in payment by the local butcher for a medicine to treat his rheumatism.

Rand eyed the drink, then Annie. She rolled her eyes and reached for his glass, took a sip, then offered her drink to him. He shook his head and reclaimed his own. *Suspicious man.*

"Why do I want to leave Scotland? I don't. I know I will miss my homeland. It makes my heart weep to know I'll not be here to see the heather bloom on the moors in August. But then I think of all the sights and experiences that await my discovery and my heart sings with excitement."

"So you are adventurous."

"Aye, I think I might be. I've not exactly had the opportunity to test the theory."

The way his gaze made a lazy trip from her head to her toes, then back again made her wonder what direction his thoughts had taken. She suspected they weren't entirely innocent. Annie was shocked and surprised at herself to realize she didn't entirely mind. "Anyway," she hurriedly continued, "I know what awaits me here if I stay, so in essence, I have no choice."

"No choice? I find that hard to believe. What fate are you afraid of?"

She found she didn't want to tell him about the current village rumor. It was too close, too frightening to her right now. Instead, she attempted to explain by relaying details of the event that first planted the notion of leaving Scotland in her mind. "I haven't always lived in this small cottage, Rand. Up until three years ago, a fine, eight-room house stood not a hundred yards from this place. It was the home where I was born and lived with my mother, her sister, and their mother."

"And your father?"

Annie smiled humorlessly. "Munro witches canna seem to keep husbands. He left before I was born."

Rand winced, then asked, "What happened three years ago?"

"A rumor. A wicked, evil tale started by a woman who suspected her husband of adultery with my aunt. It was a lie. My aunt provided him nothing more than medicine for his rheumatism. But the wife wouldn't listen. She claimed my aunt had hexed her husband, and she worked the village women into a froth warning them their men were next. After a week of such talk, a mob descended upon us and put our home to the torch." She paused a moment in the telling until he met her gaze. "My grandmother and aunt died in the blaze."

Rand's mouth flattened into a grim line and he had a mineral glint in his eyes as he shook his head. "People can sure be stupid sometimes, can't they? I don't understand."

"I do, to a point. Superstition is firmly entrenched in the Scotsman's mind and I won't naysay it. I have my own set of superstitions you won't see me ignoring. What I canna forgive is the failure of the villagers to listen when my aunt proclaimed her innocence loud and long. Aunt Janet was a witch because her mother was a witch, and her mother before her, back through the ages, so the villagers felt no responsibility to consider she might be telling the truth."

"So they killed her."

"Aye. They killed her because of who she was, not what she did."

"Explain something to me. If the villagers are so concerned about your . . . witchery, for lack of a better term . . . why do they come to you for cures?"

"Because my remedies work. For the most part, the people of the village and I coexist peacefully. We're not friends, but we're not enemies. But every now and again something happens to make it uncomfortable for me around here." A vision of Johnny Hart's predatory leer arose in her mind. "That's why I want to leave."

"Has something happened lately?"

She shrugged, not wishing to go into it. Even though she knew it shouldn't, the rumor embarrassed her, shamed her. It made her feel dirty.

"Annie, you have a peculiar look on your face. What is it? Did someone—ouch!" Rand's face grimaced with pain and he reached behind him. Midnight clung to his back, her claws obviously sunk deep into his skin. "Get off, you stupid cat."

"Don't call her stupid. Midnight is very smart." She had just saved Annie from his prying, had she not?

"She's stupid because I'm gonna wring her neck first chance I get."

"Dinna you threaten my pet."

"It's no threat, it's a promise," he snapped, grabbing behind him. "Yeow! She bit me. The danged cat bit me."

"Good for her."

"Get her off me."

"Turn around."

"I hate cats. I truly do."

Annie stroked her hand down Midnight's soft fur and spoke in a soothing, gentle tone. "Let the mean man loose, sweetheart. I will protect you. I winna let him hurt you. Good kitty. Friendly kitty."

Midnight released her right front paw, then extended her claws and gave Rand's back another swipe before letting go of him entirely and curling herself into Annie's arms.

"Friendly kitty my a—" He clamped his mouth shut and glared at both female and feline. "That cat is a menace. All cats are menaces. I don't know why anyone would want to keep a cat for a pet when everyone knows dogs are infinitely superior to cats."

"Excuse me? Dogs are *not* superior to cats."

"Yes they are."

She lifted her chin. "In what way?"

He snorted. "Honey, I could give you a hundred different ways."

"I haven't heard one yet."

"All right. For one thing, dogs won't claw a man half to death."

"Hah. Dogs use their teeth and do great damage. I'm surprised that a man as big and braw as you is such a whiner, Rand."

"Second, dogs are loyal whereas cats don't care if you live or die."

"That's not true. Midnight loves me. She's simply subtle about it, more independent. Cats are aristocratic in everything they do; they're not clowns like dogs."

"What's wrong with being a clown? They make you laugh. When was the last time a cat made you laugh?"

She gave his scratches and wounds a significant look and made a show of biting back a smile. His scowl thundered at her.

"You have a cruel streak in you, don't you, honey?"

Then, she did chuckle. Midnight squirmed in her arms, so she tossed her to the floor. The cat immediately jumped and climbed a nearby shelf where she sat and observed the proceedings. Rand glared at the kitty. She licked the back of her paw.

He no sooner took his wary attention away from the animal, than she attacked yet again, this time latching onto his chest. "That's enough!" Rand shouted, grabbing her and shoving her toward Annie. "Put it on a leash or something or I swear, next time she digs her claws or her teeth in me I'm gonna bite back."

"I don't know what's gotten into her," Annie said, clucking her tongue at her pet. "She's truly the most friendly cat. She's lived with me for over a year—since shortly after my mother died—and she's never scratched a single soul."

"She's been saving it all up for me," he grumbled, rubbing his hand back and forth across his chest. "Although, to be honest, it's not the animal's fault, but yours."

"Mine?"

"The drug you gave me. Or, the . . ." he sneered the word, "spell."

Now Annie wanted to scratch him. Instead, she set Midnight on the floor and shook a finger at her, speaking sternly, "Go to your basket."

To her shock and surprise, the cat did as she was told. Head and tail both held high, the cat glided regally toward her basket, pausing long enough to hiss at Rand as she walked past him. "I think you've made her mad."

"Good. Maybe she'll stay away from me." *Ah-ahchoo.*

Rand flexed the muscles in his back and worked his shoulders around as he rubbed harder at his chest. "I need some more of that salve of yours. This time it's really starting to bother me. Would you mind?"

"Such a bairn," she scolded as she retrieved the jar of ointment. "Take off your shir . . . oh my."

Annie's eyes widened at the sight that met her eyes. Puncture wounds from each of Midnight's paws were clearly visible on his back; a swipe of scratches pearled red blood across his front. But that's not what took her breath away. While the sight of his broad naked shoulders would have stolen her breath at any time, it was the vivid red welts rising right before her eyes that made her speechless.

These were no ordinary hives. This condition looked . . . painful.

Midnight did this? She must have something on her claws. She must have stepped into something on my worktable.

"You need more than ointment this time, I'm afraid. You'll need to soak in a bath mixed with oats and some soothing herbs. Is your skin burning, Rand?"

He nodded. "Itching, too. All in all, I think I'd prefer a gunshot. But you say bathing in this stuff will help?"

"I believe so."

"Then give me your buckets and I'll go for water."

Annie shook her head. "No, I thought to melt snow over the fire. I prefer to drink water from the running burn, but for bathing, snowmelt is fine. I'll step just outside to get it if you'll pull the tub in front of the fire. It's heavy."

He nodded and they both went to work. With each minute that passed, Rand's expression grew a bit more pained. Annie tried to distract him by resuming their cats versus dog argument. "Cats are better than dogs because cats don't snore and dogs do."

His mouth twisted in a half smile. "Dogs are better than cats because they guard your home. They'll let you know when a stranger is approaching."

"Cats are better because they don't like to roll in the mud, then track it into your home."

"Dogs don't throw up hair balls."

He had a point with that one. Annie cast about for more ammunition while she refilled two pots with snow. Reentering the cottage, she sniffed disdainfully, then said, "My cat uses a straw box for her personal business as opposed to a dog who must go out in the snow and sniff around for half an hour before he finds the perfect spot to do a wizzy."

He chuckled at that, as she had hoped he would. "Dogs are always happy to see you."

"Cats are smart enough to know that you only went away for a few minutes."

"You can train a dog."

"Eventually. Cats learn the first time."

"Only what they want to learn. They're just as likely to look at you as if you're crazy and walk away."

Guid fegs. She couldn't argue with that one, either. Instead, she glanced into the bathtub and said, "Almost enough. Let me add the herbs and oatmeal, and you can get in."

"Good." His hands went to his belt buckle, and it appeared to Annie as if he intended to undress right before her eyes.

"Wait!" she exclaimed. "Ye canna strip right in front of me."

"Just add your herbs, Annie. I'm dying here."

With that, he dropped his drawers.

Five

Guid fegs!" Annie exclaimed as she quickly turned away. "What are you doing?"

"What do you think I'm doing?" Rand wouldn't have cared if the Queen of England was having tea with the President of the United States. He'd still have stripped and climbed into that bath. He felt like he was on fire. "You don't have to look, Annie, but you do need to doctor up my bath water as quick as you can."

Naked, he stepped into the metal tub and immediately realized soaking his back was gonna be tricky. "Well, hell."

"What's wrong?" asked Annie as she slowly backed her way toward him, holding a basket overflowing with supplies in her left hand.

"Nothing's wrong. I was just wishing for a larger tub." Grabbing his shirt, he wrapped it around his hips and said, "I'm covered, Annie. The good parts, anyway. Turn around and watch where you're going so you can do this faster."

Her shoulders rose as she took a breath, then pivoted. "Oh," the air went out of her in a rush as her gaze swept him head to toe, her eyes wide and filled with admiration.

Under other circumstances Rand might have preened a bit, but right now all he wanted was to drown his burning skin. "Please, Annie."

Averting her eyes, she approached the tub and reached inside her basket. "I'm adding ground oats, powdered bistort, ripple-girs, and gowk's meat. We'll have you soak for twenty minutes, maybe even half an hour, and then once you're dry, I'll apply the ointment you used before."

Rand watched her sprinkle her cures into the warm water, frowning a bit when he saw that the water was turning green. He hoped the stuff wouldn't stain his skin. "I won't come out of here looking like a shamrock, will I?"

"Of course not," she replied. "You're not Irish. Only the Irish turn green from my herbal baths. Being a Texan, you'll turn yellow."

"Yellow?" Offense bristled his tone. "Texans never turn yellow!" With that, he ripped off the shirt with a flourish, then calmly, slowly sat down. Annie Munro's face turned as red as his skin felt. It made him feel marginally better.

Water reached to just below his waist. Cupping his hands, he splashed water on his chest. The relief the water offered his blazing breast was almost immediate. He'd have groaned with satisfaction if his back weren't killing him. Well, hell, he thought as he glanced down to see the redness across his chest slowly fade. To soak his back, he'd have to slide his butt toward the end of the tub and let his legs hang over the side.

Despite the fire that was his back, he hesitated. That particular position left parts of a man hanging out, so to speak, and Rand never liked being at a disadvantage. "Annie, you'll keep the cat away from me, won't you?"

"Midnight won't bother you," she told him, her stare firmly fastened on the fireplace mantel. "I'll see to the water. Those last two pots of snow should be nice and warm by now."

As Annie crossed the room to the stove, Rand flopped his legs out of the tub and attempted to sink his back. His effort went for naught because his shoulders were too broad. He tried twisting his torso, but that only succeeded in dunking part of him. "I feel like a circus contortionist," he grumbled.

Then, when the demon-animal climbed the side of the tub and peered at Rand's privates, he'd had enough. Sloshing to a seated position once again, he glared at the cat and said, "This won't work, Annie. I don't fit. Grab a dipper along with the water. You'll have to ladle the water down my back."

"Oh, no. I couldn't."

"Why not?"

"Well, I'd have to look at you."

"Just at my back. Not at the good stuff. Not unless you want to look, that is, and if that's the case, I want you to feel free. Literally."

She sputtered, muttered, then approached the tub with a tin cup in hand. Kneeling behind him, she dipped the cup, then poured the water atop his head.

"Witch."

"Rand Jenkins, you are a muckle bold man."

"I'm a boiling bold man. Doctor my back, hynygukkis, would you please?"

She paused mid-scoop. "What did you call me?"

"Hynygukkis. It's a Scots term of endearment, right? I picked it up in Inverness."

"Makes a woman wonder what else you picked up in Inverness," she grumbled as she poured warm, soothing water down his back.

Rand's chuckle transformed into a low groan of relief as the additives in the bath water began to work their magic. Over and over and over again, Annie sent a stream of healing water running down his skin. Over and over and over again, Rand murmured and moaned and groaned his relief.

A quarter hour ticked off the mantel clock before his skin felt normal again, yet Annie continued to pour, sending one cupful of water down his front for every three down his back. He didn't even think to stop her; he was enjoying her attentions way too much for that.

It was quickly becoming one of the most sensuous moments of his life. The wash of water flowing down his skin. The rose petal scent of her filling his nostrils. The rustle of her skirt as she shifted positions and the faint kiss of her breath against the back of his neck. Then, as she leaned over to dip the cup into the water, her breast brushed his back and Rand shuddered.

"The water is cold?" she asked.

Actually, he thought it might turn straight to steam at any minute. He cleared his throat. "It's not exactly cold, but I wouldn't mind you adding another pot or two of hot water."

"Hmm . . ." Tin clinked against the stone floor and her skirt swished as she stood. "The redness and swelling is gone. I think it's time you got out and dried off so I can apply the ointment."

Her hands on his back. Decent trade. "All right."

As he went to stand, she let out a little yelp and turned her back. Rand grinned. "You got a towel?"

She marched over to a chest, removed a towel and without looking, tossed it in his general direction. It landed with one corner perilously close to the fire. "Watch it," he said, stepping from the water and making a grab for the towel as it started to smoke.

At the alarm in his voice, Annie turned around. She looked at the towel. Looked at him. *Looked* at him.

Rand reacted like any other red-blooded Texan man would under similar circumstances. He saluted. Quite impressively, if he had to say so himself.

Damned if the woman didn't go and faint at the sight.

Annie drifted awake slowly, warm and comfortable and safe. Without opening her eyes, she took silent stock of her situation. Rand held her on his lap in the rocking chair pulled close to the fire. His naked chest pillowed her cheek, the dusting of hair tickling her nose. He smelled like a dewy spring morning, and the soft rasp of his breathing was a lullaby to her ears. She thought she could stay like this forever.

Recent events came back to her in a flash. Her eyes flew open and she struggled to sit up.

"Calm down, sugar. Rest a bit more. Everything's fine. You bumped your head on the corner of a table when you went down, but I think you'll be all right. It's not much of a goose egg."

Annie wasn't worried about her head. It was her heart that was giving her trouble. At least, she thought it was her heart. What else would be the source of the warm, tingly, makes-you-want-to-moan rush of sensation flowing through her? Was this desire?

Of course it was. Just because she had little experience with passionate yearnings up until now did not mean she could not recognize the feelings when she finally felt them. She desired Rand Jenkins. And, judging by the way he'd grown to such an impressive size right before her eyes, Rand Jenkins desired her, too. So what did she want to do about it?

You could get rid of your "virgin's blood" and put that part of the rumor to rest.

The pace of Annie's heartbeat escalated. It was a thought. Better a man she wanted than one who snuck up on her during the night. Plus, as a woman without a reputation to begin with, she wouldn't be throwing anything away.

Yet, as intriguing as the idea was, she knew she would not do it. He had agreed to take her away with him, to take her to Texas where she *could* be respectable. She wanted to live as a normal respectable woman in a community more than anything. It would be foolish of her to give up her virginity now—no matter how naughtily attractive she found the notion.

His thumb stroked slowly up and down her arm, brought shivers to her skin, and made her want to squirm. Annie tried to summon the energy to leave the shelter of his arms. She failed. Instead, she snuggled back against him and sighed.

"You feeling better now?" he asked, his voice a deep, sensuous rumble.

She nodded. Despite the bump on her head, she felt better than she had for a long, long time.

"I didn't mean to scare you, sugar. You're a beautiful woman and the look you were giving me was . . . well . . . a man can't stop his body's natural reaction. However, I want you to know you never have to be afraid of me."

"I wasn't afraid."

"Annie, you fainted dead away."

She wrinkled her nose. "I didn't faint. That was a lady-like swoon. I was practicing. I've never swooned before, you see. As a rule, witches don't swoon."

Annie could hear the grin in his voice as Rand said, "Right. So why do you need the practice?"

She looked up at him. "Because I'm giving up witch-craft once I move to Texas. I intend to be a respectable lady."

"Oh really?" One eyebrow arched. "Can you do that?"

Now she stiffened and spoke with a snap in her voice. "I'm already respectable. People refuse to believe it."

"I meant, can you resign from being a witch?"

Annie had no idea, but since she wasn't one, the question wasn't a problem. She relaxed back against him. "In my circumstance, yes."

"Oh."

Long, peaceful minutes ticked by as they sat without speaking. Annie knew she had no excuse for continuing this intimacy, but it had been so long since anyone had held her, and never had she known the pleasure of a man's arms like this. It was exciting. It was risqué. It was . . . lovely.

Guid fegs. For a woman so intent on gaining respectability, she was acting extremely disreputable. Annie sighed, knowing the time had come to end this interlude.

"What's wrong?"

"Respectable ladies dinna sit on their guests' naked laps," she replied ruefully as she attempted to rise. "This is not at all proper."

He held her in place. "Now Annie, that depends on how you look at it. I've been injured and you are acting as my doctor. Doctors often see their patients in the natural state; we can excuse it that way."

She met his gaze and dryly said, "Doctors dinna sit on their patients' laps, either."

"Maybe they should. It's certainly restorative medicine for me. Besides, I'm not naked. I grabbed a blanket off your bed and wrapped it around me before I sat down with you. I'd have put my pants on, but it seems that the devil-cat decided to use them for her bed."

"She did?"

"Yep. Climbed right into my britches. I'm just tickled I wasn't wearing them at the time."

She smiled then, and his gaze dropped to her mouth and remained there as he said, "Annie, you believe me when I tell you that you needn't be afraid of me, right?"

Her lips felt swollen and she licked them. "I do."

"Do I need to be afraid of you?"

"What do you mean?"

He leaned closer. "I seem to remember a fairy tale involving witches and kisses and men being turned into toads. I don't need to worry about Sarah getting her wish to see me using a lily pad for a home, do I?"

"Are you telling me . . . ?"

Blue eyes gleamed with determination and something more. Something exciting. Something dangerous. "I'm gonna kiss you, Annie Munro. And if you turn me into a toad, I promise I'll give you warts."

With that romantic pronouncement, Rand Jenkins touched his mouth to hers. And the world as Annie knew it was forever changed.

He was the one who cast a spell when he drew her lower lip into his mouth and gently sucked it. He was the one who worked magic with the slow, sweet thrust of his tongue. He was the one who wove a spell of enchantment with nips and tickles and hotly murmured sounds of need.

"Rand," she breathed against him.

At that, his mouth turned hungry. His kissed her hard and hotly, thirstily. Greedily. His tongue plunged into her, reaching deep. Ravaging. She gasped, shuddered, and clung to him. With his kiss, Rand transformed her, swept her away to a fairyland of sensation where everything was liquid, hot and pulsing and pounding.

Annie followed without protest. She mimicked the

movements of lips and tongue and teeth. She answered him eagerly, needily, and when he groaned against her mouth the sound sent a delicious, shuddering shiver up her spine. The kiss went on and on and on and ribbons of heat unfurled within her. She pressed herself against him. She needed . . . something. Instinctively, she wiggled her bottom, wanting to get closer.

With a muffled curse, he finally broke the kiss.

"My oh my, woman," he said, breathing hard. "You witches pack a powerful punch. To think of all the years I've wasted romancing mortal women."

Annie blinked as she came crashing back to earth. She scrambled off his lap, her heart still racing, her blood continuing to pound. She stared at him, not speaking. Her right hand lifted and covered her lips.

"Annie?"

"I . . . I . . ."

Slowly, Rand rose from the rocking chair, grabbing part of the tartan and throwing it over his shoulder. Annie's gaze slid down his body, then back up, her eyes rounding even wider than before. He'd somehow managed to wrap, fold, and belt the blue, green, and black tartan blanket into a bulky version of the *feileadh-mór*, the long, belted plaid that was the forerunner of the kilt.

He was, she thought, a modern woman's fantasy brought to life. He was *her* fantasy brought to life.

She swallowed hard. "Ye look like a Highland laird of auld, Rand Jenkins."

He glanced down. "Do you think? I tried the Roman toga look first, but the wool doesn't hold a knot worth beans. Ended up using my belt to keep it on. Didn't want to risk it coming off and giving you another . . . uh . . .

swoon." He gave the cloth a tug and said, "I can't say I envy the old Highlanders. This wool is scratchy, not nearly as comfortable as wearing leather like in a breechclout. I had a lady friend once who was half Comanche, and she showed me how handy that article of clothing can be upon occasion."

Annie's mouth set grimly. She had a very good idea of just what sort of "occasion" he meant, but even as a spurt of jealousy washed through her, she couldn't help but picture how he would look standing before her dressed in nothing but a breechclout. The image was almost as intriguing as Rand-the-Highland-laird.

Except the Highlander stood before her now. In the flesh. And Annie wanted him. She wanted to lie with him on the rug before the fire. She wanted to explore these feelings of heat and hunger. But just as important as the physical desires were the emotional needs she yearned to fulfill.

Silent seconds ticked by. Annie closed her eyes. With his kiss, everything had changed. She realized she wanted to know Rand Jenkins, not only in the biblical sense, but in every other sense, too, inside and out. She yearned to become part of him, part of his life, and she longed for him to become part of hers, too. Because sometime between the time he stepped inside her cottage yesterday and this moment here and now, she had begun to love him.

Love. Oh, guid fegs, Annie Munro. Ye've gone and done it now.

How could it have happened so fast? She never did things fast. But hadn't her mother always said Munro women recognized their soul mates almost immediately?

Hadn't she fallen in love with Annie's father on the first day they met?

At least I waited for the second.

Love. If it was true, the repercussions were huge. Because loving Rand Jenkins meant that traveling with him to Texas would not be enough. Loving him meant marriage, which presented a clatty problem.

The man had cold feet.

Six

"Nothing like a good bowl of soup on a snowy day," Rand said as he brought a spoonful up to his mouth, then blew a gentle stream of air over the steaming mixture.

"Is it still snowing outside?"

"Last time I checked it was."

"That's nice," she absently replied, drawing circles in her own bowl of soup with her spoon.

Rand frowned as he surreptitiously watched his hostess. Something was wrong with Annie. She'd acted peculiar all morning. In fact, she'd acted peculiar ever since yesterday's kiss.

Rand glared down at the orange chunks of carrot on his spoon. He never should have kissed her. Here it was a day later and his lips were still tingling and the taste of her continued to haunt his tongue. Even after half a bowl of soup, not to mention that gawd-awful witches-brew sneezing medicine she'd given him to drink a while earlier.

He'd never tasted anything so bitter. It had burned going down and bubbled in his gut once it got there. But as nasty as it tasted, he wouldn't trade it for the finest French champagne. Since choking down the first dose two hours ago, he hadn't sneezed once. Nor had his eyes watered or his skin broken out in hives, not even when the devil-cat found a way to burrow down his shirt. All in all, Annie Munro's medicine was a miracle cure. So why, he wondered, did she seem so all-fired worried?

Did he haunt her mind as much as she haunted his?

He'd dreamed of her all night long. Dark dreams, sensual dreams. The kind of dreams that kept a man hot even when sleeping on a stone floor on a bitter cold December night.

He wanted to bed her. Quite badly, in fact. But he couldn't in good conscience take advantage of her like that.

One thing that had become clear to him since waking to the sounds of her packing this morning, the woman honestly expected him to take her with him when he left. She truly believed she'd pulled the tartan over his eyes with this witch's spell nonsense.

Or else, she was pretending awfully well because her situation was desperate.

That possibility had occurred to him while lying awake between dreams in the middle of the long winter night. Annie Munro made a damn poor liar, even though she didn't seem to know it. As Rand thought back over events since meeting the woman, he'd come to suspect that something had happened with that last customer, the man with the blistered face. That's when her attitude had changed, although at the time he'd been too wrapped up in his own concerns to worry about hers. After giving the matter a good bit of thought, Rand had made a few decisions of his own.

If she truly was in some sort of trouble, he couldn't go off and leave her. Neither was he about to take her with him like she'd asked. He'd just finished escorting one woman across the Atlantic and look how much fun that was. He'd be damned if he'd do it again—literally. He hadn't had a yen for Sarah Ross; he was head-over-heels in lust with Annie Munro.

No way could he spend all day, every day, for weeks on end with the little witch and not make a run at her. But the girl was an innocent, he'd bet the entire bottle of sneeze-relief medicine on that. Experienced women didn't blush like she did, didn't go wide-eyed with wonder like she did. Didn't swoon at the sight of his John Thomas like she had.

Experienced women didn't kiss like she did.

Damn, but she'd seduced him with that kiss. Fresh and sweet, yet ripe and full of promise. Innocently seductive, that was Annie Munro. And Rand would be a first-class chump to take advantage of that innocence when he had no intention of paying the honorable price for such a gift.

Marriage. He'd been down that road before, thank you very much. He had no intention of risking that route again.

With that thought uppermost in his mind, he turned his attention toward finishing his meal. When his bowl was empty and the bread and cheese consumed, he wiped his mouth with a napkin, leaned back in his chair, and leveled a look on his hostess. "Annie, what has you running scared? What did that fella do to you yesterday?"

Her spoon slipped from her fingers and clattered to the table. "What?"

"I don't believe you are witch, Annie, and neither do you. You're a talented healer, but you're a lousy liar. Why are you so intent upon leaving your home?"

She picked up her spoon and set it carefully on the plate beneath her soup bowl. For a long minute, she stared down at the table, and when she finally looked up and met his gaze, those green eyes glittered with decision. He leaned forward, anticipating.

Flatly, she said, "If I stay here, I am bound to be taken against my will."

"Taken where?"

She rolled her eyes. "Not where. How. One of them will rape me, Rand."

The word turned his stomach sour. In one smooth motion, he shoved back his chair and stood. "Who? I'll take care of 'em."

She closed her eyes and shook her head. "Ye canna battle prejudice with your fists."

"Well, I can give it a darn good try," he snapped back. Then, seeing by the look in her face that she wasn't about to name names, he flipped his chair around, straddled it, and demanded, "Explain it to me. All of it."

She told him an ugly tale of rumor and superstition and the base nature of man. When she was done, he not only understood her lies and blackmail attempts, he sympathized with her. "Is there nothing you can do to convince them you're as mortal as they are?"

She shook her head. "I must leave here. It's the only way. And you've agreed to take me, sir. Dinna try to renegotiate that."

He wasn't about to throw her to the wolves, but he couldn't let her get by without a challenge. "Wait a minute there, woman. Allow me to point out the fact that this agreement was based on your claim of having cast a spell on me, which you've just admitted is a lie. No court in the land would hold to those terms."

"So you intend to abandon me in my time of need?"

"You're no more a mind reader than you are a witch," he said with a sigh. "Now, a couple things you should know. First, my word—when freely given—is good as gold. I promise you freely, right here and now, that I will help you solve this problem. No one is gonna hurt you, Annie, not even me. Which brings me to my second point. I don't dare take you back to Texas with me. You wouldn't be safe."

"Why not?"

"I'm just as much a mortal as you are, sugar. I'm a man with a man's needs, and the fact is, I'm mightily attracted to you. It's simply not a good idea for us to make such a lengthy trip together in close company." Damned if those witchy eyes didn't brighten with interest.

"Are you saying I tempt you?"

"I thought you picked up on that yesterday." Damned if those peaches-and-cream cheeks didn't ripen with color.

"Yes . . . well . . ." She closed her eyes and licked her lips.

Rand grabbed his glass and took a quick gulp of water. When she opened her eyes and their gazes met and held, he had a distinct impression that he'd have been better off with whisky than with water.

She looked him straight in the eye and asked, "Would temptation necessarily be a bad thing?"

He choked on the water. "Annie!" he protested once he caught his breath. "Please. I'm trying to protect you here. I'm trying to be noble."

"What if I don't want you to be noble?"

At that he did go in search of something stronger. Stalking away from the table, he grabbed her whisky bottle from a shelf, held it up and said, "Have you tampered with this?"

At her negative response, he poured a splash, tossed it back, then tipped the bottle once more. Fortified by drink, he faced her. "All right, since we're speaking frankly, by telling me this story about hair burning and virgin's blood, you have confirmed my suspicion that you're still an innocent. I won't take your virginity, Annie, no matter how much the idea of bedding you appeals to me. That crosses the line for me; I'd be honor bound to marry you. I told you about my cold feet, honey. That hasn't changed."

Her chin came up, her shoulders squared, and her eyes narrowed. "Excuse me, but I don't remember volunteering to warm your feet."

In the interests of acting like a gentleman, he decided not to call her on that one. "Let's just figure a way to solve your problem, shall we? I agree you need to leave here, but are you certain you want to leave Scotland? It's a big country."

"America is bigger. I'll always be a Munro witch in Scotland."

He scratched his head in thought. "Jake. He's the one to help. I'll take you to Rowanclere as soon as the snow lets up. In the meantime, let's talk about the cats, shall we? You need to go ahead and give me the second antidote."

Annie pushed away from the table, stood, picked up her dishes, and carried them to the washtub. As her plate sank into the sudsy water, she said, "I can't."

"Yes, you can. I'm giving you my word that I'll help you. There's no sense prolonging this nonsense. I'm just about sick to death of cats, Annie. Yes, I'm not sneezing or scratching anymore, but I still collected four of the critters between here and the stream when I went out for water. It's gotta stop."

He saw her shoulders rise, then fall, as she took a deep breath before saying, "You don't understand. The cure is not an infusion I brew at will. A special ingredient is needed to rid you of what causes the cats to be attracted to you."

Rand didn't like the sound of that. "What ingredient?"

She wiped her hands on a towel, then turned to face him. "You'll need to drink of the Cream of the Well."

Cream of the Well? Rand felt both a rumble of nerves and a rush of anticipation.

Damned if whatever she was talking about didn't sound downright nasty.

Annie was packed and for the most part ready to leave by the time the storm blew itself out shortly after noon. As sunlight broke through the clouds and sparkled off the icicles that dripped from the roof, Annie said a silent prayer of thanksgiving. She'd have made the trip to Rowanclere village tonight no matter what the weather, but she certainly preferred traveling beneath a clear sky than in the midst of a raging snowstorm.

She sat cross-legged in the middle of her bed, quietly sipping her afternoon tea and making notes about her treatments and supplies to give to Gillian Delaney. The Lady of Rowanclere would see the medicines put to good use.

A faint snore rose from the direction of the fireplace where Rand lay stretched out on the rug taking a nap. Midnight lay curled around his feet, her little eyes shut in slumber.

"That's it, sweetie," Annie softly said. "I need all the help I can get warming up those appendages."

The man was being annoyingly stubborn about the entire process. Had she known how difficult he'd be about the customs of Hogmanay, she'd have chosen a different approach to her plan. In hindsight, she should have at least considered the possibility he would discount the customs and superstitions of her country.

"Hardheaded man," she murmured.

"You're not talkin' about me, are you?"

She twisted her head to see that both Rand and Midnight had awakened. Her kitty now lay stretched across his chest, purring with pleasure as his hand stroked down her back over and over again. Annie melted at the sight, continuing her plunge into love with this infuriating, intoxicating man.

After all Midnight had done to him, to see him treat her with such casual, yet caring attention made her want to weep. At the same time, it strengthened her determination to pursue her plan—and to ignore the nudges of self-doubt and shame her conscience kept trying to generate.

"Who else would I be referring to?"

"I don't know." He set Midnight on the floor beside him and sat up. "Maybe one of your customers."

"I no longer have customers. I'm closing up shop."

The Texan glanced around the cottage. "I've been thinking about that. You shouldn't simply walk away from all this stuff. I imagine you'll want it when you find a place to settle. If we boxed it up I know Jake wouldn't mind storing it at Rowanclere until you're ready for it."

Before Annie could answer, a knock sounded on her door. Midnight leapt onto Rand's shoulder as he rolled to his feet, then sauntered across the room to answer the door.

Jake Delaney grinned at Rand, then gave the cat a pointed look. "Does this mean you won your battle or lost the war?"

"A little of both," Rand replied with a smile in his voice. "Come on in, Delaney. What brings you out on New Year's Eve?"

"It's Hogmanay over here," the former Texan said as he stepped into Annie's home and removed his hat. "Good afternoon, Annie."

"Welcome, Jake." Then, in an effort to be hospitable even though she knew what his response would be, she said, "May I offer you something to drink?"

"No thanks. I'm fine." Jake Delaney didn't see the quick roll of her eyes because he'd turned to Rand and said, "Since we expected you back by now, Gillian and Sarah got to fretting. I knew it would be easier to check on you than sit and listen to them carry on. So . . ." He looked around curiously. "Your eyes aren't red, and you don't seem to be sneezing anymore. What's keeping you here?"

"The cats. They won't leave me alone."

Jake glanced at Midnight. "I can see you're being terrorized by that one. What, is she purring you to death?"

Rand scratched the top of Midnight's head. She closed

her eyes and mewed. "Midnight won't let 'em near me in here, but the minute I step outside I'm fair game."

"What do they do?" Jake asked, his mouth sliding into a mocking grin. "Hold you at gunpoint or something?"

"Clawpoint. You wouldn't believe my scratches."

Jake's gaze slid from Rand to her, then back to Rand again. In a voice as dry as the marram grass roots hanging from the ceiling, he said, "So you're holed up here with the beautiful Miss Munro because you're scared of a bunch of cats?"

"Can you blame me?"

"Not me," Jake replied with a shrug. "Sarah might have something to say about it. She's anxious to leave for London and it seems she expects you to provide escort. I've about held her off as long as I can."

"London, hmm . . . I hadn't planned on going there, but . . ." Rand rolled his tongue around his cheek, then looked at Annie. "How about London, Annie? That would be far enough away from here, wouldn't it?"

Her stomach sank. He was determined not to take her to Texas. *Well, I'm just as determined to go with him.* "Nae. Too many people from here have either moved to London or visit there. My reputation would follow me."

Rand turned to his friend and said, "Annie's having trouble with the locals. Someone started some ugly talk, and she's in a pickle because of it. She wants to move away, and I told her we'd help her find a place to settle. You could make room for her at Rowanclere until we get it worked out, couldn't you?"

"Of course. Annie, you're more than welcome to stay with us." Jake looked as if he wanted to ask more, but he refrained. "So, do y'all want to ride back with me now?"

"I want to, but the lady has other plans. She's making me go out in the cold at midnight."

"Wants you for a firstfoot, hmm? So does Gillian." Jake gave his friend a quick once-over, nodded, then looked at Annie. "He will make a good one. Fits all the criteria. Male, tall, dark-haired, and healthy with no deformity or handicap. I can't say I've looked at his feet."

Addressing Rand, he asked, "You're not flat-footed, are you? That wouldn't do at all. You need a high instep that water will run under. Flat feet or crossed eyes or eyebrows that meet in the middle are symbols of the evil eye."

"What in blazes are you talking about?"

Jake chuckled. "It's New Year's in Scotland, my friend. The firstfoot is the first person to cross the threshold of a home in the New Year. The right firstfoot brings good luck to the house; the wrong firstfoot can bring ill luck if something isn't done to combat it."

Annie moved next to Rand and reached out to take her cat from the comfort of his arms. She nuzzled the kitty, then said, "Actually, evil fortune can be made to disappear by casting out the house cat. However, since Midnight here would never cooperate, I'm better off ensuring I have a lucky firstfoot."

Rand shrugged and shook his head in dismissal. "Oh. More of this superstitious nonsense like she has me doing tonight."

"It's not superstitious nonsense," Annie said, lifting her chin and shooting him a haughty glare. "How many times must we argue about this. I may not be a witch, Rand, but I believe witches exist. I believe in witches and ghaists and fairies and bogles. I believe in luck, good and bad, and in fate. I believe that most of the traditions and beliefs we

Scots hold dear grew out of the auld religion and do indeed have a basis in fact."

"That's stupid, sugar. Jake, you agree with me, don't you? All this nonsense—"

"Don't be putting words in my mouth, friend," Jake said. "I'm out of that. Annie, mind my asking what plans you have for him in addition to being your firstfoot? My wife has her heart set on his first footing Rowanclere Castle. If there's time . . ."

Rand reached out and scratched Midnight behind the ears. "That shouldn't be a problem, should it Annie? This business at the well shouldn't take long."

Glancing at Jake, he clarified, "At midnight we're doing something she calls Creaming the Well. She's trying to tell me it'll keep the cats away. I don't honestly believe it will work, but at this point, I'm willing to try just about anything."

"She's gonna give you the Cream of the Well?" Jake's eyebrows winged up.

Annie spied the knowledge in his eyes and her stomach sank.

She waited for him to ruin her plans by speaking out.

Instead, he simply asked, "Which well are you going to?"

"Laichmoray. It's closest."

"Hmm . . ." Jake scratched his chin in thought, then said, "You know, Annie, if you're moving from this cottage, you don't necessarily need a firstfoot. Why don't you use the church well in Rowanclere village? You'd have fewer maidens to compete with. After that, you could come on out to the castle and celebrate with us."

"Maidens?" Rand repeated. "Compete? Annie, what

have you not told me? I thought all you wanted to do was to get the first dip of water from the town well after midnight."

She met the challenge in Jake Delaney's gaze, then quickly looked away. Since he hadn't given her away already, perhaps he would refrain from doing so—if she didn't lie to Rand outright. "As I explained before, the 'cream' or 'flower' of the well is the first water from a well—preferably a holy or curative well—on New Year's Day. The cream is valued by many people for various reasons. Since it can be drawn only once, people often race to get it, hence the competition."

"Why maidens?"

She shrugged. "Milkmaids use it to wash dairy utensils and give it to cows to increase milk production."

She told the truth, though not nearly all of it. When she had said all she intended to say, she held her breath waiting for Jake to give her away. Instead, he said, "So Rand, can I tell my wife to expect you to firstfoot Rowanclere Castle sometime after midnight tonight?"

Rand glanced at Annie and when she nodded, replied, "Sure."

Jake leveled a flinty-eyed gaze on her and added, "You'll tell him all the rules?"

"I'll make certain he arrives with a piece of coal, a loaf, and a bottle of whisky."

"Make sure he knows not to speak until after he's wished everyone a Happy New Year. I know Rand. It'll be hard for him to stay quiet, and if he ruins it for Gilly . . . well . . . she's expecting a child. She's counting on a first-foot's good luck. I'll not have anything upset her."

"Dinna worry," she assured him while Rand slapped him on the back.

"A baby? You're gonna be a daddy? Sonofagun. That poor child."

Rand and Jake joked back and forth about the siring of a child as men were wont to do, then Jake prepared to leave. At the doorway, he said, "Annie, I do have a question about this pregnancy you might be able to answer. Walk me out to my horse?"

While she grabbed a cloak, Rand gave his friend a narrow look brimming with suspicion. Jake ignored the look, instead calling attention to the half dozen cats cautiously stepping toward the cottage. Rand muttered a curse, then after Jake and Annie walked outside, stepped back and slammed the door.

They walked without speaking to where he'd left his horse. Annie braced herself against the accusations she felt certain he would make. How could she explain? Should she confess her feelings? Would he believe her? Would he warn his friend off?

As he untied the reins, Jake asked, "Are you thinking to put a ring around that man's finger, Annie Munro? That is why the Cream of the Well is sought, isn't it? Gillian has taught me all kinds of Scots folklore and tradition. You think if Rand accepts the Cream of the Well from your hand and drinks it, he'll fall in love and marry you within the year. Am I right?"

Her hands buried deep in the pockets of her cloak, Annie kicked at a small drift of snow. Her emotions were in a turmoil. She could do no more than speak the naked truth. "I can be a good wife to him."

"He isn't looking for a wife, Annie. He's been burned in the past and he's sworn he'll never marry again. You should believe him."

She shivered and tried to pretend it was from the cold. "I know about the divorce, Jake. I know he was hurt. But I won't hurt him. I could help him heal. That's who I am. It's what I do. I'll make healing Rand my only priority." Her eyes filled with tears and she blinked them back. "Rand is . . . is . . . he's special. I can love him, Jake, and I honestly believe he can come to love me."

"Helped along by the Cream of the Well." When she only shrugged, he continued, "I can't say I believe in all your Scottish traditions, but I do believe a man can be bewitched. Don't do it. Not this way. Believe me in this. If you put a spell on him, whether from your own powers or the power of the New Year's well water, you'll regret it. He'll figure it out someday and when he does, he'll feel like he's been lied to. Again. Don't lie to him. Rand cannot abide liars, and women liars . . . well . . . you'll both end up losers."

"If you feel that way, why didn't you warn him?"

The handsome man's mouth twisted in a wry grin. "Because I saw the way he looks at you. You can do this without witchcraft or tricks. You already have a head start."

"What do you mean?"

"I've known Rand Jenkins a long, long time. Cats aren't what's keeping the man here, but a beautiful green-eyed kitten."

It took her a moment to realize he meant her. "I'm not a witch. Truly. I canna put a spell on him."

"What of the Cream of the Well?"

"He's not a believer."

"It will still be a lie." He untied his horse's reins and climbed into the saddle. He tipped his hat in farewell, then said, "I like you, Annie. I think you'd make my friend a fine wife. But do it the right way. Bewitch him on your own. You can do it, I know you can. I'm giving you this advice for your own good as well as Rand's. You see, I'm certain you can win him, and when you do, you deserve the joy of knowing his love for you is real and not the product of a Scottish superstition."

The winter wind whipped around Annie as she watched Jake Delaney ride away. Despite the fact her cloak kept her toasty warm, inside she felt cold and bleak as a gravestone.

Was Jake Delaney right?

Rand was watching a witch at work.

Standing just behind the ribbon stretched across Rowanclere village's main street, he gazed at Annie and shook his head in wonder. He couldn't believe what he had just seen.

Twenty minutes ago when he and Annie arrived at the spot in Rowanclere village marked as the starting point for the race to the churchyard well, Rand counted fourteen females lined up behind the ribbon, laughing and joking and making ready to run. Now, five minutes before midnight, only four remained.

Annie Munro had driven away the others by giving them the Evil Eye.

Rand didn't know whether to congratulate her or scold her. She had some of these gals scared half to death. He was amazed at how the Scots believed this superstition business, and as he watched the villagers react to her, his temper kindled to a slow burn. These people ought to be ashamed. How many of the women cringing from her now had recently gone to her begging for a potion or poultice? No wonder she wanted to get away from here so badly. These folks treated her as if she had an infectious disease.

The longer he watched, the more disgusted he became. Sure her waving-fingers-and-glare trick only made matters worse, but if these folks weren't so ready to believe the worst about her, they wouldn't fall for such an obvious act. Despite the brevity of their acquaintance, Rand knew beyond a shadow of a doubt that Annie Munro wouldn't hurt a flea. Why didn't the people she'd doctored all her life recognize it? The fact they didn't made him glad she'd be leaving this place.

Due to what he'd witnessed, when Rand took his position beside Annie and prepared to provide the distraction Annie had planned, he was filled with righteous indignation. Any anticipation he'd felt toward his part in this business had died when the blond girl made the sign of the cross as Annie passed by.

As muffled church bells tolled out the old year, trepidation rolled over Rand. Leaning toward Annie, he said, "I want to change my part. How about I draw my gun and shoot into the air a few times instead?"

"No. My plan is much better. 'Tis customary behavior that no one will question, yet you do it so extraordinarily well that it will effectively distract the women from their purpose."

"Extraordinarily well?" he repeated, standing a bit straighter.

"Aye," she said with a sigh. "This isna easy for me, either, you ken. I'll not like it one bit."

Rand sensed he should pursue that line of thought, but

at that moment, the church bells, muffles removed, began to ring in the New Year with joyous peals. A great, festive cheer went up from the crowd and Annie dashed off, shouting, "Now!"

"The sacrifices a man must make," Rand grumbled just before he prevented the woman beside him from following Annie by grabbing her hand.

He pulled her to him and gave her a kiss. It was a half-hearted effort on his part, but when he released the woman, he noted the dazed look in her eyes. *Extraordinarily well, hmm?*

Rand took off after the next gal, his long strides eating up the distance between them. As he ran he saw that Annie had been correct; the lane was lined with people randomly kissing other people. Something she'd said stuck in his brain, and he asked himself why Annie would be bothered by his kissing other women. Was she jealous?

That idea put an added bit of spring to his step, and he ran toward the second Cream of the Well seeker determined to put more enthusiasm into his task. Only, by the time he reached the pretty redhead, his distraction services were no longer needed because a cat had leapt onto the young woman's skirts, climbed up her dress, and tangled itself in her red curls. She abruptly stopped and attempted to deal with the tabby.

Rand didn't break stride. He immediately set his sights on the next closest female who happened to be Annie. He realized he'd have liked to stop and kiss her, but unfortunately that wasn't his mission. Especially since she was being beaten in the foot race by two more women. *Not much of a speed demon, are you sweetheart?* Rand contented himself with blowing her a kiss as he passed by.

The route to the church well snaked along the twisting village street. Having pulled away from Annie, Rand rounded a curve, and the sight that met his eyes had him slowing his run to a walk. The last of Annie's competitors sat sprawled in the middle of the narrow snowy lane. Both were wiggling and thrashing and letting out caterwauls loud enough to raise the kirkyard dead.

Both were all but covered up in cats.

"This is too damned strange," Rand muttered, reluctantly preparing to dive into the middle of the brawl. He should try to help. Shouldn't he?

Looking closer he realized these two were the ones who'd acted cruelly to Annie and his intentions wavered. When he saw that the cats were not scratching and biting, simply cuddling and tangling, he pretty much made up his mind.

Then Annie caught up with him and tugged on his arm as she ran by. "Come on."

Moments later, they arrived at the designated well. The trio of torches burning behind it offered a false picture of warmth while bringing light to the surroundings. Annie's breaths fogged on the night air as she leaned over the well's stone wall and stared down into the darkness. Rand found the look on her face arresting. The yearning in her expression made him think the well held more than just a cure for the cats, but her own hopes and dreams as well.

A shiver ran up Rand's spine and he looked away, feeling like a slimy Peeping Tom, eavesdropping on a singularly private moment. Movement up the street caught his attention. He blinked, looked again. Sure enough, at least a dozen cats bounded their way. "Well, sugar. Looks like you won the race, but I suggest you do your dipping without delay. There's a whole herd of felines headed this way, which undoubtedly means the other runners are right on their tails."

After a glance toward the street, she took a deep breath, then placed trembling hands on the crank and began to lower the bucket. Rand noted the tremor in her hands and scowled. "You're shuddering. Are you terribly cold?"

Haunted green eyes looked up at him. "I'm terrified."

"Terrified? How come?" Leaning over, he peered into the well. "I'm the one who'll be drinking this stuff. I have to tell you, Annie, the idea of tossing back ice-cold water at midnight on New Year's doesn't thrill me much. I'm already cold as a corpse, and this Cream of the Well water won't help any. Not unless you reel up a bucketful of whisky. Now wouldn't that be a trick."

The wooden crank groaned and squeaked with every turn. Rand watched it, watched her hands, and scowled. "Why didn't you wear gloves? You should have worn gloves. Want me to do that?"

"I told you earlier. I must be the one to draw the water and offer it to you. Otherwise, it won't work."

Hmm . . . something about that scenario bothered him, but he hadn't quite put his finger on it yet. "You know what, Annie? I can't believe I'm saying this, but I hope you're right about the magic in this drink. Look, my pals are back."

He pointed toward his feet where the cats were now milling about him, slinking back and forth between his legs, rubbing themselves around his ankles, and purring and mewling and meowing. A gray cat and a calico plopped themselves down, one on each foot.

"Cold feet," Annie murmured just as a splash sounded from the bottom of the well.

"Along with everything else. Hurry up, Annie."

Moments later, the water-filled bucket appeared at the top of the well. Rand reached out to grab it, but Annie stopped him. "No, I'll do it. I must do it all."

He shoved his hands into his pockets and stepped away. "Why is that, anyway? I'm the one with the cat problem."

"And your problems are just beginning if ye take a sip of Annie Munro's cream," called a voice from just beyond the light. Rand had been aware that a crowd had gathered around them, but he'd paid scant attention to them prior to that remark. The annoyance he'd experienced before the race returned with a rush. "C'mon, sugar. Give me the water so we can get out of here. I'm sure Jake and Gillian are anxious for their first luck to arrive."

"Firstfoot. The firstfoot brings the good luck with him."

"Luck I have a'plenty. It's the question of cats I'd like settled now."

Annie set the bucket on the ground, fished a tin cup from her pocket, and dipped it into the bucket. As she slowly straightened, both hands cupped around the mug filled with well water, her green-eyed gaze met his. Rand felt a now familiar surge of desire. Those beautiful, mystical, enchanting eyes. He could lose himself in them forever.

Rand's heart began to pound. His hands began to sweat. As if from miles away, he heard murmurs and musings coming from the crowd that encircled them. Louder were the purrs rising from the cats at his feet, a melody of meows with a chorus of encouragement.

Annie Munro, self-denied witch and admitted liar,

offered up the cup with trembling hands and said, "The new year signifies a fresh start. 'Tis time to make a break with the past, to leave its troubles and turmoils behind ye. May the warmth of a heart filled with love melt the cold from yer feet. A guid New Year to ye, Rand Jenkins, and many of them. Slàinte Mhoire."

"Slàinte Mhoire, Annie Munro," he replied, having learned the Gaelic for good health.

Then Rand brought the cup to his lips and prepared to drink.

Seven

Don't do it, Annie. Not this way.

As Annie watched Rand bring the Cream of the Well to his mouth, Jake Delaney's voice echoed through her mind. *Do it the right way.*

Her heart pounded; her hands grew clammy.

Bewitch him on your own. You can do this without witchcraft or tricks.

At her feet, Midnight meowed.

You'll regret it.

Rand tipped the mug and Annie's hand flew out. "No!" she cried out as she knocked the cup away, the Cream of the Well spilling and splashing in impotent drops upon the collection of cats milling about their feet. The kitties meowed. The crowd observing them gasped. One young woman wailed, "She's wasted it! Annie Munro wasted the Cream of the Well!"

Then the world seemed to fade away but for her and Rand. Her heart pounded, her breathing was shallow. Somber curiosity glimmered in his eyes. "Annie? Want to tell me what just happened here?"

What should she say? What could she say? "I need . . . I wanted . . . oh, no." She closed her eyes, allowed her head to fall forward, and fought back tears.

Frustration resonated through his voice. "All right. I can see we need somewhere private to talk."

He grabbed one of the torches, took hold of her hand, and pulled her toward the kirk. As if from out of a fog, Annie thought she heard the click of a gun being cocked, then Sarah Ross's voice saying, "No, get away from the bucket. That's Annie Munro's property, and I intend to see it's here when she returns."

The kirk's big wooden door banged shut behind her. Rand led her to a box seat and told her to sit, then he used the torch flame to light lamps and chase away the gloom inside the church. He disposed of the torch and approached her, his mouth grimly set, his ice blue eyes narrowed in determination. "Now, you want to tell me what all that was about?"

Not particularly, no. But Annie knew she owed him that much. Again, Jake's voice floated through her mind. *Don't lie to him. Rand cannot abide liars.* And, *I'm certain you can win him, and when you do, you deserve the joy of knowing his love for you is real and not the product of a Scottish superstition.*

Annie cleared her throat. "I need to explain something about the cream."

"I figured as much. Is it poisoned or something? Was the entire cat-cure claim something you made up?"

"Nae." This much she could give him. "The Cream of the Well does have curative powers. I wasn't lying about that."

"What is it, Annie? Don't you want me cured of the cats?"

"I do. In fact, I think the cream will still work for you if you dip a cup in the bucket and drink it yourself."

"All right. I see where this is going. What was supposed to happen when you gave me the water along with your pretty toast?"

She swallowed hard, then mumbled. "It becomes a love potion."

"Pardon me?"

Finally, she braved his gaze. Her heart was thumping so hard she expected he could hear it. Her mouth was as dry as old bones. Clearing her throat, she confessed. "I wanted to win you. The Cream of the Well is a love potion."

"It's what?"

"A love potion. According to custom and tradition, if a lass fancies a lad and causes him to drink of the Cream of the Well before sunset on New Year's Day, love will blossom and the two will marry within the year. I wanted you to fall in love with me. I want to go to Texas with you, Rand, but I want to go as your wife."

His eyes went wide. "My what?"

Oh my, this was harder to say the second time. She licked her lips. "Your wife. I want to marry you, Rand."

His voice emerged as a strangled squeak. "You want to marry me?"

"I do."

"Good Lord, why?"

"Because I love you."

"You love me." He took a step backward, then slumped into a pew. He dragged his hand through his hair, then sighed as if the weight of the world—or Annie's dreams and expectations—weighted his shoulders. "Oh, hell, Annie. No, you don't."

Her heart, which had been in her throat, sank to her knees.

He started shaking his head. "I understand now. Oh, sugar. I'm sorry. I didn't realize just how afraid you really are. Look, I give you my word, Jake and I aren't gonna let anything bad happen to you. You'll be safe at Rowanclere until we can find you a fine place to live. If you're still bent on coming to Texas, well, once I get home I'll do some nosing around and see if I can't find just the right spot for you to settle."

"I don't want to settle. I want to make a home with you. I'm not afraid. I'm in love."

"No, sugar, you're not." He leaned forward and took her hand in his. "Annie, I know what you're feeling. I feel it, too. You and I have a good, old-fashioned case of lust for one another. It's powerful and it's the reason I won't travel with you, because I know as sure as I'm sitting here that I'd have a weak moment and act on it. But, it's not love. We've only known each other a few days. It's not possible to fall in love that fast. We're not in love. We're in lust."

She sucked in a breath. *Right now, I wish I were a witch. I surely would turn you into a toad.*

"Annie," he chided. "Listen. I respect you, and I respect your desire to be respectable. As difficult as it will be, especially now that I know for a fact you want me as much as I want you, I think we'd best part ways as soon as possible.

You're a wonderful woman, Annie, and I do care about you. If I could fall in love with any woman, you'd be at the top of my list."

His every word was another dart to pierce her heart. Jake Delaney had been wrong. Truth wouldn't win him. At least with lies she'd have had a chance. But she had made her choice out beside the well, so now she must live with the results. The one positive note she could see in all of this was that when one spoke the truth, they need not hide what was in their heart.

So Annie stood and said, "I did not take you for a coward, sir, but I see now that I was wrong. You talk of fear ... I suggest you look into yourself. 'Tis not my fear driving events here tonight, but your own. You are afraid to take the lesson of the new year. You are afraid to let go of the pain of the past and start fresh. I pity you, Rand Jenkins, because you are throwing away something that could have filled your life with joy and laughter and love. You are throwing away me."

"Now, Annie—"

"Enough. I'm going home. Please give the Delaneys my regards and don't forget the knapsack of supplies for the firstfooting."

"Wait a minute. Hold up. You can't go home by yourself."

She stalked to the door and threw it open to reveal what must have been thirty cats congregated before the door. "Aye, I can and something tells me you will not be able to stop me. Good-bye, Rand Jenkins. Have a safe journey back to Texas."

The cats parted like the Red Sea before Moses as she exited the church. Rand made to follow, but the felines closed ranks against him, their hisses sounding more like a barrel of snakes than a group of kitties.

"Annie, wait!" he called after her.

She ignored him, hurrying out into the kirkyard and the cold winter's night. Tears clouded her eyes so she didn't see the figure that reached out to stop her.

"Miss Munro," Sarah Ross said. "Wait. Please. Rand is—"

"A fool," she snapped back. "And I've no more patience for fools right now."

Annie wasn't terribly surprised to hear Jake Delaney speak next. "Sarah, I'm glad you talked me into coming out to watch this. Make sure Rand finds his way to the castle, would you please? Gillian is fretful over her firstfoot and the damned fool friend of mine needs to see to that business. Annie, I'll see you home."

Mindful of the drunken revelers sure to be roaming the road tonight, she nodded. "Thank you."

They exchanged a minimum of words the entire way back, but at the doorway to her cottage Jake cleared his throat. "I won't come in. I don't have the proper supplies to act as your firstfoot. I want you to know . . . well . . . I'm sorry, Annie. I knew he was stubborn, but I didn't think he'd be stubborn *and* stupid. But don't give up on him. Give him some time. I still think he might come around."

Pride bruised, heart broken, she looked at him and said, "Not on my account, he shouldn't. 'Tis a hard lesson I've been reminded of this first day of the New Year, but it is one I'll not soon forget again."

"What lesson is that?"

She shrugged. "The Scots have a saying, Jake. 'True

love's fearless.' I remembered that I'm not willing to settle for anything less than true love."

The cats didn't follow Rand to Rowanclere.

It was one more strange event in a collection of 'em. When Rand had attempted to leave the church to go after Annie, they'd ganged up and blocked his way looking more like mountain lions than village cats. Once Sarah ushered him down the road to Rowanclere Castle they'd disappeared. Completely. Even the black one whose eyes reminded him so much of Annie's.

He'd arrived at the castle numb through to the bone, something he'd tried to pin on the weather. He did his firstfoot duty for Gillian, bringing good luck to Rowanclere Castle by adding a coal to the fire, placing a loaf of bread on the table, then pouring whisky for everyone and saying the toast Annie had taught him, "Lang may yer lum reek," which translated to "Long may your chimney smoke," meaning long may you live. But as the Hogmanay party commenced and the partygoers grew more festive, Rand's mood sank to melancholy.

Sarah noticed and joined him on an isolated bench in the corridor outside the castle's great hall. She handed him a whisky. "Are you ready to talk about it yet?"

"What were you doing in the village?"

She took his drink from him, took a sip, then handed it back. "Jake let slip what she intended to do. I wanted to watch."

"Why?"

"I don't know. Maybe because all these Scottish traditions fascinate me. Or maybe because I'm a wedding planner by profession and thought I might need the

Cream of the Well information someday. However, I think the real reason I wanted to see what happened at the church well tonight was because of the way Jake said you looked when you were looking at her."

He didn't want to ask. He couldn't stop himself from asking. "How's that?"

"He said when you looked at Annie Munro the ghosts were gone from your eyes."

Rand stared at the amber liquid in his glass. Were those the reflections of his ghosts he saw on the surface? Or were they his fears? Was he the coward Annie claimed him to be? He rotated his wrist, causing the liquid to swirl, watching the small whirlpool the motion created. He imagined himself sinking, sucked into the maelstrom.

"What happens when you reach the bottom, Sarah?"

"The bottom of what?"

"Just . . . the bottom. It's when the cold migrates upward from your feet to freeze your heart and soul."

"Oh, Rand."

"I'll tell you what happens." He tossed back his drink, then slammed the empty glass on the bench. "You gotta find yourself a witch, that's what. A witch's powers will beat out a ghost's every damned time."

Sunlight beamed from a cloudless sky, warming the air and reflecting off patches of ice as if sparkling diamonds lay scattered across the land. Standing at her cottage window, Annie gazed out toward the distant hills, sipped her tea, and reflected upon the events of the past few days.

She was tired in both body and spirit. After returning home last night, she'd slept in fitful stretches and arisen midmorning with the weight of every hill in the High-lands on her shoulders.

What should she do next?

She did not want to accept help from Rand through the Delaneys, but the cost of pride would be high. Was she willing to pay it? Was she ready to stay here and play the village witch and fight off rumormongers and would-be attackers until one of them eventually won?

And what of the wound to her heart? How long would it take her to forget Rand Jenkins? Perhaps she would never forget him. Perhaps her heart would simmer with anger and resentment toward him for years to come. She took hope in the notion. Better that than pining with unrequited love for the rest of her life.

"Ach," she muttered, turning away from the window. The words "unrequited love" had a pitiful sound to them, and she simply refused to be pitiful. "Remember, Annie Munro, if the man was too mellheidit to value the gift of your love, then he's nae the man you thought he was. You deserve better."

In saying it, she tried to convince herself she believed it. She also made the decision to accept the terms of Rand's offer of help. Addressing Midnight, she said, "No sense allowing pride to bring me to grief. Tomorrow, we go to Rowanclere Castle."

An hour later, an unexpected knock at her door made her wonder if she'd made a mistake in staying this long. Annie stared hard at the door, bothered by her sudden fear. Finally, she called out, "I'm no longer providing service as a healer. Take your troubles to the howdie. She has healing skills, also."

But the knock sounded again.

Annie made a face at the door. "Please, just go away."
Knock. Knock. Knock.

She folded her arms and tapped her foot, determined to wait her visitor out. *Knock knock knock. Knock knock knock. Knock knock knock.* "Oh, all right!"

Grabbing an iron skillet suitable for head-banging if needed, she marched over to the door and flung it open. "I am not—" She broke off abruptly upon identifying her caller. The skillet slid from her hand to clatter against the floor. *Rand.*

Without asking her leave—without speaking at all—he stepped inside carrying a large picnic basket. Annie caught a whiff of something spicy as he headed straight toward the fireplace, fished a piece of coal from his pocket and added it to the fire, then walked to her small dining table where he set down his basket and flipped back the lid.

She cleared her throat, tried to find her voice, but the pounding in her heart got in the way.

He pulled a loaf of bread from the basket and set it on the table. Next came a bottle of whisky, and an unusually slow-witted Annie finally realized he had brought traditional firstfoot gifts.

But apparently, that wasn't all.

He pulled a small crock from the bag, the steam from which quickly proved the source of the spicy smell. Following that, he placed a silk lady's fan on the table, then a second amber-filled bottle. He took a glass, added ice, then filled it with liquid from the second bottle. Then, lifting the first bottle toward her, he finally spoke. "A good New Year and many of them, Annie Munro. Am I the first?"

"The firstfoot?"

"Yes."

"Aye, you are."

"Good." He uncorked the bottle of whisky and took a swig. "That means I have some luck going for me. I'm a superstitious man, you know, and I figure I might need a measure of luck here today. So . . ."

He drew a deep breath, exhaled in a rush, then lifted his left foot and held it out toward her. "I guess that brings me to this old dog."

Old dog? Annie shook her head, unable to translate his Texanese.

"It's my second foot. Now, you need to know right off that this is the last time I expect Texas to come in second to Scotland as long as we're together. Here," he handed her the crock. "It's Jake's sister's recipe for chili, which is the national food of Texas and a much better New Year's gift than a loaf of bread."

"It smells wonderful."

"Gillian's chili is good—not on a par with Chrissy's yet, but she's trying." Next, he flipped open the fan and waved it in Annie's face. "This takes the place of the coal. In Texas, you'll find yourself more often wishing for something to cool you down than something to heat you up, which brings us to this."

Rand handed her the glass and said, "Whisky is the Scots tradition, but this is pure southern comfort. Take a taste."

She sipped, then grimaced. "Tea over ice?"

"Can't beat it on a hot August day."

She set down the glass. "I'm sorry. I'm afraid my patience is thin this day. Please get to the point of your visit."

"Food, drink, and fuel for the fire—Texas-style. A Texan firstfoot."

"Oh." She tried to smile. "How nice."

He rolled his eyes. "You're not getting this, are you? I was hoping doing a double firstfoot would bring me a double dose of good luck. I think I'm gonna need it. You might not have recognized it, but I'm trying to grovel here. I don't have a lot of experience at it, so bear with me."

Grovel? Annie blinked twice. "Did you say 'grovel'?"

"Yeah. It might take me a try or two to get it right."

"Certainly, take all the time you need." Annie waved a hand magnanimously even as she thought she had better sit down before her suddenly watery knees gave way. Rand Jenkins had come to grovel. What did that mean?

"Not gonna make it easy on me, are you?" Rand cleared his throat. "All right, then, here goes. Annie, you said some hard things to me last night. You'd better learn something about Texans right off, Texan men in particular. We don't like bein' told we're yellow. Especially when in our guts we know it's the truth. Now, you told me to take a good hard look at myself, and that's what I did. It was hard, but I did it, and I saw the trouble big as life. You were right. I had a yellow streak running right up my backbone with a little detour through my heart."

At the mention of his heart, Annie's climbed to her throat.

"However," he continued, "I'm pretty sure you were wrong about what created that yellow streak. I'm not afraid to let go of the past. I loved my wife and she hurt me, that's true, but if I let her ruin my ability to love again, well, I'm smarter than that."

"You are?"

Now he sent an exasperated glare. "Yes, I am. Letting her rule my heart that way would give her too much power over me. Shoot, she's not even in my life anymore, why should I let her have any say in it? No, the woman didn't make me afraid to love again, but she did something else almost as bad."

At that, Annie's eyes went wide. "What was it, Rand?"

"She stole my dreams, Annie. She stole my dreams of home and family right out from beneath my feet. That's when they started getting cold."

The warmth of hope sparked inside of her in that place that had been so cold. "You want a family?"

"Very much. Always have." He paused, grimaced. "This is the hard part to talk about. She had a child with her lover before our divorce was final. I was . . . well . . . jealous. Had a pea green stripe running right alongside the yellow one. Had a red one, too, because I was so angry. With three stripes running up my back, you've got to understand why it took me by surprise to find the blue one managed to paint over the others."

She gave her head a shake. He may as well have been speaking Greek. "I don't understand you. What is blue?"

"True blue. The color of love. The color of my love for you."

His words caused her head to spin. The hope within her blossomed. "Are you saying . . . ?"

He cupped her cheek in the palm of his hand and stared down at her. Then slowly, he dropped to one knee. "I needed to call it lust to feel safe, but I know it's more than that. I love you, Annie. Will you marry me?"

She closed her eyes, hardly believing her dream was coming true. "Are you sure?"

317

"Positive. I didn't think it could happen this fast. Shoot, I didn't think it could happen at all, but it has. You own my heart. You've warmed my feet. You're like my own pair of tartan wool socks."

"Wool socks? Oh, Rand." A sense of giddiness filled her as her heart took flight. "That's the most romantic thing anyone's ever said to me."

"What can I say, I've always had a way with words." He gave a wink that was pure wickedness, then reached for her and pulled her down beside him. "I'm even better with my hands."

Heat flared inside her. She wanted to cry and laugh and dance for joy. Instead, she teased him by saying, "I don't believe it."

"Annie, Annie, Annie." He shook his head and clicked his tongue. "That sounded like a challenge."

Eyes drifting shut, she lifted her face for his kiss, waiting for it, aching for it.

He didn't kiss her.

Her eyes flew open. He grinned smugly, wickedly. Curse the man. "I'll put a spell on you."

"You already have. I'm spellbound. Charmed. Enchanted. But I want the words, witch. Give them to me. I need them."

Her smile could have lit the entire Highlands. "And I need you, Rand. I love you. I will be honored to marry you."

"Good, I'm glad that's settled." As his mouth captured hers in a senses-stealing kiss, he swept her up into his arms, and carried her to the bed. There, wrapped in each other's arms, lost in the joy of discovery, they set about practicing the magic of true love.

* * *

Midnight purred with satisfaction as she climbed the outside wall of the cottage up to the rooftop. She took her place at rafter's peak and let out a loud yowl. Moments later, she was joined by upwards of a dozen cats in a myriad of shapes, sizes, and colors.

Midnight sat back on her haunches and extended her front paws. With a melodious meow, the cat transformed into an ethereal figure of a beautiful dark-haired woman.

One by one, the other cats followed suit. Midnight, once known to humans as Elspeth Munro, addressed her kinswomen. " 'Tis done. My daughter has captured his heart."

"Was there any doubt?" asked her sister, Tabitha Munro, recently the tabby cat who'd done such a fine job of tripping Rand Jenkins.

"He was a stubborn one," said another.

Tabitha nodded. "Aye, which is just what she needs. She's a stubborn one herself, denying her heritage all these years. I'll never understand how the child could remain so totally blind to the truth. I'll miss her though. Dreadfully."

"This was what she wanted," another Munro woman said.

Yet another added, "This is what she needed to make her happy."

"Aye," Tabitha said with a sigh. She looked toward her sister and asked, "So what now, Elspeth? Is our work here finished?"

"Aye, for now." A slow, secretive smile stretched across her face. "They'll return to us someday, of course, and wait until you see what plans I have for my granddaughters."

USA Today bestselling author GERALYN DAWSON lives in Texas with her husband and three children. A three-time RITA finalist, Geralyn has received a Career Achievement Award from *Romantic Times* magazine and The National Reader's Choice Award. Her books have been chosen "Top Ten of the Year" by both Romance Writers of America and the *Detroit Free Press*. All her books reflect her strong belief in the power of love and laughter.

The Matchmaker

PAM BINDER

One

A matchmaker was the last thing Kathleen MacKenzie needed today.

The lyrical sound of bagpipes filled the modern-day streets of Edinburgh, as though reminding her not to worry about such matters. She sat in the cushioned window seat that overlooked the Royal Mile and saw Harriet Maclaren, Edinburgh's unofficial matchmaker, walking toward her bakery shop. Kathleen took a deep breath. The sweet old woman was persistent.

Morning sunlight spread over this ancient city that had the ability to embrace the future without forgetting its past. The tradition of having a matchmaker was one of the ancient ways that had survived in Edinburgh. It was another reason Kathleen loved it here.

The aroma of cinnamon, chocolate, and brown sugar floated in the air. Kathleen smiled. Everything was ready. She had been baking since dawn, and now all there was to do was wait for her customers. The first would be Harriet, but that was all right. Kathleen had avoided her before, and today would be like all the others. After all, she had a bakery to run. She did not have time for anything else.

Her father had died in a plane crash and after her mother's death, Kathleen had willingly taken over. The bakery shop had been in her mother's family since before the time of Mary, Queen of Scots. Kathleen set her book, *Forever Amber,* in her lap. The novel written by Kathleen Winsor, had been her mother's favorite, and rereading the classic somehow made her feel less alone. They both shared a love for historical novels. Her mother had died over three years ago, just a short week after Kathleen had graduated from the University of Edinburgh.

Tears welled in her eyes. No one had been surprised that her mother had waited until her daughter graduated from university. Her friends said everything she did was planned well in advance and suggested she was probably at work reorganizing heaven. Kathleen wiped the tears from her eyes and glanced over at an eight-by-ten-inch chalkboard with today's to-do list printed in white. She smiled. Making lists was another thing she had in common with her mother. Kathleen had also inherited some of her father's traits: green eyes, as well as a light Scottish brogue. She liked being a combination of the two.

Kathleen glanced over at the grandfather clock that stood straight and proud by the entrance to the shop. It was almost nine A.M. The time her shop opened for business. She slid off the window seat, lifted the hinged lid, and placed her book with a stack of others. She straightened her ankle-length print skirt and tucked in the matching blouse. The style fit the whimsical ambience of the shop. Normally she wore this type of clothing from force of habit, but of late it fit her mood.

She shrugged away the strange feeling, that she was becoming more attracted to this ancient city. She walked over to the entrance and unlocked the door to her bakery shop. It was called Kathleen's, after generations of women who shared that name. Lace curtains blew softly against the open windows, and the tables were covered with starched, white linens. The bakery was situated just a short distance from the Palace of Holyroodhouse, the summer residence of the Queen and a popular attraction for tourists. The grandfather clock announced the hour, and at the same moment a soft bell chimed. The door opened and Kathleen welcomed the spring day and her first customer.

She smiled. "Good morning, Harriet."

" 'Tis all of that, lass, and more." Harriet hugged her worn canvas bag to her ample breast. Her eyes crinkled up in a smile. "I have pictures of a new crop of men I wish to show ye. I snapped the pictures myself. Much easier than trying to draw their likeness. The men are all fine, hard-working, reliable sorts. Even a few that are easy on the eye." She winked. "If you get my meaning."

Kathleen walked behind the waist-high counter and the glass cases filled with a variety of fruit-filled scones. "Aye, Harriet, I know exactly what it is you mean. But my answer is the same as it was during your last visit. Since my mother's death, I've had to run this shop alone. 'Tis the height of the tourist season. I donna have time to think of romance. And one of these days you shall encounter someone who does not approve of your taking pictures of them."

Harriet shook her head. "Will na happen, lass. I'm only interested in the ones with the kind eyes. But as usual, ye've changed the subject."

Harriet walked over to a nearby table by the window and sat down. She put her bag beside her and rummaged around inside. She pulled out a handful of pictures. "Ye've been saying the same thing about romance for longer than I can remember. Your mother was of a like opinion." She arched an eyebrow. "Before I found her match."

Kathleen laughed. Harriet liked to take credit for bringing together all the happy couples in Edinburgh. Kathleen remembered her mother telling her about the chance encounter with her dad. However, if her mother never disputed Harriet's claim, neither would she. She smiled and pulled herself back to the present.

Harriet waved a picture in Kathleen's direction. "The boy's name is Liam Campbell. Fine man, solid stock."

Kathleen put her lace-trimmed apron on and tied it around her waist. She waited for Harriet to add that Liam probably was as bland as bread pudding and thus a perfect match for Kathleen. She shrugged the thought away. She did not know what type of man she wanted, so how would Harriet?

The door chimes rang again, and Kathleen glanced toward the sound. It was her American. She wiped her palms on her apron and felt her heart skip a beat or two. He looked good this morning, but then he always did.

He wore a black leather bomber jacket, faded blue jeans, and carried a long narrow parcel under his arm. As usual he was talking on a cell phone and seemed oblivious to everything and everyone around him. She'd overheard him say once that he was staying at the Balmoral Hotel. It was one of the most exclusive and expensive hotels in Edinburgh. He might be wearing blue jeans, but she'd be willing to bet there were gold-colored credit cards in his wallet.

For the past two weeks he had stopped in her shop, right after it had opened, and ordered the same thing: a cup of black coffee and a plain scone. He liked his coffee in a paper cup with a lid, so he could take it with him, and a scone on a plate.

Kathleen reached for the coffeepot on the warmer and poured the steaming brew into a cup. She put a buttery pastry on a china plate covered with painted yellow rosebuds and waited for him. Kathleen pressed her hand against her stomach and tried to ignore the prehistoric-size butterflies that seemed to be fluttering about. Her schoolgirl crush was bothersome. 'Twas a good thing he was leaving soon.

The American paused at the counter. He reached for his wallet in an inside jacket pocket. "Hey, Bob, hold that thought." He set his phone on the counter and pulled out British currency. He smiled. "I remembered this time."

She laughed, remembering yesterday's conversation. "I donna mind exchanging your U.S. dollars."

He lowered his voice. "I know you don't, but you always remember my order; the least I could do was bring the right money."

He set his wallet on the counter. He handed her the currency and his fingers brushed against the palm of her hand. The contact sent a warm shiver through her. He leaned forward. He smelled as though he had just stepped out of a shower. Her heart pounded. She tried to remember to breathe.

The voice on his cell phone screeched through the air. "Hey, Duncan, you there?"

He drew back and picked up the annoying contraption. "I'm here. Now go over the details again." He put the plate on top of the paper coffee cup and walked over to the table in the far corner of the shop.

Kathleen let out her breath slowly. She watched him tear off a chunk of the pastry and pop it into his mouth.

She heard the click of a camera. She flinched and looked in the direction of the sound. Harriet put the camera down and smiled. She motioned for Kathleen to join her.

As Kathleen walked over to Harriet, she decided the woman did not have a subtle bone in her body. Kathleen sat down in a chair opposite her.

Harriet put her camera in her bag. "Who's the tall, dark, and handsome lad?"

Kathleen shushed her. "He'll hear you."

Harriet shook her head. "Not likely. He seems too preoccupied with his phone conversation." Harriet winked. "However, the lad noticed you. And well he might. Ye be as bonnie as your dear mother. God rest her soul."

Kathleen laced her fingers together in her lap, uneasy about the compliment, but pleased she shared one more thing in common with her mother. "Thank you, but you canna be serious about the American's interest. He walked straight in and sat down. We barely spoke. 'Tis the same each day. He comes in for a scone and a cup of coffee."

Harriet stuffed the pictures back into her satchel and rummaged around. "I'm not so sure. Over the years I've acquired a certain feel for such matters. But the young these days are always too busy. Well, ye know what the ancients say? If ye dinna find the time for love, it will find it for ye."

She searched through her bag and pulled out a gold brooch set with a large red stone. " 'Tis called The Dragon's Fire and belonged to a feudal lord who had it made for a woman whose love would never be his. The jewel is not for ye, but 'twould be perfect for a lass who lives not far from here." She replaced it in her bag and continued her search.

Kathleen leaned forward and peered into the bag. There was a wide assortment of jewelry mingled with photos of men and women.

Harriet smiled. "Ah, there it is." She drew out a long gold chain with a crest-shaped pendant dangling on the end. Sapphires, emeralds, and rubies adorned the piece of fine jewelry. She held it up to the light. " 'Tis a copy of the jewel given to Lord Darnley on the occasion of his marriage to Mary Queen of Scots. That would be around 1565 or so." Harriet looked in the direction of the Palace of Holyroodhouse. "Strange things are happening there these days. The new elevator they installed for the Royals use keeps stalling between floors." Harriet took a deep breath. "No matter." She handed the pendant to Kathleen. "Consider it a belated birthday present."

"Harriet, I canna take this. It is too expensive."

"Nonsense, lass, 'tis just a copy."

The jewels winked and sparkled in the light, as though to dispute Harriet's easy dismissal of their worth.

A chair scraped against the wood floor. Kathleen glanced toward the sound. Her American was leaving.

He stood and walked over to the kitchen area behind the counter and put his empty plate in the sink. It was this small gesture that captured her attention the first time he had come into her shop. She did not expect her customers to clean away their own dishes, but his unconscious offer of help made a lasting impression. It set him apart from all the others.

Her American smiled toward her as he left the bakery and headed in the direction of the palace.

Kathleen took a deep breath to hide her disappointment. "I don't see how you can say he is interested in me. As I said before, he only comes in here for the coffee."

Harriet reached over to the window, pulled the lace curtains aside, and peered out. "Then why would the lad be throwing it in the waste receptacle?"

Kathleen followed her gaze. Sure enough, the American had thrown the coffee away. "That does not prove a thing. Maybe he was finished."

"Hum, or maybe he has another reason to visit your bakery shop."

"That is nonsense."

Kathleen wanted to add that Harriet was being too obvious. The American was not Kathleen's match. At the very most he would make the perfect subject of a wonderful mist-shrouded dream. She paused. Well, maybe he warranted two or even three dreams. Anyway, he was not for her.

She put the pendant over her head and walked to the counter. She paused. The American had left his wallet. She picked it up and turned toward the door.

Harriet nodded. "Well, well, what do we have there? The American has forgotten his wallet." Her voice was devoid of emotion, but her eyes twinkled with mischief. "Ye will have to return it to the lad. Go after him, child, I'll mind the shop until you return. And remember, that just like the Darnley Jewel, everything in life has its match."

Kathleen slipped the leather wallet into her skirt pocket. "And what of the customers?"

Harriet glanced around the shop. " 'Tis no one about, lass. Go, go quickly, before it is too late. And donna worry about a thing." She paused. "Wait, lass. I almost forgot." She reached into her bag and pulled out a sprig of heather. She handed it to Kathleen. "See ye give it to Callum at the palace. He likes to wear it on his jacket."

"Harriet, can it be that ye are interested in Callum?"

"Fiddle-faddle. Ye ask too many questions. Now off with ye."

Kathleen smiled and hurried toward the door.

Harriet called out to her. "Take as much time as ye need, Kathleen MacKenzie. And remember, If ye dinna have time for love, it will find it for ye."

Duncan MacGreggor threw his cup of coffee in a wastebasket along the side of the street and denied himself a glance in the direction of the bakery shop. The owner had been on his mind too much of late. He'd heard one of the customers speak her name. Kathleen, it fit her perfectly. It made him think of castles and fighting for honor. The way she looked only completed his image. She had green eyes and jet black hair. And she spoke with a soft Scottish brogue that made him want to listen to her all day. He guessed that if she read the dictionary to him, he would still be mesmerized.

It was not the first time he wished he was not leaving so soon. But he was. A few years ago he wouldn't have let that stop him, but of late he'd wanted more. Besides, he didn't have time to get to know someone. At least the way he wanted to know Kathleen.

Duncan combed his hand through his hair as though trying to banish her image. He paused outside the window of a shop on the Royal Mile on the way to the Palace of Holyroodhouse. A replica of a Scottish claymore lay propped on a stand. It was just like the one he carried under his arm. Only his was real. It had cost a fortune, but it was worth every cent.

As a teenager he'd often skipped school and ridden his bike to the medieval reenactment fair in Carnation, Washington. Always athletic and big for his age, he'd talked someone into showing him how to wield a blade when he was ten years old.

He remembered his first reenactment tournament fight and the roar of the crowd. A pretty damsel would wring her hands and yell for him to save her. It was during those times he wished he'd actually lived in the Middle Ages, when all you had to do was rescue the damsel in distress to be a hero.

Maybe that was why he'd developed so many games with Arthurian legends for his company, Vision Quest. He could immerse himself in a world where good conquered evil. Of late the lines had blurred.

The gray buildings seemed to blend in with the sky. The day had started out clear, but rain clouds were blocking out the morning sun. Eight hours difference between Seattle and Edinburgh, Scotland. It would be five P.M. in Seattle. He took a deep breath and punched in the direct line to the head of mergers and acquisitions at Vision Quest.

His call connected. "John Forseith here."

Duncan smiled to himself. The man always sounded as though he were talking with a mouth full of jelly beans. "John, I've briefed Bob on the details and am on my way to meet with Robertson. The guy insists I meet with him at the palace to sign the contracts. I thought I'd take along one of my swords to sweeten the pot."

Duncan waited while John congratulated him, and then the man shouted to someone in the office. He could hear the muffled cheers. Duncan wished he could be as pleased as everyone else, but this was just another acquisition in a long line of buyouts. What he really missed was creating new characters and designing games. It had been a long time since he'd come up with a new concept. Maybe all his ideas had dried up.

John came back on the phone. "Well, you've done it again. How does it feel to be on the brink of yet another takeover? When this hits The Street, your stock will set new records."

"Terrific. I'll let you know when the papers are signed. I'm booked on a flight that leaves tomorrow. I'll call you when I get in."

Duncan ended the conversation and put his cell phone in his jacket pocket. He walked past the scrollwork iron gates and the deserted courtyard of the palace. It was still too early for tourists. However, in about an hour, the place would be swarming with people. He almost wished he'd made the appointment for later in the day. Duncan liked being around people.

The doorman, dressed in a green plaid kilt and dark navy blazer opened the door for him. "Morning to ye, Mr. MacGreggor. Nice to see ye again."

"Good morning, Callum. Is Mr. Robertson here?"

"Aye. He said I should send ye up straightaway. However, the stairs are blocked off. A section of the ceiling fell down during the night. It should take a good part of the hour to clear. I have received special permission for ye to use the Royals elevator."

"Thanks." Duncan had been in Edinburgh long

enough to realize that getting permission had not been easy. He appreciated Callum's effort. But the Scots were like that. Duncan had felt right at home the moment he'd arrived.

He followed Callum over to a room that had been converted into an elevator. It was like that in these old buildings. Small rooms and closets were often transformed into bathrooms or elevators.

Callum pressed a button on the panel by the door. The sound of grinding metal screeched through the room as the doors opened. Callum shook his head. " 'Tis been screeching like an Irish banshee of late. Nothing to worry about, though. It will get you where ye need to go."

Duncan stepped past him into the dark paneled interior.

Callum held the doors open.

Duncan leaned his sword against the back wall. "What are you waiting for, Callum?"

"There be someone else I'm expecting." He paused and glanced toward the entrance to the palace. "Aye, there she be." A smile spread across Callum's face. "And a good morning to ye, Kathleen MacKenzie."

Her face was flushed from running and her hair had pulled free of the tight ponytail she always wore. If possible, she looked even lovelier than when he'd seen her in the bakery.

She paused and handed a sprig of heather to Callum. "Harriet asked me to give it to ye."

The man held it up to his nose. "Aye, the sweetest fragrance in all the world." He smiled. "Kathleen, have ye met Duncan MacGreggor? He has traveled a great distance. All the way from America."

She nodded. "Not formally, but he is the real reason I am here."

Kathleen rushed past Callum, stepped into the elevator, and held out Duncan's wallet. "You forgot this."

He smiled. "Thanks. Must have too much on my mind." His fingers touched her hand as he reached for his wallet. Time seemed to hold its place as he looked into her deep green eyes. Her mouth parted in a smile that stole his breath away.

Over the erratic beat of his heart he heard the elevator doors slam into place. The room lurched. Instead of moving upward, Duncan had the sensation the elevator was moving toward the basement, if the Palace of Holyroodhouse had such a thing.

The lights flickered and the elevator picked up speed. Duncan braced himself against the wall. "What's going on?"

His sword clattered to the ground. Kathleen lost her balance and pitched forward. He reached for her and held her against him. The elevator increased its speed once more. Duncan had the sensation of falling and rolled so that he would cushion Kathleen's fall.

Two

The elevator came to an abrupt stop. The lights were out, and Kathleen lay on top of him. If he was dreaming, he didn't want to wake up. Her body was pressed against his and her hair smelled like a meadow after a spring rain. He could feel her breasts against his chest through the layers of clothing they wore.

Duncan swallowed and put his hand on the small of her back. He had wanted her from the first moment she'd smiled at him at the bakery shop two weeks ago. She'd asked if he wanted a cup of coffee. He'd never acquired a taste for the beverage, but on that day he'd gladly have drunk the whole pot by himself.

He felt the steady rise and fall of her chest against his. She was so close her warm breath caressed his face. He wanted to kiss her and felt the pull between them like an invisible thread. He rose slightly and brushed his lips against her mouth.

The feather-soft touch jolted him. It was as though he were experiencing his first kiss all over again. He felt her body mold against the length of him, felt her lips part. The kiss deepened.

She abruptly pulled away from him. "I dinna know why I . . ." She took a breath of air and let it out slowly. "Do ye believe the danger has past?"

He rolled to a sitting position and wanted to tell her that he was afraid it had just begun.

Loud shouts broke through the silence and screams rippled through the air.

Kathleen scrambled to her feet. "What was that sound?"

He stood. Glad to refocus his thoughts. "Maybe someone's seen a ghost. Is Holyroodhouse haunted?"

"Aye. There are spirits aplenty. But I fear 'tis something else."

The noise was coming from beyond the elevator doors. Angry shouts mingled with a woman's cry for mercy.

Kathleen's voice sounded urgent. "Someone should help the poor woman."

A dark foreboding wove through Duncan. It was one thing to have an elevator malfunction, but when you added loss of electricity and combined it with a woman's screams, something just didn't feel right.

He remembered arriving in Heathrow two weeks ago only to learn that one of the express trains to London was being searched for a bomb. He combed his fingers through his hair. "Maybe the palace is under attack?"

Kathleen made a humph sound. " 'Tis impossible. The palace is one of the Queen's summer residences. The security is excellent. Besides, this is only the month of May and the Royals are not due in Edinburgh until July. Are ye suggesting the terrorists will take up residence until they arrive?"

"Good point. But how do you explain the elevator and the screams?"

Her voice lowered. "I cannot."

The plunge of the elevator had disoriented him; he didn't know which way he was facing or where the control panel was located. "We have to find a way out. We'll start in opposite directions and work our way around."

The darkness was so complete he couldn't make out her form or the outline of the interior of the elevator. What bothered him was that if light couldn't seep into the room, chances were that neither could air.

Kathleen raised her voice. "I believe I've found the doors."

Duncan crossed over to her. It didn't take long in the small space. He was behind her, his chest against her back. He felt her turn her head toward him. Survival should be his number one priority, but pulling her against him and kissing her was gaining ground. He opted for sanity. They wouldn't last long in these small quarters without air.

Duncan extended his arm toward the wall. His hand touched hers and together they followed the outline of the doors until he felt the separation between the panels. They worked well as a team. He hadn't had to tell her what to do; she'd just sensed it.

He put his fingers alongside the seam. He worked out in a gym and lifted weights but wondered if his strength would be enough to open the doors. He braced himself and pulled the panels in opposite directions. The door burst open. He stepped back. That wasn't right. He didn't have time to dwell on the dilemma, as the image that greeted him seemed to steal the breath from his lungs.

The dark paneled room was lit by candles in silver chandeliers. Three women clung to each other on a cushioned bench that was draped with red and gold velvet. He followed their gaze. A half dozen men were stabbing a lifeless body that was slung over a table. Blood flowed to the floor and pooled around shattered dishes and discarded food. He whispered, "Holy, shit." He felt Kathleen tremble beside him.

She swallowed. "This cannot be happening. The reenactment looks so real. Do ye see how they are dressed? They wear clothes that date to around the sixteenth century."

He sensed she didn't believe this was a reenactment any more than he did. Duncan hastily unwrapped the sword he had brought as a gift for Mr. Robertson. It was meant to soften the blow of the man's losing his company in a merger. Now there would be blood on it.

He tightened his grip on the hilt of the blade. "I don't know what this is, but it's not like any reenactment I've ever seen. The blood looks real. Stay here."

There were at least a hundred reasons why he should heed his own advice. He knew he wouldn't listen to any one of them. Someone was in trouble and that's all he needed to know for him to risk life and limb.

Duncan raced toward the center of the room. He grabbed a man by the shoulder, just as he was about to stab his victim again. Duncan doubled his fist and hit him in the jaw. The man slumped to the wood floor. Somewhere in the back of Duncan's mind it registered how many men he was up against. It didn't matter. Once again he'd taken action before he'd thought it through. The men who remained, paused. Good, he had their attention.

A man dressed in a short dark coat and leggings stuffed his bloody knife into his belt. "I shall teach ye not to interfere in what is not your concern." The man drew his sword and lunged toward him.

Duncan blocked the man's attack with his blade. The sound of steel on steel rang through his ears. The contact of his weapon vibrated through his arms. This was real. It was not some strange reenactment. He fought to hold on, to defend his position. He pushed the improbability of the situation out of his mind. He had to keep his mind clear.

He heard Kathleen scream out his name.

One of the others had joined his comrade and swung his blade toward Duncan. He sidestepped out of the way.

He heard loud voices and the clatter of footsteps in the corridor outside. The men he fought drew back and motioned to the others. They stumbled over each other and fled down a narrow staircase at the opposite end of the room.

Silence wove around him as he sheathed his sword and bent down beside the bloodied man. He felt for a pulse. There was none.

The tallest of the women rushed over to the dead man. She wore a long gold dress with ropes of pearls wrapped around her neck. And she was very pregnant. The other two women stood behind her, wringing their hands and sobbing. The pregnant woman held the dead man to her breast as tears streamed down her cheeks. His blood soaked her dress and pooled on the dark wood floor.

Duncan fought back the bile that rose to his throat. The man had been brutally murdered. Nothing was making any sense. He straightened. Kathleen? Where was she?

He turned and saw her standing at the entrance to what moments before had been the elevator. Her face was as white as chalk. She was looking at the inside of the small room.

Duncan walked over to her and reached for her hands. "We need to get out of here."

She gripped his arm. "Something very odd is going on here. I cannot explain it." Her voice lowered. "The markings on these walls are different. Familiar somehow. And there is more." Her words tumbled out in a rush. "I recognize some of these people from the pictures that hang in a gallery at the palace. It sounds crazy, but I think we just witnessed the murder of Riccio. He was a friend of Mary, Queen of Scots. Mary's husband, Lord Darnley, was jealous of Riccio's friendship with the Queen. Darnley and his friends killed Riccio in front of her."

"You're right. That does sound nuts. Now, let's get out of here."

Men, dressed in dark-green-and-blue kilts, burst into the room. They rushed in and surrounded Duncan, pointing their swords at his chest.

A man with a flaming red beard growled out his words. "Who be ye?"

The brogue was thicker than anything Duncan had heard during his brief stay in Edinburgh.

The woman on the ground raised her chin. "Lord Hepburn, do not treat him thus. He has saved us. Do not waste your time questioning him; it is the others I will see punished." She pulled the murdered Riccio closer to her. "I know who is behind this treacherous act, and he will pay."

Lord Hepburn bowed low. "Aye, Your Majesty." He offered his hand and helped her to her feet. He turned to Duncan. "I still would know how it is you were in the private quarters of Her Majesty the Queen."

Kathleen touched Duncan's arm as though to keep him from answering the question.

She curtsied and bowed low. Her Scottish brogue was more pronounced than usual. "We were lost, my lord."

Duncan turned to her. "We weren't . . ."

She interrupted him and motioned for him to bow as well. "Aye, husband, we were indeed lost. And for that, we beg Her Majesty's pardon."

Duncan arched his eyebrow. "What are you talking about?"

Kathleen ignored him and turned to Lord Hepburn. "We are the new cooks. We must have taken a wrong turn along the way."

Lord Hepburn sheathed his sword. "I do not remember the hiring of new staff?"

Queen Mary rested her hand on her belly. "You are too suspicious, Lord Hepburn."

He bowed to her. " 'Tis only that I put your welfare above all else."

A smile flickered across the woman's face. "And for that you have our trust. Now see that these two have a warm place to sleep and clothes to wear. The garments they wear are unsuitable. The west wing has chambers aplenty. The hour is late. Tomorrow would be time enough to acquaint them with the cookroom."

"Aye, Your Majesty. It will be as you wish."

The Queen raised her chin and headed slowly to an adjacent room. Her two women bowed their heads and followed her. When they had disappeared from sight, Lord Hepburn turned toward them.

"The Queen may believe your story, but I do not. Nevertheless, I shall do as she wishes. But know this: I will be watching you." He motioned for them to follow him down a torchlit corridor.

Duncan gripped his sword with one hand and put his other around Kathleen's waist. He leaned toward her. "What's going on?"

She lowered her voice. "We must wait until we are alone."

He pulled her closer against him. He realized that he must feel exactly as Alice must have felt in Wonderland after she slid down the rabbit hole.

Kathleen shuddered as Lord Hepburn opened the door to a cold, dark room and shoved her and Duncan inside.

The man walked over to the hearth, threw a log on the embers, and coaxed the dying fire to life. A bed hugged the far corner, and there was a large table with a ceramic pitcher of water and a large bowl.

Lord Hepburn growled out his words. "This be your sleeping quarters."

Kathleen watched as Duncan walked over to the bed and tested it. He lifted the mattress and blankets. A latticework of rope served as the springs for the crunchy mattress. He looked toward Lord Hepburn and smiled. "Comfy."

Lord Hepburn growled low and left the room. The door slammed shut behind him.

Kathleen stood statue still. "Ye should not provoke him."

He put his sword on the bed. "Sorry, force of habit."

Kathleen clenched her hands in a fist at her side. "Well, please make an effort. If it has escaped your attention, we are not in Kansas anymore."

He laughed. "Actually, I was comparing this to *Alice in Wonderland,* but I could live with *The Wizard of Oz.* "

She refused to smile at his joke. This was serious. "How is it that ye can remain so calm?"

He shrugged. "I'm more the explode on impact, rather than the slow-burn type."

"That would explain your trying to save Riccio." Despite how infuriating it was that he was not rattled about their predicament, his calm behavior was indeed helping her.

"This canna be happening to us. I was only going to be gone for a few moments. I left Harriet to mind the shop. She must wonder where I am."

"Actually, I was thinking the same thing myself. Any ideas?"

She crossed her arms over her chest. "Ye really donna have any idea about where we are, do ye?"

"In the twilight zone?"

She nodded. "Very close." His attempt at humor lightened the dark clouds that had threatened to smother her the moment she realized what had happened to them. The only way to tell him was to use the direct approach.

She straightened. "One summer I worked at the palace conducting tours. The time period around the reign of Mary, Queen of Scots, was the most popular. I learned many things that were not in my history books, such as her favorite foods and that Lord Hepburn was in love with her. However, it was a dangerous time for a woman, even a queen." Kathleen paused. "Duncan, we have traveled back in time to where a woman's place is tenuous at best. That is why I told them we were married."

He walked over and pulled her into his embrace. "You did the right thing."

Kathleen pulled away and looked into his eyes. They reflected hidden strength and tenderness. His arms felt warm around her and made her feel less afraid. She remembered his kiss. And wanting it to go on forever.

She smiled. "Ye believe me, then?"

He scrunched up his eyebrow. "Not really. Time travel is something that happens only in theory or in a science fiction movie."

"Then, how, sir, would ye explain our presence in this world?"

He nodded slowly. "Good point. Any ideas how to find our way back?"

"Not a one."

The fire crackled and spit a small piece of wood onto

the stone hearth. It flared a bright gold before going out. Duncan stared at it and then walked over and picked it up. He knelt down and tossed it in the fire. "One of the first games I ever created involved a character by the name of Sabaston who was trapped in an alternate universe. It was a simple premise. Fire would burn the walls that separated him from his world. The fire was on the first level and the wall on the tenth. Sabaston had to place the fire in a container and bring it to the tenth floor."

Kathleen took a deep breath. "That sounds simple enough." She wondered why he was telling her about a game when their lives had been turned upside down. "Continue."

He tossed a log on the fire. "Anyway, each level was designed to extinguish the fire if he hadn't selected the right container for the fire." Duncan reached for an iron poker that was beside the hearth and stirred the embers. "I've got to believe some sort of logical mechanisms got us here. All we have to do is find the key. Sort of like the problem faced by Sabaston."

Duncan stood and dusted off his hands. He glanced toward the window and combed his fingers through his hair. "If things weren't weird enough already, we seem to have lost most of the day as well. It's dark out. We'll get a good night's sleep and tackle the problem in the morning. I'll sleep on the floor."

Kathleen took a deep breath. "Do not be silly. We will share the bed."

He arched his eyebrow. "Are you sure?"

She nodded, anxious as well to change the subject. "Are there people who will miss ye when ye donna return?"

He brushed a strand of hair off her face. He grinned.

"My stockholders. The price of the shares of my company will take a beating if I turn up missing."

Kathleen couldn't believe that the value of his stocks was the only thing that the people he knew would worry about. She ignored the way her heart warmed as she remembered Duncan fighting to help the man who was attacked. She had almost expected him to don a suit of shimmering armor. At that moment she realized what she had tried to ignore and what Harriet had guessed. She was attracted to the American and, damn his deep brown eyes, it was getting worse.

She cleared her throat. "Why donna ye tell me how it is that ye know how to wield a sword?"

Duncan shrugged. "I learned how in those reenactment-type festivals they have where I live. It was more fun than school."

"What was wrong with school?"

"Boring. I tried computer games, but they weren't interactive enough for me. College was better. I picked the classes where all the professors cared about was the final exam. Your turn. Tell me about you."

"There is not much to tell. I attended the University of Edinburgh and took over the bakery shop when my mother died."

"Ever want to do anything else?"

"Ye mean like climb Mount Everest, or bunge-jump from an airplane?"

"I'm serious."

"So am I. I want to do all of it, but first I have bills to pay."

Duncan pulled off his coat and dropped it on the floor. He flopped down on the bed.

"Are ye going to leave your coat on the floor?"

"Sure, why not?" He closed his eyes and laced his fingers together over his chest.

She liked the way his T-shirt stretched across his well-defined chest. He opened his eyes, and she realized he had asked her a question she had not answered.

Kathleen cleared her throat. She needed to find something to talk about to clear her head and calm her breathing, even if it sounded silly. "If we are to live here together, even for a short time, we should at least set some boundaries. I do not want to be stumbling over your clothes every time I walk into the room."

He grinned. "I was never very good in the neatness department, but I have a feeling that you are. Let me guess, color-coded hangers."

The fire crackled cheerily in the hearth and gave off a warm glow. And seeing him on the bed was doing terrible things to her imagination. She kept trying to imagine how it would feel to lie next to him. It had been her idea to share the bed. He looked as though he had all the willpower in the world.

"And what is so terrible about wanting to live an orderly life? It might do ye some good." She knew the words came out harsh, but she couldn't help it.

He shook his head. "Me. What's wrong with me? You're the one who probably writes out a schedule before you start the day."

Kathleen tapped her foot on the floor to keep from blurting out that she did not make a list at the beginning of the day, but the night before. There was a big difference.

"I will not let ye make me feel guilty about being

organized. It is because of that skill that my bakery is so successful."

He rolled to a sitting position and sat on the side of the bed. "You're right. Having organizational skills in business is important. That is why I hire people like you to do that for me."

"What do ye mean, 'people like me'?"

"You know, organized, cautious, methodical."

"If the next word out of your mouth is 'boring,' I shall run ye through with your own sword. Besides, I know about men such as ye. Risk takers, reckless. Ye probably are the type who would leap off a cliff before checking to see if there was water to cushion your fall."

He kept grinning at her. Her heart beat so loud she thought for sure he must hear it. The fire in the hearth was blazing, and the room was warm, too warm. She looked over at him. He sat on the bed so calmly, yet she felt as though every nerve in her body were on fire.

He grinned. "You know more about me than I thought. Do you also know what side of the bed I like to sleep on?" Kathleen had been right. In fact, he thought he remembered jumping off a cliff in Hawaii and then being relieved to see a deep lagoon beneath him. That experience should have been a wake-up call. It wasn't. After all, he'd survived.

"We are not sleeping together."

He rubbed the back of his neck. "Okay, I'll take the floor."

"Don't be silly. We can roll the blankets and put them between us."

He looked at her and thought about saying a brick wall wouldn't be strong enough to keep him from thinking of her, but decided now was not the time. He needed to control himself. She was obviously annoyed with him. Of all the people to get stuck with, he was probably her last choice. The firelight made her skin glow. He swallowed. This was going to be the longest night of his life.

Three

Kathleen rested her hand on a man's warm chest and snuggled closer. She felt his heart beat against her fingers. Its rhythm matched the beat of her own. The bed was feather soft, and the blankets seemed to wrap protectively around her. This dream was so real. The fantasy was almost complete. She did not want to wake up.

It had not started out that way. She vaguely remembered dreaming of being transported in an elevator to the sixteenth century with the American. That was odd. She thought fantasies all took place on remote Caribbean islands. A vision of tanned bodies entwined on white sandy beaches and soft, fragrant breezes drifted into her thoughts.

The clatter of horses' hooves on cobblestones pulled her fully awake. Her pulse rate increased. A tapestry hung on the far wall, and light streamed in through the slats of the wood shutters over the window. It had not been a dream.

She raised herself up on her elbow. To make matters worse, if that were possible, she was lying next to Duncan MacGreggor.

Her heart felt as though it were slamming against her chest.

Duncan stretched in his sleep and reached for her. He pulled her next to him and nuzzled the base of her neck. Her pulse rate beat off the charts. She wanted to melt against him, feel his lips once more against her mouth.

She pushed against him. What was happening to her? She had never spent this much time thinking about a man before. It must be their circumstances. She had to focus. They had to find their way back to their own time. She had the unpleasant thought that getting off a deserted island would have been easier.

Kathleen shook him gently. "Duncan, please wake up." She raised her voice. "Duncan MacGreggor."

He stretched on his back, rubbed his eyes with the back of his hand, and opened them slowly. He glanced toward her, sucked in a deep breath, and pushed himself to a sitting position. "Who?" He rubbed his eyes again and looked around. His eyes widened. "Holy shit, it wasn't a dream."

She shook her head. "No, it was not. It is very real."

"Too bad. Parts of the dream were pleasant. Didn't want to wake up."

Kathleen felt uneasy at his comment. Had something happened last night that she had not remembered? "Duncan, what do ye mean?"

He reached over and cupped the side of her face with his hand. "Don't worry, nothing happened."

She sighed. She did not know if it was with relief or regret. "I thought we made a barrier between us last night."

He flung the covers off and swung his legs to the floor.

"We did, but with the fire out, this place was as icy as the North Sea. You were shivering and I was cold. I decided you wouldn't mind using the blankets to keep us from freezing to death." He grinned. "Did you know that your lips turn blue when you're cold?"

Kathleen smiled. "That is how my mother knew it was time for me to come inside. If it was cold, my lips would turn the color of a spring sky."

He looked over his shoulder and stared at her mouth. "Hmm, always did like the color blue."

Kathleen felt her heart do a somersault. She sensed he was just trying to make light of their situation with jokes. Somehow that knowledge was even better than the strange compliment.

He stood and muffled a curse. "This floor is like ice. I'll build a fire. I always think better when I'm warm. We need to find a way back. Perhaps the best thing to do is to try and explore the castle without drawing attention to ourselves."

He rubbed his arms, rushed over to the hearth, and blew on the dying embers. A puff of ash blew on his face.

Kathleen covered her mouth with her hand to stifle a laugh.

He turned slowly toward her and wiped the soot from his face. "It's not funny."

She chewed lightly on her lips to keep from telling him the obvious. She doubted he would appreciate her suggesting to him that he'd blown too hard. "Do ye need my help?"

He grinned. "All I can get."

She slid off the bed. Her toes curled when her feet touched the floor. Duncan was right. It felt like a sheet of ice beneath her feet. She hurried to the hearth and sank down beside him.

He ripped off a piece of the hem of his shirt and stuffed it near a glowing coal.

She leaned forward and blew gently on the dying embers. They glowed amber red. A spark ignited the cloth.

Duncan added dried twigs that lay beside the hearth and tore off another piece of his shirt.

The fire crackled to life.

He sat back on his heels. "We make a good team."

She nodded and followed his gaze. They did indeed. The little fire was licking around a chunk of wood and it was gaining strength. She reached out and put her hands toward the flames.

He stood and brushed off his hands on his jeans. "Could you tend the fire? I need to find whatever passes for a bathroom in this century. Will you be okay here for a while?"

She smiled. "I think I can handle it."

He smiled slowly. "I think you could handle just about anything. Most people, given our circumstance, would be gibbering idiots by now."

"If I did behave that way, ye would be left alone to try and figure out a way back to our own time."

"I like the way you think." His voice lowered. "Don't worry, we're going to get out of this."

His words made her believe anything was possible.

He reached out to her and then hesitated.

Duncan walked over to the door and opened it. A plump woman stood in the threshold. She wore a gathered red-and-yellow-plaid skirt and a crisp blouse, and carried a bundle of clothes.

Kathleen stood slowly. They had bluffed their way past Mary, Queen of Scots, and Lord Hepburn last night. This test would be more difficult. Kathleen guessed from the manner of clothes that the woman wore that she was a servant in the palace. The hardworking people of this century, or for any other for that matter, were very observant. Very little escaped their notice.

The woman curtsied to Duncan. "Good day to ye. Your wife, be she awake?"

"Yes, she is. Is there something wrong?"

The woman chuckled. "Nay, lad. I was instructed to ease ye and your wife into life at the palace."

"Okay, I guess it's all right." Duncan nodded and walked around the woman and down the corridor.

The woman walked in and deposited her bundle on the bed. "Name's Martha. That man of yours is mighty protective. Almost as though he would not let me pass. I like that quality in a man." She paused. "Strange manner of speech, if ye donna mind me saying. Where be he from?"

Kathleen was well aware of the thinly veiled third degree the Martha was putting her through. There might be a smile on the woman's face, but her intent was very serious. She wanted to find out about the strangers that literally popped into the Queen's chambers last night. Kathleen tried to guess a place the woman might not be aware of.

Kathleen blurted out the first exotic country she could think of and prayed the woman had never been there. "Egypt. My husband is from Egypt."

Martha shook her head slowly. "I have heard of the place, but I have not ventured out of Scotland. Egypt, I am told, is an odd place. Full of wondrous things. It is a distant land. No wonder your husband has an accent I do not recognize." She glanced around the room. "Ye have made a fine impression on Her Majesty, and she has given ye a grand chamber. I heard what your husband did. The castle is quite astir. Will ye still be wanting to serve in the cook-room, or are your sights a mite higher?"

Kathleen knew exactly what Martha was saying and what was at stake. But she and Duncan were alone in the sixteenth century and the last thing they needed was ene-mies. If Martha thought that she and Duncan were opportunist, word would spread. It would be safer to befriend Martha than count on the fickle approval of the Queen. Besides, Kathleen did not know how long they would be here. However, she did know that not long after Mary, Queen of Scots, gave birth to her son, she would find herself in the Tower of London. Yes, it was much safer to put in a hard day's work and keep a low profile until they could figure out a way back.

Kathleen stood. "I have no wish to be other than I am, a cook."

A broad smile spread across Martha's face. "Aye, 'tis good. We can use your help. The Queen and her men are a hungry lot." She motioned to the clothes on the bed. "I have brought ye something more suitable to wear. The dress you wear cannot keep ye very warm in this damp place."

"Thank ye. There is something else. Do you have . . . ?" Kathleen searched for the word for bathroom, but couldn't remember what it was called in this century. Kathleen started again. "I need to relieve myself."

Martha nodded. "Of course, the garderobe is right

beyond the tapestry. Ye are most fortunate to have one in this chamber."

Kathleen smiled to herself. Duncan was searching for the bathroom and it was right here all along. She walked over to the wall Martha had indicated and spread the tapestry aside. She held her breath, afraid to breathe too deeply.

The "garderobe" was basically a hole in a raised platform in the middle of the alcove. Intellectually she knew indoor plumbing was still in the experimental stages in sixteenth-century Europe. Some castles and manor houses were better equipped than others, depending on how well-traveled their architects. Obviously, the guy who designed this room went in for the basics.

She listened as Martha chatted on and on about how wonderful the garderobe was, and how lucky Kathleen and Duncan were that it was in their chamber. If Kathleen ever made it back to her own time, she would never complain again about the size of her own small bathroom. Or, for that matter, that the water pressure in the shower was unpredictable. The closest she would come to duplicating a shower in this century would be if someone stood over her and dumped a bucket of water over her head. An image of Duncan doing just that caused her face to flush. She busied herself with fixing her hair in a long, single braid. She could not understand what had come over her. When it came to thoughts of Duncan, her imagination was running amok.

Kathleen straightened her skirts and tried to take a deep breath. She was cinched into a tight-fitting bodice contraption. But she counted her blessings. One advantage of not being one of the privileged nobility was that she did not have to wear a corset. This was tight enough.

She hurried to keep up with Martha. "Do ye know what is keeping Duncan?"

"Aye, Lord Hepburn requested an audience."

Kathleen did not think that was such a good idea. She had not had a chance to tell Duncan about the history of this time period. She hoped he would be all right.

She followed Martha down a torchlit corridor and through the rooms used by the Queen to entertain visiting dignitaries. Kathleen smiled to herself. This was the same route used by the tour guides when they escorted the tourists. She wished she had paid more attention to the placement of the furniture when she was a tour guide herself. Regardless, there were obvious differences. The furniture gleamed as though it were brand-new. The colors of the tapestries that hung from the walls were vibrant; their images seemed to spring to life as she passed them. She glanced out the window. The gardens looked very similar to the way they would look in her time.

She paused. Duncan was down there. He was talking to Lord Hepburn.

Martha reached for her arm and pulled her forward. "Come away, lass. There is much to be done."

Kathleen pointed toward the window. "Do ye have any idea what Lord Hepburn can be saying to my . . . husband?"

"Nay, but ye can be glad that ye are married and to a lad who, as evident by the way he fought last night against Riccio's murderers, is skilled with a sword." She whispered, "'Tis well-known that Lord Hepburn is bold, particularly when it comes to the ladies of the court. Of late, however, he has been most attentive to the Queen." Martha tugged on her arm. "Do not concern yourself. Perhaps Lord Hepburn has asked your husband to join the guard. 'Twould be an honor."

Kathleen looked over her shoulder. Duncan and Lord Hepburn had disappeared from sight. She must warn Duncan not to get involved any more than he had to. Because he was an American, she didn't know how much he knew about English and Scottish history.

She followed Martha down a flight of stairs. It opened into the cookroom, which was alive with activity. The walls and brick ovens were whitewashed, and the air was warm and mixed with the aroma of baking bread. A boy of about ten or eleven sat by the hearth. He slowly turned the iron spit of a roasting pig. Fat hissed as it dropped onto the flames. Dried ropes of garlic hung from the oak beams, along with clumps of dill and rosemary.

Martha motioned toward a long table that was covered with flour. "Our Queen has a love for sweets. She also wishes variety. I think it has increased since she has grown large with child. She is always speaking about how fine the food is in France. I believe she misses her life there, and the Perhaps you can make a sweet to please her."

Kathleen rolled up her sleeves. She felt right at home. There might be a time difference of over four hundred years, but the ingredients that went into making mouthwatering desserts were still the same. Besides, Kathleen already knew the Queen's favorite dessert. Kathleen looked around. She needed to search the pantries to see if the necessary ingredients were available. Perfect. She reached for flour, sugar, and a bowl and returned to the table, working the ingredients into a dough.

The door slammed open. Duncan, dressed in a red-and-black kilt, walked into the room carrying a load of wood. Activity seemed to come to a crashing halt as everyone paused to look in his direction.

Martha leaned toward her and whispered. "Well, I'll be. I thought for sure your husband would be out prancing around with Hepburn's guards instead of doing chores." She winked. "Although, I am not complaining. I have never seen a man wear the plaid so well."

Kathleen leaned against the table. Her legs felt like overcooked spaghetti. Living in Scotland, she saw men dressed like that every day. It must be the heat in the cookroom. She pushed away from the table and decided she'd better keep herself busy.

She cut off a slice of warm bread and ignored the stares as she walked over to Duncan. He appeared oblivious to all the attention his entrance had caused. She handed the bread to him.

He set the wood down, reached for the bread, and took a big bite. "It's very good. Is this your doing?"

She shook her head. "Martha made it this morning. She has put me in charge of desserts."

He smiled. "Good choice."

She warmed and then felt like a schoolgirl with her first crush. She cleared her throat. "Who gave you the plaid?"

He leaned closer to her, and for a moment she forgot to breathe.

Duncan leaned against the wall. "Lord Hepburn gave it to me. It was a good thing I'd taken part in medieval reenactments as a teenager. Otherwise, I'd never have known how to wear the fabric like a kilt." Duncan straightened and adjusted the plaid around his waist. "The blasted thing is scratchy without anything on underneath. And to make things worse, it took Hepburn a devil of a long time to find boots large enough for my feet."

She felt her face warm and was thankful she could blame it on the nearby oven. Kathleen remembered an old wives' tale that compared the size of a man's feet to his . . . She swallowed and tried to think of something else.

Returning to their own time should be a subject complicated enough to distract her. It was one thing to fantasize about being stranded with a man that looked as delicious as Duncan and another to have him here in the flesh. But she was also a realist. The sixteenth century was a dangerous time even if you belonged here and knew the rules. However, for them it was life-threatening.

Kathleen put her hand on the wall for support. She felt as though the floor of the cookroom were spinning.

Duncan interrupted her thoughts. "Are you okay?"

She nodded. "We need to figure out how to get back home. It's not safe for us here."

"You got that right. Hepburn is suspicious of my accent. He mumbled something about what the Scots do to English spies." He shuddered. "Not pleasant."

The door creaked open, spilling sunlight into the cookroom. Two more servant girls came in and started work on peeling apples for a pie. It was getting too crowded. Kathleen did not want to be overheard.

She motioned for him to follow her to the other side of the oven. "Martha was surprised you were not with Lord Hepburn and the rest of the Queen's guard."

Duncan finished his bread and began stacking the wood beside the brick oven. "He asked, but I declined. I thought I'd learn more if I was able to move around doing odd jobs rather than under Hepburn's watchful eye." Duncan grinned. "I don't believe he's in the habit of hearing the word *no*. I think he was annoyed." He shrugged. "But I have that effect on people."

"So, ye have said." She wanted to add that he had never annoyed her.

The buzz of conversation died down. Kathleen suspected the servants had overheard Lord Hepburn's name and were curious about what she and Duncan were discussing.

She touched Duncan's arm. "Maybe we should talk later." She paused. "Please try and stay out of his way. Lord Hepburn is a powerful enemy."

Duncan tucked a strand of hair behind her ear. She shivered, despite the warmth of the cookroom, and fought the impulse to lean closer to him.

He smiled. "I'll take your word on Hepburn's influence. You're the expert here. But you'd better know something about me, staying out of trouble was never my strong suit. My dad used to say the reason I started my own business was because I had a problem with authority."

Kathleen had a sudden image of a boy of about twelve sitting waiting outside the principal's office. She wished she had known him then. She smiled. "Was your father right?"

He nodded. "Pretty much. I'm sure I gave him some uneasy moments. He raised me after my mom died of cancer."

Kathleen heard the loneliness in the tone of his voice. She knew how it felt to lose someone you loved. She reached for his hand. "I'm sorry."

He squeezed her fingers lightly. "Thank you."

Pots and pans clattered to the floor and the sound combined with that of Martha scolding one of the women for careless behavior. Kathleen turned to Duncan. "I had better get back to work."

"Okay, I'll see you later tonight."

Duncan turned and wove his way around the table and people bustling around the cookroom. She smiled to herself. Kathleen had been a model student and had never strayed outside the lines of authority. Once a teacher had written in Kathleen's high school annual that she should do something adventurous over the holiday. Kathleen had to ask her mother for suggestions on what to do that would fit that suggestion. However, she was getting an image of Duncan as a young man. It must have been hard without a mother's gentle hand. Maybe that was why he was a regular outside the principal's office.

Kathleen saw Duncan pause and smile at the boy who was turning the roasting pig on a spit over the fire. Duncan bent down and whispered something to the young man. Duncan then stood and walked to the door. He turned toward her and waved before disappearing up the stairs that led to the courtyard.

She waited until the door had closed behind him before walking back to the pantry. She tried to remember what she had been doing before he came in, but her mind had turned to mush. It came to her. She was going to make a dessert for the Queen.

Martha walked over to her with a platter of dried

salmon. She set it down and motioned to the boy by the hearth. "Your husband has made quite an impression on my grandson. Most treat him as though he were a fly on the wall. Duncan will make a fine father someday. Ye are most fortunate."

Kathleen stuffed her hands into a bowl of sticky dough and plopped it onto the flour-coated table. She kneaded and punched the dough.

"What troubles ye, lass?"

Kathleen punched it again and tried to keep her thoughts from Duncan's scratchy plaid. She shook her head. "I am fine, Martha. I just want to make sure I don't make any mistakes."

Martha patted her on the shoulder. "Do not worry, lass. As long as your dessert is sweet, the Queen will take a fancy to it."

Kathleen nodded and rolled the dough into a thin sheet. She had not been talking about desserts.

Four

The whitewashed brick ovens warmed the cookroom, and the candles on the ledge over the hearth cast flickering shadows upon the walls. Evening settled in as Kathleen braided the last loaf of dough. Martha hummed as she finished drying the platters and stacking them away in a wood cupboard.

The meal had been a great success. The Queen had announced that she had never tasted desserts so grand.

Kathleen smiled, knowing the secret ingredient had been the chocolate packaged in an elegantly ornate chest, she had found stashed in the pantry.

Martha dried her hands on her apron, and Kathleen saw her glance toward the window. She gasped and motioned for Kathleen to join her.

The old woman pointed toward the courtyard. " 'Tis my grandson, Jeremy, and your husband."

Kathleen peered out the window. Beneath the light of a wall-mounted torch, Duncan sat on a stone bench. The boy from the cookroom was perched on his knee. Jeremy's eyes grew wide as Duncan spread broad strokes over a piece of parchment paper. Even from this distance Kathleen could tell that Duncan was drawing a horse.

Jeremy laughed as Duncan handed him the piece of charcoal and gestured to the page. It looked as though Duncan was teaching the boy how to draw.

Martha drew back from the window and wiped her eyes with a corner of her apron. " 'Tis the first time I have heard my grandson laugh out loud since his mother's death. 'Tis been hard for him."

Kathleen watched as Jeremy bent over the parchment and tried to duplicate Duncan's drawing. She smiled. She doubted Duncan's stockholders were aware of this side of his character.

Martha sniffled and patted Kathleen's hand. "Keep that husband close to ye. There is much more to him than meets the eye."

"Aye, I am beginning to see that as well."

" 'Tis good ye do. There are times when we are so close we canna see the value." Martha tucked a strand of gray hair inside her cap and walked to the door. She paused and turned toward her. "Ye have done a fine job today; the Queen was well-pleased. See that ye are to bed early. We begin again tomorrow."

Kathleen nodded and walked to the long trestle table. She spread a damp cloth over the loaf of sweet bread she had braided. "There are a few more loaves to prepare for tomorrow. I will make sure the cookroom is clean before I leave."

Martha smiled. "Such a hard worker. Both ye and your husband are a good match. It was a blessing ye found the palace."

The older woman turned and disappeared up the stairs. Kathleen wondered if she suspected. That was ridiculous. It was hard for Kathleen to grasp what had happened and that she had lived through the experience.

Kathleen stretched her lower back. She was probably just tired. She was used to long hours in her own bakery, but at least there she had the luxury of setting the timer on the stove and having a cup of tea. In the sixteenth century, she could not quit until the last person was fed. And in a household this large, that could take all day.

She busied herself with braiding more of the sticky dough. Instead of a loaf shape, she designed a heart. She stepped back and smiled to herself. Hmm, not bad.

Footsteps echoed over the stone stairs. She looked toward the sound. It was Duncan.

She hastily scooped up the dough and formed it into a ball.

He smiled as he ducked under the low-hanging beam and walked toward her. "I was hoping I'd find you here."

She felt her heart beat faster in her chest. "I thought I'd get a head start on the morning meal for the Queen."

Duncan walked toward her and sat on the corner of the table. He pinched off a piece of the dough and plopped it in his mouth. "Not bad."

"It will be better when it is cooked."

He shrugged and reached over and snatched another piece. "I like it the way it is now."

Kathleen concentrated on dividing the dough into three sections. She braided the long strips. "That was kind of you to take an interest in the boy."

Duncan shrugged. "Actually, I did it to keep him out of trouble. While we were talking, it looked as though he was trying to slide the roasting pig off the spit and into the fire. If what I suspected was true, I think he figured that if the meat dropped into the fire, it would be ruined, and he would be out of a job. The reality was that he would've been discovered and punished."

"That was very observant." Kathleen pinched the ends of the long strips together. This time the shape of her loaf of sweet bread was not as imaginative as before.

"Thanks." He pinched off another piece of raw dough.

She slapped his hand away. "Ye should not eat it raw. 'Tis not good for ye."

He grinned and leaned forward. "I like living dangerously, or haven't you noticed?"

She set the loaf aside and reached for the remaining mound of dough in a nearby bowl. "But what I donna understand is why ye suspected the boy in the first place?"

"Because it's something I would've tried." He smiled. "And with the same outcome, might I add. Luckily a counselor discovered three things about me. One, that I was bored; two, that I liked computers; and three, that I could draw. I combined them all into a business. All it takes is someone to give you other options. That's what I was trying to show Jeremy."

"There are many who would not have gone to the effort."

"No one gave up on me. I just think I should repay the favor whenever I can."

Kathleen set the braided loaves on a wooden paddle. Without needing to be asked, Duncan opened the oven door. Warm air surrounded her as she slid her creations on the iron shelves. His arm brushed her shoulder as he closed the door. The contact sent shivers through her.

She had admitted she was attracted to him physically from the moment he had walked into her bakery. He seemed the perfect candidate for a fantasy: tall, dark, with well-defined muscles. But there was more to him than the physical appearance. Each time she uncovered a new layer of his personality, another one, even more interesting than the last, appeared. She discovered she wanted to know as much as she could about Duncan MacGreggor.

She turned toward him. "Why don't you tell me more about your business."

Duncan rubbed the back of his neck. Vision Quest had begun as an interactive, kid friendly, computer game program. However, it had evolved into a cutthroat corporation. He wished that he could instead tell her he'd saved the rain forest, or discovered the cure for cancer. In the past, he'd not cared what other people thought about what he did. But that was before he'd met Kathleen.

He walked over to the fire and threw a log on the flames. He stared at them until they blurred to a color of amber and blood red.

He dusted off his hands. He might as well tell her and see that look of disappointment in her eyes. It would probably be for the best. "I buy companies that are in financial difficulty. The merger always benefits my company, Vision Quest." He stood and blurted out the rest. "Our main focus is adding business. The majority of the time we don't take all the employees in the new company."

"Ye don't sound as though ye believe it is such a fine thing to do."

He looked toward her. She was not judging him, like so many others had. Kathleen was just asking him if that was what he wanted to do with his life. Wisps of hair had pulled loose from her braid and she had a smudge of flour on her nose. She looked delicious.

She smiled. "Perhaps 'tis none of my business."

Kathleen had a way of lighting up a room. The realization hit him that he wanted it to be her business. He had the overwhelming need to pull her into his arms and kiss her.

He shook his head to try and clear his thoughts. "There are parts of my business that are still exciting, or at least they used to be when I was creating and designing games. I don't like letting people go. But the truth is that I have to keep acquiring businesses to keep my company alive and vibrant. It used to be that I could inspire the programmers with new concepts for games. I've lost my touch. So the next best thing is to try and get as much raw talent as I can."

"If ye could come up with new ideas, ye would not need to always buy other companies, or try to hire away their programmers."

"Yup, that's it exactly." He leaned against the wall. "That's the problem. I can't think of any more ideas for games."

"It sounds a lot like 'writer's block.'"

He nodded. "That's a good way to put it. Another is that I've run out of ideas. I even thought that coming here, to the land that seemed to have invented the concept of legends, would help. So far, it hasn't."

She smiled. "I think ye are trying too hard. 'Tis similar to when I decide I need a new bakery item for my shop. The harder I try, the less I feel like cooking. I discover my best recipes when I am concentrating on something else. For example: You tasted one of my latest creations just a few days ago."

Duncan pushed away from the wall. He knew exactly what she was doing. She was trying to cheer him up, to give him encouragement. He'd been on the receiving end of advice all his life, long enough to recognize the tactic. He walked toward her. This time he didn't want to miss a word. He loved that she was making the effort. Most people didn't bother.

He looked at the smudge of flour on her nose. His fingers itched to wipe it off. He opted for conversation. "Which one of the scones was it?"

" 'Twas the one that was laced with cinnamon and dusted with powdered sugar."

He smiled. "It was great. I think I went back for seconds."

Her eyes crinkled up in a smile. "Thank ye, and yes, ye did. The idea came to me while I was pasting a bunch of old photos my mother had taken of me while I was playing in the snow. I was about three or four and had my head tilted toward the sky. My eyes were closed and my mouth was open. I was catching snowflakes. They looked scrumptious, like powdered sugar. It was then the idea for a new recipe came to me; the Cinnamon Snowflake Scone."

"You're amazing. I'll have to try your idea." He leaned toward her. "You also have a smudge of flour on your nose."

She smiled. "That happens a lot in my line of work." She reached up and wiped it off with the back of her hand. Instead of fixing the problem, the flour smudged across the side of her face. "Is that better?"

"Not yet, but it's getting there. Wait, I know what's the problem."

He smiled and grabbed a handful of flour and threw it into the air. It floated through the air like fine snow and settled in Kathleen's hair and on her shoulders.

She brushed off some of the flour. She laughed. "What are ye doing?"

"Trying to find a little inspiration." He shook his head. "Nope, nothing yet. I guess we need more flour."

"Ye are mad, Duncan MacGreggor."

He nodded. "Some people have called me worse."

She smiled. "Why should ye have all the fun?" She reached for a handful and flung it in his direction. He ducked, but not before a fine layer coated his hair.

His eyes widened. "So that's how it's going to be?" He grabbed another handful and dumped it on her head. He pulled her into his arms. "I always wanted to see if you tasted as good as your scones."

"I have a secret fantasy as well."

Kathleen suddenly put her hands on his shoulders and kissed him.

Her boldness pleased him. He leaned forward until their lips met. She tasted of flour and sugar and woman. Her mouth parted as he deepened the kiss. She molded against him.

She pulled away abruptly. "Do you smell something?"

His lips caressed her mouth. "Burning passion."

Kathleen pushed against him and rushed to the oven. "My bread."

She reached for a hand towel and opened the oven door. Smoke billowed out. "They are ruined."

"So is my ego."

"What are ye talking about?"

He shrugged. "If I was kissing you soundly enough, even the thought of being in the path of a runaway freight train shouldn't have distracted you, let alone smoking bread."

She looked over her shoulder. "I am ignoring ye. Please, hand me the wooden paddle. I must see what can be done."

"Actually, I think I would do better with a bucket of ice water." He handed the paddle to her.

She laughed and the loaves slid off the paddle onto the floor. One of them rolled under the table.

Duncan knelt down. "Found it." He grabbed it and dusted it off. "Good as new."

Kathleen slid the others on the table. "We canna use that one." She looked at the remaining loaves. "Well, they are not burned at all. Maybe it was something in the oven that was smoking."

He leaned forward. "Or maybe I was right in the first place and it was us that was on fire."

370

She smiled. "Do ye always have such a one-track mind?"

He put his hand over his heart. "It's one of my greatest virtues." He reached for her. "Now, where were we?" He pulled her toward him.

She pushed against him. "Duncan, someone will see us."

"It's the middle of the night."

"And that is the point. Martha arrives here early, very early. We have to clean up the cookroom before she arrives. 'Tis a mess."

He nodded and nuzzled her neck. She smelled so good.

She groaned. "Duncan, what about the cookroom?"

"You started the kissing thing, remember? I'm just trying to improve upon it."

She laughed and untangled herself from his arms. "We really have to clean."

He nodded and reached for a towel draped over a chair. "You're right. There's flour everywhere. Your clothes are covered with it." He brushed the front of her dress with the towel. His fingers lingered over her breasts. Her nipples hardened.

She raised her chin and kissed him. He felt as though someone had cranked up the heat in the cookroom.

Kathleen's voice was whisper soft against his lips. "Ye are covered as well."

She slowly wiped the remnants of flour off his face with the tips of her fingers. Then she brushed the flour from his shoulders, his shirt, the front of his plaid.

"Duncan."

He groaned. He loved hearing her say his name. "Yes, Kathleen."

"How fast do ye think we can clean up the cookroom?"

He grinned. "I'm prepared to set an all-time world's record."

Five

The cookroom was spotless. Kathleen watched Duncan lean the brooms against the wall. The remnants of the flour storm was completely swept away, except for the traces covering the two of them. She smiled. She remembered the complete abandon she had felt when she dumped the flour on his head, and the mischief reflected in his eyes. He made her feel like a desirable woman as well as a reckless spirit, all at the same time.

He walked toward her, and her heart forgot to beat. She felt happy just being around him.

"Duncan, I am impressed. Ye worked very hard and the cookroom sparkles." Kathleen felt him move closer to her and put his hand on the small of her back.

"Well enough for a reward?"

She laughed and let him guide her out of the cookroom and up the stairs that led to their chamber. Their moments together seemed like a golden enchantment. She had never felt as free to say or do whatever came to her mind as she did when she was with Duncan. He embraced life and viewed it as an adventure.

Today had been perfect. There were times she even forgot that she did not belong in this century, that neither of them did. She glanced over at him. His expression was lost in the shadows. She wondered what he was thinking. He had not mentioned if he had discovered a way for them to return to their own time. She knew she should want to go back, but when Duncan held her in his arms, she did not want anything to change. Not even the time.

As they reached the corridor, moonlight streamed through an open window and spread ribbons of light over the floor. It seemed to guide their path as Kathleen felt Duncan put his arm around her shoulders and pull her closer. Light wove gently around her as he turned her toward him. Flour dusted his face, remnants of their food fight.

She brushed his cheek with her hand and whispered, "Ye are still covered with flour."

His eyes reflected the moonlight as he leaned toward her. "So are you, but I have a weakness for anything that tastes like scones."

She smiled. "So, it was only my pastry that attracted ye to the bakery shop."

"Not exactly." He paused. "Kathleen, we haven't talked about returning."

Her voice was low. "I know. We should be trying to find a way home."

He nodded. "I was working on that problem today. I brought wood to the Queen's chamber. The Queen granted me special permission to be in her chambers because of how I tried to save her friend, Riccio. However, they consider me a servant, so they pretty much ignored me." He raised an eyebrow. "I was surprised how much it bothered me. I've never been ignored in my life. The teachers were always afraid I would do something when their backs were turned. My employees are another story. They think they have to hang on my every word."

Kathleen's life had taken a different path. She had a lot of time to be by herself. She did not think either path was enviable. She squeezed his hand. "What did ye learn in the Queen's chamber?"

He shook his head as though to clear his thoughts. "I went to the room where we arrived and looked around. The walls are covered in sections of dark wood paneling. In each section is a different family crest. Their details are carved and painted into the wood, but that was it. I couldn't find any kind of controls or levers. I think that means we're back to square one."

She did not know what effect their being here would have on history, and she did not want to be responsible for altering time. They did not belong here.

Katherine took a deep breath. "Do ye have any other ideas?"

Footsteps echoed over the wooden plank floor. Duncan straightened. "The guard is walking his rounds."

Duncan whispered. "I think I overheard that they like all the servants tucked in bed by this hour. This is a suspicious time. If someone isn't where they're supposed to be, all hell breaks loose. We'd better hide."

Duncan reached for her hand and pulled her behind one of the tapestries that was hanging on the wall. She was pressed against him and could feel the gentle rise and fall of his chest. She knew she should be disappointed he had not found a way to return. But she did not want to go home. Not yet.

She heard the footsteps gradually fade away, until all she could hear was the beat of her own heart. She peered around the tapestry. The guard was nowhere in sight. It was safe to leave.

She followed Duncan to their chamber and hurried inside.

The room was dark and ice cold. A single candle burned on the mantel. The fire had died down during the day, and only a few embers glowed in the hearth. The wood shutters were wide open, letting in the night air. Spring in Scotland could still be bitter cold.

Duncan hurried over and latched the shutters. He then turned his attention to the fire. Kathleen rubbed her hands together to warm them as she watched Duncan. He was hard at work to make their little room comfortable. She smiled to herself. Their chamber already had a welcoming feel to it that had nothing to do with the temperature. Her mother had once told her that when you were with the right person, a house became a home. She had never fully understood that concept, until now.

Kathleen walked over and searched for more candles in a cupboard beside the window. She had an idea that might just produce so much heat that a fire would not be necessary. She opened the door and reached for the candles that were stacked on a shelf. Grabbing a handful, she retraced her steps to the fire.

Duncan had succeeded in nursing the embers into roiling flames. The fire crackled in the hearth and already she could feel its warmth. Or was it Duncan's effect on her that made her feel warmer? She smiled. Well, she planned to make the fire higher.

She knelt down, lit the candles, and placed some of them on the mantel. She placed a few more on the table beside the bed as well as on the window ledge. Their light combined with the glow of the fire and cast a romantic golden haze over the chamber.

Kathleen slowly turned around in the room that was now filled with a fantasy of light, warmth, and magic. "'Tis beautiful."

Duncan stood and walked toward her. "Yes, more beautiful than anything I've ever seen." He gathered her in his arms and whispered her name. "Kathleen."

She closed her eyes. The sound of his voice vibrated through her in a loving caress. She remembered the first time he had come into her shop and ordered a cup of coffee. She had wondered what it would be like to be held by him, to feel his arms around her.

He cupped her face in his hands. "Kathleen, I want to make love to you. I know we haven't known each other long . . ."

She put her fingers over his lips. "I want the same thing."

Duncan drew her closer still. Her mouth parted and she felt a swirl of emotions as he pressed his mouth over hers. He deepened the kiss and picked her up in his arms as though she were as light as a breath of air. She wove her arms around his neck as he walked over to the bed.

He laid her down gently. She felt the urgency in his kiss as he pulled her against him.

He hesitated and then yanked his shirt over his head. Seams ripped, fabric tore, as he removed his shirt and threw it to the floor. The muscles in his chest and arms flexed as he moved toward her slowly, unaware of the mess he had made.

Kathleen laughed and tried to concentrate on his dark eyes and not the expanse of bare chest that glowed bronze in the candlelight. "Your shirt is ruined."

He grinned. "Never liked clothes much. How about you?"

She smiled and felt her pulse quicken. "I agree. Clothes are completely overrated."

He laughed and the deep sound warmed her. She was suddenly as anxious as he to rid herself of her clothes.

She sat on the edge of the bed and unfastened the sleeves of her gown. And then the outer shift. He placed a warm kiss on the swell of her breasts. Her fingers would not work properly. They fumbled at the ties. He kissed the base of her neck. She could not breathe. She had too many layers of clothes to go, far too many. She worked to untie her bodice. Duncan was not helping. He was distracting and making it harder for her to work.

He kissed the base of her throat, the mounds of her breasts, sending hot shivers through her veins. It was hard to breathe. The ribbons that laced her bodice were knotted too tightly. The harder she pulled the tighter they became.

"Wait, 'tis stuck."

He took a deep breath and smiled. "Every man's fantasy."

"Clever." She nibbled on her lip to keep from laughing and pushed against him.

He pretended to lose his balance as he fell to the floor on top of the pile of clothes. He unwrapped his tartan from around his waist and held out his arms toward her. "Join me. There's more room down here."

Lord help her, he was naked . . . and ready. She concentrated on untying the knot. Her fingers felt clumsy. Calm yourself. You have seen lots of naked men before. Well, maybe not lots of them, but what was the mystery? They all had the same body parts. She stole a glance at Duncan and felt her face warm. Well, maybe some parts were bigger than others.

She cleared her throat. "I canna get my bodice undone."

He knelt beside her. "Let me help." His fingers brushed against her breasts and lingered. Her breathing was ragged. Her heartbeat thundered in her ears. He leaned toward her and took the ribbons in his mouth. He broke the silken threads with his teeth.

She sighed. "Ye did it. I am undone."

He winked. "Not yet, but soon, very soon."

He helped her remove the bodice and lowered the linen strap of her shift over her shoulder. He kissed her bare skin. Her body warmed to his touch as she leaned toward him and caressed the nape of his neck.

Duncan pulled the linen shift slowly over her head. He sucked in his breath and whispered, "Wow. If I'm dreaming, I never want to wake up."

Flames curled around the wood in the hearth. Warm air pulsated from the fire, and waves of heat drifted toward her. She wanted this sweet fantasy to last a lifetime.

He kissed her, and she felt as though she were floating in warm currents of air. She had never felt this way before. No one had ever taken her to such heights.

He put his arm around her waist and gathered her against him. She drew in her breath as her bare skin touched his. His touch ignited the flame within her. She pulled herself against him. She could feel his hard muscles beneath her touch, feel him moan and whisper her name.

He groaned and covered her mouth with his. His movements were slow, gentle, as though the night would go on forever. She did not want it to end. As though he heard her thoughts, he slowed the urgency of his kisses even more. His touch was feather soft as he caressed her skin, her breasts, inflaming her body with ever increasing heat and desire.

The intensity of the fire spread through her. His lips felt hot against her mouth. She pressed herself closer to the flame.

His strength surrounded her, combining with her own. He entered her and time and place no longer existed. There was only one reality that was important, the one where they were together, forever.

Six

Kathleen sat on the edge of the bed. Her fingers trembled as she pulled the linen shift over her head. The fabric felt like fine silk against her skin. She shivered with pleasure, remembering Duncan's touch.

She glanced over her shoulder. He was sleeping soundly. His slow, even breathing seemed in stark contrast to her own. Instead of feeling sated after their lovemaking, she felt wide awake. She stood and walked to the window. A lone candle on the mantel lit her way and the fire warmed the chamber.

Kathleen felt a strong attraction to him. She crossed her arms over her waist. Everything was happening so fast. She glanced over at Duncan once again. He was "easy on the eye," as Harriet would say. At first that was what

Kathleen had convinced herself was the reason for the attraction. But what she was feeling was based on more than mere physical attraction.

She wanted to know everything about him. She enjoyed hearing about the type of boy he was growing up. She wanted to know if he had a favorite food or a favorite color. He was wonderful with Jeremy, but did he want children of his own? She paused at the windowsill and gripped the stone ledge. The fantasy had taken a dangerous turn. Maybe it would be easier if all she felt for him was blind lust.

She swallowed and opened the wooden shutters. It was clear, and a fine dusting of stars crowded the night sky. A spring breeze carried the fragrance of heather toward her. She welcomed the cool air against her skin. She needed to return soon or her heart would be lost forever.

Kathleen heard the soft pad of footsteps as Duncan approached. He put his hands on her shoulder and turned her toward him. "Can't you sleep?"

She shook her head. "I was thinking. Tomorrow we should try to find our way back. Ye told me about the character in the first game ye designed. What was his name?"

"Sabaston."

"Aye. Well, Sabaston needed to find something that would break through the barrier to his world. Maybe that is what we need as well."

He yawned and rubbed his eyes with the heel of his hand. "Sounds logical. I'd be willing to bet half of my company's assets that the answer is somewhere in that room where we arrived." He combed his hand through his hair. "But I think better when I'm awake. How about we tackle this problem in the morning?"

Kathleen nodded and forced a smile on her face as the reason for her wakefulness reappeared. She realizd that she cared for Duncan and returning to their own time might mean that she would lose him. If they were successful in returning, this enchanted moment in time would end and the monotony of her life would resume. Duncan would return to his life and she to hers. She needed to at least admit that that much would come to pass.

Perhaps she should stop dwelling on the downside and take a page out of Duncan's book. He lived for the moment. She would as well and enjoy whatever time they had left together.

She kissed him on the mouth and whispered, "Let us go back to sleep."

He smiled. "Actually, I'm not thinking about sleep anymore."

Duncan pressed his lips against hers and pulled her closer. She could feel his warm skin through the thin shift she wore. The fragrant air and the magic of the moment wove around her until her only thoughts were of the here and now.

Morning sunlight streamed through the open window. Kathleen stretched on the soft bed and glanced over at Duncan.

His dark eyes were open and he was grinning. He whispered, "You were talking in your sleep."

She laughed. "I was not."

He propped himself up on his elbow and shrugged. "It's okay. It was actually entertaining. But who's this Fred guy?"

Kathleen rolled over on her side to face him. The remnants of last night's concerns were locked safely away. Right now she felt warm and safe beside him. She could tell Duncan was teasing by the way his eyes flashed with mischief. It was easy to imagine how hard it had been for his parents and teachers to keep one step ahead of him. And all the while secretly enjoying the adventure, as she was now. She tugged on the hair on his bare chest. "I donna know a Fred. Ye are making it up, and I do not talk in my sleep."

He scrunched his eyebrows together. "Maybe you said John."

"Now, I know ye are teasing me. The two names do not even sound similar."

He reached for the long gold pendant that lay between her breasts. She tingled as his fingers touched her skin.

The smile faded from his face. "Kathleen, is there a Fred or John in your life?"

She reached over and kissed him lightly on the lips. "No, not really. I dated a little at the University of Edinburgh, but since my mother's death, and with running the bakery shop, I have not had the time."

He laid the pendant back in place and cupped the side of her face. "I know it sounds selfish, but I'm glad there's not some guy pacing the floor waiting for your return." His eyes crinkled up in a smile. "I might have to challenge him to a duel."

She laughed. "And what of ye? If ye talked in your sleep, what names would you call out?" She had kept her voice light, but the seconds seemed to last a lifetime as she waited for his response. She hoped there was not someone special.

"Your name is the one you'd hear." He kissed her and stretched out on the bed. "No one is waiting for me,

Kathleen. I was being truthful when I said the only people that would miss me were my stockholders. I think the women I've dated see a tattoo on my forehead that says, 'This man is unreliable.' "

She knew in her heart that once this man committed to someone, it was for all time. The feeling was so strong it sent a shiver through her. Kathleen brushed his hair off the place he had indicated. "The tattoo is not there now."

He kissed the palm of her hand. "I think you may be right. You have a strange effect on me, Kathleen MacKenzie." He kissed the tip of her nose. "Now, tell me about the pendant. It looks like a family heirloom. I want to know everything there is to know about you."

Kathleen reached for it. "Actually, it was given to me the day we traveled back in time."

Duncan arched an eyebrow. "Really, by who?"

"It was Harriet, the matchmaker."

"What?"

"Well, that is what a lot of the people in Edinburgh call her. It is as though she feels it is her duty to find everyone someone to love."

"Whoa, I didn't think people like that existed anymore." He laughed. "Some of the guys I know would never visit Scotland if they knew she was around. How good is she anyway?"

Kathleen paused and looked over at him. "Odd, you know I have never thought about that before. But every couple she has ever brought together is still as deliciously happy as the day they first realized they were in love."

Duncan reached for a strand of Kathleen's hair and tucked it behind her ear. "How long has she been doing this?"

She smiled, loving the feel of his touch against her skin. "I remember as a small child she would come into my mother's shop, sit down next to a young man or woman and rummage through her stack of pictures."

"You've mentioned your mom. What about your dad?"

"He died a few years before my mom. He was a pilot. On his way home he was caught in a storm and veered off course." She felt tears brim in her eyes. Whenever she thought of her father, he was laughing. He could find the sunshine in the gloomiest day. She took a deep breath. "His plane crashed in the North Sea."

Duncan wiped the tears from her cheek with his thumb. "I'm sorry. I wish I could have known him."

"So do I. I think ye would have liked him." She cleared her throat. "It was hard. Mom was never the same after that. I moved back home after I graduated from the University of Edinburgh. There are living quarters above the bakery shop. One day I found her slumped over in her chair by the window. The doctors said she had a heart attack. I think they were right. She missed my dad too much to go on without him."

Fresh tears spilled from her eyes. She brushed them away. "Oh, my. I donna know what came over me. I have never cried like that in front of someone before."

He pulled her toward him. "I'm glad it was me you chose. Do you want to talk about your parents?"

She shook her head. "Maybe at a later time."

He nodded. "I can wait. Tell me more about this matchmaker. She sounds like a character."

Kathleen wiped the tears from her eyes. "Harriet is the one who gave me the pendant ye asked about. It is a replica of a broach to commemorate the marriage of Lord

Darnley and Mary, Queen of Scots. When Harriet gave it to me, she also said that like the Darnley Jewel, everything in life has its match."

Duncan straightened. "Interesting. Don't you think it's strange that she gave you a replica of something that is connected to Mary and Darnley and, poof, we find ourselves in their time?"

Kathleen glanced over at him. "Aye, now that ye mention it. 'Tis strange indeed. The coincidence is too strong. That must be the connection. When a person finds their match, they no longer feel alone. Could it be that the Darnley Jewel needs something to make it complete?"

Duncan nodded. "Or be restored to its rightful place." He paused. "We need to find that jewel."

"Most likely it would be in the Queen's bedchamber. The place is well guarded. No one is allowed in her private quarters without permission."

A rooster crowed in the courtyard below the window. Kathleen flinched. "I had better hurry. Martha will be expecting me in the cookroom. I donna want her to suspect anything out of the ordinary. We should go about our business. Ye need to report to Lord Hepburn."

He nodded and kissed her. "I'd rather spend the day in bed with you, but I have a feeling that servants can't call in sick."

She laughed. "Ye learn quickly."

His expression grew serious. "The more I think about this Darnley Jewel, the more I think it may hold the key to our return. Tonight, when the palace is asleep, we'll sneak into the Queen's bedchamber."

"Ye must be joking."

"I'm dead serious."

385

Kathleen squeezed Duncan's hand. "Lord Hepburn is very protective of Mary. 'Tis not only that she is his queen. He secretly loves her. He was not pleased that we just appeared unannounced in her supper chamber. I donna know what he would do if he caught us in her bedroom. 'Tis too dangerous."

Duncan kissed her lightly. " 'Dangerous' is my middle name."

"Maybe ye should change it?"

He laughed. "Very funny."

"I am serious."

He smiled. "Don't worry. I've got everything under control."

Kathleen watched as he pulled his torn shirt over his head and adjusted the plaid around his waist. She knew his words were meant to calm her. They had only made her more concerned than ever.

"Perhaps we should go over the plan."

Duncan kissed behind her ear. "Later would be better. Right now I've more important things on my mind."

He pressed his lips against hers, and thoughts of the matchmaker and the pendant dissolved from her thoughts.

Seven

A silence had descended on the palace so complete that Kathleen believed she could hear Duncan's thoughts. She followed him down the shadow-draped corridor to the Queen's chambers and wondered if he still thought this was such a good idea to search for the Darnley Jewel. But it was the best lead they had. If it did in fact resemble the pendant Harriet had given her, the real jewel must be the key to sending them back to their own time.

However, if they were discovered, Lord Hepburn would not give them a chance to talk their way out of it this time. Of that fact she was certain. She paused. They had reached their destination.

Duncan lowered his voice. "Are you sure no one is on guard?"

Kathleen nodded. "They are with the Queen in the audience chamber. A dignitary from the court of Elizabeth has arrived."

He pushed on the door and it creaked open. "I wonder if we should warn her that her half-sister will one day imprison her in the Tower of London?"

"We can not interfere with history. Something about the events of time being immovable. At least that is the theory held by one of my professors at the University of Edinburgh."

He went over to the hearth, reached for a candle on the mantel, and lit it over the flames. Light spilled into the room.

"You're right. I think I heard the same thing. We probably couldn't change history if we wanted to."

Duncan's words were comforting. There were tragic events that she wished could be altered. But was not certain if doing so would change the world for the better or for the worse. Maybe people had built on past events and mistakes and were the better for it. She hoped so.

Kathleen glanced around. In the candlelight, the room seemed more enchantment than real. Rich tapestries, woven with gold threads, covered every inch of the walls, and red velvet curtains framed the Queen's bed. "This is beautiful. I have always dreamed of sleeping in this room, but it was roped off from the public and the fabric looked too fragile to touch."

Duncan walked over to her and kissed her on the lips. "I've got an idea." He reached for her hand. "Why don't we try the bed. We might not fall on the floor this time."

Kathleen smiled, remembering how enthusiastic their lovemaking had become last night. Indeed, they had landed on the floor in a tangle of arms and legs and laughter. "We must not. We do not have the time."

He arched his eyebrows. "I can do fast."

She put her hands on her hips. "Duncan, that is not what I meant."

"Okay, you're probably right. But you really should try to give in to your impulses once in a while." He kissed her on the tip of her nose. "There's a king-size bed in my room at the Balmoral. It will give us all the space we need." He winked. "And they have room service."

She forced a smile on her face. He seemed so certain that they would be together. However, she was convinced she would not fit easily into his world. He liked to go wherever the road would take him, while she did not like to travel without a road map.

Kathleen shook the dark foreboding from her thoughts and concentrated on the task at hand. She went over to the hand-carved dresser and started to search through the contents. Silk ribbons and undergarments were stuffed inside. Nothing else.

Duncan looked behind a tapestry. "Have you ever heard of a secret chamber in the Queen's room?"

"I am not sure. Do ye think that is where she keeps the Darnley Jewel?"

He shrugged. "If it's as valuable as you say, I'd sure hide it where I could look at it whenever I wanted. I'll keep looking for a secret room. Let me know if you find anything."

Kathleen went over to the wardrobe in one corner of the room and opened the door. Satin and velvet gowns hung in bright display. She felt along the shelf for a false bottom. Her fingers touched a knob. Excited, she pressed down harder. A door sprang open.

Blue velvet lined a drawer that was covered with earrings, bracelets and necklaces of every imaginable description. They sparkled in the candlelight. Rubies, diamonds, sapphires, and emeralds winked back at her. Everything a best-dressed queen in the sixteenth century could desire. Everything, that is, except the Darnley Jewel.

Disappointed, she shoved the drawer back into place. Where else could the Queen have put a pendant?

She glanced over at the Queen's bed. Would Mary keep an expensive piece of jewelry hidden under her mattress? Kathleen thought of the story of the princess and the pea and smiled. That was only a fairy tale. Anyway, it was worth a try.

"Duncan, I am going to look under the mattress. I could use some help."

He met her on the opposite side of the bed. Kathleen brushed her hand between the goose-feather mattress and the wood plank frame.

Duncan looked under the bed and sneezed. "Doesn't anyone dust in this century?"

Kathleen shushed him. "Be still. Someone will hear

ye." She smiled. "I think the answer to your question is no."

He stood. "I didn't find anything. How about you?"

She shook her head. "Nay, just dust bunnies."

He laughed. "I'll finish searching behind the tapestries."

Kathleen nodded and watched him walk to the far corner. Although he was keeping their conversation light and cheery, she sensed he was as worried as she that they would not find the Darnley Jewel.

She dusted off her hands on her apron and concentrated. There must be something they were overlooking. Her mother had liked to wear decorative pins but was always forgetting to remove them from her clothes. She would go to look for them in her jewelry box, and then remember they were still on a dress or jacket. Could the answer be that simple?

Maybe the Queen's ladies forgot to take her jewels off her gowns. It was unlikely, but worth investigating.

Kathleen walked back to the wardrobe closet and opened the doors again. She searched carefully through the gowns one by one.

Duncan emerged from behind one of the tapestries on the far wall and walked toward her. "Did you find anything yet? I found an alcove behind the tapestry near the window, probably used for eavesdropping. But no hidden passageway or place to hide stuff."

"I have not had much luck either." She paused as her fingers grazed metal. She looked closer. Multicolored jewels set in a gold broach twinkled in the candlelight. Kathleen removed it and held it up to the light. She pulled her pendant from around her neck to compare the two side by side.

Duncan whistled and shook his head. "Except for their size, they're identical. There has to be a connection."

She smiled. "I think ye are correct. I wonder how we are to use it."

"We'll figure that out later. Now let's get out of here."

Kathleen heard voices coming from the hallway. She quickly put her pendant over her head and held on to the Darnley Jewel. The voices grew louder. She and Duncan were trapped.

Duncan quickly shoved her over to a tapestry near the window and pulled it aside. "Hide here. I'll draw their attention away from the room, and when it's clear, you can slip out. I'll meet you at the room where we arrived."

She shook her head. "We will face them together. Like we did before."

Duncan put his hands on her shoulder. "Kathleen, please. Lord Hepburn let us go a first time; he will not be so lenient a second. Do this for me."

"Duncan, I do not like your plan. Besides, we are not even sure the Darnley Jewel is the answer."

He kissed her on the mouth. "It has to be. It's the only idea that makes any sense." He pulled the tapestry into place.

Kathleen was cloaked in darkness. She clenched her hands in a fist at her side to keep them from trembling and heard the door bang open. Muffled shouts echoed through the chamber. She recognized Lord Hepburn's voice over the sound of others. She guessed there were three or four guards that had accompanied Lord Hepburn into the Queen's chamber.

"Duncan MacGreggor, are ye lost, again? 'Tis fortunate a light was seen coming from the Queen's chambers, else ye could have continued with your mischief undetected."

Duncan raised his voice loud enough for people in the next room to hear. She figured he was making sure she could hear him.

"I was just checking to see if Her Majesty was in need of more wood for her fire."

One of the guards shouted to Lord Hepburn. "Someone has searched through the Queen's wardrobe. The doors were left ajar."

Another man's voice rang out. "And the mattress and coverlet have been disturbed."

Lord Hepburn growled. "It is plain MacGreggor intends to steal from Her Majesty."

Duncan interrupted. "That's not true. Why would I ..."

"Silence. I will not tolerate a thief in the Queen's household." Lord Hepburn barked out orders. "Seize him. We will secure MacGreggor in one of the cells below the cookroom. And on the morrow he'll be taken to Edinburgh's dungeon. Maybe that will teach him that 'tis a major offense to steal from our Queen."

Kathleen heard a muffled curse from Duncan. A chair or table overturned, and glass shattered. It sounded as though a war were being waged.

She clutched the jewel in her hand and felt the gems cut into her palm. Duncan was right. His only hope was if she remained hidden. She leaned against the back wall of the alcove to help support her trembling legs. It sounded as though something was being dragged from the room. She slid slowly down the wall and felt warm tears stream down her face. She would find out where they had taken him. He had to survive. Kathleen did not want to believe anything else was possible. All she had to do was wait until the men left and then follow them to where they were taking Duncan.

Kathleen heard the door slam in place and scrambled to her feet. She tucked the jewel inside her bodice. The next sound turned her blood cold.

Keys rattled as she heard the door being locked from the outside. She was locked in.

Kathleen pulled the tapestry aside. There had to be another way out. Maybe she should have tried to help Duncan after all. At least they would be together. She shook her head. That was not true. Men and women prisoners were never kept together. She would never have seen him again. That could not happen. She had to find a way to escape.

She rushed over to the window. It was a three-story drop onto a stone courtyard. If she was lucky, she would only break both legs. She turned from the window and paced back and forth in front of the bed.

She paused. Of course. She could tie the bed linens together and use them as a rope to shimmy down to the ground. It always worked in the movies. Well, most of the time, anyway. Now all she would have to worry about was the guards on duty. Minor detail.

She walked over to the bed and pulled off the top cover.

The lock in the door clicked. Kathleen froze. Her heart thundered in her chest. She had to hide. She ducked under the bed and got a mouthful of dust. Duncan was right. Dusting was not a priority in this century. She covered her mouth with her hand to keep from sneezing.

The door creaked open. She held her breath.

Seconds ticked by. She heard footsteps on the wood floor.

A young man whispered her name. The door opened wider. "Kathleen, 'tis me, Jeremy MacDougal. I saw ye go in with Duncan."

Kathleen let out her breath and scrambled out from under the bed. She had never been so happy to see anyone in her life. She rushed over to him and hugged him to her.

"Jeremy, thank goodness." She knelt down and grabbed him by the shoulders. "Lord Hepburn has taken Duncan. Do ye know where they have taken Duncan?"

Jeremy grinned, displaying the gap left by two missing front teeth. "Aye, I made sure I knew the exact location before I came back for ye. Pretty clever, huh?"

She nodded. "Very clever indeed. We have to rescue Duncan. Will ye help me?"

The boy frowned. "He is heavily guarded. Do ye have a plan?"

Kathleen stood slowly. "Nay, not as yet, but let us leave this place before the Queen or Lord Hepburn returns. We canna help Duncan if we are caught as well."

Kathleen closed the door behind her. What she needed was a foolproof escape plan. However, creating one was not second nature to her. The one time she had planned to try and skip a class, she had been caught. She obviously did not have the credentials for this type of work.

She watched as Jeremy walked silently in front of her. He turned and looked over his shoulder and grinned. Suddenly things did not seem too dark. She could not ask Duncan—he was being held a prisoner—but she could ask Jeremy. She would be willing to bet that the young man would be almost as clever at devising an escape plan as Duncan.

Kathleen took a deep breath. At least she hoped so.

Eight

Kathleen entered the cookroom behind Jeremy and paused to let her eyes adjust to the low light. On her way from the Queen's chambers to the cookroom, Kathleen had discarded numerous plans to rescue Duncan. She had finally settled on one that Jermy felt would work.

Martha sat beside a cold hearth and wrung her hands together. The woman stood and turned abruptly. "I was worried for ye. Young Jeremy brought the news that Lord Hepburn had taken Duncan. "Why would Lord Hepburn do such a thing?"

Jeremy walked over to a wood barrel that was against the far wall. He opened the lid and pulled out a red apple. "Lord Hepburn claims Duncan is a thief. Caught him in the Queen's bedchamber, he did."

"Oh, dear God. This is very bad. Lord Hepburn is so protective of the Queen. What are we to do?"

Kathleen walked over and put her hand on Martha's shoulder to try and quiet the distraught woman. The last thing Kathleen needed was a case of hysteria. Everyone needed to think clearly.

She cleared her throat. "Martha, I have a plan, but I will need your help to free Duncan."

Martha's eyes widened. " 'Tis madness. Duncan is well-guarded."

Kathleen took a deep breath. "I know, but we still have to try."

Jeremy spoke with a mouthful of apple. "I heard some of the guards talking. Lord Hepburn wanted most of them sent to Edinburgh Castle. If ye want to free yer husband, now would be the best time."

Martha folded her arms across her chest. "Why would Lord Hepburn leave the palace unprotected. That makes little sense. And who is to guard the Queen if her men are clear on the other side of the city?"

Jeremy finished his apple and tossed the core in the hearth. "Something about 'it was the Queen's time.' Dinna make a wit of sense to me."

Kathleen squeezed Martha's arm. "Could the Queen have gone into labor?"

Martha nodded slowly. "A mite early, but with all the excitement over Riccio's murder, 'tis possible."

Kathleen paced back and forth in front of the trestle table. This information could not have come at a better time. It meant her plan had a chance at success.

Kathleen turned to Martha. "We dinna have much time, but if we work hard, the plan just might work. First we need to get a fire started, the ovens as well. Next . . ."

Martha interrupted her. "Slow down, lass. Jeremy and I will gladly help ye free that lad of yours. He showed my grandson a kindness when all others ignored him. But ye will need to take a breath and explain this plan of yours to us slowly."

Kathleen glanced toward the open window. Only a few hours remained before dawn. She hoped it would be enough. She motioned for Jeremy and Martha to join her on a bench beside the hearth. This would be dangerous for them all. After she had laid out the plan, she would give them the choice. She would understand if they were reluctant to risk their lives for people they had just met.

The gray light of dawn seeped in through the window of the cookroom as Kathleen paced in front of the oven. Jeremy lay asleep beside the hearth and Martha was busy preparing the meal for the guard.

A rooster crowed in the courtyard. Startled, Kathleen flinched and leaned against the trestle table. She held on to the edge. It had been a long sleepless night trying to refine the plan to save Duncan. She had changed into the clothes she had worn when they arrived and instructed Martha to hide Duncan's. They must be ready.

Kathleen tightened her grip on the edge of the table. She did not even know if he was still alive. In a short span of time he had grown more important to her than returning to her own century. Somewhere in the hours before dawn, she had realized that she would not go back without him.

Martha removed a pheasant from the spit over the hearth and laid it on a pewter tray. The rich aroma filled the air. "Dinna worry, lass."

Kathleen felt as though there were a lump in her throat that threatened to choke her. "Duncan could be dead."

"Nay, that is news that would have spread like the plague through the streets of London. We will see the plan to its end. All is ready."

Kathleen shoved her hands into the folds of her long

dress. She remembered hearing once that having a weak plan was better than no plan at all. She hoped that was true, as what they had plotted held as many holes as a sieve.

Jeremy stretched and sat up. "Is it time?"

Martha walked over and tousled the boy's hair. "Nay, lad, not as yet, but soon."

Kathleen reached for the wooden paddle and removed the loaves of bread from the oven. She turned and slid them onto the table. "I still wish we did not have to involve Jeremy. 'Tis too dangerous."

"I do as well, lass. But we need his skill."

"I hear ye talking behind me back. I am as brave as any man. And ye need me."

Martha nodded slowly. "The lad speaks true. There is no one else."

Jeremy climbed up on a three-legged stool. "I still think I should run the guard through with Duncan's sword."

Kathleen looked over at the boy. He was barely ten and the sword he talked of was longer than he was tall. Yet, she suspected that he would attempt the impossible, just the same. Duncan had shown him a kindness and earned Jeremy's loyalty. She did not want to diminish Jeremy's determination. In reality, he was the key ingredient in the success of their plan. She just hated putting him in danger. She prayed Martha would be successful in getting the boy to safety.

She smiled. "There is no need for you to use Duncan's sword. The part you will play is more important."

He nodded and seemed to sit taller on the stool.

Kathleen reached for a knife and cut the freshly baked

bread. It was soft and hard to slice, but she did not have the time to let it cool. If their plan was to succeed, she had to put it in motion while the Queen was away at Edinburgh Castle. Lord Hepburn would be at Mary's side and had delayed Duncan's punishment until he returned. But the man would return as soon as the child was born.

Kathleen shivered. She wished she had not taken the tour of the torture chamber at Edinburgh Castle when she was at the university. She remembered the detailed descriptions and the devices used. Very few people survived, and those that did were crippled both mentally and physically for what remained of their life.

She glanced over at Martha. Her hands trembled as she arranged sprigs of parsley and steamed potatoes around the roasted pheasant. Despite the woman's brave words moments ago, she also knew the risks were great. Freeing Duncan was only a small part of the plan. The hope was to do it in such a way that Martha and Jeremy would not be implicated. There was much at stake.

A cool breeze drifted through the window, and morning sunlight brightened the room. She wished her spirits could as easily be changed as the appearance of the cook-room. The castle's inhabitants would be awake soon. They were running out of time.

Kathleen walked over to Martha. "Is Duncan's sword well hidden?"

"Aye. Just as we discussed."

"And our clothes?"

Martha patted Kathleen's arm. "We have gone over the details until I fear I could recite them in my sleep. All that remains is to see it through to the end." She hugged her. "Take care, lass."

Kathleen kissed Martha on the cheek. "Thank ye. I will never forget your kindness."

Martha cleared her throat. "Nonsense. Ye speak as though we will not see each other again. Now off with ye, before we lose our nerve. Jeremy will not fail ye. The skill he acquired before I took him into my home will prove of value this day."

Kathleen swallowed her tears. She picked up the platter of steaming food and walked down the narrow steps to the chambers below the cookroom. It was where prisoners were held before being transported to the dungeon in Edinburgh Castle.

The stone walls were damp and cold and seemed to press in on her. The air smelled musty. Something furry skittered across her shoes. She shivered and tightened her grip on the tray. In the pale torchlight she saw red eyes blinking back at her.

It was a rat.

She shuddered and hurried forward to the end of the corridor. As foul-smelling as this place was, she knew it was better than the dungeon in the castle.

The pinched-faced guard stood as she approached. A set of keys dangled from a belt around his waist. He had a scruffy beard and narrow, beady eyes that reminded her of those of the rat she had just seen. The comparison made her uneasy.

He growled out his words as though he were speaking with a mouthful of gravel. "What have ye brought?"

She closed her hands around the pewter tray and fought the impulse to throw the steaming food in the man's ugly face. His words confirmed her worst fears. However, instead of reducing her to a sniveling mass, it strengthened her resolve. Duncan must be freed before Lord Hepburn returned.

Kathleen's voice quivered. It was the first part of the plan and one of the most critical. "I have prepared food for my husband. Ye canna deny him nourishment."

The guard's expression darkened. "This food be too fine for the likes of him. Even if it were to be his last meal." He sneered. "And I hear it well may be." The guard reached for the food. "I'll see it doesn't go to waste."

He set the platter on a wooden table by his chair. He sat down and tore off a wing of the roasted pheasant. Fat dripped down his hand as he took a bite. "Are ye going to stand there and watch me eat?"

She wrung her hands together in what she hoped was a convincing display of desperation. Actually, it was not that much of a stretch. "Ye must allow me permission to see my husband."

He shrugged and motioned with his head. "Ye can see as much as the bars will allow. Talk to him if ye want. He's been pacing back and forth enough to wear a path in the stone floor."

There was only silence. The pacing had stopped. Perhaps Duncan had recognized her voice. She took a deep breath and walked to where the guard had indicated. Iron bars were set in a small opening in the door. Duncan's expression was lost in the dark shadows. The plan must work. It was his only chance.

He whispered and gripped the bars. "What are you doing here? You have the Darnley Jewel. You should be on your way home."

She reached for his hand. Their fingers intertwined. "I am not leaving without you."

"Kathleen, please, I want you to save yourself. I'll figure out something."

"You have a plan?"

His smile did not reach his eyes. "I'm working on it."

The guard burped loudly and shouted over to her. "Make it quick." He reached for the wine and took a generous drink.

She whispered. "Duncan, be ready for anything." She kissed him on the lips. The touch of his mouth on hers was urgent, as though he felt it was their last. She fought back the warm tears that welled in her eyes.

A mind-numbing scream rippled through the air. She recognized the voice. It was Jeremy's. The next part of the plan was in motion. Footsteps echoed over the stone floor, followed by shouting.

The guard stood and wiped his greasy mouth on his sleeve. "Who goes there?"

Jeremy burst through the dark corridor. His eyes were wide; he waved his arms in the air. The young boy ran straight for the guard. Before the man could react, Jeremy had plowed into him. The guard lost his balance and staggered back. He tried to pry the boy off him, but Jeremy clung to him as though attached with glue. They spun around in a wild dance.

Duncan whispered. "What's going on?"

"It begins." Kathleen moved closer toward the guard and the shouting Jeremy. She kept just out of reach and waited. Jeremy brushed against her and pressed keys into her hand. Jermey was very skilled. Everything had happened so fast she had not seen Jeremy take the set of keys from the guard.

She backed the short distance to where Duncan was

held prisoner. The game of cat-and-mouse Jeremy played with the guard frustrated the large man. He yelled at the boy to hold still. Kathleen knew Jeremy would not stop distracting the guard until she had accomplished her goal.

Kathleen backed against the door to Duncan's cell and put the key in the lock. She turned it slowly. The tumblers clicked. She froze. She prayed the guard had not heard the sound. She sighed with relief. The man was too absorbed with trying to disentangle himself from Jeremy.

Kathleen motioned for Duncan to wait. She edged closer to Jeremy. In order for the final stage of the plan to succeed, the key must be returned to the guard. She did not want the guard suspecting it was ever out of his possession. She did not want Jeremy blamed for Duncan's escape.

Footsteps echoed once more down the corridor.

Martha appeared. Her face was flushed from running, and she waved a wooden spoon in her hand. She shook it in the guard's direction. "Ye have found the lad. Now I will give him the thrashing he deserves. Ate all my berry tarts, he did. Thank ye for capturing the little thief."

The guard held the boy still. "Keep him out of my sight or I'll do the thrashing for ye."

Jeremy spun out of the guard's grasp and backed toward Kathleen. She quickly pressed the keys into the palm of his hand. The boy closed his fingers around it and zigzagged back toward the guard. The man tried to grab him.

Jeremy ducked and then darted out of the guard's reach. "Ye willna catch me." He raced passed the guard and sidestepped as Martha raised her spoon. Jeremy grabbed the pheasant from the tray and ran toward the stairs.

The guard growled. "Thief. Ye have stolen my dinner."

Martha sobbed. "Sir, ye must help me catch him."

The guard shouted after Jeremy. "Ye willna make a fool of me, brat."

Kathleen waited until the guard and Martha had disappeared from sight. Jeremy and Martha had played their parts well. A horse was waiting for Jeremy to take him to the safety of Martha's clan. The Highlands would be a good place for the boy to grow to be a man.

She turned toward Duncan and opened the door. "There is not much time."

He swept her into his arms. "You're amazing. I told you to save yourself."

"I wasn't listening."

He smiled. "Is this a trait I need to know about?"

Despite the danger, she felt her mood lighten. She returned his smile. Kathleen grabbed Duncan's hand. "There is a back staircase that leads to a corridor beside the Queen's supper chamber. This is the one that Lord Darnley used to escape after he and his friends killed Riccio."

He cupped her face in his hands and his expression grew serious. "When they discover I have escaped, they will come after us. They will kill us both. Jeremy is in danger as well."

She shook her head. "He is safe. I will explain later, but now we must hurry."

Kathleen turned and led him toward the stairs. She fought back the coil of fear that wove around her. Duncan was right. When it was discovered his prisoner had escaped, Lord Hepburn would order them killed on sight. She shuddered and opened the door to the stairway. She could not think of that now; they still had a long way to go to reach their own time.

Nine

*T*orchlight flickered over the uneven stairs as Duncan reached for Kathleen's hand and moved in front of her. If there was danger, he wanted it to come to him first.

Her hand was warm in his and a wave a protectiveness wove through him. He gently squeezed her fingers. He had never felt this way about a woman before. He'd never let them get that close. Duncan believed if he ever committed to someone, she would try to build walls around him. However, with Kathleen, he could be freer than he'd ever been in his life. He felt as though he could slay a fire-breathing dragon.

Duncan reached the landing and pushed open the door slowly. A dark corridor lay before him.

Kathleen rushed past him.

He reached for her, but she was too quick. He whispered. "Where're you going?"

She glanced over her shoulder. "To fetch your clothes and your sword."

She hurried to an alcove. Leaded glass windows were covered with floor-to-ceiling velvet curtains. Kathleen pulled aside the draperies, exposing a large oak chest.

She unlatched it and opened the lid. "I am not sure, but

perhaps we need to be dressed in the clothes of the twenty-first century to successfully return. I remembered a movie starring Christopher Reeve. It was called *Somewhere in Time.* He was in the past with the woman he loved until he found a coin from his century, and, poof, he traveled forward."

She threw a bundle of clothes in his direction. "Of course, he was not happy about it. He had left the woman he loved behind. He spent what remained of his life trying to return to her. It is just a story, but I do not want to take any chances."

"I'll try anything." Duncan changed his clothes and saw Kathleen reach once more into the chest.

She pulled out his sword. "There it is. This is heavy."

Duncan buttoned his jeans and quickly reached for his sword. He leaned it against the wall, pulled his T-shirt over his head, and shoved his arms into his leather jacket.

He heard shouting coming from the stairs.

Two guards burst through the door and headed toward them. Duncan reached for his sword and pulled Kathleen behind him. "Go to the room. I'll be there soon."

The tone of her voice did not waver. "No. We will go together or not at all."

He tightened his grip on the sword. "Then I guess, fair damsel, I'd better fight well."

The guards ran toward him. Bloodlust reflected in their eyes. Their intent was to kill both him and Kathleen. Even knowing that didn't change his resolve. He would avoid killing the guards . . . unless he had to.

The faster of the two screamed a war cry and raised his blade. Duncan blocked the attack. The sound of steel on steel echoed through the air. Duncan spun around as the second man lunged forward. Duncan knew he was fighting well, but there was no time to pat himself on the back. Already he could hear the sound of other men approaching.

Duncan hit the first assailant with the side of his blade. The man held his head and stumbled back. The second man yelled. Duncan lunged forward and wounded him in the arm. Blood flowed from the wound. The man hesitated. Duncan seized the opportunity and hit the man in the jaw with his fist. The man dropped like a stone to the ground.

Duncan grabbed Kathleen's hand. "Let's go."

He ran toward the Queen's private supper chamber and passed the spot where Riccio was murdered.

Kathleen shouted. "There it is."

The small room seemed to beckon him. He raced toward it, with Kathleen close by his side. He stepped inside and turned to Kathleen. "Let me see the Darnley Jewel."

She pulled it out of her pocket and handed it to him.

It felt cold in his hand. Odd, he'd thought it would radiate with heat. He took a deep breath. "When I was creating games, it was always the obvious that held the answers."

He glanced around the wood paneled room. Into the wood was carved the coats of arms of the major Scottish clans. He had no idea what he should be looking for. He turned toward Kathleen. She was touching the panels.

Duncan shook his head. "There has to be a connection between the jewel and this room. I think we're close, but there seems to be a missing piece to the puzzle."

She paused. "I know."

He leaned forward. "If we get back, I want you to come to the States with me. You'd love it there. I have a house on Lake Washington, a boat . . ."

She touched his arm. "My home is here, in Scotland and my shop. It has been in my family for generations. I could not bear to sell it. But neither one of us will see our home if we dinna find our way back."

He returned reluctantly to his search. He felt an invisible barrier had been thrown between them. It had never occurred to him that she would not want to leave Scotland. After all, he could offer her everything money could buy. He shrugged the dark foreboding away. She was right. First they had to reach their century.

His fingers touched an indention in one of the panels that seemed to match the outline of the jewel. It was in the center of the Queen's coat of arms.

Duncan felt his pulse rate increase. He placed the jewel in the space. It fit perfectly.

Duncan stepped back and glanced toward Kathleen. "Now what? Do you think we should say a few magic words?"

She smiled. "I am sure Harriet knows a few. She is certainly not what she seems. In fact, my first order of business will be to ask that dear sweet old woman how she was able to send us back in time. The only magic words I know are bibbidi, bobbodi . . ."

The room lurched forward. The doors slammed shut.

Duncan pulled her into his arms. "Maybe this is it."

"Or maybe we will be thrown further back in time."

He tilted her chin toward him and lightly kissed her lips. "As long as we're together, I wouldn't mind where I am."

The room lurched again. Duncan wrapped his arms around her as the room began to spin.

The doors to the elevator opened slowly. Light spilled into the small enclosure and the flash of a camera blinded him.

They were back.

Duncan pulled himself to a sitting position. Kathleen was beside him. That's all that mattered.

Callum extended his hand. "Ye dinna look none the worse for wear, as ye American's say. But then, ye were only trapped since yesterday morn." He reached down and picked up the Darnley Jewel from the ground and slipped it into his pocket. He winked. "I shall see it is returned."

Kathleen scrambled to her feet and straightened her skirt. Her eyes widened. "Yesterday? But that is not possible. We were gone longer. I am sure of it."

Callum arched an eyebrow. "Time is a curious affair. It has its own set of rules. Or at least that is what Harriet, Edinburgh's matchmaker, is always telling me."

Duncan put his arm around Kathleen's waist and together they walked out of the elevator. He smiled. "Callum, you won't believe where we've been. It was the most exciting . . ."

Callum put his finger to his lips as though he wanted them to keep their voices low. "Aye, lad, I would." He nodded toward the reporters. "But do ye really want to share your news with the likes of them? They heard about a wealthy American being stuck in the elevator overnight and thought there'd be a story in it."

Duncan felt as though the walls of the palace were closing in. "Then you know."

"Aye."

A camera flashed; the light seemed to blind Duncan. Maybe it was a dream. Maybe he'd hit his head. Yes, that must be it. But then why was Callum acting so strange and where had the Darnley Jewel come from?

People crowded around him, separating him from Kathleen. He shouted toward her. "Wait. Where're you going?"

"I have to see to my shop."

"I'll call you."

He regretted the words the moment he'd spoken them. They sounded like a brush-off. Her expression told him that was how she'd interpreted them as well. Damn, that's not what he'd meant. Duncan watched her turn away from him. He didn't know the words to stop her. He wished he did.

Callum raised his voice and shouted over the hum of conversation and the flash of cameras. "Ye have your story. Off with the lot of ye. Let the lad have room to breathe."

The authority in Callum's voice worked like magic. The crowd gave out a collective sigh of regret that the excitement had ended and filed out the door.

Duncan turned toward Callum. "Thanks. I was feeling smothered."

He smiled. "Now ye can go after that lassie of yours."

"It's not that simple. I live in the States and she lives here."

"That's nothing more than geography, lad."

Duncan did not respond. It was no use trying to explain to Callum the responsibilities that both he and Kathleen had with their businesses. From his comment, Callum was probably someone that believed that love conquered all. That might have been the case in past generations, but things were different now. People were different.

Callum slapped him on the shoulder. "I have to make sure the reporters find their way out. Think over what I have said."

A man, wearing a rumpled cotton suit that looked as though it had been slept in, edged toward Duncan. It was Robertson, the man he'd had an appointment with yesterday morning. It seemed more like a lifetime ago than twenty-four hours.

Robertson frowned. "How did you manage it? Confined in that elevator all this time? Your shirt's torn, but other than that, you look pretty good. Of course, the companionship of that bonnie lass must have been pleasant."

Robertson didn't wait for Duncan to respond. His words tumbled out as though he loved the sound of his own voice.

He indicated the sword that lay on the floor of the elevator. "I see you've brought the blade from your collection. Looks authentic. Even has fake blood. Nice touch."

Duncan glanced down at the sword as if in a fog. At that moment he knew it was not a dream. "My blade is not a replica. It was forged in the sixteenth century. And the blood is real."

Robertson cleared his throat. "Interesting." He scratched the back of his neck. "Your office has been calling me every half hour since we discovered you were stuck in that blasted elevator."

As if on cue, Duncan's cell phone rang.

Duncan reached into his breast pocket. His phone was

back. A cold reminder of his life. The voice squawking at him on the other end belonged to John Forseith.

Robertson motioned over his shoulder. "Why don't you take the call upstairs? It'll be more private, as well as give us a chance to close the deal you came here for in the first place." He laughed. "We'll use the stairs."

He nodded. Duncan looked toward the door Kathleen had used moments before. She had vanished from his life as easily as she'd walked into it. Perhaps it was for the best. After all, he had a company to run and so did she.

"Robertson, hold on. I have to get my sword."

Duncan turned and walked back into the elevator and reached for his blade. He tightened his grip on the hilt of the sword. The sixteenth century had been just as he'd imagined it would be when he was performing in reenactment festivals in high school and college. Full of nonstop excitement and intrigue. He'd even found the woman of his dreams. Too bad the fantasy had to end.

He heard a whirring sound, as though the elevator had been engaged. Duncan glanced over at the control panel. All of the buttons were lit. The room shuddered and the doors slammed shut.

Kathleen glanced over her shoulder. Reporters and curious tourists had separated her from Duncan. Through the din of conversation and rapid-fire questions directed at him, she could hear the phone ring: his phone.

She saw him reach into his jacket pocket and answer it. She felt as though her world were falling apart. It had not taken him long to return to his life. Now it was time for her to return to hers.

She turned and walked out into the mist-shrouded

streets of Edinburgh. She could hear someone playing bagpipes further up the street and saw tourists standing in line to buy tickets for the tour of the palace. She glanced over her shoulder one more time. Duncan had disappeared from sight. He was probably finishing the business he had come to Edinburgh to complete. Everything was just as she had left it.

No, things were not the same. She was different. She had survived the most fantastic adventure of her life, and fallen in love with a dark prince. Even if she had known her heart would be lost to him, she would still have stepped into the elevator. After all, happily ever after only happens in fairy tales.

Callum shouted her name. She turned and saw him running toward her.

He came to an abrupt stop in front of her. His face was red from running and he was out of breath. "Kathleen. Something terrible has happened. I tried to stop it, but it was no use. It happened too fast."

Kathleen put her hand on his shoulder. "Take a deep breath and calm down. What is the matter."

" 'Tis Duncan. He has returned."

Kathleen felt as though her heart had stopped beating. She had not thought he would return to his home so soon. He must have caught a cab to the airport. The least he could have done was say good-bye.

She swallowed back her tears. "Duncan must be in a hurry to return to his business."

Callum shook his head. "Nay, lass. Not the States." Callum lowered his voice. "Duncan has returned to the sixteenth century."

Kathleen felt as though the ground trembled beneath

her feet. She held on to Callum's shoulder to keep from falling. That was impossible. Then her thoughts cleared. She took a deep breath. "For a moment I thought ye meant that Duncan had returned to the sixteenth century. But that is impossible."

Callum nodded his head vigorously. "That is exactly what I meant, lass."

Ten

The next few days blurred together in a frenzy of activity. No one could find Harriet. It was as though she had disappeared off the face of the earth. Workmen had fixed the elevator at the palace, but when the doors were opened, Duncan was not inside.

Kathleen paced back and forth in her crowded bakery shop. She felt restless. Where was he?

Morning sunlight filtered through the lace curtains of the bakery. The drone of conversation mingled with the clinking of spoons against cups and china plates. When word had spread that Kathleen had spent the night trapped in the palace elevator with the handsome American, her shop became more popular than ever before. For once she did not welcome the added business. All she wanted to do was search for Duncan. But as Callum had pointed out to her, how do you search for someone in the sixteenth century when you are in the twenty-first?

Kathleen closed her fingers around the pendant that

Harriet had given her. If Duncan had traveled back to the sixteenth century, Lord Hepburn had no doubt been waiting. She closed her eyes and tried to block out the image of Duncan imprisoned in Edinburgh's dungeon. Why had he gone back inside the elevator?

She needed to get her mind off her dark thoughts. Callum had assured her he would let her know the moment he found Harriet . . . or Duncan.

She reached for an earthenware bowl and mixed flour and milk together. Maybe if she created a new scone recipe, the distraction would help get her through the day. She held the bowl and stirred the stiff mixture vigorously with her wooden spoon. She paused and pinched off a corner of the thick dough. It was bland and tasteless. It needed something. She scooped up a generous cup full of chocolate chips.

She looked over her shop. The counter tables were filled with couples talking while they sipped their coffee and tea and ate gooey pastries. She was doing a vigorous business today. It was the height of the tourist season and once more, word of mouth had spread. She was a success. She could not have cared less.

Kathleen heard the sound of the door chimes. She looked up expectantly, hoping it was Callum. A couple wearing matching fanny packs and laden down with plastic shopping bags entered her bakery.

Kathleen dumped the chocolate chips into the mixture and set the bowl down as the tourists reached the counter. She filled their orders, raspberry scones and mugs of steaming hot coffee, and watched as they found a table in the corner. She resumed mixing the dough.

The door chimes rang out again.

It was Harriet.

Kathleen dropped the bowl on the floor. It shattered on the tiles. She ignored the sticky mess as well as the customers and rushed over to Harriet.

"Where have ye been? Callum and I have been looking for ye. Have ye heard? Duncan is missing."

"Slow down, lass. I am bone weary and have to rest for a spell."

Harriet walked past her and sat down by the window. She hefted her bag of photos and trinkets onto the table. The contents seemed to jingle together like the notes of a flute.

Harriet sighed. "Sorry it is that I was not able to greet ye when ye and Duncan returned from your adventure, but I was hard at work. My latest pairing was the hardest to date. I am getting too old for this line of work. 'Tis time I passed it on. And 'tis not done as yet. The lass refuses to take The Dragon's Fire broach. Can ye imagine such a thing?"

Kathleen sat down opposite her. The woman was babbling, as usual. It was probably more matchmaker stuff, but Kathleen did not care. She had to find Duncan.

She leaned forward. "Dinna ye hear me? Duncan is missing. He did not return with me." She paused. "Well, he did return, but then he went back. What are we going to do?"

The phone on the wall rang. Kathleen ignored it. There was nothing more important than finding Duncan. She only hoped he was still alive.

Harriet put her hand on Kathleen's. "Are ye going to answer the phone, lass?"

"If it is important, they will call back."

Kathleen decided to take another tack with Harriet, since the woman had not responded to the dilemma that Duncan was missing. Maybe if Kathleen found out how the elevator worked, in relationship to time travel, she could find Duncan on her own.

Kathleen lowered her voice. "There is something much more important than answering a telephone. I need to understand how ye were able to send Duncan and me back to the sixteenth century."

Harriet rubbed her forehead. "My, but this generation is a tiresome lot. It used to be that my matches would just be grateful they had found each other." She frowned. "But not ye. All ye want to know is the why and how of it. Your mother did not question me."

Kathleen clenched her hands in her lap to keep them from strangling the old woman. She wondered if Harriet was deliberately avoiding her questions. "I do not want to discuss my parents; please tell me how it is that ye managed to send Duncan and me back in time?"

Harriet winked. "Trade secret, lassie. Trade secret. Now tell me why ye dinna stay with Duncan when ye first arrived from your adventure?"

"How did ye . . ."

Harriet shook her head. " 'Tis not important, just answer my question."

They were wasting precious time, but Harriet was the only one who could help her find Duncan. Kathleen took a deep breath to help her stay calm. " 'Tis complicated. There were a lot of people. Duncan was busy with a business associate and I had to check on my shop."

Harriet frowned. "Nothing is more important than making time for love." She leaned back in the chair. "Tell me, lass. If ye were to find Duncan, would ye still put your business before him?"

Kathleen felt tears brim in her eyes and shook her head. "No, of course not. Please, Harriet, please help me rescue him. I fear that Lord Hepburn holds him prisoner and I . . ."

Harriet reached over and patted her hand. " 'Tis all right, lass. Yer American will be along straightaway."

"What are ye talking about?"

The bells chimed, and framed in the doorway was Duncan. The sun was at his back and he seemed larger than he had the last time she had seen him. He was talking on his cell phone, immersed in his business affairs.

Harriet chuckled, grabbed her bag filled with photos, and stood. "Well, well, I have done all I can with this match. I'll be going now. There is much to do, much to do."

The old woman walked toward the door and paused beside Duncan. She patted his arm and whispered something to him before disappearing out the door.

Kathleen cleared her throat. She could not imagine what Harriet would have said to Duncan, but whatever it was, it had made him smile. It seemed as though he walked in slow-motion toward her. She focused on his eyes and the effort to keep her breathing steady. He was alive.

The conversation in the shop merged until she could no longer distinguish individual voices over the beat of her heart.

He reached the table and put his cell phone in his jacket pocket. He grinned. "Hello there."

She stood so abruptly the chair toppled over. "What do

ye mean, 'hello'? Where have ye been? Callum and I have been frantic. I thought ye were dead, that Lord Hepburn had killed ye."

He shrugged. "He tried, but we managed to reach an understanding. I'll tell you all about it over dinner."

Her nerves were a jumbled mess. She warred between wanting to throw her arms around him or hit him over the head with a pot of coffee. She put her hands on her hips instead. "I was worried about ye. I have not slept for three days. All the scones are burned on the bottom. And ye stand there calmly and tell me that Lord Hepburn and ye reached an 'understanding'? Ye were on an adventure and I was worried sick. How is it that ye were thrown back in time in the first place?"

He rubbed the back of his neck. "Harriet said something about I hadn't had my priorities straight."

"So she sent ye back?"

He nodded. "Sounds crazy."

"It sounds like Harriet."

He was looking at her with an intensity that took her breath away. In the last few days she had discovered that she loved him. She knew it was illogical. They had not known each other very long. She had relived every moment they had spent together. But love needed time to grow, she rationalized. How could you build a life on something that happened over such a short period of time? And yet, she knew the answer. She had only to hear it from him. But first there was something she had to do.

She raised her voice to be heard over the din of conversation in her shop. "I have an announcement to make. I would like everyone to leave, now. My shop is closed for today."

Kathleen watched as her customers mumbled to themselves, picked up their belongings, and hurried out the door. No doubt they thought the owner had lost her marbles. Actually, it was just the opposite. Today she had finally discovered what was really important.

As the last of the customers left the shop, she walked over to the counter. She knew he would follow her. There were things they needed to discuss. Kathleen reached for the carafe of coffee and turned toward him. "Coffee?"

He shook his head. "I don't like the stuff."

Her pulse rate increased. "Then why did ye order it each time ye came into my shop?"

"I thought it was obvious."

She ignored the hammering in her chest. Get control of yourself, she cautioned. He had not said the words. She reached into the glass case by the counter for a pastry. "How about a scone?"

"Not sweet enough." He paused. "Kathleen, it's you I want."

He was almost there.

His cell phone rang. He reached for it, opened the lid of the coffee carafe, and dropped his cell phone into the steaming brew. He grinned. "I never liked the thing. It was always going off at the most annoying times, like now."

Her heart thundered in her ears. That was the answer she wanted. He had put her before his business.

She saw the love reflected in his eyes; it mirrored her own. She knew the answer, but she wanted him to say it out loud. She smiled. "Why did ye do that to your phone? It might have been an important call."

Duncan reached for her hand. "I returned last night and decided to sell my business to the man here in

Edinburgh. As soon as the decision was made, I started coming up with new ideas for games. But even that was overshadowed by thoughts of you. I tried calling you, but you wouldn't answer your phone."

He came around the counter and pulled her into his arms. "I love you, Kathleen. I think I loved you the moment I walked into your shop, but I was too blind to see it. You are what is important. Everything else is an illusion. I have decided to start over, do it right this time." He paused. "With you. What do you think of the idea?"

She kissed him lightly on the lips and whispered, "I love ye, Duncan MacGreggor, and I love your plan. As Harriet would say, we have all the time in the world on our side."

PAM BINDER lives with her own personal champion, her husband of thirty-two years. Jim and Pam share their empty nest with over 2500 books that range in scope from Dr. Seuss's *Cat in the Hat* to William Shakespeare's *A Midsummer Night's Dream*.

The Christmas Captive

PATRICIA CABOT

Prologue

Gone. She was gone.

He could see it with his own eyes. He did not need to hear her maid's pathetic sniffling—nor her insistence that she'd known nothing of her mistress's intention to flee— to assure him of that fact.

Not that she'd taken much with her. Her room looked exactly as it had for the decade she'd dwelt in it, except that the dolls she'd once collected had been replaced by other fripperies associated with the fairer sex: her clothes press was filled to capacity with every sort of dress imaginable—summer, winter, morning, walking, carriage, and evening dresses; riding habits and ball gowns; pelisses and negligees. The drawers of the enamel jewel box on her dresser were similarly packed, crammed to overflowing with the ropes of pearls and gold chains his mother had left her.

It was a trousseau that would have sent any other girl swooning. Wasn't it just his luck that he'd been saddled with the one fiancée in the world to whom an impressive trousseau meant exactly nothing?

Less than nothing, actually, if what she'd chosen to take

with her was any indication. And that, a quick check of the room revealed, was only what she'd brought with her that cold November day ten years earlier when, as a recently orphaned eight-year-old with hair as red as flame and eyes as blue as a summer sky—but lashes as black as boot polish, which ought to have been his first indication of the trouble that would lie ahead—she'd first set foot in MacLean Hall: the clothes on her back, her mother's wedding ring, and her father's pocket watch.

Oh, she was gone, all right. Those possessions, though meager, were all that the wretched girl cared about—and apparently all that she seemed to think she would need to get by on her own in the world.

Well, those few belongings, and, of course, twenty thousand pounds.

Considering that the money was actually vested in the funds, he could not, he supposed, rightly accuse her of thievery—especially since the fortune was hers, left to her by her doting, though sadly deceased, parents.

Still, it was twenty thousand pounds that, if he'd played his cards closer to his chest, might have enriched his own admittedly empty coffers.

Which could perhaps explain the fine rage he went into upon learning that his betrothed had escaped . . . though it did not, of course, excuse it, nor the fact that he chose to vent this rage upon the ungrateful girl's innocent maid.

"Where?" Seizing the peasant woman by her spindly shoulders, he gave her a shake that sent her mobcap flying. "Where did she go?"

The maid—Nan, he thought she was called—wept even harder, and insisted she was as surprised as he was.

"I didna even know she was thinking of going, milord," Nan told him, with a sob. "She said nothing of it to me—and she tells me everything! But not a word, not even when I turned down her bed last night. Chattin' about what Cook was serving for Christmas supper, she was, and how much she was lookin' forward to it. Then when I brung her her breakfast—just like I've done every morning since she first come here, excepting for when she went off to school—I found her g-gone!"

His lordship, unconvinced, gave her another shake.

"Do you think me a fool?" he thundered. "I know how girls prattle to their maids. She said something to you. She must have. Where is she headed? Edinburgh? London? Not back to that godforsaken convent I made the mistake of sending her to for an education, I hope. . . ."

"I dunna know!" Nan's voice had risen to a shriek. "Oh, please, milord, I swear on my mother's grave I dunna know where the mistress went off to."

He had no way of knowing whether the maid was motherless, as she claimed. He hardly knew a thing about her, even though he'd hired her ten years earlier, as nurse to his troublesome ward. Now that the ward was full grown—and his bride-to-be—Nan's role had shifted to that of abigail. But as to her parentage . . . Well, he certainly did not release the woman because he felt any sort of compassion for her allegedly motherless state.

No, he released her because her mewling cries had begun to grate upon his nerves. The girl was clearly hysterical—as evidenced by the manner in which, the moment he released her, she sank to the floor and began to weep upon his boot toes, thanking him for his kindness in sparing her a beating.

But kindness had nothing to do with it. He simply hadn't time to beat anyone at the moment. It was imperative that he find his runaway bride, and that he did it before she got to the Post Road. Given enough of a head start, it would be nearly impossible to trace her from there.

He ought, he told himself, to have locked her in the night before. He'd been a fool not to think of it. She was, for all her contrariness, a sly one. That damned education he'd paid for—well, that the five percent interest from her investments had paid for—had been much too thorough. What those nuns had been about, teaching Platonic principles to impressionable young women who then felt encouraged to toss treatises on the absolute into gentlemen's faces, as his ward had done just last night, he could not imagine.

But it wasn't going to help her in this instance, her familiarity with the Socratic dialogues . . . not unless—and this he had good reason to doubt—Socrates had given Plato a few words of advice on the best methods of escaping from one's legal guardian.

Wrenching his foot from the hysterical maid's clinging arms, he bellowed for his man to bring his greatcoat, then have the hounds unloosed.

He was, he decided, going hunting.

One

"*B*ut what's it *for?*" Niall asked.

"It's not *for* anything." Euan cast his brother—younger by two years—a look of annoyance. "Must everything have a purpose?"

"I generally think it rather nice," Niall replied. "I like an ordered universe."

Euan snorted at this. "Well," he said, "good luck with that."

Niall supposed he could not blame his brother for snorting. There was, it was true, very little order in Euan's universe. That could easily be seen at a glance. Four of his five children were running, higgledy-piggledy, in front of them, often colliding with one another or the half dozen dogs that also accompanied them, then pitching headlong into the deep snow. These brief disappearances from view did not seem to trouble Euan, who continued to trudge along, but they rather alarmed Niall.

None of the children had yet sustained any serious injury, however. They kept popping up again out of the snowdrifts each time they fell, as if nothing had happened, and hurrying along again. Only the eldest, Collin, the young Viscount of Kenworth, was attending to the adults in their midst, and he said, with all the wisdom afforded by his ten years, "*I* know what it's for. 'Tis for hanging bits on."

"Bits of what?" Niall asked, with interest.

Collin shrugged. "Candles. And tin stars, too. We tried gingerbread ones once, but the dogs got to 'em. And that was that."

Niall, still unsatisfied, said, "Aye, but what's it supposed to symbolize?"

"For God's sake," Euan burst out, impatiently. "What does it matter? We've just got to find one and mark it for Fergus to come back and collect, do you ken? Then we can go back home and have a nice hot toddy by the fire. Until then, keep your eyes open for a decent tree. If I come back without having found one, Irmgarde'll have my hide."

Niall raised his dark eyebrows at this mention of his brother's wife. "Irmgarde? I highly doubt that."

"Aye, well, you've never seen her at Christmastime, have you? Not you, no." Euan let out a bitter laugh, smoke trailing from the cheroot he kept clenched between his teeth. "When's the last time you came home for a holiday? Always away at school, you were, then off to Paris, to study under those bloodletters—"

"They're physicians, Euan," Niall said, in a mild tone. "Not bloodletters. There's a bit more to the science of medicine than just letting a patient's blood, you know."

Euan grunted. "Not from what I've seen. All I'm saying is, if you hadn't been off attaining your bloodletting degree, you would have noticed that, since I got married, Christmas has taken on a whole new meaning in my life."

It certainly had, Niall reflected. Not that it had had any meaning at all, before, to either of them. Their father, the strictest of authoritarians, had ruled Donnegal Manor and all of its properties with an iron fist. One of his most intractable dictates had been that on his personal calendar, holidays such as Christmas, which he considered papist in the extreme, simply did not exist. An excuse, Henry Donnegal had called the date, for dishonest men to forgo a day's labor and drink more than was good for them. His contempt for the holiday was so deeply seated that one December 25 in Niall's memory, his father had actually dismissed a housemaid for daring to wear a sprig of holly on her apron.

It was a conviction His Grace had not been alone in holding. Few Scotsmen Niall had known held much truck with Christmas, or any other holiday, for that matter, except for honest Scottish ones, like Hogmanay. Anything treading too close toward "papishness" had a tendency to make staunch Presbyterians nervous.

The irony of it all, of course, was that Henry Donnegal hadn't been a Presbyterian. He hadn't, if the truth be known, even been a Scotsman—at least, not by birth. He'd been awarded the title of Duke of Camden for his services to the throne during the war against the French, and had taken the honor—and his responsibilities as a nobleman—very seriously.

And though, despite the Scottish wife Henry took and the Scottish sons she promptly birthed, there was initially some ill feeling between the duke and his closest neighbor, the Earl of Sutherland—a proud Highlander who had looked very much askance at the tartan Henry had had designed for himself, and whose son had made it a point in later years to terrorize Euan and Niall at every opportunity—Henry Donnegal had adapted quickly to his new life and seemed not to remember that he had not actually been born a Scot. . . .

But now Henry was dead, and Euan had succeeded him as duke, bringing his German bride and their ever-expanding brood to the manor house in which he and Niall had been born and brought up. And holiday celebrations at Donnegal Manor, Niall was learning, were well on their way to becoming commonplace—particularly one of the most papish holidays of all.

"Irmgarde's determined to make this the best Christmas the children have ever had," Euan explained, with no small amount of solemnity. " 'Tis their first, you know. Well, first in their new home, anyway. She wants to do it right. I don't pretend to ken a thing about it," Euan went on. "I only go along with it and keep my mouth shut. Otherwise, you know, she'd skin me alive."

Niall tried to picture his small, flaxen-haired sister-in-law—whom Euan had married over their father's intense disapproval, since Irmgarde was neither titled nor an heiress and, most offensive to the duke of all, a *foreigner*—skinning anything, let alone her very large husband, and failed. She struck Niall as being the most even-tempered of creatures, putting up quite cheerfully, and for more than a decade, with living on a virtual pittance, in a cottage that was much too small for her quickly growing family, since the old duke had seen fit to cut off his eldest son for marrying against his wishes, just as he'd cut off Niall for pursuing a career in medicine.

But though their father had tried, he'd been unable to keep Euan from inheriting the title and manor house after his death, nor had he managed to spend all of his sizable fortune so that nothing would be left for his sons to enjoy. For the first time in their adult lives, the brothers were able to live comfortably, even well, and though they were supposed to be in mourning for their father's passing, it was extremely difficult—for Niall, at least—to remember to pin on his black armband each morning.

"What about *this* one?" Una, Euan's second eldest

child, lurched towards a fir tree that had to be at least twenty feet high. *"This* one, Papa."

"Too big," Euan declared. "And," he went on, continuing a conversation Niall had thought finished, "I don't suppose you'll ever spend another Christmas with us, after this one. Where are you off to, now that you're officially licensed for bloodletting? Borneo?"

Niall smiled. "Not quite that far away, I think. But I do want to go where my services can be of some actual use to somebody." His tone hardened. "I'm not going to set up practice in London, or even Glasgow, where all I'll ever see are businessmen complaining of gout, or ladies of ennui."

"Oh, no," Euan said, knowingly. "Not you. You won't be happy until you've managed to find a cure for typhoid—not to mention all the other contagions that exist in the world. You'd better find a woman before you go, though."

Niall stumbled over a root, hidden in the snow, and only just managed to save himself from falling flat upon his face by grabbing hold of his brother's arm.

"What?" he said, when he'd managed to regain his balance, certain he could not have heard Euan aright.

The duke continued stolidly along. "You heard me. Let me see, who do we know with eligible daughters?"

"I do not need," Niall said, torn between amusement and horror over the idea, "your help in finding myself a wife, Euan, nor am I in any sort of position to marry at the moment—"

"Nonsense." Euan was warming to the subject now. "You've got five thousand a year now. Why, there's not an unattached woman in England who wouldn't swoon at the thought of five thousand a year."

Niall shook his head, bemused at the turn the conversation had taken. "Euan, I'm not getting married now, or anytime in the near future."

"Why not? 'Tis not as if you're an ugly fellow. You're decent looking enough. I'm certain there are lots of—"

"I know there are." Niall glared at his feet. "I am sure there are any number of young women in Irmgarde's acquaintance who would make perfectly suitable wives— for the average man. But not for me. If I were to take a wife—which I have no intention of doing—'twould have to be a woman who'd be willing to put up with a good deal of hardship. And that quite rules out any of the girls I've met lately in Paris or London, or even Glasgow, for that matter. Do you know"—Niall's indignation came through in his scandalized tone—"that I've yet to be introduced to a single young woman who fully understands what typhoid is, let alone knows how to spell it? All they seem capable of talking about is balls and gowns and what Lady Hanson said to the Earl of McKonnickey last Tuesday. I certainly don't want to spend the rest of my life listening to *that.*"

This tirade was followed by a moment of silence, during which all that could be heard was the crunch of snow beneath their feet and the panting of the dogs. After a moment, Euan said, "Well, dear *me.* I had no idea your taste in women was so exacting, Your Royal Highness."

Slightly ashamed of his outburst, Niall said, " 'Tis very well for you to talk. You found the only woman worth marrying, you know."

"True," Euan agreed. "Still, there have got to be others like her out there."

"There aren't," Niall said firmly. "Believe me. I've looked."

He had, too. But all the young women Niall had met at the functions he had attended—concerts and suppers and balls—had only served to impress upon him the fact that there was something seriously wrong with the way young women in both France and England were educated. They seemed to know nothing of math and science and only a very little about art and literature—but everything there was to know about their neighbors. It was, Niall had decided, tiresome in the extreme.

Not that he didn't appreciate a pretty face and a nicely curved bosom. He had certainly been attracted to a fair number of the girls he'd met.

Until, that is, they'd opened their mouths.

Reflecting upon this depressing state of things, Niall was only dimly aware that the dogs had begun barking and that Collin was shouting at them to be quiet.

"Barley!" the boy cried. "Samson! Dolly! Get back here at once!"

Niall looked up from the trail his feet were making through the deep snow. "What's wrong with the dogs?" he asked.

Euan said, "Fox, most likely. Maybe Gypsies. There've been some camping down by the sheep meadow."

"What about *that* one?" Una, who was pulling her glum-faced little brother Rory along by the hand, pointed at a ten-foot fir tree a little way ahead of them.

"Ah," Euan said. "Aye. That looks like the one. Good eye, Una. Collin, bring the axe, and we'll mark it for cutting."

But Collin was still attempting to control the fractious dogs, who seemed to have become wholly transfixed by what they'd discovered in a hollow section of the trunk of an enormous oak tree. It was a tree Niall recognized. Struck by lightning a hundred years earlier—at least according to Fergus, who'd been woodsman to the Duke of Camden for as long as Niall could remember—the sturdy oak, nearly four feet round and almost a hundred high, hadn't fallen. Instead, a long fissure had formed in part of its trunk—wide enough for a boy, grieving over the death of his mother, to slip through, and enjoy a few hours of solitary weeping.

Aye, Niall knew that particular tree quite well.

Whatever—or whoever—had taken shelter in that hollow now was probably regretting his decision. The duke's dogs scampered back and forth in front of the tree, tongues lolling, tails wagging, barking as if they would never stop.

"Och," Euan said, disgustedly. "Cease that infernal noise now, you mangy animals, or I'll have the pack of you shot."

Chuckling, Niall called out to his nephew, "Well, Collin? Can you see what they've found there? Fox? Or a rabbit, maybe?"

"No," the boy replied, at length. " 'Tis a *lady*."

Two

*H*is nephew, Niall realized, when he'd come close enough to see for himself, was not wrong. It *was* a lady. Or a woman, in any case. Niall could discern the edge of a dark skirt peeping out from the hollow part of the tree trunk.

As he watched, a face appeared, framed by what

436

appeared to be a fur-trimmed bonnet. The woman peered cautiously around the side of the fissure, then, apparently not yet realizing she'd been spotted, ducked back into her hiding place, the abruptness of the motion causing the dark skirt to sway, revealing numerous petticoats, flashing as white as the snow all around them.

The dogs barked madly, and Niall caught a glimpse of gloved hands making subtle shooing gestures.

Euan let out a rude exclamation.

"Gypsy," he said, under his breath. "Now there'll be no end of bother. We'll never be getting home for that toddy."

Niall wasn't certain what his brother meant. Their father had certainly never tolerated Gypsies, despite the fact that they had never caused him, nor the residents of Kilcairn, the neighboring village, any trouble. Whenever a caravan had shown up, the duke had sent hirelings to chase them away, often with sticks and occasionally with rifles.

But Euan, Niall was sure, would never be so hard-hearted.

A second later, however, he saw what his brother meant by "bother," when Collin, wading through the pack of dogs, addressed the woman hiding in the tree.

"Please, miss." His nephew's polite little voice carried towards them across the snow. "Don't be frightened of our dogs. They won't hurt you. Can we help you? Are you lost?"

Euan groaned at this display of childish generosity. "This is all Irmgarde's fault," he grumbled. "Her and her damned Christmas spirit. Drummed it into the children's heads, she did."

The woman must have said something in reply to the

boy's queries, but Niall couldn't hear what it was over the sound of the snow crunching beneath his feet as he followed his brother.

"No, really," Collin was saying, as Niall approached. "You can have it. I don't need it. I'm not poor, you see."

"I assure you, sir—" The voice that came from within the tree trunk was definitely *not* that of a Gypsy. It was quite without a Romany accent. In fact, it sounded to Niall like that of a Scotswoman. Odder still, an *educated* Scotswoman. And there weren't many of those in this isolated part of the country. "—I do not need your money."

Collin, Niall saw, when he'd managed to make his way through the sea of dogs to his nephew's side, was holding a shiny gold sovereign in his outstretched mitten. The boy had on his face a look of extreme distress.

"Please," Collin said. "You've *got* to take it. 'Tis Christmas Eve, you know."

"I am perfectly aware of the date," the woman replied, very tartly indeed. "I am not, however, in need of charity, sir; though I do thank you."

Niall was forced to knee several dogs out of the way before he could get close enough to see the person with whom his nephew was having this extraordinary conversation.

And then, once he'd caught sight of the face of the woman who'd taken refuge in his childhood hiding place, he froze, quite unconscious of the dogs pressing against his legs.

This, he said to himself, *is no Gypsy.*

"But it's a *pound,*" Collin was saying, in a heartbroken voice. "An entire pound. You can buy quite a bit with a pound, miss."

" 'Tis very generous of you, sir," the girl said. Because she was, indeed, a girl, and not a woman. Not a day, Niall was certain, over twenty, if even that.

And she was—not to put too fine a point on it— lovely.

"But as I explained," the girl went on, "I am not a beggar. I am in fact quite well off. See for yourself."

And she opened the reticule she held, an expensive-looking one, trimmed with beaver skin, to match her bonnet. Tilting the bag, she held it out for Collin to see. The dull glint of gold lining the bottom of the purse was unmistakable.

"There you are," she said briskly, closing the bag again. "As you see, I am in no need of your munificence, young man; though I do thank you for the thought."

Munificence. Niall repeated the word to himself. "Munificence," she had said. It seemed exceedingly odd to him, hearing so long a word fall from such feminine lips. He was better used to hearing words no more taxing on the tongue than "yes" and "no" and "oh" from girls as pretty as this one.

"I beg your pardon, madam."

It was the duke speaking now, wearing his most lordly demeanor. Euan was, it was clear to Niall, excessively bothered by this girl's interruption of their outing. He had tossed away his cheroot and now stood with his shoulders thrown back and his head held high—in spite of the blowing wind and snow. "But I am wondering if you are aware that you are on the private property of His Grace, the Duke of Camden."

The girl tilted her heart-shaped face—framed by the stylish and expensive beaver-trimmed bonnet, from which several strands of bright auburn hair had escaped—towards Euan, and said, haughtily, "Of course I'm aware of it. I am . . . why, I am on my way to see him."

Euan looked considerably taken aback. "The Duke of Camden? You're on your way to see him?"

"Indeed I am," the girl replied. "So you needn't concern yourselves with me. Good-bye."

But in spite of her dismissive tone, she did not leave the shelter of the tree, and Euan, regarding her—much to Niall's embarrassment—as if she were an exhibit in a zoo, did nothing more than shift his weight from one foot to the other.

"Have you ever," Euan asked, "met the duke before, madam?"

"Of course I have," was the indignant reply. "Many times. Not that I see what business it is of yours."

Niall knew, even before he heard Euan inhale, exactly what was coming. His brother's temper ran as hotly as Euan insisted his wife's did. If anyone's hide was going to get a skinning that day, it seemed likely it was going to belong to the girl in front of him, and courtesy of the new Duke of Camden.

Accordingly, Niall stepped between his brother and the very rude young lady standing in the tree hollow.

"The duke is dead, madam," Niall explained. "I am his son, Lord Niall Sylvester Donnegal, and this is my elder brother, the new duke, Jervis Euan MacInerney Donnegal, Duke of Camden, Earl of Glenridge, and—"

"Dead?"

The girl's voice was no longer in the least bit rude. It shook, in fact, with suppressed feeling. And it did not seem to be shaking with trepidation at Niall's having pulled out all of his and Euan's names and titles, either, an act ~~that~~ often served to awe those who happened to overhear it.

But the girl did not appear to be awed at all. She seemed to be suffering from a shock of a different kind entirely.

"The duke is *dead?*"

It was then that, for the first time, Niall noticed the girl's eyes—brilliantly blue, and very large. Their size was emphasized by a certain small miracle of nature Niall had once heard his mother, on noticing the trait in a crofter's child, describe as fairyish: long black eyelashes coupled with bright red hair. It was a combination held in great suspicion, he knew, in this part of the world, local lore asserting that anyone born with it was certain to be a changeling, a fairy child placed, in the dead of night, in the cradle of a human baby.

But fairies, as any good Scot knew, were incapable of weeping. And as Niall stood there watching, the cobalt eyes belonging to the girl in front of him filled with tears.

Harboring no great affection for his late father himself, it was quite unsettling to meet a complete stranger who had cared enough for the old man to grow misty-eyed at news of his passing.

"Um," Niall said. "Aye. Well, I'm afraid so. You oughtn't— I mean, 'tis hardly your fault if you didn't hear of it before now. 'Twas quite sudden. If, er, you have some business with the duke," Niall ventured, frantically trying to think of something comforting to say, since the girl seemed genuinely distressed, "perhaps we could help. We—"

"*No.*" The strangled-sounding, monosyllabic statement

came out from beneath the lowered bonnet-brim. She had ducked her head so that her face was hidden from view. *"Not him, too."*

At least, that's what Niall thought she said. It was hard to tell, she murmured the words so softly.

Niall, bewildered by this, said, "I can assure you, madam, that he went quite peacefully. In his sleep, I'm told—"

"When?" The bonnet came up, and that cerulean gaze fastened on him with an intensity he found disconcerting. "When did he die?"

"Well, several months ago, actually," Niall said, uncomfortably. "Last August, in fact."

"And I saw him last in July," she murmured, as if to herself. She'd lowered her eyes again, so that those thick sooty lashes curled against her cheeks. When she spoke again, it was so softly that, again, Niall wasn't certain he heard her correctly. But he thought she uttered the words, *"my fault."*

But that didn't make any sense at all. How could this young woman be in any way responsible for his father's death?

A second later, she'd regained her composure and looked up.

"I am truly sorry to hear that your father is gone," she said gravely. "I hope you will both accept my deepest sympathies. He was a very kind man. He will be sorely missed."

Niall exchanged glances with his brother, and realized by Euan's slack-jawed expression that the duke was just as confused as he was. Here was something neither of them had ever before encountered in their lifetimes: someone who'd actually liked their father . . . someone who even claimed the old man had once been kind! Niall could not remember his father ever having been kind to anyone, with the possible exception of his dogs and horses, of whom he had seemed enormously fond. That he might also have been fond of this slip of a girl did tend to boggle the mind a bit. Henry Donnegal, if Niall remembered correctly, had not had much patience for youth, and not the slightest appreciation for beauty.

But perhaps Niall had not known his father quite as well as he'd thought.

After a glance at Euan revealed that the new duke was entirely too stunned to reply to the young woman's clearly heartfelt expression of sympathy, Niall took it upon himself—a burden he did not exactly resent—to say, with all the gallantry he could muster, "It is comforting, indeed, madam, to know that in our father's declining years, he was so well attended by his neighbors. And now if you are certain that the new duke can be of no aid to you, perhaps you will allow me to escort you home? For I fear the wind is rising, and it is not a clime well-suited to travel, particularly for young women abroad without an escort."

The blue eyes grew quite a bit bigger at this. And in those sapphire depths, Niall saw what first the rudeness, and then the tears, had kept hidden from them up until that moment.

She was frightened.

Almost desperately so, he thought. And not of the dogs, though that would have been understandable. Unless one had been told that the pack of them were good-natured, even docile animals, one wouldn't have known it, as they were a vicious-looking lot.

But no, it wasn't the dogs that frightened her, for even as he watched, one of her gloved hands moved to stroke the ear of nearby Dolly, a wolfhound nearly as tall as she was.

It couldn't possibly be *him*. Nor even Euan, for all his posturing. Oh, they were intimidating, he and Euan, as tall as they were, and both of them dark as Gypsies. Certainly any woman would be a little ill at ease, coming across the two of them on a blustery day in a secluded wood.

But they were surrounded by *children,* one of whom would not give over tugging on the tail of her father's greatcoat and crying that she wanted to be carried, while two others had begun to pelt one another with pinecones, snowballs apparently being unsatisfactory missiles. Surely two men in the company of so many children could not frighten a girl who had lived through an interview with his father, whom Niall had always considered the most intimidating man he'd ever known.

But there was no doubt about it. The girl was frightened.

And if it wasn't of the dogs or their masters, what could it be?

"Oh, no," she said hastily, in response to his offer, none of her fear showing in her tone. She'd overcome—or was pretending to, at any rate—both her mysterious trepidation and her shock at hearing of his father's death. Now she was all that was natural and breezy—on the outside, in any case.

"I thank you for your kindness, my lord, but I do not need an escort. I am actually headed for the Post Road, so if you don't mind my trespassing a little longer—"

"The Post Road?" Niall stared at her. "I thought you said you were on your way to see my father?"

"Yes, yes, of course, but now that I know he is—"

"You cannot be thinking of traveling, in weather like this?"

"Oh, 'tis nothing," the girl assured him. "I have done it many times."

"Alone?" Niall raised his eyebrows. The idea of such a young girl traveling alone was quite shocking to him. He had never heard of such a thing. "What can your family be thinking, allowing you to go so far by yourself?"

"I believe," she replied, a bit tersely, "that they are thinking that I am a rational creature who is perfectly capable of getting from one location to another on her own without needing to be supported by a man."

Niall blinked. Good Lord! So she was one of *those!* He'd never have known it, to look at her.

"Let us, at least," he persisted, "escort you to the road, and wait with you until the post chaise arrives."

"You are very kind," came her steady reply. "I wouldn't dream of imposing upon you in such a manner. I am perfectly capable of finding my own way. Good day to you both, my lords."

Niall and his brother once again exchanged glances. Niall had heard, of course, about a particular sort of modern young woman who believed that her sex should receive fair and equal treatment with his own—followers of Mary Wollstonecraft and her ilk—and accordingly routinely eschewed offers of hartshorn and masculine arms to lean upon, but he had never expected actually to meet any of these exotic creatures—least of all in Kilcairn. But here, on his very own property—or rather, his brother's—was a girl who seemed to be suffering a strong case of this fairly rare malady.

And she had been on friendly terms with his father!

His father, who would have had a great deal to say on the subject of her—or any woman, for that matter—traveling alone.

Despite his firm belief that what she was doing was reckless in the extreme, Niall might have respected her wishes and gone about his way if it hadn't been for that fear he'd glimpsed in her eyes, coupled with her reluctance to come out from the confines of that tree. Something—or someone—had terrified her, despite her efforts not to show it.

Euan, however, had not seen the fear and seemed to have grown tired of the game. This was probably due to the fact that five-year-old Margaret was still hanging solidly from his arm, crying that she wanted to go home.

"For God's sake," Euan snapped, when Niall continued to hesitate, "if she doesn't want our help, she doesn't want it. We've other affairs to attend to this morning, if you'll recall."

Niall wanted to curse at his brother's cold manner. For the girl immediately wrenched her gaze from him and fastened it instead upon the duke.

"Then I do urge you to see to them," she said, coolly. "I will remove myself from your property presently."

Euan, apparently, needed no more urging. He had never, unlike his brother, been troubled by that which was not easily explained, and had little natural curiosity.

He was also, Niall thought bitterly, happily married and had no eye for any woman other than his wife.

"Fine." Euan lifted the axe and started back toward the tree Una had picked out. "Collin," he called back over his shoulder. "Come along, Collin, and help me mark this tree. The lady does not require your aid."

But Collin stayed exactly where he was. This might have been because his uncle Niall did not move, either. And Niall did not move because the girl in the tree, despite her bidding them good day, had stayed exactly where she was, as well.

He could see her resolve weakening, though. The steely determination he'd glimpsed in those azure eyes— side by side with that inexplicable fear—was slipping away. His will was a force against which, she seemed to be finally realizing, there was no defense.

Recognizing that he was winning, Niall maintained his position, even when his brother, some dozen yards away, shouted, "Would you let the girl alone? I'd like to get home before noon, you know."

But though the dogs barked in response, Niall did not budge.

Finally, after several long moments had ticked away, during which Niall could not help but notice how biting the wind had become, the girl said, "All right. You may escort me to the road. But I won't have you wait with me. Really, it isn't at all necessary."

Niall relaxed his stance and, unfolding his arms, said politely, "Then let us make haste, for the snow seems to be coming down harder than before."

The girl did not even glance at the white stuff falling all around them. "Aye," she said. And then, hesitantly, she asked, "Only would you be so good as to bring me something that I might use as a walking stick? I, um, twisted my ankle not too long ago, and I'm afraid it might still be a little tender."

Niall waded through the sea of dogs until he was about a foot away from the hollow within which she huddled;

then he stopped, bowed, and presented her with his elbow.

"I would be honored," he said, "if you would lean upon my arm."

Up close, he saw that not only were her eyelashes, through no trick of artifice, really every bit as black as coal, but her lips were a bright cherry red, stained that way by the cold. The color that suffused her smooth cheeks, however, deepened at his approach, and he realized it was a blush.

And just as she'd tried to hide her fear from him, she tried to hide her shyness, as well.

"Honestly," she said, keeping her hands firmly clenched upon the strings to her reticule. "That isn't necessary. A stick will suffice."

Collin, to Niall's annoyance, immediately ran off to look for one. Niall, however, kept his arm stubbornly extended.

"I insist," he said, looking directly into those indigo eyes. "Miss . . . ?"

Even white teeth clamped down on her lower lip. She'd dropped her gaze, as if intimidated at the boldness of his own, and now stared at his arm. Finally, after a long moment, she reached out and laid her fingers through the crook of his elbow.

"Mairi," she said, and he did not miss the fact that she pointedly avoided giving him a surname.

Then, some of the determination returning to her face, she took a step toward him . . .

And promptly lost consciousness, those cobalt eyes rolling back up into her head, and her body pitching forward, right into his hastily outstretched arms.

Three

"Is she dead?" Euan asked, after a moment of stunned silence.

"No, of course not." Niall knelt beside her, where he'd laid her upon his greatcoat in the snow. "Just fainted."

Collin, looking appalled, asked, in horrified tones, "From hunger?"

"I don't think so," Niall soothed his nephew. "You saw her purse. She's not a beggar. She's quite well off."

"What's wrong with her, then?" Euan wanted to know.

Niall, after only a cursory examination of the patient, soon found out—and when he did, he lifted the hem of her skirt an inch or two to show the duke. Euan looked, then sucked in his breath. Niall lowered the skirt before Collin, alarmed by his father's expression, could see anything.

"What?" Collin demanded. "What is it? Let me see. Why can't I see?"

" 'Tis nothing," Niall said. "A dog bite, I think."

Collin set his jaw indignantly. "Dolly would never!" he declared. "Nor Barley either!"

"It wasn't one of our dogs, Collin," the duke said. "Come along. We're going home."

The younger children, who'd been dumping snow down one another's backs, stopped and stared at their father.

"But what about the tree?" Una asked.

"Fergus will fetch it later," the duke said. Under his breath, he murmured, "And I'll make sure he brings a bloody rifle with him."

"It couldn't have been a wolf," Niall assured his brother in a low voice. "She'd have said something—"

"But if it wasn't any of our dogs, and it wasn't a wolf, then what?" Euan raised his voice. "Margaret, put that snow down. We're going."

"I don't want to go." Collin folded his arms across his chest in unconscious imitation of his uncle at his most intractable. "I want to stay with the Gypsy!"

Niall made haste to remove the temptation from his nephew's sight by wrapping the senseless girl in his coat and then lifting her into his arms. "She isn't a Gypsy," he said. "And we're taking her with us."

"Are we?" Collin looked delighted. "Do you mean we get to keep her?"

This caused his father's scowl to deepen. "No, we do not get to keep her. She isn't an injured marmot, for God's sake."

But his son didn't seem to hear him. "Are you going to carry her all the way back to the manor house, Uncle Niall? Do you want me to help?"

"I've got her," Niall assured his nephew. "She's just a little thing—"

"Will she spend Christmas with us, then?" Collin wanted to know. "Will she?"

Euan had hoisted his youngest child, three-year-old Rory, into his arms and seized the hand of his second youngest in a grip that seemed to be making the little girl teary-eyed. "She'll want to spend Christmas with her own family, I'm sure. We'll just keep her until she's well enough to tell us where she lives, and then we'll take her there."

"Why can't we keep her?"

"Because," the duke said, "she belongs to someone. She's just run off, or something."

"You don't know that." Niall had not meant to speak quite as sharply as he did, and quickly lowered his voice. "She came here to see Father—"

"Act your age, Niall." Euan shook his head disgustedly. "She was obviously taking the shortest path she could find to the Post Road. Paying a call on Father was just something she invented so we wouldn't accuse her of trespass."

"Maybe she's lost," Collin offered charitably.

"There are only a few places she could have come from," Euan said, helping Margaret struggle through a particularly deep snowdrift, "on foot like this."

"I hope you aren't suggesting," Niall said, dryly, "that we strap her into a pony cart and wheel her from door to door until someone claims her."

"Old McCardle," Euan continued, as if his brother hadn't spoken. "His sister's visiting. Might be one of his nieces. There's the vicar, too. He was entertaining relatives from town, last I heard."

"What about Lord Sutherland?" Collin suggested.

Niall, despite the gravity of the situation, let out a laugh that was echoed a second later by his brother.

"I think not," Euan said.

"Why?" Collin looked puzzled. "MacLean Hall's just across the burn. . . ." Then, noticing his father's disapproving glance, he added, "Not that I've ever been there."

"Collin . . ."

"Well," the boy said, "I never crossed the burn."

Euan frowned at his eldest son. "And you'll see that you don't. Place is haunted, you know."

Niall threw his brother a disapproving look. "Euan, what are you—"

"Aye, haunted," Euan, undeterred by his brother's disapproval, went on. "Haunted by the evil spirit of old Sutherland, who didn't like your grandfather very much."

"Why?" Collin wanted to know.

"Because he considered your grandfather a pretender—not a real Highlander, since he was born and bred in England."

"Am I a real Highlander?" Collin asked.

"Real enough," Euan asserted.

"Then why should I have to worry about an old ghost?"

"It's not the ghost you need to worry about," Euan explained. "It's his son . . . young Sutherland, who is very much alive, and doesn't like us either."

"Why?"

"Because he doesn't like anyone. Used to pelt us with rocks, didn't he, Niall, every time we came anywhere near the burn. A thoroughly unpleasant boy who has grown into a thoroughly unpleasant man. I know——" Euan brightened suddenly. "She's got a reticule. Let me see if there's anything in that bag that will tell us who she is."

A search through the girl's reticule provided no hint of her identity, though it did confirm that she was, in fact, far from the penniless beggar Collin imagined her—she was carrying a great deal of money with her, along with an old-fashioned man's pocket watch, and . . .

"That," Euan declared, looking down at the small pearl-and-diamond ring in his hand, "is a wedding ring."

"Not necessarily," Niall said.

Euan tossed the ring back into the velvet pouch and pulled the drawstring closed. " 'Tis a *wedding* ring, Niall," he said. "She's married. She's run off. Her husband's probably out combing the woods for her as we speak."

Niall said, with a calm he wasn't quite feeling, "You've been reading too many novels."

"I know a wedding ring when I see one"—the duke ignored the remark about his novel reading—"and that's what that is."

"Well, why isn't she wearing it, then?"

Euan appeared momentarily stumped. Then he brightened. "Because she intends to sell it."

"You're daft."

"And you've gone simple in the head if you can't see what's staring you straight in the face. She's left her husband, and he's likely to come after us with a rifle—"

"Oh, for God's sake, Euan—"

It was Una who declared, with all the truculence she'd inherited from the grandfather she had never known, "Mama."

Both men broke off and looked down at the little girl.

"Mama," she said again. "Mama will know what to do."

Niall threw a triumphant look at his brother. "Exactly. That's precisely what we'll do. We'll take her to Irmgarde. Thank you, Una."

"You're welcome," his niece replied.

It was at this point that the girl in Niall's arms abruptly regained consciousness, her eyelids fluttering and then flying all the way open, as if she'd been startled by something she'd seen in her mind's eye.

"Oh," she cried, as soon as she became aware of her surroundings—and of Niall's proximity. "What happened? Where are we?"

"Don't be afraid." Collin grinned up at her. "You fainted. We're taking you to Donnegal Manor. You'll like it. 'Tis very grand."

"Donnegal Manor." Color was rapidly returning to the girl's face. "Donnegal Manor? But I don't want to go there. Oh, put me down. Put me down at once!"

On the word *once,* she gave Niall's chest a healthy pound with a doubled-up fist, proving that she was quite fit again. Though the blow did not trouble Niall in the least, the duke was not so sanguine.

"I say, Niall," he said, looking concerned. "You had better put her down, I think."

"So she can do what, Euan? 'Tis clear she cannot walk—"

"I can," the girl insisted. "I *can* walk. I only hurt my foot a little."

"A little?" Niall let out an incredulous laugh. "It looks as if it was mauled by a bear."

"Just my boot," she assured him. "The skin wasn't broken."

"It was a dog?" Niall asked. "Not a wolf, surely . . ."

"No, a dog. He grabbed hold of my foot and wouldn't let go. I tripped, but he still didn't let go, and so I ended up twisting my ankle."

"He nearly chewed your boot off," Collin, who'd finally gotten a look at the boot in question, said with obvious admiration.

"I'm quite sure it looks worse than it is. Really, my lord, I'm quite all right. If you would just put me down now—"

"No," Niall said simply.

"Um," Euan said. "Niall, I do believe the lady seems to have some objection—"

"What do you suggest I do, instead, Euan?" Niall interrupted. "Leave her here to freeze to death?"

" 'Tis only a little sore," the girl assured him, through determinedly gritted—but audibly chattering—teeth.

"And that's why you fainted?" Niall demanded. "Because your ankle is a *little* sore? No. Either you tell us where you live, and we take you there, or you resign yourself to being taken to Donnegal Manor." Niall took a firmer grip on her slender body. "And that's an end of it."

She looked as shocked as if he'd slapped her.

"But I *can't* go to Donnegal Manor," she said.

"I don't see why not. That's where you were headed in the first place, was it not? To see our father?"

"Aye, but—" Niall was startled to see that once again there tears glistening in those thick black lashes. "—but that was before . . ."

"Before what?" Niall asked.

"Before I knew he was dead." Her voice rose piteously. "Oh, *please* let me down. You don't know what you're doing."

"He does, actually," Collin assured her. "He's a blood-letter, you know. Licensed and everything."

"Physician," Niall corrected his nephew. To the girl, he said, "And I *am* licensed—"

"I don't need a physician. Oh!" She swung her head around to appeal to Euan, who apparently struck her as the more rational of the two brothers. "Oh, do make him put me down, Your Grace."

"Um," Euan said, in a manner quite disconcertingly unlordlike. "Niall, are you certain this is wise? The lass clearly doesn't care to—"

"We're taking her with us," Niall said, his jaw clenched, "and I don't want to hear another word about it."

The duke, with a glance at the girl's dismayed expression, tried again. "But—"

Euan broke off, silenced by a single menacing glance from his brother.

And that was the end of the matter—between Niall and the duke, that is. Between Niall and the girl, it was only the beginning.

Four

*T*he girl who'd asked him to call her Mairi—but since he very much doubted that was her real name, he could not bring himself actually to do so—was, Niall soon discovered, an accomplished arguer. She argued convincingly and well during the course of their walk back to the manor house, citing Plato's treatise on virtue, insisting that Niall was in grave danger of throwing the cosmos into disorder by ignoring her wishes, and that his father's death ought to have been a warning to him that disharmony in the cosmos can end in catastrophe—though what his father dying of gout had to do with Niall's insisting upon removing her from the perils of frostbite, he could not imagine.

Though her little speech was very dramatic and even, as he remarked to her when it was finished, quite entertaining, it did not in any way dissuade him from what he was convinced was the only sensible course of action.

And when she finally realized that, "Mairi" stopped arguing and took to looking angry instead . . . though on her, even anger looked perfectly charming.

Her dire warnings concerning his late father, however, did manage to persuade Collin that the girl in his uncle's arms was indeed a Gypsy—a real live Gypsy woman whom they'd happened to capture just in time for Christmas, and who could prophecy the future . . . a future so filled with gloom that the boy took it upon himself to comfort her.

"You'll like it at our house," Collin took pains to assure her as they trudged along through the snow. "We have very nice Christmases, with stockings and oranges and dancing. Much better, I'm sure, than you get in your Gypsy camp. Mama will see that you get plenty to eat, so you needn't worry about having to beg . . . at least, not for a while, anyway."

This last comment brought a very healthy amount of color to the girl's face. Niall couldn't help noticing, because she was clinging very tightly to his neck, as if she didn't quite trust him not to drop her, and her face was, in consequence, very close to his.

"I'm not a Gypsy," she insisted.

Collin gave no appearance of having heard her assertion, although the woods were perfectly still, except for the gentle hiss of the snow falling all around them and the sound of it crunching beneath their feet.

"Christmas," Collin went on to explain, "is about sharing. Mama says even if you don't have very much, you should share what you have at Christmastime. Last Christmas, we didn't have so much, because Papa wasn't a duke yet. Still, we shared what he had. But now that he's a duke, we really have quite a lot. So you needn't worry there won't be enough for everyone. We have plenty, and we don't mind sharing."

Una, overhearing all of this, chimed in with, "Mama especially doesn't mind sharing. Why, she might even let you try on her tiara. She has one, you know, now that she's a duchess."

Niall was unable to restrain a smile at his niece's guile-lessness. He glanced down to see what "Mairi" thought about it and was relieved to note that her expression, which had been mutinous before, had turned thoughtful.

"I would be very grateful to you," she said, speaking not to the children, but to Niall, "if you were to bind my ankle."

Surprised into speechlessness by this sudden capitula-tion, Niall kept walking, noticing that the uppermost floors of Donnegal Manor were becoming dimly visible before them.

"But then I really will have to be on my way," the girl went on. "You've got to believe me, 'tis vitally important I leave Kilcairn today."

Euan, rambling along beside them, a sniffling Margaret in one arm and a squirming Rory in the other, grunted at this piece of information.

"Well, you won't be leaving any time soon in this muck." He tilted his head meaningfully toward the sky, from which massive white flakes were falling at a rapid pace. "The post certainly won't be able to get through it. Not before tomorrow, nor for a long bit after that, if it keeps up."

This discouraging piece of information seemed to dis-tress the girl so much, she looked ready to burst into another Platonic dialogue.

Fortunately, Niall was able to distract her by saying, "Oh, look. There's the house now."

With a single candle burning brightly in every window—another Christmas mandate of the new duchess—Donnegal Manor had never before looked so welcoming, rising out of the mist. Each golden flame did its valiant best to relieve the midwinter gloom that threatened to engulf the otherwise colorless landscape.

Inside, they soon found, the hall was just as inviting, with preparations for the tenant ball well underway. Irmgarde was understandably astonished to discover what they'd brought home with them, but bore the shock admirably, very calmly directing that a divan be placed before the great-hall fire, and then insisting upon standing beside it, holding on to the girl's hand while Niall unlaced what remained of her boot.

"You oughtn't," Niall said chidingly, after a thorough examination proved the skin was indeed unbroken and that she had, as she'd maintained, only twisted it, "have tried to walk on it."

"I didn't know," the girl said, wincing as he gently rotated her foot, "it had gotten *that* bad. I walked on it a little after I first fell, and it seemed all right. . . ."

"But then it got too sore for you to go on," Niall said, with a knowing look. "So you holed up inside that tree to get out of the wind, hoping if you stayed off it, it would get better. Only it got worse. It had a chance to swell inside your boot. And then when you tried to walk on it again—"

"I fainted." She stared mournfully down at her bare toes, which peeped out from beneath the full hem of her wool traveling skirt. "I don't suppose I'll be able to put weight on it for some time."

"Your ankle is very badly sprained," Niall said, severely.

"Your boot seems to have kept the brute's teeth from breaking the skin, but there's significant bruising—"

"Are you absolutely certain"—Irmgarde interrupted her brother-in-law worriedly—"that it wasn't a wolf, my dear?"

The girl raised her cobalt gaze towards the duchess and said, "Aye. 'Twas only a dog."

"A dog that ought to be shot," Niall asserted. "I cannot imagine who could be keeping such a brute, but rest assured, when I find out, I'll see that the animal is destroyed."

"Oh, I think he's learned his lesson," the girl said. "I kicked him rather hard in the head, poor thing. He ran off yelping, and I didn't see him again."

"Thank goodness." Irmgarde handed the girl a cup from a tray one of the maids presented her with. "Here, dear, you must drink this and try to get warm. And I've laid your boots and stockings by the fire where they can dry. They were soaked through."

The girl took the cup with a polite thank-you, but Niall noticed her fingers were shaking . . . and not, he suspected, from the cold. No, that fear—that inexplicable fear he'd glimpsed in her eyes—was still there. Suppressed, maybe, for the moment, but still very much alive.

Well, and why not? She had been through an ordeal. She ought, by rights, to have been in hysterics when they'd come across her. But the only time she'd really lost her composure had been when she'd wakened from her faint and found herself in a strange man's arms—and when he'd informed her he was taking her to Donnegal Manor.

If only he could have borrowed some of her *sangfroid*. Because, frankly, Niall was worried.

He was worried for a number of reasons—Euan's assertion that she was a runaway bride, which he could not seem to get out of his head, amongst them. But the primary cause was that the ankle before him was quite the prettiest one he had ever seen.

Or at least, it would have been, if there hadn't been a perfect mate to it, not a few inches away. And that ankle was even more appealing, since it was not in the least swollen or discolored. Still, even the injured ankle was lovely, and this was worrying, as well.

Because it was important, he knew, that he maintain a professional demeanor. Ogling his patient's feet was not the way to go about doing that.

And so he resolutely turned his attention to setting a splint for her.

It was difficult, however, to pay full attention to the task at hand when his heart was hammering loudly enough that he was certain everyone in the hall could hear it. How was it that he could find himself so powerfully attracted to this girl he had only just met? Worse, to a girl who he was not even certain had told him her real name and who appeared to be in some sort of grave trouble? He had no room in his life for this kind of nonsense.

And yet, there it was. This "Mairi" who'd appeared so magically on his brother's property drew him as had no other woman he'd ever met, and continued to do so, despite the fact that every time she opened her mouth, something strange invariably came out. . . .

Or was it perhaps *because* she was so different from the other girls he'd known that he found himself so inexplicably attracted to her? Here, anyway, was one young lady who seemed about as unlikely to utter those simple statements Niall had grown so tired of hearing upon the dance floor—all those yeses and noes and ohs—as any of those other girls he'd so disparaged were likely to recite the whole of *Parmenides* from memory.

He was just tying off the splint when the front doors burst open with a bang.

His patient, gasping in a manner that could only be called terrified, whipped around in her seat just in time to see a large man, covered from head to toe with snow, come stomping into the great hall. Wind swirled snow in a cyclone all around him, and it took a minute to see that he dragged behind him an equally snow-covered fir tree. At the sight of him, the children, who'd been playing hide-and-seek beneath the tables, burst out into shrieks of joy and darted towards him.

"Good heavens," the girl said, seeming to recover herself, all the color she'd lost returning in a flood. "Who is *that?*"

"Just Fergus," Niall replied, eyeing her curiously. "With the Christmas tree."

It wasn't his imagination. Her shoulders sagged with relief. . . .

Then just as abruptly tensed up again.

"Fergus," she said, watching as the woodsman, with the help of the duke and several footmen, attempted to right the tree. She'd flattened a hand to her chest, as if to still a heart that had begun to race. "Oh."

Niall couldn't help but observe, "You say that as if you were expecting someone else."

She turned back toward him. "Of course not," she said. "Really, who could *I* be expecting?"

He said, seriously, "I wouldn't know, now, would I? I don't even know your name."

"You do." She actually looked hurt. "I told you. 'Tis Mairi."

"Mairi what?"

That brought a smile. "Just Mairi," she said, keeping her gaze on Fergus and his struggles with the tree. "This is the first time Christmas has ever been celebrated in this house, I'm quite sure."

Niall, not completely oblivious to her careful change of subject, wryly agreed.

Something in his tone must have given away his true feelings on the matter, since she looked at him rather sharply and said, "You don't approve?"

Niall shrugged uncomfortably. "It seems a bit . . . frivolous."

She burst out laughing. It was the first time he'd heard her laugh. The sound of it startled him . . . then did something rather curious to his spine. His worries, it seemed, were only just beginning.

"Oh, if you only knew how much you sounded like your father just then," she said with a smile.

Niall frowned. In no way did he wish to be associated with his father.

"He told you Christmas trees were frivolous as well?" he asked glumly.

"Oh, of course. But I assure you, as I assured him, that their origins are actually very serious in nature."

Niall blinked at her. Irmgarde had drifted off to direct the placement of the dining tables, which in a few hours would be groaning from all the food piled atop them. The duchess did not seem nearly as concerned about the fact that she was harboring a possible runaway in her home as Niall thought she should be. She actually told him to "stop worrying so much," insisting that the girl appeared, overall, "sensible enough."

But how was Niall supposed to stop worrying, when statements like, "their origins are actually very serious in nature," kept popping from the girl's mouth?

"The fir tree," she went on to explain, "like the shamrock, is representative of the Holy Trinity . . . turned upside down, of course. The candles I imagine your sister-in-law will put on the branches represent the stars in the heavens, as Martin Luther observed them one night on a midnight stroll. Papish, your father said, when I told him this. But not frivolous, necessarily. Though I don't suppose you, as a man of science, will agree."

Hoping to disarm her into revealing her identity, he inquired, "And when did you meet my father?"

"Oh, years ago," she said. "I remember he asked why I wasn't in the nursery, and I told him I'd graduated from the nursery and was going away to school. You'd have thought I'd said I was off to sell oranges for a living, he got so angry. He shouted that one might as well throw money down a well as spend it on educating a girl. And then he—"

She broke off and glanced sharply in his direction.

"Why, you're trying to draw me out," she declared indignantly.

Niall couldn't help grinning at that. "And I almost succeeded."

To his surprise, however, the grin seemed to discomfit her. She looked away from him, into the fire, and he did not think it was because of the heat from the flames that her cheeks took on a distinctly brighter hue.

He said carefully, "Madam, I apologize. That was ignoble of me."

When she raised her gaze again, he saw that those cerulean eyes were unnaturally bright.

"Don't you see?" she asked in a husky voice. "I *daren't* tell you. I know you mean to be kind, but there isn't anything you can do to help me. And it would be better—really, it would—if you went away."

"Went away?" He raised his eyebrows. "But, madam, I live here."

She dropped her voice another notch. "From *me*, I mean."

"From you?" He shook his head perplexedly. "But why?"

She almost told him. He could tell from her expression. She'd been mentally weighing her words, taking care how she formulated her response. Her brows—black as her eyelashes—knit, and a tiny wrinkle appeared in the center of her forehead. Niall, not at all certain what to expect, leaned forward, realizing as he did so that his palms were damp and not, he was certain, as a result of the heat emanating from the fire in the hearth just a few feet away. . . .

His sister-in-law called to him imperiously.

"Niall, come, would you?" Irmgarde sounded annoyed. Small wonder, too. When he glanced in her direction, Niall saw, with a spurt of irritation of his own, that his brother, Fergus, and several footmen were all struggling, in as haphazard a manner as he had ever seen, to right the enormous tree.

"In a moment," Niall said to Irmgarde. He turned back toward his patient . . .

And saw in an instant that she'd changed her mind. She wasn't going to tell him a thing.

"You had better go," she said to him politely.

Niall, desperate to recapture the intimacy he thought they'd shared for a moment, said, with forced playfulness, "If 'tis any comfort to you, my father was impartial in his contempt for the concept of education. He didn't approve of it for boys, either."

She nodded. "Oh, aye. He and I used to argue about it. He didn't approve of very much, your father. And he certainly wouldn't have approved of *this.*"

On the word *this,* she tilted her head toward Irmgarde, who was clapping her hands and saying that she wanted the tree in the corner by the windows, not by the sideboard. Only she seemed momentarily to have forgotten the English word *sideboard* and was having trouble making her wish known. The result was that the footmen—and her husband—were dragging the tree up and down the great hall.

"Aye," Niall said. "This probably would have killed him, if he'd lived to see it."

This was not, however, the right thing to have said, since the girl paled again and went inexplicably silent.

"Niall!" his brother called to him.

Niall hurried to oblige his brother . . . but not before mentally cursing himself for being every kind of a fool.

Five

*M*airi had not killed Henry Donnegal.

She told herself this very firmly. She had not killed him, nor was she responsible in any way for his death. How could she be? His death, though unfortunate, to say the least, had nothing—nothing whatsoever—to do with her.

It was ridiculous, this idea about a curse. There was no such thing as a curse. Everyone knew that.

Superstitious claptrap. That's what it was. She knew that now. She was an educated woman and no longer an impressionable child who might be controlled with talk of fairies and curses. The duke had died through no fault of hers. And that was all.

That's what she told herself, anyway.

The difficulty, of course, was in believing it.

Still, she tried. To distract herself, she looked about and marveled at the changes that had taken place since she'd last sat in this great hall. Never in her life had she seen a household as chaotic as the one belonging to the new Duke of Camden. Things had certainly never been this disorganized when Henry Donnegal had been alive.

Granted, Mairi had only visited Donnegal Manor a few times before—when her guardian had been away and she'd been quite certain he wouldn't find out about it. The duke had formed, in his later years, a great enthusiasm for fishing and could generally be found hip-deep in the river that separated his property from the one belonging to her guardian. She had often come across His Grace on her morning rambles, in the summer months, when she'd been home from school. The last time she'd actually been inside the manor house had been years earlier . . . so many years earlier that she doubted anyone would recognize her. Even her guardian, Alistair, had told her she'd grown disgracefully tall since the last time he'd seen her. . . .

Disgracefully tall and, she supposed he was thinking now, disgracefully willful.

But no matter how tall Alistair might accuse her of having grown, she'd still never top anyone in the Donnegal household, with the exception of its very youngest members. Why, even the duchess, with her impressive crown of flaxen braids, looked as if she'd tower over Mairi by a good two or three inches. Mairi had stumbled, she realized, into a lair of giants.

Very loud giants.

Which was just fine, she figured. Her escape was less likely to be noticed in all this noise and confusion.

For she had to escape, of course. She certainly couldn't stay. Donnegal Manor was far too close to MacLean Hall for comfort.

And now there was this new duke to consider, with his pretty wife—German, Mairi thought she was, which certainly explained the transformation the great hall had undergone. The last time Mairi had seen it, the room had been filled with stags' heads and decaying tapestries. Tattered coats of arms, sewn onto flags, had hung from the rafters twenty feet overhead.

Now the stags' heads and tapestries were gone. In their place, maids were hanging boughs of evergreen and holly. Men on ladders were removing the tattered flags and draping the rafters with rich red swathes of velvet. It was as festive a room as Mairi had ever seen, and she remembered that Germans were very partial to Christmas celebrations.

She found herself hoping fervently, in spite of every logical argument against such a fantastic idea, that this new duke, with his Christmas-loving wife and towheaded children, was not going to follow in his father's footsteps, and die because of her.

And his brother . . . his very stubborn, very handsome brother. She would not be able to bear it if he—

"Gypsy Lady."

Startled from her dark thoughts, Mairi turned and found herself being addressed by the duke's eldest son, Collin, whom she'd learned was a viscount.

"Are the potatoes," the boy asked politely, "to your liking?"

Mairi looked down at the plate of food in her lap. Tea, the duchess had explained apologetically to her, would be light, because Cook was so busy preparing delicacies for the evening meal. Her Grace had hoped Mairi did not mind roast beef, German scalloped potatoes, pudding, glazed carrots, herring in cream sauce, and baked oysters, all washed down with Madeira.

If this was what the Duke and Duchess of Camden considered a "light tea," Mairi shuddered to think what they considered a heavy one.

"The potatoes are very good," Mairi said, to Collin. "Only I wish you wouldn't call me Gypsy Lady."

"Shall I call you Fairy Lady, then?" Collin looked hopeful. "Because that's what Sileas says you look like."

Mairi knit her brows. "Who is Sileas?"

"Rory's nursemaid. She's over there, by the tree."

Mairi followed his gaze, and saw the rosy-cheeked peasant girl to whom he referred fiercely scolding his little brother for some unseen malefaction.

"I don't need one," Collin informed her, proudly. "A nursemaid, I mean. So, are you?"

Mairi, still confused, looked back at him. "Am I what?"

"A *fairy* lady. Because, you see, when I tell all my friends that we had an actual fairy lady stay for Christmas, they'll be quite jealous. So please say you are one. *Please.*"

Mairi, looking regretfully down the length of her body at her splinted foot, resting atop the pile of furs at the end of the divan, heaved a sigh. Was she a fairy lady, then? She hardly thought so. Even if there were such a thing, she doubted she'd qualify as one. A fairy would not have a frightening guardian trying to force her into marriage. And even if she did, well, a fairy would certainly never fall and injure herself trying to escape him.

It was all her own fault, of course. How stupid of her to have tried to run from Boris. She ought to have remembered he'd only think it a game. Alistair *would* send the dogs out after her, as if she were a fox or a stag that needed bringing down. Only she had thought she'd be far from Kilcairn by the time he was informed that she was gone. . . .

She hadn't counted on all the snow. She had taken the shortest path to the road, the one that crossed the Duke of Camden's property, but there the snow was deepest, having been blown into thick drifts.

And there Boris had found her. Boris, whom she'd known since he'd been born, had always been able to find her, primarily because she tended to carry treats for him and the other dogs in her pockets when she was home.

Alistair knew that only too well. One look at the enormous hound, and she'd become convinced the dog's master could only be right behind. And so she'd turned and tried to run. . . .

Well, the mercy of it was that Alistair had *not* been right behind. She couldn't imagine what had caused this small miracle: her guardian was enormously proud of his hunting skills. She supposed the snow was to blame. Perhaps his mount had lost its footing and fallen . . . hopefully on top of its rider, but Mairi suspected this was too much to ask.

Still, even after she'd managed to convince the dog she had no treats today and ordered him home, then dragged herself to the shelter of that tree, she'd clung to the hope—ridiculous, she knew now—that all was not yet lost. The Post Road was just across the Duke of Camden's horse pasture, not at all far off. She could make it, if she went slowly enough. . . .

She hadn't counted upon the duke's misguided—though admittedly well-intentioned—sons stumbling across her and scooping her up as if she were a lost kitten. She appreciated their kindness—particularly that of the younger son, Lord Niall—but it changed nothing: she still needed to escape, and the sooner, the better.

But just *how* soon she failed to realize until, a few seconds later, Fergus, the woodsman, approached her divan and stooped into a low bow, clutching his cap in his hands.

"Yer ladyship?" Only it was more of a statement than a question.

And before Mairi had time to dissemble, the old man's face had broken into a craggy smile. Pulling politely on a forelock that was every bit as red as Mairi's own hair, the woodsman said, "It *is* you, then, Lady Mairi. I thought as much, but I couldna likely believe it; you've grown so, if you'll excuse the impertinence. Just a wee lass you were when I last saw you."

Mairi looked frantically across the room. No, she did

not think anyone could have overheard, what with all the scraping forks and chatter. Well, except for the viscount, but he only looked perplexed and asked, "Do you know the Fairy Lady then, Mr. Fergus?"

"Fairy Lady?" It was Fergus's turn to look perplexed. "You oughtna be calling her ladyship a fairy lady, milord. Why, she's—"

Mairi said, quickly, "I believe you are mistaken, Mr. Fergus."

Fergus had grown a little hard-of-hearing since she'd last seen him. He went on, earnestly, "Remember how much yer ladyship loved the heather that grew along the Donnegal side of the burn? Couldna keep you away from it in springtime, for all Master Alistair didna like your wanderin' so far from the hall. . . ."

"Mr. Fergus," Mairi interrupted him, urgently. Then, when she'd got his attention, she gestured for him to lean down. When he'd come close enough for her lips to reach his ear, she whispered, "I do remember you, of course, and I am very glad to see you—and very saddened to hear of your master's death. Only might I ask, sir, that you keep our acquaintance to yourself for the moment? For you see, these kind people do not know me, and I have reason to wish to keep it that way."

"Ah." Fergus nodded. "Of course. His lordship wouldna be too happy to know you were here. Lord, no. A prouder Highlander never lived. Why, I'll never forget the last time I saw him. 'Twas two summers ago, when Master Alistair bought that horse from old Mr. McCardle and found he'd turned lame. Right up to McCardle's doorstep he took tha' poor animal, and shot him, straight between the—"

"Oh, do not," Mairi could not help crying out. For the

horse had been intended as a gift for her, and when she'd learned what Alistair had done upon discovering that the animal was lame, she'd been horrified—and convinced, once again, that the curse did in fact exist.

The cry she'd inadvertently let out had not been a particularly loud one, but it nevertheless brought the duke's brother to her side, a questioning expression on his face.

Oh, no, she thought to herself. Not *him* again. What was it about Lord Niall that sent her reaching, instinctively, for her hair? She was certain it must look very blowsy, and longed for a hand mirror. A good deal of it, she knew, had come out of the plait into which she had hastily arranged it that morning. She imagined that, because of the heat and damp, her thick red hair, which had an alarming tendency to curl, must be standing out all over her head like a halo. . . .

Not, of course, that she cared how anyone thought she looked. Outward appearances were only that, and no measure of one's internal worth.

Only Lord Niall did look so disturbingly . . . nice. Before her introduction to Plato, Mairi had been an apt student of physiognomy, and Lord Niall's was particularly striking, as it incorporated all of the traits considered ideal in the male specimen, including an aquiline nose, firm chin, square jaw-line, and sloping, but not low-hanging, brow. Like his brother, but unlike his sister-in-law and nieces and nephews, he was dark-haired—thick, wavy dark hair, that fell below the points of his shirt collar. He looked, in fact, like any one of the stylish young men who had come to see their sisters on their name days at the convent school Mairi had attended, the only days male visitors were allowed.

But none of those young men had had occupations. Quite the opposite. They'd led lives of idleness and luxury.

And yet this young man, who was dressed quite as opulently as any of her schoolmates' brothers, was supposedly a physician.

It hadn't seemed at all possible. Mairi had refused to believe it, at first. The idea of allowing this stylish young man—well, all except for his hair, which was too long to be truly stylish—to look at her naked foot had quite shocked her. What would Mother Superior—had she still been alive—have thought? The nuns had always been very careful to warn their young pupils about the lasciviousness of men, and one of their direst warnings had been on the dangers of allowing any man—even a member of the medical profession—to catch a glimpse of one's ankles.

But though Mairi had watched carefully as Lord Niall examined her, she did not see even a hint of lust in his eyes—which were every bit as gray, she couldn't help noticing, as the winter sky outside. Still, there'd been nothing in them but the most professional interest. He had, she decided, very nice eyes, though it was strange to see such light eyes in such a dark complexion. . . .

But no stranger, she supposed, than her own eyes, which were ringed by black lashes that the nuns had constantly accused her of darkening with coal. As if she would bother going to such trouble! For what? She did not have any desire to draw more attention to herself than her untamable red hair and far-too-blue eyes already engendered on their own. She was, as Alistair had always been only too eager to point out to her, a fairy thing . . .

Born under a fairy curse.

Looking down at her now with those curiously light eyes, the duke's brother asked, "Is everything all right?"

"Everything is very well indeed," Mairi replied, a bit too quickly. "The potatoes are quite to my liking."

This assertion caused the corners of Lord Niall's mouth to turn upwards. "Are they, now?"

But anything else he might have said was lost when his nephew, pointing an accusing finger at his father's woodsman, declared, "Mr. Fergus knows the fairy lady! He called her Lady Mairi!"

Mairi felt a wave of warmth surge into her face. Poor Fergus, she noted, when she glanced in his direction, went just as red.

"He was only joking," she said, quickly. "Of course Mr. Fergus doesn't know me. How could he?"

"He said how much you've grown," the viscount pointed out.

The woodsman said something, but it was uttered in so low a voice no one could possibly have heard him. Lord Niall had to stoop and ask the woodsman to repeat himself.

"I . . . was . . . mistaken," Fergus said again, this time enunciating distinctly, though still quite unable to meet anyone's gaze.

"There," Mairi said, feeling a surge of relief. She reminded herself to slip the woodsman a sovereign at her next opportunity. "You see? It was just a little mistake."

"So you *are* a fairy, then?" Collin asked, hopefully. "Can you do magic?"

The boy's uncle must have seen by her expression that she'd had quite as much of this as she could take, since suddenly Lord Niall said, "Collin, go and play with your sisters and brother."

And though Collin was not his own child, Lord Niall's commanding voice nevertheless carried enough authority that the boy felt compelled to leave, and in some considerable haste. He was followed no less speedily by Fergus, who muttered something about having some things to attend to and excused himself. . . .

Only to be called back by Lord Niall, who demanded, with as much imperiousness as he'd addressed his nephew, "How do you know this lady?"

The woodsman, abashed, stood crumpling his cap over and over in his hands, unable to look the younger man in the eye.

"I dunna know her, milord," he said. "I only thought I did."

"Well, who did you *think* she was, then?"

"I'm certain Mr. Fergus has duties that need attending to," Mairi said hastily. "Don't you, Mr. Fergus?"

The old man gave an awkward bow, and said, "Aye, that I do, mil—miss. Beggin' yer pardon, milord."

Fergus left the great hall with impressive speed for a man so advanced in years. As soon as he was gone, Mairi tilted her face—her cheeks cherry red, she was sure; she always blushed when she was angry—up toward the duke's brother.

"He told you he was mistaken. Why did you have to bully him so?"

"Bully!" Lord Niall looked down at her incredulously. "Asking a few questions of a servant one has known for years is hardly bullying, madam. Besides, if you felt Fergus was being so cruelly put upon, why did you not spare him by simply telling me what it is I wish to know?"

Mairi, disliking the logic of this question, frowned at him. "Why is it so important for you to know who I am, anyway?"

"I should think that would be obvious," he said, his light-eyed gaze steady on hers.

She felt a strange sort of shivery sensation all up and down her arms as she looked into those silver eyes. It was the same way she'd felt when he'd smiled at her a little bit ago. It was an alarming feeling. *Wolf eyes,* she thought. That's what he has. Why hadn't she noticed it before?

She had never actually seen a wolf, of course, but it seemed to her that only a wolf would look at her that way, so boldly, as if he'd like nothing better than to eat her.

But she was fairly certain no wolf's prey had ever felt as she did just then, as if being consumed by such a sleek, powerful beast might not actually be such a very bad thing. . . .

She shook herself. Good Lord. What was *happening* to her?

She dropped her gaze.

I should think that would be obvious, he'd said. What did he mean? What *could* he mean?

"Enlighten me," she said, and congratulated herself on the coolness of her tone.

"As a gentleman and a physician," he said, "I feel I have a moral obligation to offer you my protection. And I cannot do that if I don't know what it is, precisely, I am protecting you from."

Oh. So that was all he meant.

"Then you'd best believe me, Lord Niall, when I say that my health and safety are best guaranteed by my speedy removal from the area." *As,* long habit forced Mairi to add mentally, *are yours.*

That, she saw, caused those wolf eyes to blink. Suddenly, he did not look half so sure of himself.

"If you would simply *tell* me," he said, sounding very concerned indeed, "what it is that you are running away from, perhaps I could be of some help to you."

She shook her head. "You might try to make me go back—"

"That," he said, and she was gratified to see that he looked distinctly shocked, even hurt, at the suggestion, "I would never do. Not if you didn't wish it."

"You are very cavalier about my wishes," Mairi reminded him. "I told you I didn't want to come to Donnegal Manor, but you brought me here anyway."

"But you will be quite safe here, and well taken care of, far better than if you were alone on the Post Road, or worse, Edinburgh or London—"

"Nay, I'd be safe in London," Mairi insisted. "Because there, anyone might hide, with perfect anonymity, forever. Here, every moment that passes brings me closer to discovery."

And you, she added silently, to certain death. Because though the curse might very well be fantasy, the person who'd invented that fantasy was quite real, and he would not be happy with anyone who, however innocently, lent his quarry aid. . . .

"Why can't you ken that it's for the best that I go?" Mairi demanded miserably.

The two of them stared at one another. She had to crane her neck to look into his eyes—those unsettling silver eyes, so unlike the eyes of any creature belonging to polite society; they were very much the eyes of an inhabitant of the woods—because he towered over her so. Still, she would not lower her gaze. . . .

Even when he looked away from her face, distracted by the quick rise and fall of her chest as she fought to suppress a powerful impulse to scream and throw things. It was a terrible curse, to be born a redhead—she had no more control over her temper than . . . well, a fairy queen in a children's tale. To be cursed with red hair was almost—in some ways—more terrible than the other curse, the one she'd supposedly been born under. Because at least that one she hadn't the slightest control over. Her temper, she knew, was another matter entirely.

With an effort, she refrained from screaming, and only seized the edges of her pelisse and pulled them over the area that appeared to have captured his attention so fully, depriving him of a view of what seemed, if she wasn't mistaken, quite fascinating to him.

This decided movement apparently brought home to him what he had not realized before—that he had been staring quite rudely at her breasts. He started visibly, wrenching his gaze back toward hers, then opened his mouth to say something—an apology, Mairi suspected—but was interrupted by the duchess, who swept toward them with a cup in either hand.

"Niall, taste this punch, will you? Euan thinks it's too sweet." She placed one of the silver cups in her brother-in-law's hand, then bent to offer the other to Mairi. "Do you like punch, dear? Will you try this and tell me what you think?"

Mairi took the cup, its silver sides cool beneath her fingertips.

But Lord Niall, who did not have as much excuse for short-temperedness as she did, being neither redheaded nor the victim of a lifelong curse, tossed the contents of his cup into the flames—causing them to flare hotly—then walked away without a word.

Mairi was not particularly surprised by Lord Niall's behavior, as she'd begun to suspect that he was as much of a wolf thing as she was a fairy thing, so this sort of rude behavior might be expected of him.

But she was apparently mistaken in this assumption—or he did not act like a wolf all the time—since his sister-in-law, observing this abrupt departure, wondered aloud, "Why, whatever could be the matter with Niall?"

Mairi shrugged. "Isn't he always that way?"

"Certainly not!" The duchess looked after her brother-in-law with a troubled expression on her face. "What were the two of you talking about?"

Mairi said softly, "I won't tell him who I am."

"Oh." The duchess took the cup from her. "Yes, I'm certain that must be troubling for him. Niall dislikes a mystery. He's very fond of order."

Mairi, feeling horribly guilty, cried, "It isn't that I don't trust him. It's just that I shouldn't like to see him—any of you, I mean—hurt."

The duchess raised her fine blond eyebrows. "Is it really as bad as all that?"

Mairi, realizing how she must have sounded, said hastily, "I don't mean to worry you overmuch. Only the sooner I go, the better, I think. Do you think that the last post chaise has passed yet this evening? Or might I still have a chance at catching it?"

The duchess did something very unduchesslike then. She snorted.

"My dear, how can you even think of such a thing? There'll be no more post chaises. Not tonight, and probably not tomorrow, either. The snow is still coming thicker than ever. No one could travel in such weather."

Mairi felt something inside of her constrict. "Do you really think so?"

"I know so. Why, I am doubting many of the tenants will be able to find their way here for the ball tonight. But, dear, if the post cannot get through, nor our tenants, then surely whoever it is you are trying to escape from— and do not tell me that is not the case; I can see it in your eyes—will be delayed by the snow, as well."

Not, Mairi knew, Alistair. The snow had already stopped him from finding her once, just that afternoon in the woods. He would not allow it do so again.

"Besides," the duchess said, moving around the couch to the hearth to gather up first Lord Niall's empty plate and then Mairi's, "you cannot think of traveling with your poor foot in splints."

"I *must* go," Mairi breathed. "I *must* get to London as soon as possible."

"London? But it is so far!"

It wasn't, for Mairi's tastes, far enough, actually. She would certainly be found in Glasgow or Edinburgh, but at least it would be more difficult in London. And Alistair wasn't likely to think of her going there.

"Well," the duchess said, dubiously, in response to Mairi's determined look, "I suppose you know best. You have friends in London, I assume?"

"No," Mairi admitted. She didn't know anyone, anyone

at all. Alistair had seen to that. Wretched man. Why, he hardly deserved to be called a man at all. Monster was more like it.

Her gaze strayed towards Lord Niall, who stood well across the hall, his back to the rest of the room as he gazed out of the windows, at the falling snow.

Now that, she told herself, *is a man.*

The duchess must have noticed the direction of Mairi's gaze, since she said suddenly, "Niall was offered half a dozen positions in London."

Mairi, realizing she'd been caught staring at the woman's brother-in-law, tore her gaze quickly away from him. "Oh?" she said, in a tone she hoped sounded extremely disinterested.

"Yes," the duchess said. "But London is much too healthy for him, as is Kilcairn. He is looking to find a cure for typhus, you see, so he intends to settle in as squalid a place as he can find, where they suffer a great deal from that disease."

"Typhus?" Mairi sat up a little straighter. "You mean enteric fever?"

"Yes," the duchess said with a sigh. "I believe the two are one in the same. And there hasn't been a case of typhus in Kilcairn, I understand, since it killed Euan and Niall's mother—the last duchess, I mean."

Mairi murmured, "I had no idea."

"No," the duchess said. "Of course you wouldn't. They don't like to talk about it. Now, dear, let us discuss something I know *you* won't like to talk about, and yet I feel I must ask it, and I hope you will answer me truthfully. This man you're running from—and don't bother denying there is a man. I know there is—is he your husband?"

Mairi couldn't control a sudden shudder that ripped through her body, though she was not in the least bit chilled.

"Not yet," she said, to the floor.

Six

*Y*ou are not," Euan observed, "enjoying yourself."

Niall shrugged and gazed out across the hall. The last of the tenants having arrived, the tables had been pushed back, and now the dancing had begun.

It was a strange and wonderful thing, the idea of dancing taking place in the great hall of Donnegal Manor. Nothing like that had ever occurred before, at least not in Niall's memory.

The crofters, who'd at first looked ill at ease, even suspicious of this invitation from the new duke, were now taking enormous enjoyment out of all of the food and drink and decorations, the musicians and the gifts, all of which had been arranged for them by the new duke and duchess.

Only Niall could not find pleasure in any of it. He could not even tap his toe to the rhythm of the reel the musicians were playing.

" 'Tis the girl, isn't it?"

When Niall didn't even bother to turn his head, let alone reply, the duke sighed.

"I knew it. We ought to have left her where we found her."

Niall turned his head at that. "And allowed her to freeze to death?"

"Oh, she'd have been all right," Euan assured him.

"I know what you think," Niall said, bitterly. "You think this husband of hers, the one you've invented, would have come along looking for her soon enough, and she'd have been well off our hands."

"Aye," Euan said. He lifted an apple off a nearby tray and bit into it. "Well, I did think that. Until she told Irmgarde she's not married."

Niall glanced sharply at his brother. "No?"

"No." Euan chewed noisily. "Running from a fiancé, apparently. That's eminently preferable, I think, to fleeing after the deed is done. I'd much sooner be left at the altar than on the honeymoon, wouldn't you? That'd just be demoralizing."

Niall was still in shock. "A fiancé?"

"Hope it's not the vicar. Though I could understand her reluctance. He's a bit on the dry side. Still, I don't imagine he'll be at all happy when he finds out we've been harboring his fugitive bride-to-be. Probably preach a sermon about it and make us an example to the rest of the congregation. Irmgarde won't like that. Here"—the duke put down his apple—"go and take her a piece of pie." He shoved something into Niall's fingers.

Niall looked down at the plate in his hand. "Irmgarde?"

"Not Irmgarde, you fool. The girl."

"Pie?"

"Yes, pie." The duke put a hand to the back of Niall's neck and physically turned him toward the great hall's hearth, beside which Mairi still lay upon her divan. "No woman can resist a piece of pie."

Niall eyed the slice upon the plate. "I think it's going to take more than pie, Euan, to warm this particular young lady's heart. She seems to think we're keeping her prisoner here. She quite hates us."

Me, he corrected himself. Hates *me*.

"Nonsense," Euan said, heartily. "No woman can resist a man with pie."

"This," Niall said, "is only going to look like a pathetic attempt to win her good opinion."

"Must you," the duke asked, shaking his head, "question everything? 'Tis just a piece of *pie*, for pity's sake." The duke gave his brother a push.

Niall narrowly avoided colliding with a quartet of dancing crofters, who laughed merrily at the interruption and made way for him to pass. Feeling ridiculous, he skirted the edge of the dance floor, passing table after table of savory delicacies—paper-thin slices of smoked salmon; goose, sausages, and pheasant; roasted potatoes and buttered sprouts; bread sauce, dishes of thick cream, brandy butter, toffee, cookies dusted with sugar, and, of course, pudding, all laid out upon his father's treasured silver, tempting the palate and titillating the appetite . . . and succeeding remarkably well, if the dazed looks on the crofters' faces were any indication.

Wending his way past all these tables, Niall finally reached the enormous fireplace—tall enough for a man to stand in.

But instead of finding Mairi alone, as he'd hoped, he found her instead surrounded by children. Some of them he recognized as his own nieces and nephews, but the majority were strangers to him.

"You," the girl was saying to one of them, looking down at a child's small, outstretched hand, "are going to be the Empress of China."

Irmgarde, who happened to be passing by, stopped long enough to follow the direction of Niall's gaze and say, with a shake of her head, "It's Sileas's fault."

Niall shook his head. "Sileas?"

"The children's nurse. Collin overheard her mentioning some sort of fable concerning redheaded people who are born with black eyelashes. Apparently, they are—"

"—said to be from fairy stock," Niall finished for her. "Yes, my mother used to say so, as well."

Irmgarde raised her eyebrows, and Niall knew it was because she was surprised to hear him mention his mother. Neither he nor Euan did so often.

"Well, in any case," Irmgarde went on, "Collin took the information to heart and began begging the poor girl to tell him his fortune. Apparently he has his Gypsies and his fairies a little mixed up. But the girl is being very sporting about it, as you can see. I suppose she thought it was easier simply to go along with Collin's wishes than to resist." Niall did not miss the slyness that crept into his sister-in-law's gaze as she glanced up at him. "That is often the only way to deal with Donnegal men, I've noticed."

Niall gave the duchess a very sarcastic look. "Here," he said, handing her the pie her husband had given him. "I don't want this." Then he turned to go.

Irmgarde detained him with a single touch of her hand. "Don't go," she said. "Don't you want to have your fortune told?"

Niall looked at the girl. The firelight lent her pale skin a creamy tone and brought out the golden highlights in her thick mane of hair. She had made no effort that he could see to restrain the unruly red curls, letting them instead tumble all down her back and shoulders. The effect was a startling one: she really did resemble something otherwordly, a wood nymph or pixie. It wasn't hard to see why the children believed she really could read their fortunes.

"Pirate," she proclaimed over the outstretched palm of Euan and Irmgarde's youngest boy. "You will sail the seven seas, and have a very long mustache."

Rory asked excitedly, "Shall I kill people?"

"A great many people," the girl replied gravely, a proclamation that caused a good deal of envious groaning as Rory danced away, delighted.

"Make way," Irmgarde called.

Suddenly, Niall found himself being propelled through the throng of dogs and children by a very determined duchess. "Make way, make way," she cried.

Then, stopping directly before the divan, Irmgarde addressed the girl who called herself Mairi. "Will you tell the pirate's uncle his future now?"

If the girl was surprised—or repelled—by this request, she gave no indication. Instead, she indicated the low embroidered footstool by the side of her couch.

"By all means," she said serenely. "If he will but be seated . . ."

Niall, however, could not be so calm.

"It is not necessary," he said, gently but firmly extricating himself from Irmgarde's grip.

"Of course it isn't necessary," the duchess said. "It is diverting, however, and you will enjoy it."

"I do not care to know my future," Niall insisted.

"You are a singular creature, then," Mairi remarked. Her tone was mild, but those eyes of hers were not. They glittered with intensity. And there were twin spots of hot color in either of her cheeks. "I would give anything for a glimpse of mine."

"You are not well." Niall found himself, in spite of his earlier protest, sinking down onto the footstool, and raising a hand to her smooth white forehead. "You have a fever."

"The fire is too hot." The girl reached up with both hands and removed his fingers from her brow. Turning his hand so that she could see his palm, she said, in a knowing voice, "Oh . . ."

The children drifted away, chagrined that their game had been interrupted, their turn usurped by an adult . . . but Irmgarde's promising them that there were gifts laid out for them near the Christmas tree proved a therapeutic balm for their disappointment.

Conscious that he and the strange girl they'd found in the woods were alone with one another again, Niall felt a little of the same unease he'd experienced before, when he'd set her ankle. It was shameful, this attraction he felt for her, a girl he had not met until that morning. And a patient, as well! What was wrong with him? His mentors had held such hopes for him, and here he was at his first real test, failing miserably. . . .

"I see," the girl said, gazing down at his palm, "a future full of good works."

"You needn't waste your time," he said evenly, although he did not pull his hand away. "I don't believe in palmistry."

"Of course not," the girl murmured, her eyes still hidden from view by those impossibly long lashes as she bent over his hand. "Because you are a man of science. Only I come from elfin stock, you know, so I see things differently."

Holding his hand cupped in one of hers, she ran her fingertips lightly along the lines in his palm. The feather-soft touch caused a shiver to race up and down his spine.

He wondered if she had the slightest idea how she affected him.

"You are planning," she said, "on going somewhere very far away."

He was surprised, in spite of himself. "Yes, I am."

"And once you get to where you are going," she went on, still staring down at his hand, "you intend to work very hard. You will cure a great many ill people."

"Aye," he said. "But then, I'm a physician, after all. That's what I do. You wouldn't"—he grinned at her, though she did not notice, since the full of her attention was focused on his palm—"necessarily have to have come from elfin stock to have predicted that."

She ignored him.

"You will make many sick people better," she said. "Especially . . . people with enteric fever."

He was so shocked he did not even think to try to get his hand back. He merely sat there, blinking at her.

It was true, he thought. What he'd been thinking all along, what his mother had said, all those years ago, about that crofter's child with the light hair and dark eyelashes: She was not of this earth. She was a changeling.

And then he remembered that he'd seen Irmgarde in deep conversation with her not two hours earlier.

He felt ashamed of his heavily beating heart as he said,

as evenly as he was able, "My sister-in-law told you, didn't she?"

The veil of lashes came up, revealing those matched azure pools.

"Aye, of course she did," she said. "But you believed me for a moment. Don't pretend you didn't."

He managed a smile. He did not want to look as if he couldn't appreciate a joke, even one at his own expense.

But it must not have been a very convincing smile, since she released his hand and slumped back against her couch, out of the firelight and into the shadows, saying, "Oh, now I've offended you."

"Not at all," he hastened to assure her. He leaned forward until his elbows rested on his knees. "I——"

"No, I have, I have offended you. I *am* sorry. I want you to know that I admire your ambition very much. It . . ." She hesitated, then seemed to come to some sort of internal decision, since she plunged ahead with, "A wave of it struck my school last autumn, you know."

He knit his brows. "A wave of what?"

But she didn't seem to have heard him.

"One of the girls," she went on quickly, "developed a little sore, and Mother Superior thought nothing of it . . . our smocks were wool, and very scratchy, and girls used to finer fabrics often developed skin irritations. But the next morning the girl with the sore woke with a very high fever. By that time, however, it was too late . . . fourteen of the other girls and ten of the nuns, including Mother Superior, had come down with fevers as well."

"Typhoid." He stared at her. "Are you talking about *typhoid?*"

"Of course." She moved, and now her face was no

longer in shadow. He could see that it wasn't fever that glittered in those remarkable eyes, it was pain—and an entirely different kind of pain from the kind that she'd endured while he'd been splinting her ankle. That had been physical. This was something much deeper.

"In the end," she said so softly that he had to lean forward in order to hear her, since the musicians had launched into another merry country reel, "the only ones who didn't get sick were me, Sister Mary Alice, and the gardener."

"Good God." Niall was appalled. She had just related a tale of heart-aching poignancy in the same amount of time it would have taken an ordinary girl to describe an outing to her modiste.

He blurted the first thing that occurred to him without pausing to think it over first. "Your family must have been frantic with worry for you."

She blinked at him. "Oh, I didn't tell them about it, of course."

"Why ever *not?*"

"I knew they'd only make me come home. And I wanted to try to help." One of the dogs stirred in its fitful gaze before the fire, sat up, and laid its head close to the girl's hand. She reached out obligingly and stroked its ears. "There was no one else to do it. And it . . . well, it seemed only fair." She shot him a quick, almost nervous look. "I mean, considering that I never fell ill at all."

Niall stared at her in wonder and surprise. Had there ever, he asked himself, been a more astonishing creature than the one seated before him?

"Wasn't"—Niall was almost afraid to ask—"there a physician?"

"Oh, there was," she assured him, thoughtfully working a burr from the fur behind the dog's ear. "But the fever had spread all over the valley. We weren't his only patients by far. And there's not much you can do for typhoid, you know, except try to keep the patient's fever down with cold compresses and, of course, not let her eat any solid food—"

He stared at her. Feeding a sufferer of typhoid tended to be fatal, as even the smallest morsel of solid food could cause hemorrhaging or even a perforation. But the medical community had only just begun to recognize this fact and were having a difficult time convincing its own members, let alone the public, of the value of starving this particular fever. Niall's own mother had died during the course of her own bout with typhoid, and he was convinced it was from being fed bread dipped in milk . . . something a physician had recommended.

The problem, of course, was that the patient could starve to death during the course of her illness, which was often of six or seven weeks' duration. And it was difficult indeed for family members to resist the cries of a hungry loved one. . . .

"What we did, Sister Mary Alice and I," the girl was saying, "was add well-beaten eggs from the convent's henhouse to the ale Mother Superior kept in the storeroom. Then we spoon-fed it to the patients. And that seemed to work very well indeed. Quite a few of them recovered. Not"—here she had to pause to swallow before going on—"Mother Superior, unfortunately, but more than half the others. . . ."

But even that small amount, Niall knew, was a miracle. He wondered if the survivors knew how close they'd come to death—and how much they owed their survival to the efforts of this girl and a single nun . . . a fact that, in itself, he found difficult to believe.

The miracle was not that so many had survived, but that any had lived at all. The sheer labor involved in treating a typhoid patient was enormous, when one took into account the washing up, the changing of bedding, the ladling out of water—for the patient's thirst was tremendous, the fever being extremely dehydrating—not to mention the emptying of chamber pots. Niall had seen highly motivated households give up after just a few days of such labor on behalf of a half dozen patients . . . and she'd mentioned that there'd been three times that number.

That this girl, with the help of only one other, had succeeded in successfully nursing so many back to health was surely a further sign of her otherworldly origins. For certainly no ordinary woman would have stayed in such circumstances, when she might easily have written to her family and secured passage home. He'd known physicians who'd refused to enter typhoid-stricken households. That this girl not only had chosen to stay in one, but had worked so hard to save the lives of the patients inside it, told him something about her, something he was certain she had not meant to reveal . . .

Which was that beneath that very charming and delicate exterior lurked a stouter heart and stronger stomach than belonged to most men, let alone females . . . not to mention a will that could only be made of iron.

"So you see," Mairi went on, apparently oblivious to how impressed he was by what she'd just described, "I did not mean to make light of your aspiration. I admire it very much. And I predict"—a hint of something gamine crept into her expression as she smiled at him—"that you will be successful in your endeavor."

A curious sensation came over him. It was almost as if he'd seen that impish smile before somewhere . . . only of course, he couldn't have. Not *that* smile, not *her* smile.

But the sensation was so strong—*déjà vu,* the French called it, an illusion of having already experienced something once, though one was actually experiencing it for the first time—that he had difficulty shaking it and even found himself wondering if what he was remembering was some long forgotten dream. She certainly seemed the sort of creature a man might dream up, with her shapely ankles, ivory skin, and startlingly blue eyes.

But never, not even in his dreams, could he have imagined a woman who looked as she did, yet had shown such a penchant for arguing Platonic critical theory. . . .

And who could have shown such bravery in the face of a typhoid epidemic.

"And what of your future?" he heard himself ask, his tone not quite as teasing as he'd meant it to be.

She raised delicately winged eyebrows. *"My* future?"

"Aye. It seems only fair, considering that you know my life ambition, that you tell me yours. I, unlike you, possess not a drop of Gypsy blood, so I am at somewhat of a disadvantage in predicting your destiny."

"Fairy blood," she corrected him. Still, she did not seem displeased with the question. At least, she smiled again.

"No one's ever asked me that before," she said. "What my secret life ambition is, I mean."

"Surely," he said, knowing he was feeling entirely too

pleased with himself for having made her smile, but unable to help himself, "you have one."

"I don't know." She looked down at her own palms, turning them toward the fire so that she could trace the soft lines in them. "I've never thought about it. Actually, it never occurred to me that I had much of a choice."

"But you do now," he pointed out.

"Aye," she said, her tone faintly surprised. "I suppose I do."

"May I make a suggestion?"

She looked up from her hands. She was still smiling. "If you wish."

He could not quite believe what he was thinking. He could not even say how such a thought had occurred to him. It was the height of all that was disruptive and chaotic. There was no place for such a fantastic idea in his ordered universe.

And yet . . .

And yet consider how much better it would be—how much better everything would be—with this girl, this girl with her gamine smile and summer-sky-colored eyes. . . .

What was happening to him? He couldn't help wondering if what she'd said about being from fairy stock might possibly be true. Was he slowly being bewitched? How else was he to explain this extraordinary thought that had come to him? One moment, his mind had been traveling along the same old comfortable roads it had always traversed, and the next, it had veered onto this alarming, unfamiliar territory. He was not a man to behave recklessly, to do anything on impulse. Yet here he was, with a woman he had met less than twelve hours ago, a woman whose surname he did not even know . . .

But it didn't matter. None of that mattered in the least to him.

Had she done that, with her fairy magic?

But, no, that was impossible. He didn't believe in magic. Magic was something people had used in the past as a way of explaining what science had not yet made understandable to them. But everything, it turned out, had a scientific explanation. Everything had a purpose. Christmas trees, for instance. And the candles on them. It would be easy to look at such things and only wonder at their beauty and not ever consider that they might have a purpose.

But not for Niall. He had never been able to look at anything and not wonder at its ultimate function in the universe.

And it had become quite clear to him suddenly what Mairi's function in the universe was.

He reached out and seized the hand she'd laid upon the dog's head.

"Come with me," he said, in a deep voice.

The smile never wavered, though her gaze grew puzzled. "Come with you where?"

"To Skye."

"Skye?" Her eyes widened. "The *Isle* of Skye?"

"That's where my practice is," Niall said, with an eager nod. "Where it's going to be, I mean. I know it probably isn't the sort of place you've ever imagined living, and I'll admit it is a bit isolated, but I'm told that it can be very beautiful, particularly in the summer—"

The smile flickered and, before his very eyes, went out.

He tightened his grip on her fingers. He realized he hadn't put it quite the way he'd meant to. He tried again.

"The people there are wretchedly poor," he said. "And

it's one of the areas hit hardest by typhoid every year. I'm going there to find out why. And since you aren't afraid of the disease, and showed so much sense and compassion in the face of it . . . Well, I thought you might . . . might be willing . . ."

She cocked her head and studied him.

"You want me to go," she asked curiously, "as your nurse?"

It was his turn to stare. Nurse? He was asking her to be his wife, and she thought he wanted to hire her!

Well, and why wouldn't she, with all his talk about her sense and compassion? He should have complimented her on her beauty first, and then on her bravery in the face of life-threatening illness. . . .

What was he doing? What was he *doing*? Maybe it was better he simply let it drop.

"Er, no," he heard himself saying. "No, that isn't . . . that isn't what I meant at all."

Something in his voice—since he couldn't seem to make his words convey his meaning—must have tipped her off to his intention, since suddenly she went quite pale. A second later, she was tugging on her hand, trying to free it.

"Oh," she said, looking everywhere but at him. "Oh . . ."

He had, he realized, made a gross error in calculation. How could he have been so stupid? He'd been too precipitous, too hasty. He ought to have waited. . . .

And yet who knew how long they had together?

No, he had to do it, and do it now. Something extraordinary was happening. He did not have to be a scientist to see that.

But he had gone about it all wrong. He wasn't an unseasoned schoolboy, after all. He had some experience with women—though that experience was not perhaps as varied as other men's. Still, even he knew that the idea of living on a plague-infested island in the middle of nowhere held little appeal for the average woman. He needed to sweeten the pot. Women were rational creatures, despite what some of his learned peers might claim. She would, of course, wish to live in the kind of comfort to which she'd become accustomed. This was only natural. He did not blame her in the least for hesitating.

"I have five thousand a year," Niall informed her. "You would of course have the best of everything—"

But this had not, apparently, been the source of her hesitation. She appeared more astonished than ever. Her small mouth dropped open, and she stared at him with something that he couldn't help thinking was very like horror.

"Are you asking me"—her voice cracked—"to *marry* you?"

"Well, yes," he said. "Of course."

He felt her fingers leap convulsively in his grip.

"Are you mad?" she asked, keeping her gaze firmly on her lap. "You don't even know me."

"I think I know you rather well," he said gravely. "I know that in spite of what one did to you today, you aren't afraid of dogs—that you're fond of them, even. I know from what you just told me that when someone you love falls ill, you'll do whatever you have to in order to see that he—or she—pulls through . . . even if what's necessary proves to be messy or unpleasant. I know that you are kind and patient with children, no matter how often they accuse you of being a Gypsy . . . or"—he couldn't help grinning a little—"a fairy."

She'd raised her gaze to stare at him incredulously as he spoke. But when he moved his thumb over the ivory-smooth skin on the back of her hand, as he did then, her eyelids dropped once more, shielding from him those translucent depths.

"And I know," he went on, in the same deep, serious voice, "the way the firelight brings out the golden high-lights in your hair. I know that when I touch you, like I'm doing now, your cheeks turn a deeper shade of pink—" She bent her head so that some of her rich red hair fell forward, hiding those offending cheeks from him. He continued, undeterred, "—and when you smile, it's not just with your lips, but with your eyes, as well. So you see, Mairi, I actually know a great deal about you. A very great deal."

He saw her throat move as she swallowed. His words, as he'd meant them to, had affected her.

But not enough.

"I'm sorry." She lifted her gaze to meet his, and he saw the tears trembling on the ends of her eyelashes. "But I cannot possibly marry you."

He was not surprised. How could he be? It was, after all, so very odd, his proposing to her like this, after such a short acquaintance. And she clearly wasn't one of those flighty girls who might be swept away by the heady triumph of securing for herself a duke's son.

Still, he would not give up.

Her name, he thought. Say her name. And so, still leaning forward, he said, "Mairi."

She looked away. But her slender shoulders hitched

beneath the puffed sleeves of her gown. That, he decided, was better than nothing.

"I *cannot*," she said, again, whispering the words fiercely, as if not so much to convince him, but herself, of the truth of them.

And now he knew what the hitching shoulders had meant. She was crying, albeit silently. A tear dropped from her cheek and splashed onto the bodice of her gown . . . the same bodice he had stared at, he knew, a little too fixedly not long before.

Was she still angry with him for that? he wondered. Did she think him some sort of rutting wretch, like the man—surely not the vicar, but some foul old baronet her family had undoubtedly arranged for her to wed—she was running from? He had behaved ignobly. . . .

But no worse, he supposed, than any other man, in a similar situation—and far better than some. What was more, she liked him. He knew she did, from the way her pulse, even now, was staggering beneath his fingers, and a blush was ebbing and flowing across her cheeks. She was not insensible of the fact that he had some physical charms. . . .

And he did not believe she was the type of girl who would allow her indignation over one impropriety on a man's part to blind her to the advantages of marriage to him.

So what was she crying for?

"You don't have to give me an answer tonight," he said. "Take all the time you need. Only promise me you'll think about it."

" 'Tis not possible," she said, to her lap. And with a tug, she freed her hand from his. "I'm sorry."

This sounded distressingly final. For the first time,

something like fear began to grip him. He'd recognized, of course, that hers was an uncommonly strong will—hadn't she been determined, back in the woods, to walk upon an ankle that was all but broken, stubbornly refusing, until the very end, his offers of aid? If she was as determined not to consider his proposal as she'd been not to accept his help . . .

He was in trouble. Grave trouble.

Niall wasn't used to feeling anything but the most supreme self-confidence. Her refusal was a mortifying blow to his ego as well as his manhood.

But more than that, it was wrong. It was just plain wrong. He knew it, and, he was convinced, she knew it, too. They belonged together. He'd known it before she'd ever admitted her experience with typhoid. He'd known it, he thought, from the moment he'd seen her peep out from that tree.

It made no sense. It had no place in his otherwise ordered universe. But there it was.

And her refusal to concede it left him feeling, instead of outraged or insulted, strangely numb.

That was all. Just numb.

He could see that he'd genuinely upset her—though for the life of him, he could not see a single reason why any girl should be reduced to tears by a fellow proposing marriage. Still, further attempts on his part to change her mind would only be perceived, he feared, as badgering. And she had endured enough of that, he thought, for one day.

And so he straightened, and said, in a determined voice, "But nothing is impossible, Mairi. Not for me."

And then he walked quickly away, before she could

reply. Because one more word from that sad mouth, he was sure, was all it would take to make him turn around, sweep her up into his arms, and do exactly what he'd been longing to do since he'd first laid eyes on her.

Seven

*T*hings were not going at all the way Mairi had planned.

Not, truth be told, that she'd ever had much of a plan, beyond getting out of Kilcairn as soon as possible. Her injured ankle had put rather a crimp in that strategy, and it had seemed likely she was going to have to come up with a new one.

Now, however, she had no choice but to revert back to her original plan.

Which was why she was standing just inside the front door to Donnegal Manor, trying—on one foot—to lift the heavy wooden post that the butler had lowered to bar the door for the night.

It seemed rather pitiful to her that she should have gotten this far, only to be stopped by a mere piece of wood.

And while she had managed to secure a walking stick, her progress was still painfully slow. She could not rest the slightest weight on her injured foot without causing waves of pain to course over her entire body, and so she'd been forced to hop—literally hop—down the stairs. It had seemed to take her an hour merely to get to the landing. And soon it would be light out.

It had been past midnight when the festivities had

finally died down—Lord, but those crofters liked a cele-
bration—and she'd been conducted to the upstairs guest
room where she'd been expected to spend the night.
There she had forced herself to wait until she was certain
the last of the tenant farmers had gone home and the rest
of the household had finally gotten to sleep. Only then
had she risen from the bed and begun the arduous journey downstairs. She was exhausted, her ankle throbbed,
and she could hardly see two feet in front of her. . . .

But she was determined that when morning's first light
touched Donnegal Manor, she would be as far as she
could possibly get from it.

And all she had to do to accomplish this goal was open
one particularly stubborn door. . . .

"What do you think you're doing?"

Mairi spun around—well, as much as she could spin,
on one foot—and then cursed to herself, quite roundly.
For there, standing in the gloom at the bottom of the
stairs, was exactly the person she'd been praying she
wouldn't encounter.

She stared at him with as much horror as if he'd been a
specter rising from a grave.

"I—" She spoke through bloodless lips. "I'm sorry. But
I must go. . . ."

"Oh, must you?" He made no move to come near her,
merely folded his arms across his chest and observed her
from a distance, as if she were an actress performing a
scene for his enjoyment. "Go where?"

"*Anywhere*," she said, with sudden passion. "Don't you
see? Anywhere, so long as it's away from here. Every
minute you prevent my going brings you—" She broke
off, confused.

"Brings me what?" he wondered lightly.

She felt a sudden rage, quick and hot, dart through her veins. He almost sounded as if he were making fun of her. How dare he? Didn't he *know?* Hadn't he *guessed?* He'd talked about her eyes . . . but not their strange coloring, no. The way they lit up when she smiled. Oh, *God.*

"Brings you a minute closer to your death," she said, flatly, to the floor.

Lord Niall maintained toward this dramatic revelation an air of supreme indifference. "At the hands of your fiancé, I suppose."

Oh, why had this happened? Why couldn't he have been asleep, like everyone else in the house? Why did he have to come downstairs at the exact moment she was trying to make her escape? And why did he have to look like that? For he had evidently only just rolled out of bed and pulled on a pair of trousers and a shirt . . . a shirt he had not bothered to lace and that hung open from neck to navel, practically, revealing a broad and crisply-haired chest from which she could only bring herself to drop her gaze with an effort. . . .

She could not tell him. Not the truth. He wouldn't believe her, for one thing—she hardly believed it herself—and for another, she had sworn never to tell.

Before she had a chance to utter another word, however, he asked politely, "And just where did you get that?"

She looked down. He'd pointed casually to the walking stick she clutched.

She couldn't tell him that, either. Fergus had brought the stick to her, tapping shyly on the door to her room just before she'd dismissed the maid the duchess had lent to her. It was the woodsman's own walking stick, its surface smooth from years of service, but as he'd informed her, with many pulls on his forelock, she had far more need of it at the moment than he.

Little had the poor man known how immediately she'd intended to put the stick to use, rather than saving it, as he'd surely meant her to, to aid her in getting to the breakfast table in the morning.

"I found it," she lied, incapable of hiding the hint of resentment that had crept into her voice, but wincing when she heard it. For he would, of course, misunderstand it. To him, it would seem that her antagonism stemmed from the fact that he had, pretty much from the start, insisted upon keeping her here, when the truth, as she knew only too well, was that she'd have given anything in the world to stay . . . if she hadn't thought her doing so would lead to his certain death. For Lord Niall was without a doubt the kindest, handsomest man she had ever met. . . .

And for that reason, he frightened her, far more than Alistair ever had.

"You found it." Niall studied her in the semidarkness. The lights in the hall had been extinguished, all except for the fire in the enormous hearth. In its flickering glow, he could see that she looked extremely anxious . . . as well as extremely beautiful.

"Aye." The bright blue eyes were defiant. "Why not? And now you'll be letting me go."

"I suppose I must." Lord Niall's expression was difficult to read, since he stood in the shadows. But in his voice, she heard a wealth of things, including a hurt that caused her an almost physical pain. "Especially since, according to you, not letting you go would mean my untimely demise.

Although I must confess I find myself unmanned by your lack of faith in my ability to defend myself."

She shook her head. She had to tell him, in spite of how ridiculous it might sound, in spite of her oath. Even though she knew what he would say—he was a man of science, after all—she had to tell him the truth, lest he go on thinking she considered him anything less than perfect.

" 'Tis not a man I speak of," she said. Her whisper, which ought to have been lost in so vast a space as the great hall, sounded excruciatingly loud, "—but a curse."

"A curse?" He turned his head, and those silver eyes caught the light and seemed to glow. She saw the glint of teeth as he grinned. "Are you telling me now that you really are a fairy, then?"

She shook her head. Oh, it was impossible. Impossible! Impossible to believe, impossible to suggest that such a thing, in an otherwise rational world, could even exist . . . and yet impossible, in light of the facts, to deny.

She would tell him. She *had* to tell him. Alistair had always warned her that no one would believe it, and that spreading family secrets only made them worse. . . .

But Alistair wasn't here. Lord Niall was. Lord Niall, who, despite that grin, was looking down at her with those wounded eyes, so convinced she was a wicked, heartless thing. She would tell him. It would be her gift to him. So that he didn't go on thinking that she'd said no to him because she didn't care—because she *did* . . . enough to want to spare him.

"Not a fairy curse," she whispered, unsteadily. "A family curse. I know you will not believe me—and yet there's no way around it. Not when the proof is there to stare one in the face."

"Proof?" Now the grin disappeared, and was replaced with a scowl. "What are you—"

"I know 'tis fantastic sounding—and once I was old enough to know better, I took it for the nonsense it sounds. And yet . . . Well, there it is. Death does seem to take anyone I come close to . . . first my parents, who were both struck dead before I turned nine years old. And then the aunt—my guardian's mother—whom I went to live with after that. The other girls, as I told you, at the school I was sent to, and the nuns who taught us along with them. And now your father. . . ."

Niall could restrain himself no longer. He hadn't, when he'd first spied her there in the semidarkness, been certain he believed what his own eyes had been telling him. But it was no trick of the light: there she was, the very person who'd made sleep so hopeless for him he'd risen and come downstairs in search of whisky. She had put her pelisse and bonnet back on again—that rebellious mane of hair was tucked out of sight—and was leaning against a sturdy-looking walking stick, her splinted ankle, over which she'd pulled—but had been unable to lace—her boot, poised in the air in a position that could not have been easy to maintain.

Mairi. His Mairi. Preparing, it appeared, to flee.

As if that hadn't been hard enough for him to process, now she flung at him this business about a curse. Well, that just about topped everything. He had heard quite a few tall tales in his day, but this one quite surpassed them all. He didn't doubt the girl sincerely believed it: there was no question this confession was painful to her and perfectly heartfelt; her eyes were huge dark pools of melancholy, and there was not a hint of her normally saucy manner. He wondered who—and for what purpose—had been feeding this girl these ridiculous lies. Whoever it was must have started early, for her to have become so thoroughly convinced they were true.

A sharp dose of reality was what they both needed, he decided.

"Your schoolmates and the nuns died from typhoid," he informed her briskly. "You told me so yourself. And my father died of gout. I haven't the slightest idea what killed your parents or your aunt, but I can only assume they, too, passed away from causes that were perfectly natural. And I must confess myself surprised that a girl such as yourself, whom I took for halfway intelligent, would believe in anything as asinine as a familial curse." He uncrossed his arms and, flinging them open wide, demanded, "For God's sake, Mairi. Is this why you won't marry me?"

Her eyes were bright with tears as she retorted, "I will admit that in the universe of Ideas, which assure order and pattern to a world in constant flux, this curse is a fact that defies all Platonic reason. However, we cannot deny the fact that whither I go, people die. And you are only putting yourself at risk of dying as well if you don't heed—"

Niall said something that would have singed the ears had it been intelligible. But since he uttered it in a sort of growl, what came out was not at all recognizable as a word. A split second later, he'd strode up to the girl, reached beneath her pelisse to snatch her about the waist, and pulled her roughly against him.

Mairi was so surprised she let go of Fergus's walking stick. It fell with a clatter to the floor.

"Lord Niall," she said, lifting both hands to his chest as if to ward him off and then starting at the warmth of the very solid wall of muscle she felt beneath her palms.

Really, but this was a most alarming turn of events—almost as alarming as when she'd wakened from her faint and found herself in his arms. Only that time she supposed he'd had a right to come so close—after all, he'd been trying to help her.

But this time she was quite obviously not in need of medical attention.

"Really," she whispered. "You mustn't. Didn't you hear what I said?"

"About the curse?" he asked. His wolf eyes seemed to be glowing particularly silver, which was unsettling. "Oh, yes. I heard you."

"Then you must know," Mairi murmured, "you must know what you're doing is . . ."

Only she couldn't go on. She was much too distracted. He smelled, she realized, with something close to panic, like freshly laundered linen. Oh, why did he have to smell of one of her favorite scents? And was that his heart she felt beneath her hand? It must be a very large heart, to be beating so strongly, so fast, against her palm. It was racing almost as quickly as her own. . . .

Really, why was it necessary for him to be so warm, and to smell so nicely? She wouldn't have the slightest problem pushing him away if he hadn't smelled so very good. And she knew she had to push him away, because the girls at school had talked about men like him, men who tried to kiss them. Though, looking up into his face, Mairi couldn't imagine what was wrong with simply letting him kiss her if he wanted to, since he had such a nice mouth.

". . . foolish?" he asked. That nice mouth was smiling now, though there was a muscle leaping in his jaw, and his eyes were still much too bright.

"Extremely foolish," Mairi murmured. His thumb was moving gently along her spine. This, like the scent of him, was very distracting. Almost as distracting as those very nice lips, hovering just a few inches above hers. "You might very well end up dead."

"Has it ever occurred to you," he wanted to know, "that I might consider it well worth it?"

And then she noticed that his wolf gaze had dropped away from her eyes, down toward her lips. Oh, dear, she thought. He's going to kiss me. I really should . . . I simply must . . .

Stop him.

But when that mouth actually came down over hers—and he did something with his hands, so that her arms were suddenly around his neck—she couldn't do it, couldn't stop him . . . didn't *want* to stop him.

Instead, she felt something she'd never heard the girls at school talking about, something that was probably a result of her wicked fairiness:

And that was a very strong desire to kiss him back.

Oh, she knew it was wrong. She knew that, no matter what he said, kissing him was wrong, and not only because it was inviting certain death, but because nice girls simply didn't let men they hardly knew snatch them up and kiss them.

But, oh! What a delightful thing, kissing was. Why hadn't anyone ever mentioned this before? Mairi had been most violently opposed to kisses—but then, the only person who'd ever offered to kiss her before had been Alistair, rather recently, in fact, and being kissed by him had held no appeal whatsoever.

Being kissed by Lord Niall, however, was perfectly

charming. Especially when, apparently realizing she was not going to stop him, he started kissing her even harder. His freshly-laundered-shirt smell enveloped her, and one of his hands moved to push her bonnet back from her head—so gently, as if he were afraid she might break.

Or maybe not, because a second later he had buried that hand deep into her hair and was kissing her *very* hard, his tongue tapping inquisitively against her closed mouth, as if to ask if it could come in.

And though Mairi was quite certain that letting Lord Niall put his tongue in her mouth was as good as signing his death warrant, she couldn't bring herself to stop him. And when she finally opened her lips to him, with a helpless sigh, it seemed to cause an explosion of passion from him—as if her small murmur of appreciation for the way he was kissing her had been something else entirely, an invitation to do more than kiss her, which it hadn't . . .

Still, she certainly didn't mind when he began kissing her throat and neck, and then lowered his head to, of all places, the front of her dress, with a sort of groan, and a hand to follow . . .

Eight

*A*nd then several things happened at once.

Mairi reached up to prevent that hand from doing what she was certain it intended to, something that Mother Superior quite definitely would not have approved of, and Lord Niall lifted his head, as if realizing he'd gone too far, and started to say something.

It was at this point that the dogs, collapsed in a disordered heap in front of the dying fire, stirred and then as one rose and commenced to barking with enough volume to wake the entire house.

Startled, Mairi tried to break free from Lord Niall's hold, fearful that someone must be approaching and might see them in such an intimate embrace. But Lord Niall held on to her, only turning his head to snap at the dogs. "Quiet!"

But the dogs went right on barking, streaming toward the front doors.

And when, a second later, an urgent pounding occurred upon the doors, the reason for their sudden outburst became apparent.

Mairi, in his arms, went pale.

"Oh, don't," she whispered urgently. "Don't open it!"

"I have to, or they'll wake the whole house," Niall said, murmuring the words into her hair, the cascade of curls he'd released when his blundering fingers had destroyed her coiffure. He wondered how he had gotten this far in life without ever having felt as he did now . . . because for the first time he could remember, he actually felt alive. Every nerve in his body seemed to be humming, tingling with excitement. Holding this warm and slender girl in his arms seemed the most natural and yet the most important thing that had ever happened to him. He would never let her go. No matter what happened.

The banging on the door grew even more imperative.

"Don't," Mairi pleaded.

"He'll beat down the door if I don't," Niall said. He

gave her a crooked grin. "This would be the fiancé, then, I take it?"

"Don't open it."

But he only chuckled, and then, placing a bold hand upon her lower hip, he half-lifted, half-steered her into the darkness of a corner just behind the door, where there stood a suit of armor that had come with the house, though his father had always liked to tell visitors it belonged to a long-dead ancestor.

"You wait here," Niall said, giving her a firm kiss on the forehead. "And let me do the talking."

She reached out just as he was moving away from her, and seized both his hands.

"Niall," she said, and the sound of his name on her lips did something to him. It was all he could do not to snatch her up into his arms again.

But the incessant pounding on the door called him back to himself. He gave her fingers—such slim, cool fingers—an encouraging squeeze, then dropped them.

Wading through the sea of dogs, Niall made his way to the door, cursing whoever stood on the other side of it. If it was this man Mairi was running from, all well and good. Better to have it out with the chap now than later.

But if it was anyone else, calling so early on this, the holiest of days—and interrupting what had surely been the most blissful few minutes of his life—Niall didn't think he'd be able to be responsible for his actions. . . .

But when he lifted the bar and threw open the door, letting in the frigid breeze, and saw standing on the step a red-haired man he not only recognized, but had thoroughly despised since childhood, he forgot all about his violent intentions and could only stare.

"Sutherland?" Niall glanced from the man—enormous now that he was full grown, topping Niall by a good two inches and what looked like fifty pounds or so—to the horse behind him, a black stallion with steam pouring in great white clouds from his nostrils as he panted. The animal's ink black muzzle was foam-flecked. Niall wasn't surprised. Sutherland had always been too hard on his horseflesh.

"What the devil are you doing here, and in the dead of night?" Niall demanded. "Are you drunk? Go home, man."

But when Niall attempted to slam the door closed in disgust, he was barred from doing so by a single booted foot, which Lord Sutherland thrust just inside the jamb.

"Not so fast, Donnegal," the earl snarled. He flung out a long arm and shouldered the door open enough to admit him. Niall, startled, took a step backwards, which was apparently all the invitation the earl needed to step inside the manor house, where his gray-eyed gaze flicked first over the motley assortment of tail-wagging dogs, then coolly across the hall.

"You aren't welcome here, Sutherland," Niall said, in a voice that was every bit as cold as the frigid wind blowing in through the door he continued to hold open.

Sutherland threw back his head in a sneer. "Oh? And who's going to throw me out, I'd like to know? You?"

"If need be," came Niall's chilly reply.

"I'd like to see that." Sutherland began working off his black leather gloves. "I've heard about you. You went away to study . . . what was it, now? Ah, yes, medicine, that was it. And I can't say I've ever heard of a medical man who could wield a blade."

Niall lifted a single black eyebrow. "We aren't called bloodletters for nothing, you know."

Alistair MacLean, Earl of Sutherland, was not, Niall recalled, the brightest fellow who'd ever graced the earth, though he had a sort of animal cunning that occasionally resulted in acts of absolute genius—and, invariably, malevolence. His primary occupation as a boy had been inventing ways to torment Niall and Euan, whenever he'd happened to come upon them in their youthful ramblings. It did not appear as if much had changed now that he had taken his father's place as Earl of Sutherland.

"Not *that* kind of blade," MacLean said, looking annoyed. Then, his gloves successfully removed, he stood, impatiently slapping them against his thigh. "Well? Where is she?"

It was only then that Niall realized just why, precisely, Alistair MacLean had invited himself into Donnegal Manor, a place he had never visited in all his life, though he lived less than a mile from it.

He was Mairi's fiancé.

Niall felt something explode inside his head. It was as if every blood vessel there had suddenly burst. He knew such a condition was medically impossible, but that's what it seemed like.

Alistair MacLean, the Earl of Sutherland, was Mairi's fiancé. *His* Mairi. His Mairi was engaged to be married to Alistair MacLean.

"Well?" Sutherland continued to slap his gloves against his thigh. Because he was wearing, in spite of the weather, his kilt, the leather did not make much noise as it hit the gold-and-scarlet wool. One result of all the blood vessels exploding in his head, Niall noticed, was that he found himself wondering if the earl's knees hadn't been mightily cold on his way over, something Niall was certain would not have occurred to him if his brain had not been on the verge of a massive hemorrhage.

"And don't bother to tell me she isn't here," Sutherland said. "For I heard from one of your brother's own crofters that last night, you gave a party—some sort of Christmas party, if I heard correctly, and if your father isn't spinning in his grave over that, my name's not MacLean—and that at this party, there happened to be a Gypsy girl—"

Niall felt the cold now. The wind was cutting through the thin material of his shirt, and where it hung open, his skin already felt like ice. He gave the portal a heave, and it slammed shut, cutting off the howling wind.

Suddenly, the hall seemed a good deal quieter. He could hear only the crackle of the fire on the hearth and the panting of the dogs.

"And what of it?" Niall asked, in a deceptively mild voice. "If I choose to entertain Gypsies, that's my own business, I think."

The earl shrugged his massive shoulders. "Certainly. Only from what I understand, this Gypsy matches rather closely in description my ward, who happens to be—"

"Alistair."

The soft voice sounded peculiarly loud in the vast, echoing chamber. Hearing it, Niall cursed to himself. Why couldn't she have kept quiet, as he'd asked? A simple request, and yet seemingly impossible for her to have carried out. It was all well and good for these modern young women to crave equality of the sexes, but they tended to forget one simple fact:

One of those sexes tended to go about fairly well

armed, as illustrated by the sword hilt on which one of the earl's hands casually rested.

Sutherland turned and looked past Niall, into the shadows where Mairi stood.

"Ah," he said. "There you are. Well, come out now. Enough of this nonsense."

"Stay where you are, Mairi," Niall said.

"I can't." She took a single painful step into the shifting light from the fire, then stood still, looking at Sutherland with eyes that were, in the semidarkness, unreadable. "He'll kill you, given half a chance."

Sutherland seemed to like this assessment of his character. He chuckled.

"So," he said to Mairi, "I see you were quite serious, then, when you said you'd sooner die than marry me. Certainly flinging yourself on the mercy of this namby-pamby has got to be akin to suicide, don't you think, Mairi?" Then he squinted at her. "What did you do to your foot?"

"You should know," Mairi said, evenly. "You're the one who unloosed the dogs."

Sutherland looked surprised. "Found you, did they? But didn't manage to bring you down? I ought to have the lot of them shot." Then he began methodically to put his gloves back on. "I don't know what Mairi's been telling you, Niall, but I think you should be aware that she's my cousin, and that she's been entrusted to my care. So don't be thinking of doing anything brash." He bared his teeth in a broad grin. "Though 'twould be a pleasure to have an excuse to thrash you, like in the old days. My ward and I will be going now. My regards to your brother. Tell him"—the earl flung a mocking look in the direction of the Christmas tree—"I like what he's done with the place."

Niall moved so that he was directly between the earl and his ward.

"Go if you want to," he said, in the same mild voice. "But you're not taking her with you."

Sutherland paused in tugging on his right glove and lifted an inquisitive brow.

Mairi said, in a stricken voice, "Lord Niall, please. You've been very kind. But you heard what my cousin said. I won't see you hurt."

"Aye, Niall," Sutherland said pleasantly. "Listen to the lady. Wouldn't want to cause undue injury to those healing fingers, now, would we? Might ruin your livelihood."

Niall remained exactly where he was.

"The girl stays," he said.

"Niall!" Mairi's voice, in which up until then she'd managed to suppress the fear she was feeling, now shook with it. "Oh, you're mad! You don't know—"

"If you want her"—Niall, ignoring Mairi, folded his arms across his chest and glared at the earl—"you'll have to go through the 'namby-pamby,' I'm afraid."

Sutherland sighed. "Now this is simply too much. Have you been taking a nip too many at the Christmas punch, then, Donnegal? For I'm as likely to leave her here as I am to put one of those fool trees up in my own house."

"Nevertheless," Niall said, "she stays."

"She doesn't!" Sutherland shook his head, dumbfounded. "Do you not ken who she is, man? A *MacLean*. Lady Katriona Mairi Berthollet, daughter of my own father's sister and her husband, the Duc de Begnac, who left her, after they met with that unfortunate boating accident, first in my mother's care, and then after her death, in mine. And if you're thinking that I'd let the likes of you have her, well, you can just think again, man. I'd sooner have her marry a monkey than a pretender like yourself."

"My understanding," Niall said, "is that you want to marry her yourself."

Something in Niall's tone must have given away his true feelings about the lady, since a slow grin spread across the earl's face.

"What have you done, then, Mairi?" he asked, as he began peeling his gloves off again. "Gained yet another admirer, I see. And encouraged him, too, from the looks of things. Tisk, tisk. You had to know nothing could come of it." He shook his head. "You'll have to forgive her, Niall. She's always been a bit of a wild, wicked thing. A fairy changeling, in fact, we've always thought her."

"Yes," Niall replied. "I've heard all about *the curse.*"

"Ah, the curse." Sutherland grinned even more broadly beneath his thick red mustache. "She's told you, then? Yes, tragic, is it not? So beautiful, yet so deadly."

"You don't seem to be letting it deter you from seeking her . . . affections."

"Aye." The earl, his gloves shed, tossed them onto a nearby chair, and then drew his sword with a flourish. "But then you see, Mairi's unfortunate curse doesn't seem to have any effect on me."

"I'm certain it wouldn't," Niall said. "Seeing as how you invented it."

"Ah, now, that hurts." Sutherland shook his head. "Always so suspicious, was little Niall. And now he's all grown up, but he hasn't changed a bit, I see." The grin grew broader. "As unprepared as ever for a fight. Well, do not be afraid, Mairi. I'll only use the flat of my sword on him, now, how's that?"

Mairi shouted furiously, "Alistair, you *cannot* think to lay your blade upon an unarmed man! 'Tis unconscionable!"

Sutherland lifted a shaggy red brow. "Allowing her to get an education," he remarked to Niall, "was the worst mistake I ever made."

And then the earl lunged.

Niall, weaponless as he was, ought to have experienced a little trepidation at being attacked thus. But since all he felt was a complete rage that blinded him to all other emotion, he welcomed—even looked forward to—the fight. Driving his fist into Alistair MacLean's face was something he'd fantasized about a good many times, and now that the opportunity was upon him, he had no qualms whatsoever about the matter . . .

Except when the earl, frustrated by the easy way Niall was avoiding the swings of the broadside of Sutherland's blade, turned the hilt in his hand and made a very determined jab for Niall's heart.

Mairi's scream cut through the stillness of the great hall and caused the dogs, who'd retired once more to the fireside, to rise to their feet again.

Niall avoided the life-threatening thrust by seizing a chair and holding it over his chest, so that the point of the blade entered, not his heart, but the eye of a bird embroidered on the chair back.

"I suppose," Niall said lightly, "that by killing me, you think you'll be adding yet more credence to this story you've concocted about Mairi being cursed."

Sutherland gave the sword a savage yank and liberated

it from the chair, staggering away just in time to spare himself from a swing of Niall's fist, which came perilously close to his face.

"I didn't concoct anything," Sutherland declared loudly. " 'Tis an old family curse, and a perfectly true one."

"Aye," Niall said, unimpressed. "So I've heard."

"Everyone the lass comes close to perishes. I'd think about that, Donnegal, if I were you."

"Oh, it doesn't worry me," Niall said. "It might surprise you to know that I don't believe in curses. The educated generally don't, as a rule."

"More fool you, then," Sutherland said. He swung the sword, and this time Niall, tiring of the game, reached out and wrapped his hands over the earl's, where they clutched the sword hilt, then dragged him forward until the two men stood just inches apart, each trying to break the other's grip.

"Here's what I think about your curse," Niall said conversationally, through gritted teeth. "I think when Mairi's parents died and she came to live with you and your mother, you decided you were going to try to get your hands on as much of her money as you could—I assume your parents left you something, didn't they, Mairi?"

"Twenty thousand pounds," came Mairi's prompt reply, from somewhere in the darkness. "Oh, won't the two of you stop this ridiculous fighting? Niall, I *want* to go with him—"

"No, you don't," Niall said. "Twenty thousand pounds is a lot of money, isn't it, Sutherland? I imagine you couldn't wait to get your hands on it. How old was she when you decided you were going to marry her when she came of age? Nine? Ten?"

Alistair MacLean hissed, his face so close to Niall's that he felt the earl's spittle on his jaw, "I *will* kill you, Donnegal."

"Oh, I haven't any doubt you'll try. But let me finish first. I imagine that even at the age of nine, Mairi was about as willing to marry you as she is now. Which is to say, not very. And you got frightened, didn't you? Frightened someone else might take her from you. And so you invented this curse. To a ten-year-old, I imagine it was all very convincing. And she wears the scars of it so close to her heart, even today, that she was terrified at the thought of setting foot in this house lest she bring a plague down upon our heads—"

Sutherland, with a terrific burst of strength, managed to shove Niall away from him. He immediately raised his sword above his head and announced, "You'll die for this, Donnegal."

"Right," Niall said. "The same way the nuns and schoolmates, and even my father, died. How fortuitous for you, that typhoid epidemic must have been. And then my father's gout. But here's where your little game falls apart, Sutherland."

The earl, with a roar that had all the dogs growling, came at him.

Niall had known, of course, that he was enraging the man, but he hadn't been aware that Sutherland's passion had reached this height. This time, there was no nearby chair for him to seize, and the earl was bearing down on him with all the fury of his ancestors. The MacLeans were rumored to have been fearsome—and unscrupulous—warriors.

Niall braced himself for the attack. . . .

And then something clattered and skittered across the floor.

He looked down. An ancient, and very rusted, sword lay at his feet. It was the sword belonging to the suit of armor in the corner.

In a single athletic motion, Niall stooped down and lifted the sword Mairi had thrown to him. He raised it just as the earl's own blade came crashing down above his head.

Alistair MacLean had swung at him with such ferocity the sword Niall held broke into two pieces. Clutching what remained of the blade by its hilt, he waved the jagged metal in the face of his opponent.

"Do you want to know what was wrong with your little plan, Sutherland?" Niall asked, circling the earl cautiously.

"I should have killed you back when we were both lads," MacLean said, with a sneer. "That's what."

"Not exactly. It was simply too complicated. Your hope was to keep Mairi in your power by making her think that if she left you, the curse she was under would kill whoever she ended up with."

"And so far," Sutherland leered, "it has, now, hasn't it? Including you . . . if you'd just hold still."

"There's a flaw in your logic," Niall informed him. "And that flaw is this: A curse didn't kill those people. Accidents and illnesses did. Occam's razor, my good man. Occam's razor."

The earl, beginning to tire, was panting every bit as loudly as the dogs. "What in the hell are you talking about? What's a razor got to do with it?"

"Occam's razor." Niall made a tisk-tisking sound.

"Don't tell me you don't know who Occam was. Shame on you, Alistair. Mairi? Care to enlighten his lordship?"

"William of Occam." Mairi's voice, after a moment of bewildered hesitation, came out of the darkness. "Born in 1285. A scholastic philosopher who rejected the reality of universal concepts. Now will you please put down those swords before—"

"There you go," Niall said. "William of Occam, Alistair. I think he sums up your problem very succinctly. ' 'Tis vain to do with more what can be done with less.' That's his most famous razor, or axiom, if you like."

"I'd like to apply a razor myself," Sutherland snarled. "To your sorry throat."

"Not that kind of razor, I'm afraid, although you can be sure the witticism is not lost on me. What I meant was that with all things being equal, the simplest explanation is probably the correct one. And in Mairi's case, that means there never was any curse. Was there, MacLean?"

The earl bared his teeth. It was rather amazing how closely he resembled, at that moment, a furious canine. A second later, he had flung himself at Niall.

And this time, Niall was caught off guard. He'd been looking at Mairi, who'd limped once more into the dim light thrown by the dying fire and was gazing at him with eyes that had gone dewy with appreciation for stating out loud what a part of her had so long suspected . . . but that childish superstition had kept her from fully believing.

But her gratitude was nearly his undoing. Because while he was basking in it, the earl's blade appeared as if from nowhere and plucked his own neatly from his fingers, sending the broken sword flying across the hall, until it landed with a crash in the midst of the dogs.

Once again unarmed, Niall turned, and faced his enemy. Alistair MacLean grinned at him.

"And now," the earl said, "here's a little razor of me own. All things being equal"—he raised his sword above his head—"the only good Donnegal is a dead—"

Only the earl of Sutherland did not get to finish this statement. This was because Mairi, seeing with alarm that Niall had lost his weapon, had stooped and seized the first thing that came to hand, which in this case happened to be the walking stick Fergus had loaned her. This she quickly tossed to Niall, who caught it and, without pausing to consider what he was doing, hurled it with all the force he could at Alistair MacLean's head.

The stick connected with Lord Sutherland's temple at the exact moment he swung his sword. In the end, the blade, which had been in the MacLean family for generations, fell harmlessly to the floor, followed shortly by its current owner, whose heavy body made very nearly as much noise as it struck the flagstones.

Nine

I say," called a familiar voice. "Good show!"

Niall turned and saw his brother, wearing a dressing gown, standing on the stairs beside his similarly attired wife and any number of servants, all carrying candles and murmuring excitedly to one another, having been roused by the disturbance in the great hall.

"Quite a nice blow you got in there," the duke went on

cheerfully as he descended the stairs. "It sounded like you'd struck a cantaloupe with a cricket bat. Is he dead, I hope?"

Niall bent to examine the earl. His color, he saw in the candlelight, was good, his breathing steady, and his pulse, beneath Niall's fingers, was strong.

"No," he said, with relief, straightening again. Much as he disliked the earl, it would not do, Niall felt, to begin his medical career with a murder on his hands. "Very much alive."

"Oh, well, that's a shame." Euan seemed—for a man roused from a dead sleep by swordplay on Christmas morning—quite cheerful. "Better luck next time, I suppose."

Niall turned around and looked at Mairi, who was staring wide-eyed at the unconscious form of her guardian. "There isn't going to be any next time," Niall said quietly.

"No," Euan said, a bit mournfully. "I suppose you're right. Still, with any luck, he might come at me one day, and then I could have a whack at him, too."

"Oh, Euan!" cried the duchess.

The duke looked startled, as if he'd forgotten up until then that Irmgarde was in the room. "Well," he said, with a shrug, "in the protection of my feudal interests, I mean."

Mairi, still staring at Alistair MacLean, murmured, "I forgot all about Occam. What with all the Plato, I simply forgot about him. But of course you're right. I was a fool. . . ."

"Well," Niall said, not at all certain where he stood now that the dragon had been slain, "it's difficult sometimes to tell where, precisely, the simplest truth lies. Especially when you've been hearing one particular version of it since childhood."

"Still—" Mairi said. She finally managed to tear her gaze

away from the unconscious man. Instead, she looked up, into Niall's eyes. "—I ought to have known better. I think I did, in a way, only ... well, I was still afraid. Just in case—"

"Just in case it might be true." Niall found himself once again unable to glance away from those sapphire eyes. "But now that you know that it's not—"

She dropped her gaze. In the glow of the candlelight, he could see that she was blushing.

"Now that you know it's not true," he said again, lifting one of her hands and holding it in both of his own, "do you think you could reconsider the question I put to you earlier? Because I'd still very much like it if you could see your way toward marrying me. . . ."

Mairi lifted the hand he did not hold and placed it upon his whisker-bristled cheek. The stubble didn't seem to bother her in the least.

"Not right away," Niall said, when a full minute had passed and still she did not reply, just gazed up at him as if seeing him suddenly in a completely different light— which, in fact, she was. "We can wait a bit, if you prefer, until you're sure—"

"Don't wait too long," Euan warned them, looking down at the earl. "He's starting to come round. In fact, just to be safe"—Euan bent down and gingerly picked up the earl's sword—"we'd better hide this somewhere."

"It doesn't matter," Mairi said, not even glancing in her guardian's direction, her gaze still riveted upon Niall's face. "There's nothing he can do to me now." Then she smiled, and her gaze turned oddly shy. "And I'll happily reconsider that question you asked me before, my lord."

Niall's heart sped up. His arms, as if of their own accord, crept around her waist.

"Niall," he said. "Call me Niall."

And very soon they were back to doing precisely what they'd been doing before Lord Sutherland had so rudely interrupted them. They did not, in fact, resurface from this very intimate embrace until someone close by cleared a throat and said, "Er . . . Niall?"

Niall tore his lips from Mairi's and looked up. The duke and duchess were standing there, looking uncomfortable. Behind them, Lord Sutherland was groaning and clutching his head. Niall, assuming his brother and sister-in-law were looking for medical advice, said, "Fetch him some ice and send him on his way. He'll be all right in a day or two," and turned back to Mairi.

Euan and Irmgarde exchanged glances. "That's not precisely what we wanted to know," the duke said. "Although it is edifying, to say the least, and we'll take it under advisement. But what we were wondering, actually—and excuse us if we seem a bit slow, but you'll understand that it is five in the morning—are we mistaken in having heard that the two of you are getting married?"

It was Mairi who answered them, although not with words. Her deepening blush, which she tried to hide against his shoulder, told them all.

"Oh, welcome," Irmgarde gushed. "Welcome to the family, Mairi."

Mairi reached out to take the duchess's hand, unaware, Niall was certain, of the fact that his day-old growth of whiskers, scraping against her mouth as they'd kissed, had turned it a very rosy pink.

"Thank you, Your Grace," Mairi said, but she didn't really appear to be paying very much attention. She was, instead, gazing up into Niall's eyes, which, she'd whispered to him at one point during their most recent embrace, reminded her of "wolf eyes." This did not, however, appear to detract from their overall attractiveness in her mind, since she could no more seem to tear her gaze from his than he could look away from hers.

"A Christmas wedding," Irmgarde said, looking delighted. Anything to do with Christmas delighted Irmgarde. "How lovely! We must have a cake. Where is Cook? Is she awake? I must go and find Cook. . . ."

And it was entirely possible that she did so. Niall had no way of knowing. All of his attention was focused on the girl in his arms, his Christmas captive, who seemed eager, even excited, at the prospect of a life shared with him, and only him.

A fact that compelled the duke to comment, "You seem to have managed to find a woman willing to go to Borneo with you after all, Niall."

"Borneo?" Mairi flung a startled look in Niall's direction.

Niall grinned at her. The twin specters of her curse and marriage to Lord Sutherland lifted at long last, Mairi was turning out to be a girl of considerably high spirits—but not high enough, apparently, for a trip to Borneo.

"It really is Skye we're headed to." Niall took her hand again. It seemed he could not bear to be without it. "Don't worry."

"Oh," she said, visibly relieved. "Of course." And then she said the word, as if to see how well she liked it. "Skye."

She seemed to like it quite a lot, if her smile was any indication.

Epilogue

"But in your strictest medical opinion—" Mairi's expression was very serious.

"In my strictest medical opinion, what?" Niall asked, lazily running a finger along the bare curve of her shoulder.

"Well, would you say—speaking solely on your merits as a doctor, of course—"

"Which I am certifiably qualified to do," he assured her. "Having well over a hundred families dependant upon my medical expertise."

"Quite. So what I'm wondering is . . ."

Outside, a sudden gust of wind whistled past the windows, shaking the diamond-shaped panes of glass in their leaded frames. Snow lay in drifts against the cottage walls. The sea—from which it seemed one could never totally escape, wherever one went on the Isle of Skye—had turned from the emerald green it had been all summer to a flat slate gray, and the burn, which had burbled merrily all through the warmer months, was now frozen solid, so that visitors to Burn Cottage did not even need to use the footbridge in order to cross the water.

But inside the cottage—despite the thatched roof—everything was warm and snug. A fire blazed on the hearth in the bedroom, casting an orange glow upon the crisp white sheets with which the bed had been made up.

Beneath these sheets, and a great many coverlets stuffed with goosefeathers, lay Lord Niall and his wife, the Lady Mairi—though here on Skye, they were known merely as Dr. and Mrs. Donnegal. They had found that the locals were much too in awe of the aristocracy ever to allow a member of it to hold a stethoscope to their chests, and so had chosen to keep the fact that Niall was the son of a duke and Mairi the daughter of one, to themselves.

"Well? Precisely what do you need my impartial medical opinion about, my dear?" Niall, noting that his wife's nightdress had a most welcome tendency to slide off her shoulders and reveal a good deal more flesh than he supposed she knew, was having trouble keeping his attention on the topic at hand.

"Her." Mairi looked down at the baby that lay on the bed between them, her blue eyes closed for the moment, her chest rising and falling in even slumber. "Don't you think—speaking as a physician, I mean, and not a doting father—that she really is the most beautiful baby you've ever seen?"

Niall reached out and touched the fluff of red hair that sprouted from the top of his infant daughter's head.

"In an entirely professional manner of speaking?" he asked.

"Yes, of course."

"Well, then, in my impartial medical and professional opinion"—he grinned at his wife—"yes, she really is the most beautiful baby I've ever seen."

Mairi nodded solemnly. "That's what I think as well. And not just beautiful. She's smart, too. When I said her name earlier, she looked right at me, as if she were perfectly aware that I was addressing her, and her alone."

"And at only a week old." Niall shook his head. "Amazing."

"You're making fun of me," Mairi said, and only then was she no longer able to maintain her somber demeanor and broke into a smile. "But here, I can prove it. Watch."

She leaned down and spoke into the baby's small pink ear.

"Brenna," she whispered. "Brenna."

Brenna Mairi Donnegal opened her eyes for a moment, blinked irritably at her parents, then promptly closed them again and went back to sleep.

"My God, you're right," Niall said. "A genius."

"Is that your professional opinion, Dr. Donnegal?" his wife asked, in teasing tones.

"It is." He leaned across his daughter to kiss his wife. "It most certainly is."

PATRICIA CABOT is the author of the critically acclaimed romances *A Little Scandal*, *An Improper Proposal*, *Portrait of My Heart*, and *Where Roses Grow Wild*. "It is a true joy to listen to Patricia Cabot's unique voice," raved *Romantic Times*, and readers everywhere can look forward to *Lady of Skye* and *Educating Caroline*, the next thrilling novel from this rising star, coming soon from Pocket Books. She is also the author of two series of young adult novels, which have been optioned for film and television. Patricia Cabot lives in New York City with her husband.